All the
Andrew Nance

All the Lovely Children
A Red Adept Publishing Book
Red Adept Publishing, LLC
104 Bugenfield Court
Garner, NC 27529
http://RedAdeptPublishing.com/

First Print Edition: February 2018

Cover Art by Streetlight Graphics

This is a work of fiction. Names, characters, places, and incidents either are the product of the author's imagination or are used fictitiously, and any resemblance to locales, events, business establishments, or actual persons—living or dead—is entirely coincidental.

Prologue

S avannah glanced at the remaining food on her parents' plates and knew she had a long wait before they could leave. "Can we throw the ball tomorrow?" she asked.

Her father looked up, a forked piece of steak near his mouth, and said, "You bet, slugger."

"Not too long," her mother said. "I want to get on the road before noon."

Savannah groaned. When her mom said, "I want to get on the road," she meant they would shut themselves up in the car for four or five hours, drive over mountain roads, and *oooh* and *ahhh* over the leaves turning colors on the trees. The locals were saying that, because of the Indian summer, the colors weren't as vivid as usual, but when Savannah's dad first drove them up to Temperance the day before, Savannah thought they were really pretty. Still, she could only look at trees for so long before it just got boring.

She gazed longingly out the big bay window of the restaurant to the park across the road. Streetlamps lit a few areas, and she could see a merry-go-round, a swing set, and a jungle gym. "Can I go over to the park while you guys finish dinner?"

"Where?" her father asked.

Savannah pointed out the window. Her parents looked out, then at one another, and her father shrugged.

"It's kind of dark over there, honey," her mother said.

"There are streetlights," Savannah said.

Her mother thought a moment. "Don't go anywhere else."

"And come back in..." Her father surveyed their remaining food. "Twenty minutes."

"Okay," Savannah said, jumping from the table and rushing toward the door before they could change their minds.

After making it outside, she paused at the curb to look up and down the street. Other than the cars parked near the restaurant, there wasn't a vehicle on the road, so she ran across. Because it was a fancy restaurant, her parents had made her wear a stupid dress, but it had two deep pockets. From one, she pulled her Atlanta Braves cap and tugged it onto her head. There were no other kids around, and no adults either, for that matter, but that just meant she'd have the playground to herself.

She went straight to the merry-go-round, a paint-faded iron circle sectioned like an orange with steel bars to hold on to. Standing beside it, she passed the bars from hand to hand and got it spinning. After waiting for the right moment, she jumped on and held tight. When it began to slow, she jumped off. The ground seemed to rock back and forth. It made her laugh. She saw a line of white benches a few feet away and went in that direction, planning to sit until the dizziness passed. She changed her mind when she spotted a path behind the nearest bench, leading into a patch of trees.

Savannah went to stare down the path. A streetlamp to her right illuminated a short distance past the opening, and she felt like she was standing before the mouth of some mysterious road in a fairy tale. She walked in as far as the light allowed, noting the line where the shadow of trees and darkness began. It was too dark, almost as black as ink. Where did the path go? She was tempted to find out and actually took another step, but then felt a little scared and stopped. Nope. Maybe she'd get her parents to bring her back in the daytime, and then she'd explore.

But something round and white caught her eye on the ground just a little farther down the path. She had no doubt it was a ball, and from what she could make out, probably a baseball. Some kids must have been playing and hit it into the woods. She'd certainly lost her share of balls. She went a dozen feet farther on the dark trail and picked it up. There wasn't enough light to make out its condition, so she ran her thumb over it. Other than a few scuffs, it felt pretty good.

She tossed the ball up a couple of times and then heard a soft sound, followed by another, and then another. Sudden fear coursed through Savannah. She couldn't tell which direction the noise came from, but she thought it sounded like three soft footsteps, like someone sneaking around, maybe even creeping up on her. She noted how loud her breathing was and how her heartbeat was way too fast. The sound was never repeated, but she was certain someone was close by. She could sense them.

Trembling, she dropped the ball. It thumped as it hit the dirt and rolled into the brush. Savannah took a step backward and then another. She wouldn't turn. She'd back out of the trail while keeping watch for anyone following. Step after slow, unsteady step, she finally crossed the border from murky shadow to the streetlight's glow. A couple more backward strides, and then she'd turn and run as fast as she could to her parents at the restaurant.

She backed into somebody. Briefly, she thought that it might've been a tree, until strong arms wrapped around her and lifted her off the ground. Something pressed against her face, and strong chemical fumes filled her nose. Whoever held her spun around so that she could see past the park, across the street, and through the restaurant's window to her parents finishing their meal.

Pulled onto the trail, Savannah was swallowed by darkness.

Chapter 1
Autumn of '82

As if being a few inches closer to the TV would make the news more comprehensible, I leaned forward. An Action News 5 reporter stood in front of the sheriff's department in the mountain town of Temperance, North Carolina, giving what few details were available about the abductions of four young girls. I watched in fascination as they flashed various images from the town where I had grown up. I knew firsthand the impact of crimes like that on a small community and Temperance in particular. The reporter threw it back to WRAL's news anchor, and after a tease for sports, they went to a commercial for a waterbed store.

Memories and emotions tangled into melancholy, and my gaze dropped to my hands, fingers interlaced around the stem of my wine glass. Though I had moved across the state to live in Raleigh, I engaged in a mental debate as to whether I should return to Temperance. I felt I owed something to the friends I'd lost over twenty years ago. I wasn't working on anything at the moment, at least nothing that couldn't wait.

My phone rang, startling me out of my thoughts. I jumped and spilled some wine on the coffee table.

"Damn it." I dropped my napkin onto the spreading puddle then got up to answer the phone. "Hello."

"It's happening again."

I gripped the receiver tightly. "Who is this?"

"It's happening again, Charly."

"Kit?"

"Yeah. Have you been following the news?"

I glanced at the TV. "I didn't hear anything about the first one. After the second, the two girls, there was a mention in the paper. I just turned on the news and saw you had another one."

"Last night. Look, Charly, I want to hire you. I want you to come up and help with the case. Work as a consultant or whatever you want to call it."

That answered the question of whether I should go or not. "What have you got so far?"

"There are four missing. The first was like in '59. Sometime between ten p.m., August eighteenth, and seven a.m., August nineteenth, ten-year-old Piper Darling was abducted from her second-floor bedroom. In warmer weather, she slept with her window open, and we figure that's how he got in."

"Damn." This was just like before. Coincidence?

"The second and third victims disappeared on September twenty-third."

"Sisters, right?"

"Yeah. Mani and Pedi Regis. One is eleven, the other nine."

"What happened?"

"Mani Regis is in middle school. After school, she went to meet her sister at Temperance Gifted Elementary. That's where their mother picks them up. Witnesses, other children, said Pedi Regis played with them on the playground until she had an argument with another girl. She ran around one of the school wings. Mani showed up, asked where her sister was, and went around the building after her. Neither was seen again."

"Any idea how it happened?"

"There's a four-foot chain-link fence around the school with woods on the other side. We found one of Pedi's shoes on the other side of the fence. Dogs picked up a scent and followed it for a mile until they came out on Weir Road. The guy probably parked there."

"Another was taken last night?"

"A family passing through Temperance, the Smallwoods, was taking a foliage tour." Carloads of flatland leaf-gawkers migrated through the mountains in autumn, taking in the bright reds, yellows, and oranges of the maple trees, dogwoods, birches, and Virginia creepers. "They booked a room for a couple of nights at the Econo Lodge and came into town for dinner at what used to be the Pine Top Restaurant. Their twelve-year-old daughter, Savannah, finished eating before her parents and went across the street to Town Center Park. When her parents went to get her, she was gone." Kit paused. "From what they've told me, Charly, this girl, Savannah Smallwood, is a lot like you were as a kid—a tomboy, a great ball player, the one picked first when choosing up teams." I heard him take a drink of something. My guess was coffee for his long night ahead. "Tell me you'll help."

"Of course." I mentally listed what I needed to do before leaving. I'd have to call Deacon, my martial arts instructor, and tell him I'd miss at least one lesson, and leave a note for the mailman. That was it. Was my life that empty? "I'll head up tonight after I pack."

"Go ahead and bill me your normal rate and travel expenses."

"I'll be in by midnight. Isn't there a new motel right as you get into town?"

"That's the Econo Lodge. I'll book a room for you."

Chapter 2
Summer of '59

I walked to the unofficial end-of-school party at Wallace Lake with my two best friends, Bobby Whist and Micah Lee Leigh. Micah's mother was kind of a nut and had given her only child a middle name that sounded just like his last.

Kids were swimming and splashing, laughing and shouting, blowing off steam that had built up in all of us during the school year. Kit Haiselton, who was a full head shorter than me and skinny as a post, ran by, screaming. In each hand he carried Roman candles that shot colored fireballs into the air.

Jeremy Driver, who lived and breathed baseball, rushed up to me. His red swimming trunks were sopping wet. "Hey, Charly. We're getting together at the field tomorrow. Need a pitcher."

"What time?"

He shook his head like a rain-soaked dog and splattered me with lake water. "Around noon."

"Maybe." I'd just gotten out of school for the summer—the last thing I wanted was to start scheduling things to do.

"Try for a perfect game like Don Larsen."

I rolled my eyes. "Why'd you have to go and compare me to a damn Yankee?"

He ran for the lake, shouting, "Because they're only the best team in the world!"

"You better run!" I called after him. The Yankees had been racking up World Series victories, seven in the past ten years, while my beloved Brooklyn Dodgers had only won one. If that wasn't bad enough, the Dodgers had moved out to California, and I still didn't know what to think of that.

Ricky Braun, Derrick Westerfeld, and Casey Lay went by, heading toward the water. "You coming, Bloom?" Ricky asked.

I shrugged. "Maybe." I had my swimsuit on under my clothes, but I didn't feel like swimming. I didn't feel like doing anything other than relishing the fact that school was out.

I looked around, but I couldn't see Bobby or Micah Lee. I wandered around for a bit then spent some time at the bonfire. After an hour or so, I got bored and went searching for them. I found Micah Lee calf-deep in the lake, staring toward Black Mountain. A bunch of other kids were doing the same.

I rolled up my pant legs and splashed over to him. "What are you gawking at?"

He raised his arm and pointed east. The sky had brightened like an impending sunrise.

"What is that?" I asked.

"I dunno."

A blazing object crested the horizon and hung over Black Mountain like the biggest diamond God ever created. I looked at those around me, all wide eyed and slack jawed. The object seemed motionless, but that was an illusion because, in the next moment, it passed overhead at incredible speed. It traveled west over Cray's Hill and disappeared behind Hallows Summit.

We'd all frozen, staring in the direction that object had gone. And we weren't the only ones shocked into silence. For a moment, there was no sound. Then a cricket chirped, and another joined it, and finally the night was filled with their song. As the surprise of what we'd witnessed wore off, we looked at one another.

Dub Mellerman broke the spell by shouting, "Hot damn! That was one of them flying saucers!"

There was a lot of mumbling as everyone considered that possibility, then Bobby said, "Ain't no flying saucer, you nimrod. That was a shooting star."

The debate began, everyone talking over everyone else, though the majority thought it was something natural like a meteor or asteroid or chunk of the moon. I could tell that Bobby got bored of the topic when he focused on Micah Lee, who'd moved thigh deep into the lake. Bobby narrowed his eyes and grinned. In the next second, he splashed through the water and tackled Micah Lee. Both of them disappeared under the surface. They came up laughing and sputtering. A free-for-all broke out, in which the purpose seemed to be to see who could get who the wettest. By the time the party was over, every one of us was soaked through.

A COUPLE OF WEEKS LATER, we were playing a sweaty six-inning game at Farley's Field. The grass was high, so for bases we used welcome mats that someone swiped from nearby homes. There was a perfectly good baseball diamond at school, but it just didn't seem right to be on school property in the summertime. It was a good game against Jeremy Driver's team, and since he was a Yankees fan, I desperately wanted to win. I was pitching at the bottom of the last inning with two outs. We were up by one, but bases were loaded, and Dub Mellerman was up. Dub could knock the skin off a ball.

On first base, Kit Haiselton started talking in a loud announcer voice with his hand near his mouth like he was holding a microphone. "It's an exciting day at the ball park, ladies and gentlemen, as the game between Jeremy's Jackals and Charly's Chumps comes to a close."

Bobby was playing first, and I gave him a subtle glance. He smiled and moved behind Kit. When I started to wind up, out of the corner of my eye, I saw Kit take a couple of steps from the base.

"That's right, ladies and gentlemen," Kit said. "Once Dub hits his homer, the Jackals will win by three, and the Chumps will take a dump."

I turned and threw the ball like a missile at Kit's head. At the last second, he fell to the ground. Bobby caught the ball and tagged Kit out.

After the game, Micah Lee, Bobby, and I ditched everyone and headed to our hideaway for a lazy afternoon. We called it our secret beach, though there wasn't any sand. The area was mostly smooth stones, a wash of high grass, and hidden by pines, white oaks, and maples. A bike ride to Wallace Lake and a fifteen-minute hike through the woods would get us to our little paradise, and none of us would dream of bringing anyone else.

Micah Lee stood and stared blankly at the water. "Did you see her last night?"

Bobby sat at the water's edge and French-inhaled before blowing a smoke ring. "See who?"

"What do you mean *who*?"

"Which girl? You have a crush on a different one every five minutes." Bobby flicked his cigarette butt in Wallace Lake. He was fourteen, as big as an eighteen-year-old, and plagued with baby-fat. Last summer, his mother's cousin had visited, riding up from Charlotte on an Indian motorcycle. Bobby was awestruck and said he'd never met anyone so cool. That was when Bobby started to dress tough. He rolled up his T-shirt sleeves, a pack of Viceroys in one, and slicked his hair into a duck butt just like his mother's cousin. But no matter how tough he acted, he couldn't hide those chipmunk cheeks.

Stepping into the water, I said, "He's got it for Alisha this go-round." I retrieved Bobby's cigarette butt and put it in my pocket. I didn't want Bobby, or anyone else, to spoil our little spot at the lake.

I didn't think Micah Lee truly had crushes on his endless list of infatuations. He was more in love with the idea of being in love. He wore a constant expression of wide-eyed worship, and sometimes, his adoration would turn my way. I could tell when he got on the hook for me because he'd start calling me Charlotte and laying on the compliments. Just a few weeks earlier, he told me my eyes were as blue as Caribbean waters, not that he'd ever seen the Caribbean, or any ocean. I slugged him for it.

"Last night at the bowling alley. Alisha was so... so..." Micah Lee's eyes glazed over, and his face turned pink. He had a funny-shaped skull, as if he'd slipped from the doctor's grip when he was born and dropped on his head. If he'd grown his hair out a couple of inches, people wouldn't notice, but his hair was always mown down to a flat-top. While Bobby and I favored T-shirts, Micah Lee always wore plaid shirts, usually orange. "I saw Alisha looking at me. I think she likes me."

Bobby hummed a few seconds then began singing "All I Have to Do Is Dream," by the Everly Brothers. I joined in on the chorus. Though we were teasing him, Micah Lee came in for some fine three-part harmony. We brought the final verse to a close, and Bobby and I fell over laughing.

Micah Lee wasn't amused. "Why do you always sing that when I talk about girls?"

Bobby smirked. "Because the only way you'll ever get a girl is in your dreams."

"That ain't funny."

Bobby shook his head. "You're whipped, and you don't even have a girlfriend."

"What do you mean?"

Bobby and I exchanged a look and snickered.

Micah Lee glared at us. "What?"

"Nothing." I picked up my Louisville Slugger and batted some rocks out into the water. "Want to come back tonight and see if that thing flies over again?"

"It ain't coming back. It was just a damn meteor," Bobby said, lying on a sketchy patch of grass and using his infielder's glove as a pillow.

Debates still raged about the object in the two weeks since its flyover. While most opinions still ran from meteor to meteorite to passing asteroid to a flying saucer from another planet, a new theory started that it was a secret military aircraft. The newest round of arguments was how big it was, which depended on how high it was, and everyone had a differing opinion on that as well, from as big as the moon and equally as distant, to the size of a small car and low enough to chuck a rock at.

I thought of something. "If anyone has ever seen anything like it, it'd be Solomon."

"Solomon," Bobby echoed.

"Yeah," Micah Lee agreed.

"Let's go."

We rode our bikes to my house and grabbed a snack while Mom yelled at us to not track in dirt. Because the quickest route to Solomon's was by cutting through a number of yards and climbing a fence or two, we left our bikes at my house and used our other mode of transportation—our feet. We had two speeds, meandering or flat out, and since we had an important destination, we ran. One of the shortcuts for our route included a pass through Old Man Altus's yard. He came out and yelled at us, and Bobby shouted something back. Elwood Altus was about a million years old and didn't like kids setting foot on his lush lawn. Though he was ancient, he was strong, able to haul eighty-pound bags of fertilizer around on his shoulders.

One time, just a few days after Micah Lee and I watched Bobby leave a flaming bag of dog crap on Old Man Altus's welcome mat, Daddy and I drove by the place, and he asked if I'd ever messed with Mr. Altus's house. I admitted that we sometimes cut through his yard, but I didn't tell him anything else. He said I should keep in mind that Mr. Altus had had a tough time of it. He'd lost a son to Korea and his wife to cancer. After that, I didn't find it fun to torment the old guy anymore. Sometimes, compassion sucked eggs.

We got to Solomon's and headed up the walk. From the street, the house resembled a ship, a tramp steamer viewed starboard-side, complete with portholes instead of regular windows.

"Ahoy!" Solomon peered out of a window. "Come aft, Charly, and bring the lads. Get yourselves a soda, and fetch one for me."

Solomon kept his front door locked. He said that was the door that bill collectors, process servers, and salesmen came to. Friends were welcome at the back door.

We paused at the gate to wrestle with the latch then ran up the ramp and into Solomon's kitchen. Bobby yanked open the refrigerator, and Micah Lee pulled out four bottles of Tru-Ade. He passed one to Bobby and one to me. I dug in Solomon's junk drawer for a bottle opener and popped the tops. We filed into the study, and I caught my favorite smell, the rich sweetness of Solomon's pipe tobacco.

"How're you rascals doin'?" Solomon smiled from behind his desk, a scarred teak monstrosity he said once belonged to an admiral. The photos on the wall, the décor of the room, and the general ambience were all of a nautical nature. Before retiring when he was in his fifties, Solomon had been a sailor and had traveled all around the world. His sister lived here in Temperance, and she'd given him a place to stay while he recuperated.

"Whatcha working on, Solomon?" I asked, indicating the paper and fountain pen on his desktop.

"My memoir," he said, holding out his hand for the soda.

Solomon Stubb was in his eighties and full of life. Under his straw-colored beard was a face sunbaked and aged into lined leather. A faded blue captain's cap covered his bristly scalp. He wore an open-necked knit shirt with horizontal stripes, and suspenders over each shoulder. He had big muscular arms, and he sounded like a pirate when he spoke.

Micah Lee handed him a bottle. "About what?"

"How I got this." Solomon flicked the small gold hoop earring in his left lobe. "Earned it the first time I sailed around Cape Horn. Terrible storm. Thought I'd die from the heavin' guts." He pointed at the sofa beside his desk, and we all sat. "So what can I do for you three?"

He rolled his chair back and spun to face us. Just above where his knees should have been, each pant leg was cut and sewn closed like the end of a sausage casing. He'd lost his legs on a ship in bad weather. A cargo container broke free and slid into another, pinning Solomon between them.

I leaned forward. "Did you see that thing that flew over town a couple of weeks ago?"

"Yep, I was out on the porch. Strange sight indeed."

I nodded. "We were wondering, since you've been every-where—"

"Have you ever seen anything like it?" Bobby blurted.

"What do you think it was?" Micah Lee added.

"Just what makes you think I can put a name to the unnamed?" He shook his head. "When you spend a life at sea, you see many strange things. You'd go mad trying to find explanations for all of them."

"What kinds of things?" Bobby asked.

"Things in the sky, things on the sea, and things below." Solomon picked up his pipe and placed it between his lips. "I once crewed aboard a hundred-twenty-foot feeder ship, and one sweltering day in the middle of the Atlantic, our boatswain's mate spied something in the water. We rushed to the rail and saw a sea creature longer than the ship and easily as wide. It rose close to our port side—not breakin' the surface, mind you—just floating underneath. An eye as big around as a ship's wheel opened in the middle of its mass and watched us watch it. After a good three minutes, the leviathan sank back to the depths."

The phone on Solomon's desk rang, making us jump.

He picked it up and barked a hello. Concern spread over his face. "How long?" He listened to the response. "Where was she? Uh-huh, uh-huh. That's not good. Where are we meeting?" He nodded. "Uh-huh, okay." He hung up and told us, "Sarah Mundy has gone missing."

We hurried to keep up as Solomon rolled out to the backdoor ramp and around to the carport. He had customized a red panel van so that he could drive using only his hands. Chrome handles were attached to the frame by the side door, allowing him to climb in and pull the wheelchair after him. Two handles were set on the rear doors, making it easier for him to load and unload cargo. A couple times in the past, when we weren't going too far, Solomon let us hang on to the backdoor handles while standing on the big bumper. It was better than any carnival ride.

"You know Sarah Mundy, right?" he asked as he pushed open the side door.

"Yeah," Bobby answered.

Living in a small town, we knew almost everybody, including Sarah, a student at Temperance Gifted Elementary. They put that part in the school's name to make the kids feel special. But since it was the only elementary school in town, there wasn't anyone to lord it over.

"Who called?" I asked.

"That was Marty. I mean Deputy Atwater." Even though he didn't have legs, Solomon was a ranking member of the sheriff's auxiliary.

"And Sarah's lost?" Micah Lee asked.

"Missing. Marty said she went to bed at her regular time. When she didn't show for breakfast this morning, her mother went up to fetch her, and her room was empty." He glanced at us then started the van. "They found a ladder up to her window."

Chapter 3
Autumn of '82

It seemed that I'd just put my head on the Econo Lodge pillow when someone knocked on the door. I opened my eyes and saw the sun was up.

"Just a minute." I picked up the slacks I had worn the night before and slipped them on. I cleared my throat and asked, "Who's there?"

"Morning, Charly. It's Kit."

I opened the door and thought about how he definitely wasn't the Kit Haiselton I knew from school. Back then, he'd been a scrawny little troublemaker. Standing in the doorway was a stunningly handsome man—a younger, better-looking version of that chiseled actor, Clint Walker. The sheriff uniform and western hat only added to the likeness.

"Kit, you could've picked any other woman in town, and she'd be overjoyed to find you on her doorstep at the crack of dawn."

He blushed, which made me laugh. The next door down opened, and a man peered out.

I said, "Sorry, sir. Just an early-morning tryst. Nothing to worry about." I pulled Kit into the room.

He snickered like the boy I remembered. "You're going to get me in hot water, Charly."

"I seem to remember a boy who was no stranger to trouble."

"We did raise some holy hell, didn't we?"

In fifth grade, Kit had brought a pocketful of cherry bombs and a pack of matches to school. He destroyed a desk, two trash cans, and one toilet before they caught him. We called him the Mad Bomber for months afterward.

"I still find it hard to believe that you went into law enforcement and that you're the sheriff."

"My second term," Kit said a bit defensively. He took off his hat and spun it in his hands. "If you don't mind my saying, I do a damn good job—at least I did until all this started up again."

"What time is it?"

"Almost seven thirty." There was an uncomfortable silence, then he said, "I've been up all night. Something happened. We found remains." He ran a hand over his head. "We found the kids. I thought you'd want to go onsite."

Kit waited for me out in his car while I got dressed. I washed my face, threw on a sweatshirt, went out, and settled in the passenger seat of his LTD cruiser. He handed me a Styrofoam cup and filled it with coffee from a thermos.

The first sip burned my tongue, but I didn't care and took another. "Just what I need."

Kit exited the parking lot, accelerated, and turned on his turret lights. "Thanks for coming."

"Thanks for calling me."

The traffic was picking up. Still, Kit drove well above the speed limit. "We don't have one damn thing to go on. And seeing as you have experience, it made sense to call." He white-knuckled the steering wheel.

I used to work for the State Bureau of Investigation, a law enforcement entity much like the FBI, before going into business for myself. "I'll do what I can, but the SBI doesn't handle abductions, not unless a local department calls them in. The only one I ever worked was drug related."

"It's not just your SBI experience." He glanced at me. "You figured out who the Snatcher was, and you were just a kid."

I blew into my coffee. "That was just dumb luck."

"I can use all the dumb luck you can muster."

"I know that finding the bodies is awful, but we'll learn things from the remains and from where they were stashed. Who knows, Kit? We might just close this case today."

He put on a blinker, slowed, and pulled over to the curb. Kit looked at me with concern in his eyes. "You don't understand, Charly. We didn't find the girls who've been abducted the past few weeks. We found the children taken back in '59."

The unexpected news brought on dizziness. Though Kit was talking, I couldn't hear him through a blood rush as loud as rapids. Even seated, I felt at risk of toppling over and had to put a hand on the dash.

He spoke louder. "Hey, you all right?"

I shook my head then nodded. "Yeah, yeah, I'm okay." I touched my forehead and felt perspiration.

He stretched a hand toward me but pulled back just before making contact. He cleared his throat. "There'll be testing to do before we can officially say it's them, but it is."

"Where? How were they found?"

"One of the dirt roads that cuts over from the county road on the other side of Wallace Lake." Kit pulled back out onto the road. "Mecklenberg County sent a couple of cadaver dogs to help search for the girls, the ones missing now. They made the discovery last night."

"After all this time." I rubbed my temples and thought about the families of those children. Would the discovery bring welcome closure, or would it rekindle past horrors? And what of the ones who no longer had families? At least I could take care of an old friend. "I'll handle Bobby's burial."

Kit scratched the stubble on his face and said, "We can't be sure yet, but it looks like the remains are all female. We'll know for sure pretty soon." At the outskirts of town, Kit turned onto a narrow two-lane road leading to Wallace Lake.

Though we'd been quiet for several minutes, it was obvious Kit was running all sorts of scenarios in his head. "I wish they'd left the old mill standing. If someone's mimicking what happened in '59, that'd be the place to look."

A few months after my encounter with the Snatcher, the town council had claimed the old mill was a danger to the community and voted to have it destroyed. In the spring of 1960, they hired a demolition company and brought it down.

"You think it's a copycat?" I asked.

"A good possibility. By the way, that's what they're calling the perp—Copycat."

"Who came up with that?"

"Who knows? Who was it that came up with the Snatcher?"

I didn't tell him it was Micah Lee, Bobby, and me.

Blue-and-red lights flashed up ahead. Massive spotlights—used the night before and now shut off—aimed down at a patch of ground twenty feet from the roadside. I counted two sheriff's cars, one highway patrol vehicle, a black sedan, and a white van that was probably from the morgue.

"Stick by me," Kit said and opened his door.

We got a dozen steps when a woman with brown helmet hair blocked our way.

Kit sighed. "Hello, Ronnie."

"Sheriff. I understand a grave has been discovered?" She wore enough makeup that she could've passed for a funeral home cadaver.

"No comment, Ronnie. Once we're sure of what we have, we'll let you know."

She turned to me and extended a hand. "Ma'am," she said to me, "I'm Ronnie Carson, *Temperance Mountain Times*. And you are?"

"Nobody," I answered.

I didn't take her hand, so she refocused on Kit. "Is this where Copycat disposed of a girl?"

Kit removed his hat. "Damn it, Ronnie. Don't go printing speculation like that."

"What would you have me print?"

"All I'll tell you is this—what we've found has nothing to do with Piper Darling, Mani or Pedi Regis, or Savannah Smallwood."

"Who do you think—"

"Excuse me, Ronnie." Kit pushed past her, and I followed.

Kit signaled for one of his deputies to come over. "Keep Ronnie away, and make sure everyone knows that the only thing they can tell her is *no* and *comment*."

The deputy nodded and hurried to inform the others.

A hole five feet deep and eight feet square had been excavated. Two gloved men were transferring bones from the hole to a body bag. Watching their labor brought about melancholy. Those remains were children I had known. One of them I had seen just minutes before she'd been abducted. We had a connection, those girls and I, tied together by violence and fear and deep human depravity. I wondered what they'd look like today if they'd lived, and I decided they'd all be beautiful and happy. Why not? It was my fantasy.

My rumination ended when a man approached. Recognizing Sylvester Caputo, I groaned.

"What is it?" Kit asked.

"You didn't tell me you brought in the SBI."

"Didn't know I had to."

I lowered my head so my hair hid my face. It had been a long road to get into the SBI, and Caputo was the man who had ended my short career. I had gone to college at seventeen, some of which was paid for with the reward I'd gotten for solving the Snatcher case. After eight years of classes at Duke, NC State, and Meredith College, I earned a criminal justice degree. I sent resumes and applications to law enforcement offices statewide, and because of my memories of one particular special agent, I sent a packet to the State Bureau of Investigation. My first response was from SBI Director Charles Dunn, and in 1972, I joined the ranks of the SBI as one of the few female field officers.

Caputo stepped next to Kit and surveyed the scene. Without looking, he gestured at me and asked, "Who's this, Sheriff?"

God, I still hated that snide tone I'd first heard back in 1975 when he'd been transferred to Raleigh from Greensboro. Feeling his eyes on me, I looked up and flashed him a counterfeit smile.

"A private investigator," Kit said.

The morning was unseasonably warm, and Caputo had his black jacket folded over his forearm, the matching tie around his neck loosened a few inches. His black hair was immaculately combed, and he positioned his head so his granite jaw looked like the prow of a ship.

Recognition came slow, but when it arrived, his look of shock was priceless. "Bloom?" He turned to Kit. "Sheriff, you can't be serious?"

"As a heart attack," Kit said.

"Sheriff—"

Kit raised his hand. "You're aware that she has a special interest in this case, right? When she was thirteen, she went toe to toe with the Snatcher and came out of it alive." Kit eyed Caputo. "She's staying."

Caputo's face reddened. "Look, Haiselton, you're the one who called us for help."

"And I appreciate your expertise, but I also called Charly."

"Are you aware of the circumstances concerning her departure from the SBI?"

I said, "No mystery. I quit."

Caputo raised his voice. "Because you wouldn't follow orders."

"I can follow orders, so long as they're not from a fool."

Kit stepped between us. "Hey! You two can have a pissing match on your own time."

I said, "No worries, Caputo. I like working behind the scenes. If I'm lucky, I won't run into you again."

He started to reply but then turned and stalked off. Arrogant, mediocre, sexist, and racist were a few of the terms that described the man. Back in the day, my fellow field agents and I figured that he knew somebody in high places. Anyone else so incompetent would have been bounced from the bureau pronto.

Kit shook his head. "Still Miss Congeniality, huh?"

"I have a dislike for misogynists."

"I guess I don't have to ask if you two have a history."

My attention returned to the remains. If things had worked out differently, my bones might have been in there as well. The thought made me weary. "Thanks for bringing me out, Kit, but I don't think I'll learn anything here that you won't. Can you take me back to the motel?"

Back in the car, Kit said, "Why don't you move to the Temperance Inn. They give the department a discount. Besides, Caputo is staying at the motel, and I get the feeling it's best to keep you two far apart."

"Yeah, okay."

"I'll call and let them know you're coming." He handed me a folder containing the case files and photos of Mani and Pedi Regis, Savannah Smallwood, and Piper Darling. "Listen. I'm glad you're here, but I have a full day ahead of me, so let's get together tomorrow." Kit glanced at me. "There's something else."

"What?" I asked, not sure I wanted to know the answer.

"The night before the first girl was taken, there was a meteor shower."

I felt the beginning of a headache. "A meteor shower? Holy hell."

Chapter 4
Summer of '59

"We should join the search party," I said.

"They probably won't let kids help," Micah Lee said.

Bobby kicked at a stone in the road. "That's stupid."

Something Solomon had said troubled me. "If they found a ladder up to Sarah's window, do you think it means someone climbed up and snatched her?"

Micah Lee shrugged. "She could have put it there before she went to bed so she could sneak out later."

"A little girl like her?" I shook my head. "The ladder would be too heavy. Plus, you know Sarah. She's not the kind of girl who'd sneak out."

"Betcha a sex fiend got her," Bobby announced, looking at his depleted pack of Viceroys. He tucked it back in his pocket, apparently deciding to save what few he had for later.

"Sex fiend?" Micah Lee asked.

"Winthrop told me about 'em. Some of them got a thing for kids, he said."

Winthrop was Bobby's brother. If someone called him stupid, it would have been a compliment. But nobody called Winthrop Whist anything to his face. Nineteen years old, tall and strong, Winthrop was a greaser, complete with a black leather jacket, oily, slicked-back hair, and a heavy pair of engineer boots. He had no qualms about fighting. Though someone his age should fight other men, Winthrop was a bully who still targeted kids. In fact, he still acted like a kid himself. He'd dropped out of school a few years earlier, but he still

hung out in the high school parking lot or lurked behind the bleach-
ers at the school's sporting events, where he'd share cigarettes and
crude laughter with juvenile delinquents who still attended school.
I doubt any of them would really consider Winthrop a friend, but
they let him hang out because they'd seen what he did to anyone who
mouthed off to him. That included Bobby. It was no secret that, when
mad, Winthrop smacked his little brother around, but Bobby still
thought his brother something of a lesser god.

"Yeah, Winthrop's right about sex fiends," Bobby said. "They lure
kids into their cars, saying they got candy or a puppy or somethin',
then they take them to a secret spot and do all sorts of nasty things."

"Grody," Micah Lee muttered.

"There aren't any sex fiends in Temperance," I said.

"Maybe he comes up from Charlotte," Bobby said.

"Why Charlotte?" I asked.

"Winthrop told me there's a park down there where perverts go
at night to suck each other off."

"Maybe a sex fiend broke out of an asylum." Micah Lee loved stories that started with news bulletins on the radio about maniacs escaping from insane asylums.

"There ain't a nuthouse anywhere near here," Bobby answered.

"The only sex fiend around here is you"—I nudged Bobby—"when you sneak a peek at those girlie magazines you got."
They'd belonged to his father, and he and Winthrop had found them
stashed in the backyard shed. I'd thumbed through most of them myself.

"Shut up," he said, blushing.

"Whaddya want to do?" Micah Lee asked.

I stopped and looked at them. "Just because they didn't ask us to
help, doesn't mean we can't look on our own."

Micah Lee grinned. "Yeah!"

"Where?" Bobby asked.

That was a good question. We'd want to go somewhere that the grown-ups might not consider right away. "Want to go back to the lake and look around Wallace Falls?"

"Yeah, that sounds good," Micah Lee said.

We ran back to my house, shortcutting through the same yards, even Old Man Altus's, got our bikes, and pedaled out to the head of the trail that led to the falls. We yelled for Sarah every couple of minutes, but the only answers came from birds, insects, and the breeze through the trees. After a half mile, the firs and pines thinned, and we came to the top of the falls.

Even though the falls were a popular hangout spot, nobody was there that day. Kids liked the falls because it offered freedom from grown-ups, plenty of places to explore, and especially because of the races. The participants, two or more, would stand on the highest rock, called the Chimney, and a wager would be made as the racers faced the falls. After a countdown from ten, the competitors rushed down, leaping from boulder to boulder, all the way to the finish line. Dangers included slippery rocks, cracks, holes, debris, competitors who shoved or tripped others, collisions, and snakes sunning on the warm rocks. The reptiles weren't venomous, but when someone was jumping a boulder and saw a snake on his landing site, he tended to lose coordination. There had been numerous injuries over the years, but the most extraordinary was when Dub Mellerman attempted a front flip from one rock to the next and landed on his face, knocking out half his teeth. Dub became something of a folk hero, and for years, we quoted his philosophical words as he sat bloody faced on the falls. "Rocks is hard."

We climbed up on the Chimney and turned in a circle, looking for Sarah.

"In case either of you are wondering," Bobby said, "I can beat you both to the end of the falls."

A veiled challenge like that usually had us hurtling pell-mell down the rocks, but we had somber business to attend to.

"Not today, Bobby," I said.

"What's the plan?" Micah Lee asked.

I glanced around one more time then called Sarah's name. When I received no response, I said, "Let's check the falls, then we can look around the lake."

On the way down, we decided to poke around in a cave that had formed when several of the boulders had fallen together in a way that created a room about twenty feet in diameter. We'd tried camping in it once, but it was too damp. I climbed in first while Micah Lee waited for a spider status report. Sometimes fat-bodied spiders claimed the cave until a storm washed them out.

"It's clean," I yelled up.

For a moment, Micah Lee blocked the sunlight from above, then he dropped to the ground next to me, followed by Bobby. I reached into a recess above my head and pulled out a wooden box bound by twine. Inside were a candle and some matches, some firecrackers wrapped in plastic, a soggy copy of *Cavalier Magazine*, and an almost full bottle of Scotch that Bobby had stolen months ago. When he had brought it, we each sampled it, made a face, and put the top on, never to open it again. We moved to the back of the cave, and I lit the candle. I tilted it to melt some of it onto a rock that was already splotched with multicolored wax. When the candle stood on its own, we got comfortable in our favorite spots.

I was considered the town's tomboy, but I really didn't care what people thought about me. Like Popeye said, "I yam what I yam." Micah Lee was a mama's boy. Bobby, on the other hand, was a modern-day Huck Finn. Both his parents were drunks, his mom the kind who drank steadily until she passed out. His father, like Huck Finn's pap, had been a mean drunk. Bobby never went into much detail, but he did tell us his father used to beat him and his brother. Mr. Whist had been a workman for the town, and a couple of years back, he had been called out to repair a broken power line. Drunk as a skunk, he ended up electrocuting himself. Bobby once told me he was glad his father had died like that. His smile had given me chills.

"It'd be cool to find Sarah," Micah Lee said.

I nodded. "Well, sure. She's just a little kid."

"No, I mean it'd be cool because it would make us heroes."

I leaned over to retie my P.F. Flyers. Yeah, it would be great to get Sarah Mundy home and all, but he was right. Whoever found her would be famous. Even more than that, the idea of figuring out who was responsible, if Sarah had indeed been kidnapped, would be the coolest part about it. It would be like solving a really hard puzzle.

Micah Lee leaned back and laced his fingers behind his head. "Maybe they'd hold a parade down Main Street with the three of us up on a float." He snapped his fingers. "You know what would be even better? If a sex fiend had her, and we saved her right before he killed her."

"Before *the snatcher* did anything to her," I said.

He stared at me for a second. "Well, sure, yeah. And we have a big fight with the Snatcher."

Bobby jumped up into a squat. "How cool would it be if we got injured rescuing her?"

"Not *too* injured," I said.

"Of course not. Maybe the Snatcher would get us with a knife in the arm or leg is all, something like that."

We went silent, imagining the glory that awaited us when battered, bloodied, and bruised, we returned Sarah to her grateful family.

Micah Lee sighed. "Yeah, I wish we could find her."

"Don't know how we'd start," Bobby said, pulling a flattened cigarette from his crumpled pack. "Besides, she's probably six feet under already."

I frowned at him. "That's an awful thing to say."

Bobby shrugged. "It's likely true."

Sometimes he said things like that just to get under my skin, so I decided to ignore it. "Come on. Let's finish with the falls and go look around the lake."

Bobby's matchbook had gotten wet, so he picked up the burnt match I'd used to light the candle, held it over the wick until it caught, and got his cigarette going. He pointed the burning match at me. "Don't say I didn't warn you when someone finds her body."

I blew out the candle and broke it from the wax. Passing it to Bobby, I said, "Shut up and put this stuff away."

Chapter 5
Autumn of '82

Taking Kit's advice, I drove to the Temperance Inn, a large Victorian home built on a hilltop. I passed through the wrought-iron gates then went up the two-hundred-foot drive to the parking area. When I was a kid, the last of the Wallace family lived there. Someone had bought the place and, by the looks of it, invested a ton of cash fixing it up. It was a lovely lavender structure highlighted with maroon and white. A porch wrapped around the first floor, and above that, spires, dormers, and gingerbread lattices loomed.

I put my bag over one shoulder, grabbed my suitcase, and headed to the front door. Inside, I passed a sitting room where two couples were playing cards, then another empty room, before I found the main desk. No one was there, so I rang the bell.

A door opened behind the desk, and a one-armed man came through it. "Good morning." He smiled, showing perfect teeth.

"The sheriff was supposed to call for me. Charly Bloom."

He grinned. "You don't recognize me, do you?"

I turned my head one way and then the other as I scrutinized the man. "I'm sorry. There is something familiar about you, but I can't place it."

He held up a finger and disappeared through the door. A moment later he returned, smiling again, but his mouth was mostly empty of teeth. He held a set of dentures in his right hand.

I remembered a boy who had knocked out half a mouthful of teeth at Wallace Falls. "Holy shit! Dub Mellerman?"

He slipped his teeth back in and held out his hand, which I didn't take. "Oh yeah." He wiped his hand on his pants. "Damn, Charly Bloom. I didn't know you were coming."

"Didn't Kit give you my name?"

"No. He said he had an investigator coming from down the mountain. Guess he wanted to surprise me."

"Surprise!" I grinned. "Well, you look good, even downright respectable with those teeth." I nodded at the empty sleeve pinned to his shoulder. "What happened there?"

"Vietnam. I may have lost an arm, but at least it got me out of that hell hole." He shook his head and leaned on his remaining elbow.

"So you're an innkeeper?"

"It's worse than that. I own the place."

"Not too shabby," I said, looking around appreciatively. "Listen, Dub. I'll be coming and going a lot. Do any rooms have a private entrance and a phone?"

Dub erased something in his registration book and wrote in another spot. "All the rooms have their own phones. I'll put you in the Mockingbird Suite. It's on the second floor at the back of the inn. There's an exit out to the fire escape you can use."

"Perfect."

Dub came around the desk and reached for my suitcase.

"I got it. Just give me directions."

Dub gave me a clumsy, one-armed hug then told me how to get to my room. I lugged my suitcase up the staircase and navigated the halls to the Mockingbird Suite. Getting the key to work took finesse, but I managed. I stepped in and put down my bag while taking in the focal point of the room—an enormous mahogany bed. The hand-carved posts rose almost to the ceiling, and the mattress was so high that I had to give a little hop to sit on it. I bounced up and down a few times and rubbed my hands over the soft comforter. Getting down, I headed across a hardwood floor covered with a couple of braided, country-style rugs, pausing to look in the dresser mirror. I sometimes felt like a child again when returning to Temperance, so I was happy to see a grown woman in the reflection. I peeked out one of the three curtained windows and then opened a door to the fire escape Dub told me about. I closed it and tried another door that opened to the bathroom.

"Yes," I muttered with a smile, and wasting no time, I turned on the water to fill the antique claw-foot tub.

While the tub filled, I undressed. A full-length mirror hung on the back of the door. "Hey, hot mama." At thirty-six, I was holding up pretty damn well. I could definitely give someone ten years younger a run for her money. Two scars were the only things marring my reflection. The first, a little wider than a wrinkle, began in my right eyebrow and angled up into my hairline above my left eye. The second was a round pucker of flesh on my left collarbone.

The rushing water got my attention, and I saw the tub was almost full. Grabbing a washcloth, I stepped in and lowered myself into liquid heaven.

After my bathtub indulgence, I got on the phone. "Hi, Grievous."

"Charly? Is that you?"

"I'm in town, so I thought I'd get in touch with Roscoe and pick his brain."

Roscoe Gunn was an old friend, old in age as well as in how long I'd known him. We became close when I was a kid, sticking my nose in the middle of the Snatcher investigation. Being a published author, he was something of a local celebrity. Grievous was his wife. Her real name was Gretchen.

"Are you here because of what's going on?" Grievous asked.

"Kit asked me to come help."

"Good. I hope you can put an end to this nightmare."

"I'll do my best."

"No doubt. Roscoe's out running chores for me, and then he's got some writing to do."

If he had writing to do, that meant he'd be at the bowling alley. He said that writers all have a favorite place to work, and his, oddly enough, was in the little lounge at the Temperance Bowl-A-Rama, surrounded by the cacophony of bowling balls crashing into pins.

"I'll see him this afternoon," I told her. We chatted a few more minutes then hung up.

I spent much of the day driving around town and looking at locales that had special meaning for me. I ended up sitting in front of my childhood home for a long time, thinking about my parents. Daddy died of cancer while I'd been in school, but at least Mom saw me join the SBI before she passed. Noting that the current owners kept the house in good shape, I headed out to Wallace Lake and hiked the falls before finally joining Roscoe, now in his seventies, at his unique place of inspiration.

I entered the bowling alley and felt like a time traveler. A handful of lanes were in use, and the rumble of balls rolling and the thunder crack of flying pins mixed with the dings of the pinball machines in the game room fed a strong nostalgia. But it was mostly the smell that launched me back to the late fifties—the leather bowling shoes and the disinfectant they sprayed in them, as well as the burgers, dogs, and popcorn from the snack bar.

It was the other bar I was concerned with, and it was there I found my old friend Roscoe Gunn. I stood in the door and watched him scribbling intently. He wrote novels freehand, and in the fifties and sixties, he authored the Jack Hazzard private eye series.

I walked to his table and said, "Hey there, good-looking. Come here often?"

He looked up and smiled.

After we got caught up, Roscoe said, "I'm glad you're here. Kit's a fine sheriff, but your expertise will be a great help."

"I hope so." I looked at him, finding comfort in his aged face. "The similarities are frightening, aren't they?"

"I've been thinking about that," Roscoe said. His eyes narrowed. "I think that maybe we should revisit what happened back in '59."

"You think that would help?"

He thought a moment and then said, "It could."

I took a deep breath, barely nodded, and said, "Okay."

He signaled the bartender to refresh his coffee and bring me a cup, and then I began a recitation of what happened back in the summer of 1959 from my perspective. Afterward, he interviewed me like a reporter, asking about certain parts of my story and how they made me feel back then and now. We'd done this kind of thing a number of times. Roscoe retired his fictional detective, Jack Hazzard, after bringing out new books based on his character's daughter, Sami, called the Hazzard's Girl series. Roscoe placed her in the FBI, though he based those books off actual cases I worked while in the SBI and then later when I went on my own as a private investigator. He took great literary liberties to turn those cases into compelling reading, and the Sami Hazzard books sold well.

Roscoe picked up his cup and took a slurp of coffee. "You know what my favorite part of how you remember it is?"

"What?"

"How we met. You didn't think much of me."

I smiled. "I didn't know you, Roscoe, just what people said about you, which wasn't flattering. And then when I learned you wrote dirty stories, well..."

Roscoe chuckled at the memory. While the Sami Hazzard books earned him a lucrative income, the earlier Jack Hazzard series did not. Back then, he supplemented his income by writing pornography that he sold to sleazy men's publications.

"It wasn't until I woke in Handsome George's arms with you beside me that I realized you were a good man."

Roscoe smiled warmly, but after a second, he cast his eyes down and cleared his throat. "I've had a rocky past, Charly, but I don't regret much. However, there's one thing I still feel guilty for, and I'm sure Solomon and Handsome George felt the same. Our advice and encouragement nearly got you killed."

"Your advice and encouragement helped get me where I am today. What nearly got me killed was thinking I was indestructible, going where I shouldn't have, and doing things a thirteen-year-old had no business doing."

Roscoe pulled a cigarette from a pack of Vantage. I took the pack and held it up with the health warning facing him.

Roscoe shrugged and lit the cigarette. "I could either quit drinking and smoke, or quit smoking and drink. Not both. I chose to quit drinking. And yes, I know it's odd since I still come to the Gutter Ball Lounge every day to write." He took a deep drag. "What you've told me is a lot more than you usually do, though it's understandable."

"This isn't for publication, Roscoe."

"Good, because I don't write ghost stories."

"You're the one who told me to tell it as I remember it."

"And that's how you remember it?" Roscoe scrutinized me. "Seriously?"

I waved away some drifting smoke. "Think what you want, but I saw them as plain as I see you. They helped me. They didn't want any more children to die."

"What you saw was due to blunt force trauma."

"Not all of them were after my head injury."

"You were dreaming then. You just said so." He put his hand over mine. "That was a long time ago. Memories change to fit desired perceptions."

I pulled my hand free. "I'd probably be dead if it hadn't been for them. And I'm not an idiot. I know I probably imagined them. But

I'm not enough of a cynic to discount the possibility that they really did help."

"I've always thought you were a natural-born detective. Maybe back then, you were figuring things out on a subconscious level, and you brought your solutions to the forefront via these dreams and hallucinations."

I smiled. "That, or they were real."

Roscoe mumbled something unintelligible, his sign that he no longer wanted to debate. "Grievous says you should stay with us."

"Tell her I can't this visit."

"Sure you can."

"I'll be in and out a lot. I don't want to disturb you guys. Tell her thanks and that we'll get together while I'm in town."

"I will."

I grinned and told him, "You do know you married up?"

"Fourth time's the charm, right?" Roscoe beamed, then his expression turned serious. "You need to look for someone to commit to, someone permanent."

"I like being on my own."

"So you say. I was hoping that thing you had with Kit would bring you back."

"A private detective wouldn't have much of a business here in Temperance."

Roscoe sipped his coffee. "No, I suppose not. Maybe you should have lured him to Raleigh. He could have joined the sheriff or police department there."

To avoid responding, I stood. "Come on. Let me treat you to an early dinner at—what is it they call the Pine Top Restaurant now?"

"Le Bistro," he said, slowly getting to his feet with an old-man groan. "Let's go. I'm starving."

We took separate cars, and he must have known a shorter route because he beat me there. The place wasn't too busy, so we got a table with no waiting. The lighting was low. Each table had a candle burning inside a red globe, and the walls were painted a light burgundy. White linen covered each table, with napkins of the same fabric folded into pyramids. The restaurant looked like a caricature of fine dining, but maybe that was because it was located in the heart of Temperance.

A waitress with big disco-style hair brought us some menus. The twenty-something-year-old wore black slacks and a black button-down shirt with Le Bistro's logo printed in gold across the left breast. Roscoe called her Violet and asked after her parents. We ordered drinks, whiskey neat for me and coffee for Roscoe.

After she walked away, I opened my menu. "Roscoe? There's no French cuisine on the menu."

"Nope."

"Why do they call it Le Bistro?"

"I have no idea. Though I love it when some of our locals say they're going to eat at *the* Le Bistro." He chuckled. "Hey, did you see Handsome George today?"

"Haven't had a chance. I'm hoping to swing by the theater before I leave."

Roscoe fidgeted with his napkin then put it in his lap. "So what do you think of Temperance these days?"

"I went sightseeing earlier, even hiked up to the falls."

"A good day for it. Warmest autumn I can remember."

"Things have changed, but not as much as I'd expect."

"Mmm-hmm. Asheville, Boone, and Blowing Rock are all high-traffic tourist towns, while poor little Temperance remains the Mayberry of western North Carolina."

"Is that bad?"

"Hell, no. The last thing I want is a gaggle of Florida blue-hairs tying up our roads."

"That might be good for the town."

He gave a dismissive wave. "We'd have to put in ski slopes or become some artsy-fartsy community. I think most people are happy with the way things are. And it's not like we're in the Stone Age. The population has grown, and we have a McDonalds and an A&W."

"Oooh," I said, pretending to be impressed.

"We have a K-Mart and a Piggly Wiggly too."

"Wow! It's almost New York."

Roscoe's grin dropped. "Not that it's all coming up roses."

"I know," I said, my mood falling. "The missing girls."

Roscoe nodded and then leaned forward. "Not just that. Times are catching up with us. They arrested some kids at the high school for selling cocaine."

"Really? That's not the Temperance I remember."

Roscoe frowned. "Last year, there was a burglary ring working in the fancier neighborhoods. Turned out to be a group of teenagers. And Temperance also has its own motorcycle gang."

"My, you are moving up in the world." I imagined kids riding around on dirt bikes with knobby tires.

"They call themselves the East Coast Thugs."

"Wow. Really?" The Thugs were the real deal. They weren't a club I'd expect in Temperance.

He nodded. "A bunch of bastards. Remember the old Claymoor place? It's about ten miles out of town, past my cabin. Big old house that looks like something from *The Texas Chainsaw Massacre*. The Thugs moved in there a few years back. They're always riding their motorcycles by my house in the middle of the night. Assholes wouldn't know a muffler if it up and bit them. I thought they were squatting, so I complained to Kit. He went and talked to them, and turns out they bought the place. They have every right to be there."

"Sorry for your interrupted sleep."

Violet returned, and as she put down our drinks, Roscoe said, "We were just talking about your uncle."

She looked at me. "You know Uncle Kit?"

I smiled and nodded. "I grew up with him."

She studied my face, and then her eyes lit up. "Wait a minute. Are you the girl who killed the Snatcher?"

I glanced at Roscoe, who shrugged, then I said, "I haven't been a girl in a long time."

Violet looked embarrassed. "I'm sorry. I mean, you're Charly Bloom, right?"

Roscoe chuckled. "What can I say? You're famous around here."

"I've read all your books!" Violet gushed.

Feeling uncomfortable, I pointed at Roscoe. "Those are Mr. Gunn's books."

"Yes." He smiled, obviously enjoying my discomfort. "But they were based on *your* life."

Violet stepped closer. "Sometimes when I read them, I think that I'd like to get into law enforcement."

"See?" Roscoe smirked. "You're an inspiration to young women everywhere."

I fought the impulse to roll my eyes.

"Uncle Kit says you two were best friends growing up."

Instead of responding, I took a drink of my whiskey. We'd been friends, but Kit had been a pain in the ass, so no, not best friends. But times changed, and people did too. And I'd be damned if I'd tell her about the fling Kit and I had a few years back.

Roscoe saved me by inquiring about the specials. He ordered pork chops, and I chose the porterhouse.

When Violet left to turn in our order, I asked Roscoe, "How many are there?"

"How many what?"

"Back to our conversation. How many East Coast Thugs?"

"There's never more than a handful, a half dozen at most. They seem to change them out like they're rotating through, except for the big guy in charge. I think he's always here."

"There has to be fifteen, twenty chapters. Their membership is into the hundreds, if not thousands. Five or six members? That isn't much of a chapter. Remember that case I worked with the bike clubs?"

"Yeah, almost used it for one of my plots. But that wasn't the Thugs, was it?"

"No. That had to do with the Storm Troopers. A group of them killed two members of the Pagans in a highway shooting on I-85. But while working it, I learned about all the different clubs in the state. The Thugs used to be a small group who liked to put patches on their jackets and ride in a pack, but there wasn't much of a criminal element about them. In the late sixties, their leadership changed, and they began expanding, both in numbers and illegal enterprises. The chapters in Raleigh and Charlotte are supposed to be mixed up in the drug trade, which probably means they all are."

"Well, the Thugs run a business in town, ECT Motorcycle and Small Engine Repair. But that's really all I can tell you about them. Hey, I got a royalty check last week. Since you're here, saves me from having to mail your cut." Roscoe took an envelope from his jacket pocket and passed it to me. In total, Roscoe had written eight best-selling Sami Hazzard books, and since they were based on my actual cases, he insisted on splitting his royalties with me. "The books are selling like crazy now that Sami has left the FBI to follow in her father's footsteps."

"I still say you're too generous." And it was true. His books sold well enough that I wouldn't have had to work if I hadn't wanted to.

"You live it, I write it. Half is fair. Plus, the Hazzard's Girl series has fired an interest in the original Jack Hazzard books. They're all back in print, and I'm selling more of them than I dreamed possible."

"I'm happy for your success, and so is my pocketbook."

Violet returned with our salads. I finished my whiskey and told her to bring red wine with my steak. We attacked small plates of baby leaf lettuce, sundried tomatoes, and artichoke hearts.

Roscoe grinned. "I have something else for you." He opened the briefcase by his chair and passed me something in a flat paper bag.

I pulled out a thick, glossy issue of Penthouse Magazine. There was a blonde on the cover, hair piled high and large breasts about to burst from her exposing top. "Really, Roscoe? This is a very strange gift."

Roscoe reached out and flipped open the cover. He tapped a listing in the index. Under the heading Fiction was the title "Hazzard's Girl on Her Own," followed by his name and a small photo of him.

"Well, hell, are you writing smut again?"

Roscoe laughed loudly, and some other customers turned to stare, making me self-conscious about holding a men's magazine in a public restaurant.

"This is priceless. You're blushing as much as when you read my writing twenty-some-odd years ago." He took the magazine, slipped it back in the plain brown wrapper, and handed it to me.

I set it on the chair next to my purse.

Roscoe picked up his fork to finish his salad. "Some of those magazines publish great short fiction, though I almost turned down the offer when they wanted to publish a chapter of the new book as a short story. Then I remembered back to when you were a kid and got offended that I wrote for girlie magazines. Sami Hazzard is based on your life, so in a way, you've just made it into a men's magazine."

I laughed and gave him a sarcastic, "I'm so honored."

Our food arrived, and we had a fine time. After we split a slice of amazing apple pie, Roscoe walked me to the parking lot.

He looked over my '72 Firebird Formula 400. "I see you're putting your money to good use."

"Most fun car I've ever had."

"Candy-apple red? Don't you stand out a tad when you're tailing someone?"

"I have a beat-up sedan for those jobs." I dropped into the driver's seat and started the engine, which idled with a growl.

Putting a hand on the roof, he bent down and said through the open window, "Charly, find out what happened to those girls."

"I'll do my best." I hoped my best would be enough.

Chapter 6
Summer of '59

S arah Mundy had been missing for two weeks. Some nights, I lay in bed, worried the same thing could happen to me. I imagined Bobby's sex fiend and all the perverse cruelties he'd perform. One night, I dreamed of Solomon's sea monster, a giant bottom dweller in Wallace Lake that rose to eat me while I was taking a midnight swim.

Micah Lee and I, and sometimes Bobby, spent hours almost every day out in the woods, looking for Sarah. We couldn't think of anywhere else to look where she wouldn't have already been found. The only thing to come out of our searches was Micah Lee getting a bad case of poison ivy.

Even though it was summer and school was out, there was a special assembly for the town kids in the Temperance Junior/Senior High School auditorium. Bobby, Micah Lee, and I, along with Kit Haiselton, sat on the curb of Our Lady of Hope Catholic Church, a small clapboard building just big enough for the town's small population of Catholics, and watched everyone show up at the school across the street.

"Anyone else's mom going nuts over this?" Micah Lee asked, scratching at the rash on his neck.

Bobby shook his head.

"My mom keeps telling me to be extra vigilant," I said.

"Meaning what?" Micah Lee asked.

I did an impression of my mom ticking off on her fingers, "Be aware of your surroundings, look out for strangers, and be mindful of safe places to run to if anything happens."

Bobby snorted and said, "Don't seem right, opening up the school in the summer."

"Coulda met over at town hall or something," Kit said.

"Ain't big enough," Bobby added, tossing the last of his cigarette into the street.

Sighing, I got up and stomped on the butt. I picked it up and put it in my pocket. "Damn it, Bobby. I'm getting sick of picking up your butts."

Kit pointed at me, laughing. "You pick Bobby's butt."

I shook my head at Bobby and Micah Lee. The only person who thought Kit was funny was Kit himself.

A police car pulled up to the curb in front of the school. Sheriff Rysdale got out of the passenger side, and a deputy, Marty Atwater, got out of the driver's side.

Bobby stood. "Let's see if they know anything."

We all got up and went into the auditorium. Usually, during the school year when the auditorium was loaded with kids, there was pandemonium until the principal and teachers got everyone under control. Now, it was like walking into a library or church or hospital. The only talk was hushed, and nobody was cutting up. Our principal, Mr. Abercrombie, welcomed everyone and spoke for a while about Sarah Mundy and how we should all pray for her family and her safe return. He added that it was important that we listen to what the sheriff had to say, and then he turned the podium over to Sheriff Rysdale.

He stood there and looked over the gathered crowd. The only sound was a random cough.

The sheriff took off his hat and spoke. "I believe all of you know what's going on, but I'll run down the general facts anyway. Sarah Mundy is missing. Evidence suggests that someone climbed a ladder up to her bedroom window and kidnapped her late at night. I would advise that, for the time being, all of you close and lock your windows at night." This brought about a general murmuring, and the sheriff looked down at the podium while he thought a moment. "I'm not saying this'll happen again, but until the kidnapper is caught, we want to be cautious. We don't know why this crime took place. As of now, there has been no ransom demand."

The sheriff opened his mouth and then closed it. You could tell he was trying to remember what to say next. There was a fairly long stretch of silence, until Marty Atwater stepped next to him and whispered in his ear.

"Damn sheriff is dumber 'n dirt," Bobby grumbled.

The sheriff started to speak again then turned to Marty and mumbled something. Marty nodded and whispered back.

The sheriff turned to us and cleared his throat. "The Temperance Lion's Club has told me that they're going to put up a reward of one thousand dollars for the return of Sarah, whether she's alive or... well... for Sarah's return."

A buzz of whispering filled the auditorium at the mention of the reward.

Micah Lee leaned over to Bobby and me, eyes wide, and whispered, "A thousand dollars. Man, oh man. We won't just be heroes if we find her. We'll be rich too."

The auditorium quieted when the sheriff spoke again. "Me and Deputy Atwater will stay here for a while. If anyone has information, please see us. Otherwise, I want all you kids to keep your eyes and ears open and report anything out of the ordinary. Until we figure out what happened, don't go anywhere by yourself, and never ever get in a car with somebody you don't know."

The sheriff put his hat back on, grabbed the lectern with both hands, and leaned forward as if sharing a secret. "Boys and girls, there's a lot we don't know right now. But there is one thing I do know with one hundred percent certainty. We will catch whoever is responsible. You have my word."

The following day, Mom got a phone call from her cousin while I was eating a grilled cheese-and-baloney sandwich at the kitchen table for lunch and reading the funny pages.

"What?" Mom said after greeting her cousin. "Are you sure?" I looked up to see Mom leaning against the refrigerator like she'd lost the strength to stand. She listened intently while clutching the phone with both hands. The concern on her face shifted into an expression that bordered on fear. "Oh dear God. What is happening to this town, Mary Beth?"

When Mom hung up, she looked at me and said, "Theresa Goodnight is missing."

Chapter 7
Autumn of '82

I stopped by Kit's office in the morning to get the addresses of the families of the missing girls. He'd arranged for me to speak with their parents. Kit also informed me that all the remains they'd found were female, so the Snatcher did something else with Bobby's body.

Out in the sheriff's department parking lot, I turned my face to the morning sun, already warm enough that I took off my sweater and tossed it in the backseat.

Since their daughter's abduction, one or both of the Smallwoods had stayed at the Econo Lodge. Mrs. Smallwood opened the door when I knocked. She would have been an attractive woman in a full-figured way if it weren't for stress and heartache. She clutched a Kleenex and stood aside without comment. The curtains were drawn, the bed unmade, and a barely nibbled hamburger sat in an open wrapper on the dresser.

"Do you mind if we talk in the coffee shop?" I asked.

Mrs. Smallwood nodded and grabbed the room key lying next to the uneaten burger.

We didn't say much until the waitress brought our coffee. I took mine black, but Mrs. Smallwood doctored hers with sugar substitute and powdered cream. I noticed the sympathetic looks directed at Mrs. Smallwood from the two employees in the shop. They knew who she was and why she was there.

I didn't take notes because that distracted from watching the interviewee, and I didn't use a tape recorder because it sometimes made them nervous. I always made a point of remembering interview details, important and mundane, so I could write them down later. I kept meticulous notes, and I had Solomon to thank for that, since he had given me my first notebook back in '59.

I started with the basics. "Mrs. Smallwood, the sheriff tells me that you're from Greensboro."

"That's right."

"Is Savannah your only child?"

She opened her mouth to respond, but a wave a grief struck her. She lifted the coffee to her lips and closed her eyes as she sipped. She put down her cup and said, "Yes."

"Are you employed?"

She shook her head. "No."

"What does your husband do?"

"He works for Jefferson-Pilot, a life insurance company. They're a good company, told David to take as much time as he needs. He's tying up some loose ends and then coming back up."

"Does your husband have any enemies?"

She blinked twice and looked as though she had a hard time understanding what I meant. "Enemies? No, not David."

Time to get to the meat of the interview. "The night Savannah went missing, you ate at Le Bistro?"

"Yes."

"And she left to go to the park across the street?"

"Yes." Her answer came out as a quiet sob. She reached for the chrome napkin dispenser and pulled out two. She quickly wiped at her eyes.

"About what time did she go to the park?"

"We told the sheriff it was sometime after eight o'clock. It was a late dinner."

"Late enough that it was dark when Savannah went to the park?"

"Yes, but they have streetlights. The park wasn't totally dark." She said it like the lights should have kept her daughter safe.

"Did you see anyone suspicious that night?"

"No."

"Did you see someone in the restaurant watching your daughter, maybe outside looking through a window?"

She wiped her nose. "No. Nothing like that."

"Are you sure? Sometimes things that don't seem important become relevant later."

She looked at the wall for a few seconds then sniffed and shook her head. "I really can't think of anything."

I realized then that she wouldn't be of any real help, but I stayed and chatted a few more minutes to make her feel as though she were doing something to assist me. Then I wrote down my number at the Temperance Inn. "Call me if you think of anything." I stood to leave.

Mrs. Smallwood said, "No one told us."

"Excuse me?"

"No one told us about the missing girls, about Copycat. If someone had told us, we wouldn't have let Savannah go."

I sat back down. One mention of the previous girls' abductions, and they would probably have kept Savannah close, especially after dark. But who should have told them? Whose responsibility was it? Should the desk clerk at the motel have informed them? Cashiers at the shops they visited? The maître d' at Le Bistro?

Mrs. Smallwood gazed at me with so much pain in her face I could almost share her heartache. She nearly sobbed as she said, "It's our fault. We shouldn't have let her go."

I scooted my chair closer and put a hand on her forearm. "It's not your fault. There was no way anyone could know..." I let the thought fade.

In any other instance, there would have been nothing wrong with letting their daughter go to the park. When I was young, we'd had so much more freedom than kids today. We'd leave home after breakfast and not have to return until lunch, and then we wouldn't have to be home until dinnertime. In the summer, when sun set late, all the kids would meet back out on the street after dinner for games like kick-the-can, hide-and-seek, or red light, green light. Most kids only had to go home when the streetlights came on.

I stood and said, "I am very sorry." I put some money on the table to cover our tab and added, "Really. Don't blame yourself."

I walked to the door of the coffee shop and turned to see Savannah's mother gazing blankly into the distance, her hands tightly grasping each other as if engaged in a frenzied prayer.

My next stop was the Regis house. I was an hour early, but sometimes I learned more from a surprise visit. Driving up the winding road of Cray's Hill, I decided not to ask the question I most wanted to ask: *In what reality did you think naming your daughters Mani and Pedi was a good thing?*

The neighborhood was not yet ten years old. Each bit of property had several acres, and the houses were anywhere from big to sprawling. Those who wished to maintain a mountain charm had built cabins, three-story monstrosities that would shame Daniel Boone.

The Regis house was a flat-roofed, glass-walled, modern design built right up to the hill behind it. It strived for Frank Lloyd Wright but came across as pretentious. Though there was a multi-car garage, two vehicles were parked in front, a Lincoln Town Car and a Porsche 911 Targa. I figured the Lincoln for the Mrs. and the Porsche for Mr. Regis. Assuming that my muscle car had more in common with the Porsche, I parked next to it.

The stairs leading to the twin front doors were redwood and chrome. I pushed a dime-sized ivory button and heard Quasimodo go to town on the bells of Notre Dame.

A moment later, a dark-skinned woman opened the door. "May I help you?"

"I have an appointment with Mr. and Mrs. Regis. My name is Charly Bloom."

Maintaining an expressionless face, she said, "Your appointment isn't until one, and it's not yet twelve. I'm afraid you'll have to—"

"Who is it, Rebecca?" a man called from inside.

The housekeeper called back, "It's nobody, sir. I'll be right—"

I leaned in and shouted, "Mr. Regis, I'm Charly Bloom!"

There was a moment of silence, and the housekeeper tried to wound me with angry eyes.

"Well, let her in, Rebecca."

She sighed to let me know just how much I displeased her. "Come this way," she said and led me to a living room.

Because of the floor-to-ceiling windows, I felt as if I were in a fish tank. A gray-haired man stood from a chair. The woman on the sofa next to him stayed seated, her head down.

He extended a hand. "How do you do? I'm Marshall Regis." He wore creased white slacks and a black golf shirt that looked fresh off the rack. I put him somewhere between sixty-five and seventy. It was obvious he worked out and ate right, and he was lucky enough to have genes that ensured him a full head of hair at his stage of the game.

I took his hand and returned his firm grip. "Charly Bloom."

"I've heard about you. You're well known in Temperance." Regis sat next to his wife and placed a hand on hers. "Ramona, dear. The private investigator is here, the one the sheriff told us about."

I stepped over to Mrs. Regis, who wore a bathrobe—a plush, expensive one. She raised her head. Her gaze was vacant. She had obviously been medicated. Like Savannah Smallwood's mother, she was an attractive woman marred by heinous circumstance. In any other situation, she would be gorgeous.

With an air of forced dignity, she asked, "Can you find my girls?"

I'd learned that promises, though cheap, were hard to keep. "I'll do what I can."

Mr. Regis indicated the chair he'd been in a moment earlier. "Please, sit down."

Once seated, I took in the room, the tasteful furnishings, the expensive art, and the quiet desperation that hummed like electricity about this couple. "I'm sorry I'm early."

"Nonsense," Mr. Regis said.

I crossed my legs and put my hands on my knee. "Mrs. Regis, Sheriff Haiselton told me that, after school, your older daughter would walk to her sister's school, and you would pick them up there."

Mrs. Regis's lips trembled. "Yes."

"Once your older daughter got there, how long would they wait until you arrived?"

A transformation took place, beginning in her eyes. The blank look was replaced by fire, and her slack expression tightened. "How dare you."

"Excuse me?"

Mrs. Regis stood and looked down at me. "How dare you insinuate that this is my fault." She was even more beautiful in her cold rage.

"Mrs. Regis, I don't know what I said that would make you think—"

"Get out!" she shouted, stepping closer.

I leaned back, worried that, in her fury, she would slap me.

Her husband stood and took her in his arms. "Shhh, sweetheart. She didn't mean anything." He turned toward the door and shouted, "Rebecca!"

Mrs. Regis went limp in her husband's arms. No longer filled with righteous anger, she seemed unable to stand without assistance. Rebecca rushed in.

"Take Ramona upstairs and help her dress," Mr. Regis said.

Rebecca came over and put an arm around the woman. "Mrs. Regis?"

"Mmm?" Mrs. Regis replied, turning and leaning on the house-keeper.

"Mrs. Regis, let's get you dressed for the day."

"Mmm-hmm."

Rebecca walked her from the room.

"I apologize for my wife's outburst, Miss Bloom. This has taken a terrible toll on her. Can I get you something to drink? Coffee?"

"No. I'm fine. Thank you." In reality, her outburst rattled me. I took a deep breath to calm myself.

He sat again and picked imaginary lint from his pants. "Ramona gets to the elementary school shortly after our older daughter gets there. That day, however, Ramona had a hair appointment. She told the girls she'd be a half hour late." Mr. Regis leaned forward and put his elbows on his knees. "She wonders if she'd gotten there at the nor-mal time if they would be safe at home right now."

"I see." The poor woman was burdened with heavy guilt. "Mr. Regis, did your daughters ever mention anything strange happening in the days leading up to their disappearance?"

"No, not that I can think of."

For the next thirty minutes, we played question-answer, but nothing struck me as helpful. His interview was much like Mrs. Smallwood's, except he admitted he had enemies.

"I was a successful businessman. My last position was CEO for Kelton-Myers. Are you familiar with the company?"

"I've heard of it."

"Based out of Atlanta. During my tenure, we owned everything from restaurant franchises to construction companies to malls, as well as a big manufacturing division. We had over a hundred twenty thousand employees. You can't run a company that big without mak-ing enemies."

"Anyone in particular come to mind? Someone who'd go so far as to take your girls?"

He shook his head. "No one specifically. There are people I fired, competitors I put out of business, and others who've come out on the losing end of a cutthroat business. I've given the sheriff and the SBI a list."

I pondered the possibility, but considering the other missing girls, I dismissed it.

Mrs. Regis returned, wearing a green dress that looked as though it would be a hit at a country club social. She was a bit more alert, so I questioned her about anything she might have seen around the school that day. Like her husband, she gave me nothing.

I checked my watch and brought the interview to an end. Mr. Regis walked me to the door.

When I offered my hand, he grabbed my wrist like a man dangling from a precipice. "I'll pay you," he said.

"Excuse me?"

"Find my girls, and I'll pay you whatever you ask."

I couldn't stand it when someone grabbed me. It was confining, almost like I was bound or restrained. I took hold of his hand and pulled it from my wrist. I didn't want to seem cold, so I kept hold of his hand. "Thank you, Mr. Regis, but I already have a client."

"Then I'll pay you a bonus."

I let go of him and started to tell him that it didn't matter who was paying me, I'd handle it the same. But I realized that this was probably the first time he'd come up against a situation that money couldn't resolve. I wasn't very good at comforting people, but I said, "Mr. Regis, I'll do as much as I can to find out what happened to your daughters."

Chapter 8
Summer of '59

Before Mom would let me leave the house, she made me promise to call her once I got to Micah Lee's.

On my way to Micah Lee's, Solomon pulled up beside me in his van. "Charly, come here." He motioned me over.

"Hi, Solomon."

"You've heard about Theresa Goodnight, haven't you?" he asked.

"Yes, sir."

"Then you should know it's not a good idea to be out and about by yourself."

I kicked at a pebble on the sidewalk. "I know, but I'm just heading over to Micah Lee's."

"Hop in. I'll give you a ride."

I climbed in his van, and when he pulled away from the curb, he said, "I'm on my way to help with the search."

"It's crazy it happened again," I said.

"We don't know that it's the same as Sarah Mundy. She might have just gone to a friend's house and lost track of time." I could tell by the way he said it that he didn't really believe it.

"Theresa doesn't have many friends, Solomon. She's so shy and all." The way Mom put it was that Theresa was painfully shy. She barely spoke and couldn't look another person in the eyes, so she went everywhere with her head down.

"Maybe she just wandered off somewhere."

"Do you know how it happened?" I asked.

"Theresa was going to the library, and her mother told her to be back by ten. Mrs. Goodnight called Sheriff Rysdale when Theresa was an hour late. He told her to wait a bit, that Theresa would probably be home for lunch. When she didn't show up at noon, both of Theresa's parents went to the sheriff's office. The sheriff has called in the auxiliary."

"She disappeared from the library?"

"Nope. She left the library. Some folks said they saw her at the park."

Town Center Park, located across the street from the library, sprawled over several acres and held a gazebo and a playground. The town hall, sheriff's department, and courthouse were across the street on the north side. The fire department and library were south of the park. Businesses, shops, a restaurant, and a diner were on the east and west sides. The park was always busy in good weather. It was hard to imagine that a kid could vanish there without someone seeing something.

"You going to search the park?" I asked.

Solomon pulled his van to the curb in front of Micah Lee's house. "Uh-huh. I suggest you and your friends stay in today. But if you run across any grown-ups who want to help us look for her, send them to the park, and tell them Theresa was wearing a pink dress with matching ribbons in her hair."

"I can help," I said.

Solomon shook his head. "No, Charly."

"I'll get Micah Lee so I won't be alone."

"No. Now, go on," Solomon ordered. I opened the door and got out. I turned to plead my case, but Solomon shook his head. "Stay inside."

I realized there was no point in arguing. He drove away, and I went to Micah Lee's front door. He answered immediately and let me in. I called my mom and let her know I made it, then we called Bobby, but no one answered at his house. Luckily, Micah Lee's mother hadn't heard about Theresa Goodnight yet, so she was fine with us leaving. We figured all the grown-ups would be searching the park, so Micah Lee and I decided to look around and behind all the businesses that ringed the park. We spent an hour checking the alleys and back entrances of every building but didn't find anything.

"Wonder where Bobby is?" Micah Lee asked as we cut through the alley between Beryl's Diner and Cosgrove's Five and Dime.

"No telling."

He looked behind three boxes stacked by the back door of the store. "We're about done."

I breathed through my mouth as I checked around the diner's stinky trash cans. "Let's look around some of the houses close to here."

"Firemen and deputies are checking around the neighborhoods," Micah Lee said. We'd seen them going from house to house.

"They're just going up to people's doors, asking them if they've seen anything. Let's really search, you know, in their backyards, in their bushes, places like that. We're always cutting through people's yards anyway, so no one will notice us."

"Even Old Man Altus's place?"

I grinned. Not only would we tromp around on the cranky old man's precious lawn, but we'd have a good reason for doing so. "Yeah, especially his place."

As we set off walking toward the residential area, Micah Lee said, "Old Man Altus is older than old."

"Older than the hills," I said.

"He's older than Methuselah."

"Older than dirt," I added, laughing.

"Older than the Earth," Micah Lee giggled.

"Older than the sun."

"Older than the universe."

"Older than God."

Micah Lee got all serious. "You shouldn't joke about God. It's a sin."

I smirked. "Your face is a sin."

"You're ugly as sin."

"Your mama's fat as sin."

We made it to the next street over and began at the Krigbaums' property at the corner of Sage and Prospect. We searched in the bushes by the house and along the stockade fence. While we were looking through junk in their carport, Mrs. Krigbaum came up the driveway in her Impala.

She parked and climbed out of her car. "Hey, Charly, Micah Lee. What are you two doing?" she asked.

"Sorry we're snooping around, Mrs. Krigbaum," I said. "We're helping the sheriff search for Theresa Goodnight." That wasn't exactly a lie. Just because they hadn't asked us, that didn't mean we couldn't help.

"I was at Ruby's getting my hair done when I heard." She clicked her tongue.

I glanced at her hairdo, solid and high, and set in place so that it looked done up with lacquer.

"Well, you can help me bring these bags in," she said, opening the back door of her car.

We loaded our arms and followed her into the house. We put the bags on her counter and declined her offer of a couple of RC Colas.

As we turned toward the door, Mrs. Krigbaum twisted the string of pearls around her neck and said, "You get out there and find her, hear?"

Mr. Littlefield, next door, was leaving as we got to his house. A short man with brown hair, he seemed to be in a hurry, but he stopped and said, "Charly, might not be a good idea for you and Micah Lee to be wandering around. Another child has gone missing."

"We heard about Theresa Goodnight," I said.

"Yeah," Micah Lee said. "We're looking for her too."

"What Micah Lee means," I quickly added, "is that we're gonna keep an eye out for her on the way to his house." I told myself that it wasn't a lie because we were looking for her, and we would end up back at Micah Lee's, eventually. But I knew deep down that if I kept stretching the truth like that, it would snap like a rubber band with dry rot and sting the heck out of me.

"Good. Call the sheriff if you see anything. I'm meeting some of the auxiliary boys to assist in the search." He was dressed for hunting with a camouflage vest and his khaki pants tucked into hiking boots.

"This is just like Sarah Mundy," I said after he drove off.

"I really wish we could solve this and find both of them."

Micah Lee's offhanded comment made my heart pick up its pace. That simple sentence from my friend gave me direction, and I suddenly knew what I wanted to be when I grew up. I wanted to solve crimes, and I could start by learning the identity of the Snatcher and the fate of the missing girls. I might have only been thirteen, but I was sure that I could accomplish that.

When we finished at the Littlefield house, we went back out to the sidewalk and saw a patrol car pull up to the curb in front of the Krigbaums' house. Marty Atwater got out and went up on the porch. Mrs. Krigbaum let him in.

"Come on," I said, nudging Micah Lee. "Let's go to Old Man Altus's place next."

The old guy seemed to have a sixth sense when it came to his yard. We had taken no more than a couple of steps onto his lawn when he opened his door, his expression fierce. He looked confused when, instead of running, we went right up onto his front porch.

"Whaddya want?" he asked with a scowl, peering at us through thick, round glasses. He had a full head of white hair parted in the middle. Though he'd shaved, he hadn't shaved well, and there were a couple of patches of white stubble on his jowls. His button-down shirt was yellowed with age, and his brown slacks were held up by suspenders. I noticed his zipper was open.

I opened with another exaggeration that some might classify as a lie. "We're helping Sheriff Rysdale look for Theresa Goodnight."

"Horse crap. Do you take me for? A twit? Whaddya kids want?"

Micah Lee took a step back and pointed down the street to Marty Atwater's squad car. "No, sir. See? We're helping them."

Mr. Altus raised his glasses and squinted in the direction Micah Lee pointed. "Someone's missing, you say?"

I nodded. "Theresa Goodnight, a little girl."

"I don't know her." He dropped the glasses back down on his nose.

"We just want to look around outside your house," Micah Lee told him. "Everyone's out searching."

I figured there wasn't much difference between exaggeration and fib, so I added an outright lie. "Sheriff Rysdale asked us to look around everybody's property."

"Outside, eh?"

"Yes, sir." I glanced at his hand and noticed he had clenched his right hand into a fist.

Mr. Altus saw me looking and stuffed whatever he held into his pocket. A couple of inches flopped out before he shoved it all in. I tried to keep my expression blank when I realized it was a strip of pink material.

He waved his other hand. "Go ahead and look around, but don't mess nothing up."

I worked at remaining calm as I led Micah Lee around the side of Mr. Altus's house. In the backyard, I said, "Remember when we talked about how we'd be heroes if we found out what happened to the girls?"

"Uh-huh."

"Get ready to be a hero."

"What are you talking about?"

I told him what Solomon had told me, that Theresa had been wearing a pink dress with pink bows in her hair. "Old Man Altus was holding a pink ribbon in his hand. I saw him trying to stuff it in his pocket."

Micah Lee's face lit up. "Hot damn! Altus is the Snatcher? It's gonna frost Bobby to no end that he missed it. Hey, did you notice Altus's fly was open? Do you think he's a sex fiend like Bobby said, and didn't have time to zip—"

"Geez! Keep your voice down. We can't let him hear us."

"What should we do? Should we break in? 'Cause maybe Theresa is still alive, and I—"

Spotting Mr. Altus's face in the window next to the backdoor, I threw an arm over Micah Lee's shoulders and pulled him close to me. "Shhh! Act normal." I moved us so our backs were to the house.

Micah Lee lowered his voice. "Whaddya mean? You said—"

"Old Man Altus is eyeballing us."

Micah Lee started to turn.

"Don't look! Damn it, Micah Lee. You can be such a spaz." I let go of him. "He knows I might have seen the ribbon, so he's watching us. We have to act normal, like we don't suspect anything. And you're right about Theresa. She might still be alive, so we have to do something quick."

"What?"

"You keep looking in the backyard where Altus can see you. I'm going to head around the side of the house like I'm searching, right? Then I'm going to run for the Krigbaums' and get Marty Atwater."

"What do I do?"

"Just what I told you, act like you're searching."

"What if he tries to get me?"

"Keep an eye on the house. If he comes out, haul ass."

Micah Lee nodded, though I knew it was hopeless. If Old Man Altus chased him, Micah Lee would trip over his own feet, get caught, and get chopped into fertilizer or whatever Altus did to kids.

"I'm serious, Micah Lee. Watch the house and keep away from Altus."

"I will." Micah Lee walked into the backyard. I could tell he was trying to look casual, but his glances at the house were pretty obvious. I hoped it would fool Old Man Altus long enough for me to get help.

I took my time, acting like I was looking along the wall of the house. When I got to the front corner, I peered around it to check the front yard. Seeing no one, I took off. Halfway across, I slipped and fell, but I jumped back up and continued to the Krigbaums' front porch. Out of breath, I banged on the door. When Mrs. Krigbaum opened it, I slid past her to get into the foyer and out of sight.

"What are you doing here, Charly?" the deputy asked, standing next to Mrs. Krigbaum.

"Old Man Altus... has Theresa... Goodnight," I blurted, panting between the words.

Marty reached out and closed the front door. "Did you see her?"

I shook my head. Not sure how to explain why we'd been there, I decided to skip the searching part. "He came out on his porch, and we were talking to him. Marty, he was holding a pink ribbon. He tried to hide it from me, but I saw it."

"You sure?"

I nodded energetically. "Yep, and I don't know if it means anything, but his pants were open."

"Okay. We're going out to my car. Mrs. Krigbaum, please stay inside."

Marty opened the front door, and keeping his body between me and Old Man Altus's house, he walked me to his patrol car. After opening the passenger door and waiting for me to get settled, he went around to the driver side.

He plopped into the seat behind the wheel and grabbed the police radio. "Frank, you there? This is Marty."

After a few seconds, a static-backed voice answered. "Go ahead, Marty."

"Sheriff, I'm with Charly Bloom. She just came from the Altus place. She says Elwood was on his porch with his pants open, and he was holding a pink ribbon."

"I'm on my way."

We sat in Marty's car. He stared at Old Man Altus's house, cracking his knuckles and drumming on the steering wheel.

"You nervous, Marty?"

"Yeah, I reckon so."

"Me too," I admitted.

"You sure you saw that ribbon?"

"I know what I saw."

"And his pants were open?"

"His zipper was down."

"What were you doing at his place?" Marty asked, looking at me with a cocked eyebrow.

I tried to decide whether to lie or to confess that we'd been doing a little searching of our own. Luckily, I didn't have to do either. I pointed through the windshield. "Look. There's the sheriff."

Marty started his car and rolled forward to park in front of Altus's house. When Sheriff Rysdale parked in front of him, Marty said, "Wait here," then climbed out of the car to meet the sheriff. The men stood together, hands on their belts, talking and occasionally glancing at the house.

After a couple of minutes, Sheriff Rysdale strode over and opened the passenger door. "Tell me what you saw, Charly."

"Like I told Marty, Old Man—um, Mr. Altus opened the door, and we talked to him."

"We?"

"Me and Micah Lee Leigh."

The sheriff grunted. "Okay. What else?"

"Mr. Altus had something in his hand, and when he saw me looking, he stuffed it in his pocket, but I saw it was a pink ribbon. And his fly was open."

"You wait here, Charly." The sheriff gestured for Marty to join him, and they headed up the walkway.

Hoping to get a better view, I slipped out to stand beside the car. The two officers mounted the steps, and the sheriff pounded on the door. Old Man Altus wore a sour expression when he answered, but that changed to surprise when he saw the sheriff and deputy on his porch.

The sheriff said something I couldn't hear, then Altus said, "You can't just barge into my home."

Sheriff Rysdale said in a loud voice, "Step aside, Elwood."

Mr. Altus hesitated a second then kind of leaned out of their way. The sheriff and Marty moved into the house. Old Man Altus started to close his door, but spotting me beside the car, he glared.

Give me the evil eye all you want, you old goat. You're not getting out of this, I thought.

I shifted from foot to foot, wishing I knew what was going on in there and hoping to see them bring Theresa out the front door. Then I remembered Micah Lee.

I ran around the house and into the empty backyard. "Micah Lee?" I whispered. "Micah Lee?" I searched wildly, checking behind every tree. I shouldn't have left him alone. I was suddenly gripped with a certainty that Old Man Altus had snatched him while I'd been getting Marty. I sprinted onto the back porch, yanked at the door, and stepped into Old Man Altus's kitchen. He was sitting at a table with the sheriff and Marty, drinking coffee.

Sheriff Rysdale stood. "Damn it all, Charly. I told you to stay outside."

"He's got Micah Lee too," I blurted.

Altus croaked in surprise or anger, got to his feet, and pointed a bony finger at me. "You're crazy." His eyes were red-rimmed, and he clutched a tissue in his pointing hand.

Crossing to the sheriff, I told him, "Micah Lee was going to stay in the backyard." I pointed out the open door. "He's not there now. Mr. Altus got him."

Altus fixed me with eyes like a snake about to strike. "Now look, you. I don't have Micah Lee hidden away, and I didn't take either of them girls."

In that moment, I knew we had Altus dead to rights. "Hold on. I only told you we were looking for Theresa Goodnight, but you said *either of the girls*. How come?"

"Because I ain't stupid, you idjit!" Altus yelled. "Everyone knows the Mundy girl's been gone for weeks. Well, now this Goodnight girl makes two, don't it?"

Marty stood and took my arm. "Let's go, Charly."

"Wait! Aren't you going to search his house?" I shouted as Marty dragged me out. "Aren't you going to arrest him?"

On the porch, Marty slammed the door and put his hands on my shoulders. "You calm down, Charly. You're acting like a lunatic."

"Dang it, Marty. He had that ribbon right in his hand."

"Don't you think that if he'd taken it from a girl he'd just kidnapped, he'd be more careful about carrying it around?"

I took a deep breath for my counterargument but couldn't think of one. Instead, I released the air, hissing like a leaky balloon. "But—"

"We looked all around. He's the only one in the house."

"But the pink ribbon... I saw it." I winced, knowing I sounded like a whiny kid.

"It's not pink. It's red. And it's not a ribbon. It's a scarf that belonged to his wife."

I gaped at him. "*Wife?*"

Marty nudged me toward the steps. "His deceased wife. He sat there crying and telling us that he holds it when he's lonely, that he can still smell her on it. It looks kinda pink, but it's really red. And his fly was open just like anyone who forgets to zip up."

"Oh man." I stopped. "Wait a minute. What about Micah Lee?"

"Why don't you ask him yourself?" Marty said, pointing.

Micah Lee was sitting on the curb across the street. When he saw me looking, he waved.

"Ah shit," I mumbled.

The front door slammed, and Sheriff Rysdale stomped down the porch steps. I imagined steam coming from his ears, and I breathed a sigh of relief when he continued past me and climbed into his car. Looking back at the house, I saw no sign of Old Man Altus.

"Charly!" Sheriff Rysdale shouted through his open passenger window.

I jumped and cautiously approached the vehicle. "Yes, sir?"

He pointed at me, so angry his finger shook. "You told Mr. Altus that I authorized you to search around his yard?"

"Um... well... what I said was—"

His face turned an even darker shade of red. "You think this is a joke?"

"No, sir. I was just—"

"You wasted my time and Marty's. There's a little girl, two now, who are missing, and we can't afford to waste time." He shook his head, started the car, and drove away.

I hung my head and tried not to cry.

"It's okay, Charly." Marty put a hand on my shoulder. "The sheriff's frustrated. It irks him to no end that Theresa Goodnight was last seen in the park right across the street from the sheriff's department. What you did was wrong, saying you had the sheriff's permission to look around, but you did the right thing coming to us about what you saw. It just didn't turn out."

I nodded, though I didn't feel any better.

Chapter 9
Autumn of '82

I grabbed a quick bite before heading to Rodney Darling's Auto Repair out on Sage Road at the outskirts of town. The shop was in the building that used to be the Esso station. The gas pumps were gone, and a chain-link fence enclosed an acre behind the garage. The Darling family had been around Temperance as long as I could remember, though when I was a kid, they were farmers and lived up on Rock Ridge and Hallow's Summit.

Both garage bay doors were open, and a man was working on a yellow Chevy Nova on a lift in the right-side bay. My car rolled over the gas station dinger hose stretched across the parking lot. As I shut off the engine, the guy came out of the garage, wiping his filthy hands with a dirty bandana. Gaunt, tan, and a few years younger than me, he wore grungy overalls with a gray T-shirt underneath, and old cowboy boots, one wrapped in duct tape.

He smiled as he approached. "Damn, but that's a fine car you got there."

"Thanks. You're Mr. Darling?"

"Uh-huh. Call me Rodney. I take it you're Miss Bloom?"

"Charly will do."

"Kit said you'd be coming. Can I get you a cup of coffee?"

After that A&W cheeseburger, heavy on the onions, some coffee would have hit the spot, but I worried that he'd have an acidic batch that'd been cooking for hours. "I'll pass, thanks."

"Suit yourself. Come on in."

He led me through the front door, and the smell of fresh coffee made me regret my decision. I looked around a room that got the occasional sweeping but not much else in the way of cleaning. A small sofa and three chairs sat to the right of the door.

He slipped around a counter that held a stack of papers and an old cash register. Picking up a percolator, he asked, "Sure I can't get you some? I just put it on."

"I think I *will* have a cup. Make it black."

"Like God intended," he said. He poured coffee into two cups and passed me the one that advertised shock absorbers.

I sat in one of the chairs. "How are you doing, Rodney?"

He'd seemed so calm when I first met him that I was taken by surprise when his face constricted in emotion. He perched on a stool beside the counter. "Not so good. It's hard, you know?"

"I'm sure it is."

He took a deep breath and regained his composure. "I'm a bit of a history buff. Did you know that a hundred years ago, one out of every five children died before they reached the age of five? Feeling what I feel, I wonder how those parents could stand it."

"You don't know for sure that Piper is dead."

He laughed without humor and shook his head. "Right after she went missing, Kit said that it's crucial we find her soon, as the odds drop quite a bit after the first twenty-four hours."

"That's true."

"After twenty-four hours passed, he said the same thing about forty-eight hours, then seventy-two hours, and then he quit saying anything about deadlines." He looked at me as if expecting some kind of encouragement. When I didn't offer any, he said, "You went through the same thing when you were a girl. I remember that. I wasn't much older than Piper is now."

"It wasn't the same thing."

"But you found out who was taking the girls. You killed him." He eyed me as he took a sip of his coffee. "Kit told me they finally found those children."

"Yes. Out on the other side of Wallace Lake."

Tears filled his eyes. "You think it'll be twenty-three years before they find Piper?"

Not wanting to answer, I steered the conversation in another direction. "Mr. Darling... Rodney, I understand you're a single parent."

He wiped his nose and, from behind his dirty bandana, responded with either "Yes ma'am," or "Yes, I am."

"Where's Piper's mother?"

"That's a good question."

"What do you mean?"

"I mean I don't know where she is." He drained his cup, and as he poured more coffee, he said, "Her name is Mary Erath, or at least, it was. Maybe she got married, or maybe she just changed it to Sunshine or Daffodil or something like that."

"Why would she do that?"

"She's a hippie, or she was when I knew her."

"Here in Temperance?"

He settled back on the stool. "No. I had a cousin who worked as a maintenance man over at that college in Boone. When I turned eighteen, I went to live with him. I got a job working in the garage at a car dealership there, Mack Brown Chevrolet. My cousin—his name is Tray—hung out with some of the college kids, and that's how I met Mary."

"Was she a student?"

He chuckled. "In the loosest sense. I don't remember her going to class more than a half dozen times. She lived in the dorms when we met, but I rented this old cabin ten miles from town, and she moved in with me. It was run down and had an outhouse, but to us, then, it was a little slice of paradise."

"I take it the pregnancy changed things."

"Not right away. I was scared, but also real happy. The first few months of her pregnancy were wonderful. She said she knew it would be a girl and picked the name Piper Dancer Darling. I used to just walk around and say the name, and Mary would laugh, saying it sounded like a song as it came off my lips.

"Anyway, things turned sour when she was six months along. Mary was into bands, and some friends were going to spend a summer following the Grateful Dead tour. Mary wanted us to go, but I pointed out that I had a good job with insurance, and she was close to her due date. She had this fairytale image of what having a baby would be like, and that was her first brush with the responsibility she faced. From then on, she got unhappier and began saying all those things people say when they want to break up. Trouble was, she was pregnant. What could she do? She didn't work. I supported us. She didn't speak to her parents, and she would have rather died than gone home to them. Her friends left without us, Piper came a couple of weeks later, and Mary left us both a few weeks after that."

"Did she ever get in touch with you?"

"Nope. No calls, and the only letter was the one she left by the crib when she took off. I was at work, and she left Piper all alone, a newborn baby. It wasn't any apology, either. No explanation other than she couldn't handle the lack of freedom."

"Do you think she might have come back for her daughter?"

Rodney shook his head. "If those other girls hadn't gone missing, if Copycat wasn't out there somewhere, I might. But I'm thinking that what happened to Piper is the same as what happened with Mani and Pedi Regis and that Smallwood girl."

"Tell me about the night Piper disappeared."

"Piper and I made sloppy joes for dinner, then we watched some TV. After that, we went outside and watched the meteor shower. She got to bed a little later than usual. When I went to wake her up the next morning, she was gone."

"And the day before? What can you tell me about that?"

He shrugged. "Same as any other day. I got up, woke Piper, we had breakfast, and I drove her to camp. During the summer, she goes to a local day camp. She likes it. When she's not at camp, my sister watches her, and sometimes I take her to the garage with me."

"Where's the camp?"

"North of town. They have kids that stay for weeks at a time, but they also take locals as day campers."

"Anything out of the ordinary when you dropped her off?"

"Not really."

"After work?"

"I close at three, because of Piper and having to get her after school or camp. I picked her up at three thirty. On the way home, we stopped at Shorty's."

"Shorty's is still in business?"

"Yeah."

Shorty's had been around for a long time. Back when Temperance County was dry, Shorty Watson opened a bar just across the county line in a dilapidated old cabin on a no-name road off I-26. The county commission approved liquor sales in the early fifties, but people still went to drink at Shorty's. When I was a kid, it was famous for hard-drinking men, loose women, and knock-down, drag-out bar fights. People used to say you had to cut your way in and shoot your way out.

"Isn't that a rough place for a ten-year-old girl?"

"It's all right in the daytime. I wouldn't take her at night. Every now and then, we'd stop in on the way home from camp. I'd get a beer, and Piper would play some pinball or darts. Shorty died years ago. His daughter, Tamara, runs it now. She loves Piper, makes her

Shirley Temples, gives her fries if she's hungry, and gives her change to play the games."

"What happened when you stopped in that particular day?"

"About the same as any other. We sat at the bar awhile, then Piper went to play some games, then we left."

I finished my coffee, got up, and leaned against the counter. "Who was at Shorty's that day?"

Rodney scratched behind his ear. "You go any day around four or five, and happy hour brings in a couple dozen folks."

"Regulars?"

"I suppose."

"Anyone else come to mind?"

Rodney thought a moment. "Three of them biker guys came in, but we left right after that."

"The East Coast Thugs?"

"Yeah."

"Do you know their names?"

"One of them is a guy from Temperance, Luke Beason. Another was big, tall but fat too, just big all around. He had black hair, long like a hippie, and a big black beard. The other fellow was kind of squirrelly, skinny, wore an old leather pilot's cap, like when they flew those biplanes."

"Did you or Piper talk to them?"

"Yeah, but it wasn't anything. Piper was playing games. The bikers got some beer and sat at a booth. Tamara said something about getting Piper better playmates. I looked over, and Luke and the big one were showing her how to make a pool shot."

It wasn't a smoking gun, but it was something I could follow up on. "What happened?"

"Nothing. I went over and said hi, casual like. The big one said they were showing her how to be a pool shark so she could win a bunch of money for her daddy. I told Piper it was time to go. I paid the bill, and we left."

"Did Piper say if they talked about anything else?"

"I asked her later, and she said all they talked about was how to play pool. I told Kit about it... after she... anyway, he talked to them but didn't think it was anything."

"Did you stop anywhere else?"

"No, we went straight home."

I retrieved a business card from my jacket pocket, turned it over, and wrote the phone number for the Temperance Inn. "Call me if you think of anything else," I said, holding the card out to him.

Any parent of a missing child would say that one of the worst things was the helplessness they felt. They'd do anything to get their child back if they only knew what that was. While I spoke with Rodney, the act of talking about it was exactly that, doing something. I saw a change come over him, recognition that perhaps there was still hope. But as he took my card, the weight of the world resituated on his shoulders. There was little I could do to help him with his burden, but I liked this man and was confident I would have liked Piper. It was uncharacteristic of me, but I stepped forward and hugged him.

Chapter 10
Summer of '59

Every time the phone rang, I worried that it was the sheriff calling to tell my parents what I'd done, but he never did. With two girls missing, Mom was really worried. She would only let me leave the house if there was someone with me at all times.

A couple of days after Theresa Goodnight's disappearance, Micah Lee and I caught up with Bobby at the bowling alley. He was manning the flippers on Arabian Nights, our favorite pinball game. There was a welt fading to yellow on his cheek, and matching bruises ran up both arms.

"Dang, Bobby. What happened to you?" Micah Lee asked.

"Pissed off Winthrop." He didn't have to say more.

Micah Lee jumped into how I'd fingered Old Man Altus.

Bobby laughed so hard he let the silver ball drop. "Oh man, I bet the ol' geezer blew a fuse." He shook his head. "I can't believe you thought it was him. That old fart couldn't kidnap a lightning bug with a Mason jar."

Micah Lee got offended on my behalf. "Hey, it's not her fault. She saw what she thought was a ribbon and put two and two together."

Bobby grinned. "And got five."

I shoved him out of the way and smacked the plunger, sending the next steel ball into motion. "Yeah, well, where the hell were you?"

Bobby moved my hand from the left flipper and took that while I played the right one. "I was hanging with Winthrop up at the old mill."

"If the sheriff caught you up there, you'd be in trouble," Micah Lee said.

Bobby shrugged. "Big deal."

The old mill dated all the way back to the 1880s when a New England textile businessman opened the factory a third of the way up Hallow's Summit. He died in 1901, and his properties and holdings fell to his son, who didn't care for business. Deciding the millions he'd inherited were just fine, he closed the mill three years later. It sat vacant for decades, rotting away.

As anyone could have predicted, kids from Temperance started hanging out up there. Back in the forties, three teenagers were running around on the third story and fell through all three rotted floors before landing on some old machinery in the basement. Their tragic deaths led to the town erecting an eight-foot-tall chain-link fence around the property and decorating it with No Trespassing signs.

"I didn't think about the old mill," I said. "We could look for Sarah and Theresa up there."

Bobby shook his head. "Don't bother. Winthrop found Dad's old .38 out in the shed. We went up and shot stuff. We looked all around too. There's nothing up there." His flipper sent a pinball into a bumper and down the gutter. "Crap."

"Cool. You got to shoot a gun?" Micah Lee asked.

I was jealous. "Maybe we can go shoot it sometime."

"I wish," Bobby said, "but Winthrop's keeping it." He looked up at me, and after a moment, he asked, "So Rysdale was mad, huh?"

"Yeah. Not sure what pissed him off more—that I made a mistake about Old Man Altus, or that I said we were part of his search party."

After a few more games, we ran out of coins and left the bowling alley. Micah Lee had to

get some things for his mom at the hardware store, so he dropped into Scruggs Mercantile. Bobby and I kept going, talking about maybe seeing if we could get up a game out at the field.

We were walking by the laundromat when Mrs. Whist's beat-up Plymouth chugged to the curb beside us. "Well, looky there. A couple of walkin', talkin' shit stains," Winthrop called out the window. He had a lisp, so the last part came out sounding like "thit thtains." He was tall, maybe six feet four, and he looked as gangly and clumsy sitting behind the wheel as he did when he stood. He pressed a nostril closed with a finger and blew snot from the other out the window. He turned back and wiped his face with the sleeve of his leather jacket.

Bobby's eyes lit up. "Hey, Winthrop. What's up?"

"My big ten inches, or at least it was until I got a look at your girlfriend there. I wouldn't bang her with *your* dick."

I wasn't eager to mix it up with Winthrop, but my mouth often took on a life of its own. "You wouldn't know where to put it if I drew you a picture."

Winthrop pushed open the car door and emerged like a trapdoor spider. He rushed me and shoved both hands against my chest, copping a feel while forcing me back. I knew I'd made a big mistake mouthing off to him, but I stood up to him with gritted teeth and fisted hands. Winthrop's arm extended like a tentacle, and he grabbed my throat. My eyes flicked left and right, but there was nobody on the street, no adults to intervene. I swung my fists, batting at his arm, but he held it straight as an iron bar and began squeezing with his long fingers. When I could no longer draw in a breath, I stopped hitting at him. Winthrop shoved my back against the brick wall of the laundromat and stepped close enough so that his body pushed against mine. I was trapped like a mouse squeezed by a snake.

Winthrop put his mouth by my ear and whispered, "I don't need a picture, skank. If I stuck my dick in, you'd think I was ripping you in two. Yeah, you'd bleed and cry like a little girl, but then you'd come back wanting more. Whaddya say, Bloom? Wanna fuck?"

His hand eased up, and I inhaled deeply, taking in Winthrop's sour breath. He moved back, and though there were black stars in my vision, I saw that Bobby had Winthrop's arm and was pulling him back.

"Hey, Winthrop," Bobby said, trying to draw his brother's attention. "Can I get a ride home?"

Winthrop stared at me while chewing on his bottom lip, turned to his brother, and then back to me. His hands clenched, and he breathed like a bear. After a second, he relaxed. "Yeah, squirt, sure." He reached a hand and slapped my cheek a couple of times, just hard enough to make a smacking sound. He smiled, licked his lips, and went to get in his mother's car.

Bobby shrugged at me then followed. "See ya, Charly," he said through the open passenger window.

"Hey, Bloom. Sit on this." Winthrop flipped me the bird then tried to lay a patch, but the old junker nearly stalled.

When they rounded the corner, I blinked a few times. I looked at my hands, and they were shaking. Winthrop had scared me bad. Walking again, I crossed my arms and put my hands in my armpits to stop them from trembling. I could still smell his breath, and his body odor seemed to cling to me.

Head down, I shuddered, and a voice called, "Charly! Hey there, kiddo. Are you okay?"

I looked up to see Solomon at the curb in his rust-red van. I walked to the van. "Hi, Solomon. I'm okay."

"The way you were shuffling down the sidewalk, I thought something might be wrong with you."

I thought about telling him about Winthrop but decided not to revisit that. "Just thinking about the lost girls and all."

He nodded and then frowned. "I should be mad at you, Charly Bloom. The sheriff certainly is."

"I'm sorry, Solomon." I rested my arms on the passenger windowsill. "I just wanted to help."

Solomon scratched his beard and gave me a wink. "I know you did."

"Still no word?"

Solomon shook his head. "Her father, the sheriff, a couple of deputies, and a few volunteers are out in the woods today. Billy Gentry's out there with his bloodhounds, but last I heard, nothing. I'm afraid she's gone, just like the Mundy girl."

I didn't want to agree, but there was no use denying the truth. "Yeah."

"Hop in, Charly. Where you headed?"

I pulled open the door and hopped into the seat. "Nowhere particular."

"Why don't you come over to the ol' steamer, and we'll eat some lunch on the deck?"

"Okay."

When we got to Solomon's house, I helped him make tuna fish sandwiches with Duke's mayonnaise and sweet pickles. His kitchen counters were built low so he could cook from his wheelchair, which meant I had to bend over to chop the pickles. He put a pocket-sized notebook and pen on a tray with the food. He put the tray in his lap, while I carried a couple of sodas, and we went up the two long ramps that ran along the back wall.

"Get the hatch, there, Charly," he said, indicating the small door at the top of the ramp.

We exited into warm sunlight on the roof. Like the rest of his home, the roof had a nautical appearance, resembling the deck of a ship. We set the food and drinks on a portion of the deck that rose a little over a foot, which he called the cabin house, and had our lunch there.

After Solomon finished his sandwich, he asked, "Still trying to solve the mystery?"

I grunted, and when he raised an eyebrow, I said, "Trying to solve the mystery of why I made an ass out of myself with Sheriff Rysdale. I can't believe I accused Old Man Altus."

Solomon patted my shoulder. "If you'd have minded me, it wouldn't have happened. But beyond that, it was a good call. You saw a faded bit of red cloth and thought it was a pink ribbon. Elwood Altus will survive." Solomon could always make me feel better.

"Yeah, but the sheriff thinks I'm an idiot."

"He doesn't think you're an idiot. But even if he did, why do you care?"

"Because I think I want to..." Right away, I wished I hadn't started that sentence, but I figured I should just go ahead and tell someone. "I thought maybe I'd be some kind of detective when I grow up."

"Like in the police?"

I nodded.

He stared at me and rubbed his stubbly chin.

"Stupid, huh?"

"No, I don't think it's stupid. It's just that I haven't heard of many police ladies. I mean, other than meter maids and secretaries."

"Yeah."

"And that's why you and Micah Lee were out scouring yards?"

"Yeah. We thought that maybe we could—"

Solomon waved away my explanation. "Wanting to be a detective is why you disobeyed me?"

"I s'pose."

He studied me a long minute. "Now that I think about it, you'd be damn good at it."

"Do you think so?"

"I said so, didn't I?"

"Thanks, Solomon."

"But now is not the time to start. Something bad is going on, something that would put you in danger if you were in the wrong place at the wrong time."

My shoulders sagged a little. "You think I should forget about the Snatcher?"

"I didn't say that, Charly. You can still hone your skills, but do it from a distance. You have a good mind, and you might help—but like I said, from a distance. Do you know what I mean?"

"I think so."

"Keep your distance, literally. If you come up with a suspect or think you may have found out where the girls are, don't investigate on your own. Something like that is too dangerous. Instead, you tell Sheriff Rysdale or me."

I nodded. "Okay."

Solomon burped. "Let's work now—at a distance."

"How?"

"Put our heads together and go over what we know about the missing girls. Maybe something will stick out."

I grinned.

Solomon wheeled back to the tray and picked up the pen and small notebook. "Write it down. Sometimes making notes will help." Solomon handed them to me and turned his wheelchair so that it faced the sun. He leaned back and closed his eyes. "Now, what's the first thing we know?"

I thought a moment. "Seems it all started when that thing flew over town, doesn't it?"

"Maybe. But I don't see how something like that would be pertinent to the case."

"So it began with Sarah Mundy's disappearance."

Solomon tapped the notebook. "Write that down."

We continued going over stuff we knew about the girls and what had happened. When we finished, I had barely filled two pages.

Looking it over, I said, "So the last time somebody saw Theresa, she was walking toward the park trails?"

"Yes, though no one saw her actually go into the woods." Solomon yawned. "Those woods in the park—it's not like there's a whole lot to them, you know? Maybe a few acres or so."

"And I know they probably searched there first."

He nodded. "The whole park was searched. But in those woods, if she screamed, someone would have heard. And if she was carried off, someone would have seen." He wheeled over to the hammock strung up over the wheel house, pulled himself up, and rolled into it. "Maybe she was kidnapped somewhere other than the park. Just because no one saw her leaving there doesn't mean she didn't. Something could have happened between the park and her house, though we've checked that route pretty well."

"Everybody thought she was going home, but maybe she was going somewhere else first," I said, scribbling.

He yawned again. "I haven't had much sleep since the Goodnight girl vanished. I believe I'll take a nap."

"Then I'll cut out. I wish I knew what else I could do."

He folded his hands behind his head. "If I can get copies of the sheriff's reports, I'll let you take a peek."

My eyes went wide. I hadn't expected something like that. "Wow! Thanks, Solomon."

"And while I don't want you to go out and confront suspects, that doesn't mean you can't talk to other people."

"Like who?"

"Have you seen Handsome George Crow lately?"

"Nope. But Bobby, Micah Lee, and I are going to the matinee tomorrow."

"Well, Handsome George is a smart man. He might have an idea or two. Talk to him about it. And you should talk to Roscoe Gunn."

"The writer? He's a drunk."

Solomon chuckled. "He writes whodunits, which means he thinks about crime. I heard he got his start as a crime reporter. He'll have insight."

"Maybe." But I was skeptical.

"If you're going to be a detective, you'll have to talk to plenty of people you don't like. Hell, Charly, maybe you'll solve mysteries like Roscoe Gunn does—in books."

I looked at the notes I'd written, closed the notebook, and held it out to Solomon.

"Keep it, Detective," he said.

Before I left the roof deck, Solomon was snoring. As I walked through his house, something was bugging me. I stopped in his kitchen and sat, thinking about what he'd said about me writing books. Those would be crimes I made up, so they wouldn't really be any kind of solving at all. Besides, Mrs. Dickinson, my last English teacher, would have a conniption fit at the idea of me being a writer. Still, there was something about writing and books that kept nagging at my brain. Then it hit me. Standing, I reached for Solomon's kitchen phone and dialed.

It rang a few times until someone answered, "Temperance Library."

"Hey, Miss Grunwald. This is Charly Bloom."

"Hello, Charly. I'm sorry, but *The Mystery at Devil's Paw* hasn't come in yet."

I may not have been much of a writer, but I was a voracious reader and always the first to check out the latest Hardy Boys adventures. "That's not why I'm calling. I was wondering, on the day Theresa Goodnight disappeared, did she check out any books?"

After a long pause, the librarian asked, "Why would you ask such a thing?" I could hear the hurt in her voice. She was a kind old lady, and I was sure she was upset about Theresa. The poor woman might have even felt some responsibility since Theresa had disappeared right after leaving the library.

"I'm visiting Solomon Stubb. He heads up the sheriff's auxiliary, you know? We were just going over some of the stuff in Theresa's and Sarah's disappearances, hoping something new would stick out."

"I'm sure Sheriff Rysdale would have asked me if it was important."

"The sheriff never asked about books?"

"No, Charly."

"We're just grabbing at any little straw. I can get Solomon if you'd rather speak to him, though he's up on his roof right now, and you know how long it'll take him to come down since it's hard for him to get around without any—"

"That's all right. I just don't think that a young girl should be worrying about terrible things like this. Tell Solomon that she borrowed several picture books. I remember because I checked her out. Would you like the titles?"

My heart beat faster. "Yes, ma'am, if it isn't much trouble."

"Hang on, sweetheart." The phone clunked as she put it down. Several minutes later, she returned. "Are you still there, Charly?"

"Yes, ma'am," I answered, trying not to sound too eager.

"She checked out *Chouchou, Curious George Flies a Kite*, and *Sam and the Firefly*."

"Thank you, Miss Grunwald." I hung up and smiled. I wasn't sure of the importance, but the fact that she checked out books was something that everyone had overlooked, including the sheriff.

I ran back up to the roof. "Solomon! Guess what?"

"What? Charly? I thought you left?" His voice was thick with sleep.

I told him about my call to the library and what I had learned.

"She had books with her?" he asked, reaching for his wheelchair.

I nodded, grinning. "Three, from the library." I held the wheelchair in place while he climbed out of the hammock. "I got the idea when you said something about me solving mysteries in books. It made sense that if she was at the library, she'd have checked out some books. Do you think it's important?"

Solomon scratched his chin. "Could be. Everything is worth looking into."

"I thought that if someone finds the books, it's a good chance that was where she was taken."

Solomon nodded. "Aye. And if they're scattered about, it could mean she struggled with her captor."

"And if she took them with her, would that mean she didn't panic because she knew the person?"

Solomon slapped the arm of his chair. "See, that right there? That's why you'll be a hell of a detective, Charly." He rolled toward the hatchway. "Let's get over to the sheriff's. He should be back soon."

WHEN SOLOMON AND I got to the police station, Sheriff Rysdale sat at his desk, talking to his deputy and some volunteers, including Mr. Littlefield in his camouflage. His office wasn't big, so it was crowded, and the two mounted deer heads and stuffed bobcat didn't help.

He nodded at Solomon and looked at me with annoyance. "What can I do you for, Solomon?"

Solomon explained about the library books. The other people in the office murmured, and the deputy patted me on the back.

Behind me, I heard a soft voice say, "Good job, young lady."

I turned and saw a man I hadn't noticed earlier. He was dressed in a dark suit and wore a fedora. "Thank you."

"Maybe we should go kick around the park again," Solomon said.

"We've already looked there," the sheriff said.

"But now we have something specific to look for," the man in the suit said.

"I suppose," Sheriff Rysdale mumbled.

Everyone filed out of the office. Since the park was across the street, we walked. I got behind Solomon's chair to push.

"Do you know who that man was?" Solomon asked me.

"The one in the suit?"

"Yeah." He craned his neck so he could look at me. "He's an SBI agent who's come from Asheville to help Sheriff Rysdale."

"What's SBI?"

"It stands for State Bureau of Investigation. It's like the FBI, but for the state. They're topnotch crime fighters, and he said you did a good job."

"An honest to goodness G-man?" For the rest of the way, I felt about ten feet tall.

Once there, we waited while the sheriff went to the library to verify what I'd learned. After he returned, we all looked around the playground for places the books could be hidden.

I pointed at a couple of barrel trashcans. "When do they empty those?"

Sheriff Rysdale scowled. "I'd have gotten to that, Charly."

Behind him, the SBI agent smiled and winked at me before turning to Sheriff Rysdale and asking, "You did go through the trash cans during your first search?"

"We checked them to make sure, you know, the girl wasn't in one, but we didn't go through every little bit of trash." Sheriff Rysdale sent someone to ask if the trash cans had been emptied since the last search, then we worked our way north to the tree line. There were only seven of us to comb through the four trails that led to the northern part of the park. Sheriff Rysdale and the SBI agent took the first, a deputy on the second, Mr. Littlefield on the third, and the remaining volunteer on the fourth.

"What about us?" I asked.

The sheriff turned. "You and Solomon can look around the sidewalks at the edge of the woods on each side of the park."

I had a feeling he was just getting rid of me, but I also realized that the sheriff might have been thinking about Solomon. Getting a wheelchair down those hiking trails would have been difficult.

Solomon and I began at the west side where the little forest grew right to the concrete. I got a stick for him to poke around with, and every now and then, I would get on my knees and push through loam and look under rocks. We found nothing, so we went around to the east side and started doing the same.

"Sheriff, I got something!" Mr. Littlefield yelled.

Remembering which path he'd taken, I ran for the north entrance to the third little trail. Somewhere behind me, I heard Solomon call for me to wait.

The sheriff trotted out of the woods. "Damn it, Charly. Hold up."

Ignoring both of them, I continued sprinting. I slowed then came to a halt when I saw Mr. Littlefield on his knees by the side of the path. He was holding up a large rock. When he looked up at me, the stone slipped and fell crooked. Peeking out from the edge of it was a blue book cover and a portion of the title—*Curious G.*

Chapter 11
Autumn of '82

As soon as I returned to my room at the Temperance Inn, I pored over the photos of the lost girls. I took my time. Piper Darling was a cutie-pie. In the picture, she wore overalls like her father's, but clean and with a yellow flower sewn under the chest pocket zipper. Her eyes were wide and so blue that they were a contrast to the mahogany hair that fell past her shoulders. Smiling widely, she displayed a Brigitte Bardot gap between her front teeth. Though just ten, it was apparent that she'd be a bombshell when she grew up—if she got the chance.

The next picture showed Mani and Pedi Regis at some social gathering. There were lots of people behind their pose, and I decided they were at a beauty pageant. They wore little chiffon evening gowns, their hair up, and their faces heavily rouged. Mrs. Regis had painted the lips on her nine and eleven-year-old daughters with prostitute-red lipstick.

I flipped to the picture of twelve-year-old Savannah Smallwood. Underneath a ball cap, her blond hair exploded in wavy locks. She had on a baseball jersey and held a well-used catcher's mitt. The picture was taken at a park or neighborhood baseball field. By her smile, I could tell that her team won that day. Thinking back to my childhood, I decided she and I would have been friends.

I splashed cold water on my face and headed back out in search of Dub. I found him kneeling in one of the gardens.

"How are you, Dub?"

"Busier than a one-armed weed puller."

I laughed and dropped to my knees. "Let me help you."

"How's your stay?"

"I love the inn, and Temperance is still an odd place."

He nodded. "That it is."

"I want to ask you about Shorty's."

"The bar?"

I had to dig a little to uproot a stubborn weed. "I'm going there tonight. I remember all the old stories, and I was wondering how careful I really need to be."

Dub sat back on his haunches and brushed the dirt from his hand. "I s'pose it can get a little rough, but no more so than any other honky-tonk. Most of the stuff we heard about when we were kids was probably made up. I imagine the worst you can expect is getting hit on by some lonesome mountain man."

In the other room, I weighed options on how to get dressed for a night at Shorty's. I slipped on a new pair of jeans and picked a dark-blue blouse. My next mental debate was whether I should put on a pair of come-fuck-me pumps, but considering my destination, I chose my good ol' steel-toe boots. To get to Shorty's, I took I-26, a twisting, turning two-lane mountain highway that allowed me to open up my Formula 400 and enjoy the feeling of centrifugal force on looping curves and that split second of weightlessness when topping a hill at speed.

My love of driving in the mountains started early and was a way of healing. The summer I was sixteen, I was still emotionally scarred by my run-in with the Snatcher. But I also had my driver's license. Other than working a part-time job at the Temperance Bowl-A-Rama, most of my waking hours seemed spent behind the wheel of my father's car. I put so many miles on it that I could remember my parents arguing as to whether they should take away my driving privileges. Mom worried that it wasn't normal and that I'd eventually get into a wreck. My father sensed that it did me good to be on the move, and that was the only time I'd ever seen him forcefully overrule my mother.

Looking back on it, I know a psychiatrist would say that my driving, the constant moving, was a form of running away from my own personal boogeyman. It didn't matter that he'd died. I'd always be on the run from him. My love of driving continued, which was probably why I owned a Formula 400. But that first summer I had my license, driving Dad's Rambler station wagon offered me more freedom and solace than any car I'd ever owned.

Still on I-26, I crossed the bridge over Morrison Gorge and took the next right onto a gravel and oil road. The road curved after a quarter-mile, and Shorty's was on the right. I pulled into the rutted dirt parking lot. There were a half dozen or more pickup trucks, the beat-up kind, and a few cars. Shorty's wasn't hopping, but it wasn't dead either. The tin-roof cabin had three smudged windows facing the front, and each was cluttered with neon signs advertising Miller, Schlitz, Old Milwaukee, Black Label, and Pabst Blue Ribbon. There were a couple of outdoor lights, but the stairs leading to the porch were in shadows, and I imagined a number of drunks had taken a header when leaving Shorty's.

I went up the steps and crossed the porch. As I opened the door, a fat man in a red flannel shirt pushed past me, mumbling indecipherable words. He stumbled down the steps but stayed upright. Entranced, I watched him zigzag to a Chevy truck, climb in, and drive off. *Good luck, Bubba,* I thought. A wall of cigarette smoke greeted me when I entered, and a brightly illuminated jukebox by the door played a Tammy Wynette ode to bad men. Shorty's was one big room. Several men hunkered over drinks at the bar. One straw-haired woman cackled with delight. Behind the bar was a large woman in a plaid western shirt with pearl buttons and her hair done up high enough that I wondered if she had to duck under the overhead beams. A gray towel sat at the ready on her shoulder. As I crossed the room, she gave me a suspicious look.

I hopped onto the stool at the end of the bar and looked over the beer taps. "Miller."

She got a woman's glass and tilted it under the tap. I knew it was a woman's glass by the lipstick smudge on it. She put it down with a glare, daring me to say anything. I returned her stare and emptied the glass in one long gulp.

"Give me another," I said, slamming the glass on the bar. "Make it a clean glass this time."

She grinned and returned to the taps. I belched and looked around. A pool table sat at the open space to the right of the bar, along with a couple of decrepit pinball machines, a dart board, and one of those bowling games where you slid a metal puck under the pins. There were a dozen tables and ten booths, and less than half had people sitting at them. To the left of the bar were the bathroom doors. I imagined how grimy they were and hoped the beer I drank didn't go right to my bladder.

"Why would a pretty little thing like you think coming here would be a good idea?" The bartender put my beer down and leaned on the bar.

"I'm thirsty," I replied.

She glared at me.

"Not buying it, huh?"

She shook her head.

"I've heard about Shorty's all my life. Decided I had to come see it for myself."

She gestured about the room. "Does it meet your expectations?"

"I was expecting blood on the floor and overflowing spittoons, but other than that, yeah."

She pulled the towel from her shoulder and wiped the bar. "You a townie?"

"I grew up in Temperance but moved down the mountain a long time ago." I put both elbows on the bar and leaned closer. "I'm a friend of Rodney Darling. I'm looking into the disappearance of his daughter."

Her eyebrows went up. "You're that Bloom girl, aren't you?"

I whispered, "Let's keep that quiet."

"I'm Shorty's daughter, Tamara."

"I'm pleased to meet you." I held up the beer like a toast and took a sip. "Rodney said that other than home, this was the last place he and Piper went."

Tamara made a pained expression. "Such a little angel. What kind of a monster would hurt a child like her?"

"Hey, Tamara. Who's that sweet thang you're talking to?" a hillbilly with tobacco-stained teeth called from down the bar.

"Shut up, Grover," Tamara snapped, and he looked away. The nearby drunks laughed at him.

I took a sip. "When you heard that Piper had been abducted, did anyone cross your mind, anyone here that day?"

She frowned and shook her head. "Can't say I suspected anyone. Most people that come here are harmless. Some think they're tough and like to get in fights, but I can't imagine who'd want to kidnap a little girl from her bed."

"Rodney said there were some bikers here?"

"Yeah, I already told Kit that a few of the East Coast Thugs were here."

"Rodney said one was real big with black hair."

"That'd be Grizz."

"Grizz?"

"As in, grizzly bear. He's head honcho of the Thugs here in Temperance."

"Another was a skinny guy in a leather cap."

"They call him Weasel."

"And he said there was a local guy with them."

Tamara let loose a blast of air like he wasn't worth mentioning. "Luke Beason."

"Do they come here often?"

"Often enough that I've had to show them the Persuader a time or two."

"The Persuader?"

Tamara reached under the bar and pulled out a double-barrel shotgun. "Persuades unruly patrons to calm down."

"No doubt."

"It's loaded with rock salt, though I do keep some buckshot handy just in case." Everyone lined along the bar eyed the Persuader until she put it back. "My daddy used it a couple of times, but I've never had to do more than show it."

"He shot people with it?"

Tamara nodded. "Rock salt. He said it produced a real attitude adjustment."

"I never saw your father. I always assumed he was a short man, but looking at you..."

"The name was a joke, because he was so tall." She snickered and got close. "He used to tell a story that he had a tattoo on his pecker that said Shorty. He said the women he bedded would laugh at him until he got excited and the tattoo grew into *Shorty's Bar and Grill, Temperance, North Carolina*. If he was really trying to impress someone, he'd add the zip code."

Laughing, I decided I liked this rough woman.

From outside came a rumbling thunder, and Tamara said, "Speak of the devil, or in this case, a pack of devils. Sounds like the Thugs have arrived."

The roar of poorly muffled motorcycle engines shut down one by one. Wanting to study these guys, I nodded at Tamara, picked up my beer, and ducked into the last booth on the other side of the pool table. Each booth had its own cheap hanging light fixture, and I licked my fingers and unscrewed the bulb over mine.

The front door opened, and I had to agree with Rodney Darling. Grizz was big, as tall as the door and almost as wide. I put his weight at three hundred fifty pounds. He crossed the threshold in a manner reminiscent of a gunfighter entering a saloon and sizing up all the cowboys within. He turned around and said something to whoever was behind him, displaying the Thugs patch on the back of his leather vest. It showed two daggers with brass knuckles for handles. The base of each knife touched and angled up in a wide V. In between the V were the crown, forehead, and empty eye sockets of a skull. Across the upper back was a banner patch, or what bikers call the top rocker, that said *East Coast Thugs* in script. On each side of the knives and skull were an *M* and a *C*, signifying motorcycle club. Underneath was the bottom rocker that said *Nomad*. Interesting. A bottom rocker denoted which chapter they belonged to. Nomad meant that he didn't belong to a specific chapter, so the Thugs didn't consider Temperance to be official. His jeans were tucked into massive boots. The comparison to a gunfighter became even more evident when I noticed an old cowboy spur on his left boot. It sent up a metallic ting with every other step.

As he turned my way, I ducked back into shadow. Two of his crew followed. One was Weasel, judging by his appearance, and the other was a muscular man with a beer gut that turned his torso into a solid barrel. His windblown hair was brown and shoulder length, and he smiled widely, displaying a broken front tooth. In the unusual autumn warmth, he wore a sleeveless denim jacket over a sleeveless black T-shirt. From his shoulders down to his wrists he was covered in black and gray tattoos. The bikers moved through the room toward the bar. Grizz was like a huge ship plowing through the sea. "Muscles" continued to grin and stared with a challenge at anyone who looked their way.

Tamara set them up with a pitcher of beer, and they headed across the floor in my direction. I pushed into the booth as far as I could and felt some relief when they stopped at the pool table and dumped a pile of quarters on the rail. They were arguing about motorcycles. I'd lived in North Carolina my whole life, and I spoke with a southern twang, but Muscles's accent was so thick that I figured he was from Alabama or Mississippi or maybe Georgia. Grizz's voice surprised me. I'd been expecting basso tones, yet he spoke with a gravel whisper, like he had laryngitis.

Weasel racked up the balls. Grizz lit a cigarette, clamped it between his teeth, and broke, sending balls cracking around the table. The game was cutthroat, and they wielded their cues with blatant machismo, overpowering each shot. Still, Grizz and Muscles shot decently, but Weasel just embarrassed himself. Pretty soon, Grizz was down to three balls, Muscles had two, and Weasel hung in with one. Muscles tried to put Grizz's twelve ball into a corner pocket but cut it too much. The twelve came to rest right in front of a pocket on my side of the table. The cue ball stopped a few inches from the opposite rail and gave Weasel a straight shot. He strutted around the table and took his time lining up his cue. Grizz stood next to him and drained his glass. Just as Weasel shot, Grizz slammed his empty glass on the rail, startling Weasel, who crashed his cue tip into the bottom of the white ball, firing it off the table and directly at me.

Instinct and years of childhood baseball took over, and I caught the ball. Muscles doubled over hysterically, and Grizz laughed with rhythmic wheezing.

Weasel cussed and tromped to my booth. He attempted to be menacing as he held out his hand. "Gimme the fucking ball."

Fate had mandated that it was time to meet the Thugs, so instead of giving him the ball, I held it by my face, working it like Humphrey Bogart kneading his ball-bearings in *The Caine Mutiny*. Weasel's expression shifted from tough to confused when he saw that I wasn't intimidated, and then it changed again when he got a good look at me.

"Damn, you're a fox."

Grizz and Muscles stopped laughing and stared into the shadowy booth.

Weasel looked at Grizz, saw his scrutiny, and turned back to me. "Hey, c'mon. Give me the ball." Aw, I made him look bad in front of his peers. I winked and handed him the ball. "Damn straight," he said.

Grizz dropped his cigarette and approached with Muscles. There was something familiar about the big man, the way he carried himself, his swagger.

Without taking his eyes from me, Grizz grabbed Weasel and shoved him to the side. "Well, well. What do we have here?" Grizz smiled, grinding his teeth.

"Someone too fine for this dump," Muscles said from behind him. His eyes were dilated and shining. "Hey, Tamara," he shouted. "I thought you only let skags like Betty in here."

The blonde at the bar turned and shouted back, "I wasn't too much of a skag for you the other night." Everyone along the bar laughed.

Grizz said, "She's got you there, Preach."

So his club name was Preach, and I could tell by his scowl that he was not amused by Betty's response.

Grizz reached for the light fixture and screwed the bulb in, brightening the booth. "How about that? A loose bulb."

"What do you know," I said, and Grizz peered at me, turning his head from one side to the other.

Preach moved beside Grizz, leaned on the table, and spoke in a honey-thick Southern voice. "How y'all doing, sweetheart? What's your name?"

I wasn't eager for this bunch to know who I was, so I deflected the question. "Where you from, smooth talker?"

"Biloxi, Mississippi."

"Are they all as dumb as you?"

"Huh?"

"You asked me, 'How y'all doing?' Any Southerner worth his salt knows that one person is 'you.' Two to four are 'y'all.' Five and over are 'all y'all.'"

Grizz wheezed laughter. Preach glared at me. The scowl he'd given Betty the skag earlier seemed tame in comparison.

Preach fell into the booth across from me and pointed his finger. "I asked your goddamn name."

Weasel sat next to me, grinning. "Yeah, baby. Tell us your name."

Grizz pulled Weasel out and squeezed in, pushing his massive belly against the table. I could have gotten past Weasel, no problem. I had serious doubts of leaving the booth with Grizz blocking my way. *Note to self,* I thought, *don't spy from booths.*

"I know who you are," Grizz said.

"Well, now that that's settled, maybe you can let me out." I felt claustrophobic.

"Boys," he rasped, "I want you to meet Charly Bloom. She's an ex-cop here in town, looking for Copycat."

I returned his gaze. "Do I know you?"

"Me?" he asked, all innocence. "Now why would you know me?"

"You ever ride with any other clubs? The Pagans or the Storm Troopers?"

He shook his furry head. "Once a Thug, always a Thug."

"Then how do you know me?"

"I don't know you. I just know who you are. They wrote about you in the paper this morning."

"The Mountain Times?"

"Yeah."

I shook my head. "Crap. What'd they say?"

"That the sheriff found a grave, and a former SBI agent and the real-life Sami Hazzard is helping with the investigation."

Ronnie Carson found out who I was.

"Besides," Grizz continued, "this is a small town. What happened when you were a kid is local legend."

I pushed against him, which was kind of like pushing against a fleshy boulder. "Let me out, big guy."

He didn't move, and his mouth shifted into an unpleasant grin. "We don't like cops around. Makes us paranoid." Though he was bearded, I saw his jaw muscles clenching and unclenching. This guy was riding something.

"I'm not a cop anymore, though I wonder why you're paranoid."

Preach snapped his fingers, getting my attention. "We don't have nothin' to be paranoid about. We're law-abiding citizens."

"What're you doing here at our watering hole?" Grizz asked. "Because you ain't going to find any lost girls here."

"I'm just drinking a beer, Grizz."

"You've heard of me?"

"You're Grizz, he's Weasel"—I pointed at them— "and he's Preach, though I think Muscles would be a better handle."

Preach whooped, thrilled by what I said, and struck a body builder pose. "Take a feel if you want." He kissed one massive, tattooed bicep. "Once you've touched one muscle, you'll want to get your hands on my biggest."

I ignored him, and Grizz said, "We call him Preach because he's such a spiritual guy."

"Yeah, I bet."

"No, really," Preach said and lifted his T-shirt, showing me a prison-style tattoo on his chest. It was a picture of an open book with a ribbon hanging down and out the open page. There were lines to signify writing, and at the top of each page it said The Bible. He poked at the left-hand side of the book where letters and numbers spelled out Leviticus 19:28. He asked, "You know your verses?"

"Some. I know that's Old Testament and that Leviticus covers ancient Jewish law."

"That's right." Preach's face lit up, delighted I knew that much. His voice turned to that of a southern Baptist preacher. "Leviticus 19:28: 'Ye shall make no cuts in your flesh for the dead, nor print any marks upon your body.'" He poked at his tattoo for emphasis.

"'Nor print any marks upon your body?'" I looked at his ink work. "Doesn't that mean tattoos are a no-no?"

There was a gleam in his eyes that made me question his sanity. "Exactly."

"So shouldn't we call you Blasphemy instead of Preach?"

"I'm show 'n tell, baby. The lord has set me here on this land to display the sins that must not be committed."

Grizz chuckled. "He puts the demon in *demon*strate, get it?"

"Let me get this straight," I said, "You get to indulge in all the sins you want?"

"By my actions I show mankind what must not be committed."

"You're doing the Lord's work?"

"Ain't it grand? And as it says in the book of Jude 1:7, 'Sodom and Gomorrah and the surrounding towns gave themselves up to sexual immorality and perversion.'" Preach sat low, his chest against the table, and in a moment, I felt his hand moving up my leg. "Let's show those around us what it is like to give themselves up to sexual immorality and perversion."

"Preach, you best get your hands off me."

His eyes were wide and glassy, and he licked his lips. His hand moved farther up my thigh. I looked to Grizz, but he just grinned. I jumped into as much of a standing position as I could manage, grabbed the back of Preach's head, and slammed it into the table once, twice, three times. The first time he resisted. It was easy after that. Grizz pushed his bulk against me, shoving me against the wall. Weasel climbed onto the table, spilling my beer, and grabbed a handful of my blouse.

Grizz hissed in my ear, "You hurt one Thug, and all the Thugs hurt you."

"Excuse me, boys," a calm voice said. Grizz eased up some, and I looked around his girth to see Betty the skag standing at our booth. "Tamara wants to know which of you to shoot first?"

She stepped aside, and we saw Tamara aiming the Persuader in our direction.

Grizz slid off me and held up his hands. "Just a little disagreement, T. Ain't no need to go all nuclear on us."

"Weasel, get off the damn table," Tamara shouted.

He climbed back into the booth, grabbed Preach by his hair, and lifted his head. Preach's mouth was slack, and his eyes rolled back.

"You and your boys behave, or I won't let you play anymore," Tamara said.

"Sure, T. No problem," Grizz answered.

Tamara put her shotgun in its place under the bar.

Grizz looked at Preach's unconscious face. "I suppose he had it coming. Shit, put his head down. He's starting to drool."

"Let me out," I said.

Grizz stood, and I climbed out of the booth. As I headed toward the door, Grizz said, "Hold on, Charly. To show there's no hard feelings, I'll spring for a game of pool."

"No thanks."

"Don't you want to ask us about the missing girls?"

I stopped midstride and turned. "Do you know anything about them?"

Grizz smiled. "Play me a game of nine ball. If you win, we'll tell you all we know."

"And if I lose?"

Grizz scrutinized me. "If you lose, pucker up and give me a kiss. And I mean a real kiss." He slid out a fat tongue, slick and red, and wiggled the tip up and down.

Through a grimace, I said, "How can a girl turn that down?"

Grizz put coins in the table and racked the balls. I wasn't too concerned. I'd seen him shoot, and I was better. I played up to three times a week. After my Kajukenbo classes, my instructor, Deacon, and I cooled down next door at the Red Lion pub and played a few rounds of pool.

Grizz and I lagged, and my ball ended up an inch from the bumper.

I sank the two on the break, and as I lined up for the one ball, I asked, "Have you always talked like that?"

"Nah, I had a great voice. Coulda been a disc jockey, it was so deep and smooth."

I shot and dropped it in a corner pocket. "What happened?"

"This," he said and lifted his beard so I could see a puckered three-inch scar on his neck.

"Knife?"

He nodded. "Thought I was a dead man. Could hardly breathe for all the blood. But they saved my worthless ass, and now I talk like Dirty Harry. Wasn't my first knife wound." He held up his hand and showed his open palm. A wide scar ran from the pad underneath his index finger to the heel of his hand. I marked it for a defensive wound. "That's the first time a blade cut into me." He pointed at my head. "How about that one?"

"Bullet grazed me."

"Someone was a crappy shot."

I pulled my blouse away from my shoulder and showed him my puckered scar. "Good

enough to get me here."

Grizz whistled in appreciation.

The three ball sat behind the five and eight, and I bounced the cue ball off a rail to smack it and free it up. "Rodney Darling said you talked to his daughter hours before she was snatched."

"Snatched? Just like the Snatcher."

I looked at him.

"Everyone is rehashing the past since the girls started disappearing."

"Let's get back to Rodney Darling's daughter."

"Yeah, ain't that some shit? Here I'm nice to some little kid one day, and the next, the sheriff is banging on my door, asking questions, insinuating that I had something to do with it."

"Did you?"

He laughed and licked his lips. "Like I'd say if I did." He put chalk on the end of his cue, blew on it, and said, "Look, I talked to the girl all friendly-like and showed her how to make a pool shot. That was it."

Weasel, leaning against the booth and watching our game, said, "Sleeping Beauty is waking up."

Preach sat up and rubbed his face where it connected with the table. He looked at us, and I winced. His left eye was already swelling up. From the look of it, the upper left edge of his eye socket took the most damage. Wouldn't be surprised if he was the proud owner of a hairline fracture. Weasel pushed the pitcher of beer and a glass over to him.

"What the fuck happened?" Preach asked.

Grizz lined up a shot. "You fell into the table." He sank the ball. "Three times." He pointed his cue at Weasel. "Get Tamara to wrap some ice in a towel, and hold it against his eye. He's ugly enough without his head swelling up."

Preach reached for the pitcher and poured a beer, though his depth perception was off, and he spilled quite a bit before finding the glass. Grizz laughed at him and made a couple more shots. He missed and left me my win. If I cut the six enough, it'd cross the table and sink the nine in the side pocket. Weasel held the ice-filled towel against Preach's eye as I stretched over the table and lined up my shot.

Grizz moved next to me. "Uh-uh, sister. No way."

From the corner of my eye I watched him drain his glass. How dumb did he think I was? I pulled back the cue and pretended to shoot. Grizz slammed his glass on the rail. My real stroke was smooth and accurate, catching the six a tad on the right so that it rolled up against the nine with just enough force to drop it.

"Shee-it," Grizz said.

I turned to him. "What else do you know?"

"Other than seeing that poor kid in here? Only what I read in the Mountain Times."

There was hubbub over by the booth, and I turned as Preach pushed the towel from his face. "I remember what happened. That bitch slammed me."

Preach launched himself, knocking Weasel to the ground. As he stormed toward me, I gripped the pool cue like an eskrima stick.

Grizz stepped between us. "Cool down, brother. T's already shown the Persuader once tonight."

His face red, Preach actually growled as he tried to get by Grizz, who took him by the throat until he stopped struggling. Grizz was as strong as he was big.

"Fucking bitch," Preach spat in choked fury.

"Well, Grizz, this is about all the fun I can stand in one night." I leaned my cue on the table, blew Preach a kiss, and headed for the door.

Chapter 12
Summer of '59

"I can't believe you thought of the library books," Micah Lee said. "Me neither," Bobby muttered.

We sat in the dark theater, ignoring the newsreel. We'd pay attention when the cartoon started.

"Only two of the books have been found. I wonder what happened to the third one?" I said.

"Did they look through the woods again?" Micah Lee asked.

"Yep. Rysdale called up a bunch of volunteers."

"Didn't find anything, did they?" Bobby said.

"Nothing."

"You did real good, Charly." Micah Lee looked at me. "You know what? You'd be a good detective."

Bobby chewed on that a moment and then smiled. "Like a private detective?"

"Yeah," Micah Lee said.

"I dunno," I added. "Maybe."

"A private dick." Bobby laughed again. "Don't you got to have one to be one?"

I thought to punch him, but the cartoon started, one with Bugs Bunny, Yosemite Sam, and a fire-breathing dragon with a cold. I laughed so hard I forgot Bobby's insult.

After the movie, I ran up to the concession stand to talk to Handsome George Crow. He was of the Bird Clan and a descendant of the Cherokees who hid in the mountains of western North Carolina to escape the Trail of Tears march to Oklahoma.

He liked talking about his ancestry and once told me, "Those of the Bird Clan were messengers of the tribe. I think that's why I like movies so much. They're messages."

Handsome George wasn't much taller than me but so handsome that adolescent girls were always fawning over him, though he pretended not to notice. His black hair was short and neatly combed, his dark eyes sparkled, and he liked western-style jackets, string ties, and fancy cowboy boots. He owned and operated the Forum Theater and let me, Bobby, and Micah Lee in for free. In exchange, we'd help him clean up after the show.

Micah Lee and Bobby pushed through the lobby doors amidst a crowd of mostly kids.

Micah Lee's eyes were wide. "*The Blob* was unreal."

"It was crazy," Bobby agreed.

"Steve McQueen will go far," Handsome George predicted.

Micah Lee went behind the snack bar, opened a door, and pulled out a broom and long-handled dustpan. Bobby picked up a trash can, and they went through the swinging doors to clean up the popcorn boxes and soda cups from under the seats. Handsome George handed me a bottle of Mr. Clean and a rag, and I got to work wiping away fingerprints, soda spills, and chocolate smears from the snack bar counter.

"Do you need help tomorrow?" I asked. I wanted to see *The Blob* again.

"Not tomorrow. I'm going to visit my mother."

"How's she doing?"

Over the past ten or so years, his mother's mind had slipped so much that he had to move her to the Golden Years Elderly Care Center. Handsome George was a good son. Even though she no longer recognized him, he still visited her regularly.

"As good as can be expected, but senility is an awful thing. She smiles at me, and that warms my heart. I remember when I was a kid, and she seemed so big, I didn't think anyone was bigger. Last week when I looked at her, I couldn't help but think how small she is."

"I'm sorry, George."

A sad smile came to him. "Growing old ain't for sissies."

I wiped the soda taps, which were always the stickiest to clean. "George, what do you think happened to Theresa Goodnight and Sarah Mundy?"

Handsome George filled a sink with soapy water. "I wish I knew. I helped search for Theresa. Watching her father fall apart just about broke my heart." He added some bleach to the sink. "So what do you think happened to the girls?"

"Well, I think about it all the time, but it's just a big mystery."

"You think whatever happened to Sarah Mundy happened to Theresa Goodnight?"

I nodded. "Bobby thinks a sex fiend got them."

"Sadly, that is a possibility."

"I can't think of any other logical explanation."

"It could be an illogical explanation," Handsome George said. "Like someone crazy." Handsome George put the mop in the sink. "Hang on a minute." He went to get the cashbox from the box office. "Come with me, Charly."

We went upstairs and through an invisible door covered with the same rich red wallpaper as the surrounding walls. A small hallway led to the projection booth, and a little farther down, we got to Handsome George's office. The walls were covered with Cherokee art—paintings, feathers and colorful twine woven into complex geometric patterns, and old photographs of his people. There were a few pieces of pottery and woven baskets on shelves and a small tabletop. A stack of movie reels and strewn paperwork were on his desk. He put the cash box in a safe behind his desk and sat. I took the chair across from him.

He leaned forward. "I spoke with Solomon. He says this thing with the lost children is consuming you."

I didn't answer him right away but looked in his dark eyes. "I feel like I can solve this." I opened my mouth to continue but couldn't explain what I felt.

"Put your hand where you most feel this passion."

It was an odd request, but I knew that Handsome George had a unique mind. So I asked myself, *Where does this need come from*? I closed my eyes and moved my hand to hover in front of my face, moved it down past my neck, shoulders, and stopped at my chest where I felt it the most. I opened my eyes and saw that Handsome George, like me, held his hand over his heart. He knew from where it sprang.

He raised his eyebrows. "Then it makes perfect sense, Charly Bloom. I'm afraid the only help I can offer is advice."

"Okay."

"Remember that reality often differs from our perceptions. You will find the answers you seek in that other truth. Sometimes you have to put your ear to the earth to get a clear sense of the inner workings of the world. Don't dismiss anything just because it seems impossible."

I had no idea what he was talking about, but I was polite and said, "Thank you. Solomon said I ought to talk to that drunk writer."

"A good idea, though talk to him early in the day when he's not tanked up."

"I guess."

"And Charly, be careful. This is not a game. Someone is taking these girls, neither of whom is much younger than you."

"I know." I stepped toward the door but stopped to ask, "What do you think that thing was that flew over town at the start of summer?"

Handsome George tented his fingers under his chin and looked aside as he thought. He finally answered, "A warning."

"What kind of warning?"

"Perhaps a warning that we should watch over our children."

I found Micah Lee and Bobby, and we left the theater.

Micah Lee looked at his watch. "Oh shit. I have to get home." Micah Lee's mother was nearly hysterical in her fear that he'd get kidnapped next.

Bobby had some mischief to get into that I wanted no part of, so even though I promised my parents I wouldn't go anywhere alone, we split up. I headed for Town Center Park. Yes, a crime had taken place there, and yes, Solomon had told me I could help with the case as long as I did so from a distance, but I figured a good detective would spend time at a crime scene. The first thing I did there was draw a park map in my notebook while sitting on a swing.

Looking around, I wasn't surprised to see that adults were keeping sharp eyes on their kids. And there weren't as many people in the park as should have normally been on a sunny day. The merry-go-round usually whizzed around nonstop with a dozen clinging kids. Now, it sat motionless, and I thought it looked kind of sad. I walked around it, searching for anything that might present itself as a clue. I widened my search around the whole playground and made my way through the trees and bushes, looking for anything of note. From there, I took the trail where Mr. Littlefield discovered the books. It started wide but narrowed considerably. Over the years, I'd used those paths countless times yet never found them the least intimidating. But now, knowing something had happened here, I thought the trees seemed kind of spooky. I'd never noticed before how much sunlight they blocked. On that particular trail, the path was so crooked you couldn't see where it opened at either the south or north side. I thought that if someone was attacked and they didn't scream loud enough, it was possible no one would know. But how would they get her from the park?

In the north field, I went and sat on the steps of the gazebo, watching a few idlers attempting to enjoy the day. Yet a sense of something sinister stained everything. I needed an edge, something to get my investigation rolling. What was it Handsome George told me? Something about putting my ear to the earth to hear the inner workings of the world. I wasn't sure if he meant it literally, but I got up and walked to the northeast side where there was a grassy hill near the gazebo. I lay on my back and put my hands behind my head like I was staring up at the sky. After a couple of minutes, I looked around. Nobody was watching, so I rolled onto my side and planted my right ear to the ground. I didn't hear a thing, but maybe it took time. So I lay there awhile. The grass was sun warmed and soft, and I became drowsy. In that velvety fog between consciousness and sleep, I heard something deep in the earth, and then it got to where I could feel it as well. I swore I heard the clank of gears meshing and the rumbling tock of gargantuan clockworks. Mental images came to me of mountain-sized gears, mainsprings, and pendulums operating at the center of the Earth. As soothing as a mother's heartbeat, it lulled me to sleep. And in sleep, the inner workings of the world showed me a child.

I sensed her first, and when I looked, she stood a short distance away, halfway down the hill. She wouldn't look at me directly. With her head down, nibbling on a fingernail, she'd cast quick glances at me. Though I recognized her, I lay still, worried that if I got up, I would lose sight of the girl in her pink dress and hair ribbons. Theresa Goodnight turned to look at another girl who stood down the hill near the sidewalk. That one, Sarah Mundy, wore pajamas. Sarah motioned for Theresa to join her. Theresa looked at me, shrugged, and ran down the hill. She reached Sarah, who grabbed her arms, and the force of her charge sent both girls spinning round and giggling without sound. Sarah and Theresa stopped and held each other while looking at me. They broke apart, Sarah lifted an arm to point at the Pine Top Restaurant, and the two girls began to fade. Theresa noticed my confusion and looked where Sarah aimed. Theresa shook her head, pointed higher, and then they were gone.

A sharp pain blossomed in my chest. I opened my eyes to Winthrop Whist kneeling next to me, my nipple pinched between his thumb and finger. He twisted, and I yelped.

"Shit, Bloom. You ain't got nothin' but mosquito bites for tits." Winthrop chuckled, spraying me with spittle when he lisped *mothsquito bitesths for tiths*.

I grabbed his wrist and wrestled his hand off. "Let go."

"But that's all right. I don't mind itty-bitty titties. Besides, the important part's down here." He cupped my crotch and squeezed.

Pain tears blurred my vision. I shoved him, and he fell back. By the time I stood, Winthrop was up and in my face.

"Don't you ever push me, Bloom."

I noticed the raised vein in his forehead. Every kid knew to steer clear of Winthrop when his vein was throbbing, but right then I was so mad I didn't care.

"You ever put your hands on me again, Winthrop Whist, and I'll kill you. I swear to God I will."

Winthrop clenched his hands into tight fists. He sputtered like he was searching for words, but he gave up as rage contorted his face.

"Hey you!" a voice called. We both turned to see a man on a nearby park bench watching us. "Are you picking on that girl?"

Winthrop wiped at his thighs and whispered, "We'll settle this later."

"Good."

"Good." Winthrop sat, pulled a pack of Viceroys from a pocket, and fired one up with a battered Zippo lighter. He looked at the man on the bench and shouted, "Nah, I ain't pickin' on no one."

My nipple ached, but my anger lessened, and I remembered the dream I had before the titty-twister. It had seemed so realistic. I turned my back on Winthrop and looked where Sarah pointed, at the Pine Top. Why would a missing girl, probably dead, be interested in a restaurant known for meatloaf, fried chicken, and biscuits 'n gravy? But had she pointed to the restaurant? I remembered how Theresa Goodnight had pointed over the Pine Top's roof.

"They were pointing west," I muttered.

"Huh?" Winthrop grunted.

Deep in thought, I was barely aware of him. "Did he take them somewhere to the west?"

"What are you talking about, Bloom?" Winthrop demanded.

"None of your beeswax."

"Took who west?"

I looked at Cray's Hill, Rock Ridge, and Hallow's Summit in the distance and didn't bother to answer him.

"You're a damn goofball, you know that, Bloom?"

I walked away without a backward glance.

Chapter 13
Autumn of '82

E xiting Shorty's into the night, I took in the nocturnal beauty of
the mountains. Tall pines blocked most of the sky, but over the
road, it looked like blackstrap molasses with a dusting of diamond
chips. I walked to the motorcycles, two Harleys and one Triumph.
Two helmets hung upside down from handlebars, another rested on a
seat. One bike was wide, fat, and low, and I imagined that belonged to
Grizz. The Triumph was lean and narrow, with an extended front end
and fenderless front wheel. It was skinny like Weasel, so I figured it
was his. Picking Preach's was easy. The first two were black, but the
third was pearl-white with gold crosses emblazoned on each side of
the tank. For all their swagger and macho names, they couldn't hide
who they were from the DMV, so I memorized their tag numbers.

My car rumbled to life, and I left the parking lot, headed toward
Temperance. Approaching the Morrison Gorge Bridge, I wondered
if any drunks ever ended up at the bottom after leaving Shorty's. The
hum of the road changed as I crossed the bridge, and I glanced to the
right, into the blackness of space, knowing the gorge dropped
well over a hundred feet to the French Broad River. Part of me felt
as if I wasted my time, but then I also thought that someone should
keep an eye on the East Coast Thugs. Perhaps I was just getting an
overall criminal vibe from them. I wouldn't be surprised if they were
involved in something illegal, but if someone asked if I thought they
abducted the girls, I'd have to say no.

I rolled down the windows and enjoyed the mountain air.
Though deer and black bears were dangers on these mountain roads,

I couldn't resist the urge to go fast. I felt in perfect harmony with the night. I looked in the rearview mirror as a car with mismatched headlights crested a hill far behind me. For a second, I was annoyed, feeling as if they'd purposefully intruded on my serenity. I'd been driving seventy to eighty miles per hour, slowing to forty or fifty for curves, yet when I glanced in the mirror, the lights were closer. I'd punch it to a higher speed, but I didn't know the road well enough. Instead, I eased up on the gas until I was cruising at fifty miles per hour. I'd let them pass. After a curve and a bit of a straightaway, I glanced in the mirror as the car rounded the curve, and one headlight swerved wide into the other lane. It wasn't a car—those were two motorcycles.

"Oh shit."

I ran through options. I could go faster and hope for the best. I could pull over and confront them, but that seemed foolhardy as I left my gun at the inn. I decided to continue at my present speed. What could they do? They were on two wheels, and I was in a car. If they wanted to mess with me, I'd have no qualms about forcing them off the road. With a strategy in place, I found myself looking forward to a confrontation.

The motorcycles pulled close enough that I heard their engines. When they got right behind me, I was tempted to slam on the brakes but decided to let them make the first act of aggression. They followed through three quick curves, down a hill, and onto a long straightaway. I watched as the right-side motorcycle dropped back. The other accelerated, pulling alongside. I looked out the window and recognized Preach on his white hog. He wore a beanie of a helmet, goggles, and a grin. His right hand on the accelerator, he raised his left, a .45 automatic in his grip.

I flung myself down into the passenger seat, and he fired. He accelerated ahead. I sat up and gripped the wheel with both hands as it jerked violently back and forth. The bastard had shot my front tire. Hitting the brakes hard might cause me to lose all control, so

I allowed the car to slow on its own. The flapping of the dead tire was loud through my open window. The motorcycle behind me kept pace, and Preach pulled up ahead, slowed, and turned back. I pressed the brake pedal. When the car slowed enough, I stomped hard, slammed the gear shift into park, and leaped out. I crossed the opposite lane and ran down a small hill into trees and brush. The motorcycle engines died. A few seconds later I heard Preach and his accomplice charging into the woods behind me. My attempts at silent running failed when I almost tripped over a small fallen tree. I stumbled into a clearing with rocks, pine needles, and oak leaves scattered about. Running through, I headed for the trees across it. Someone tackled me from the side, and we fell to the ground.

I got a glimpse of Preach as I shoved him off and stood. My bearings were all screwed up. I made for the trees, but Weasel popped out, blocking my way. I turned as Preach got up. He pulled out his .45, and I stepped forward to grab his wrist with my right hand. Stepping behind his arm, I aimed my open left palm at his elbow. He saw what was coming and twisted his arm so that I only hurt him enough that he dropped the gun. He turned and swung his left fist at my head, which I ducked. As he twisted, I drove the heels of both my palms into his kidney. Preach grunted, farted, and dropped to his knees. Weasel rushed past, diving for the gun, for which he got my steel-toe boot in his ribs. He still managed to grab the pistol as he rolled away. I rushed him as he came up kneeling, and aimed my boot for his chin. He held out his arms to block my kick, which sent the gun flying into the brush.

"Fuckin' bitch." Preach was up and rushing me.

I planted my stance and used his momentum to flip him over my hip. He howled as he slammed onto the ground. Twisting to his side, he exposed a large rock he'd landed on with the top of his spine. Dropping to my knees, I delivered three hook punches to his already swollen eye. Preach stopped moving. Weasel was on his ass, cradling his arm. I headed for him, but movement drew my attention back to Preach. He reached for something in his boot. I kicked him hard in the temple. The sound of impact was satisfying.

My back erupted in pain, and I fell. I was rolled over, and Weasel's fist flew straight at me.

I heard an incessant buzzing that morphed into a voice. "I got her, the bitch. I got the bitch. I took her down." I felt his breath on my face, and it smelled like long-rotting garbage.

I opened my eyes, but only a little so he wouldn't see I was awake. Weasel was bent over me, his face in mine, until he stood up straight and howled into the night. The fucker hit me in the back with something, and I had to give credit where credit was due. I never would have thought the skinny little pissant could pack that much power in a punch. I felt my left eye starting to swell. I was propped up, my head resting on Preach's leg, but he didn't mind because he was still unconscious.

Weasel bent down to gawk at me. "Thought you were hot shit, didn't you, bitch? Well, you aren't so damn hot now, are ya? I'm gonna fuck you up the ass, you cunt."

Weasel was just in my line of vision, and I watched him undo his belt. Then he took a small pill bottle from his pants pocket, poured white powder on the bottle top, and snorted it up his nose. He moaned in satisfaction, put the bottle back, and yanked on my boots. I almost kicked out at him but remembered Preach reaching for something in his boot. While Weasel cussed, laughed, and worked on removing my footwear, I focused on Preach's booted foot. Slowly, I brought my left hand to his leg. Weasel got one of my boots free and was too busy yanking on the other to notice my movements. I pulled up Preach's pant leg and was rewarded with the sight of a knife handle. As my other boot slipped off, I removed the knife, sat up, and planted the blade through the top of Weasel's boot and deep into his right foot. He screamed and fell on his ass.

I got to my feet, breathing hard. There was a thick tree limb just past Weasel, and I picked it up. "You hit me with this?" I asked, but he went right on bawling. I swung the limb into the side of his head, shutting him up.

My back felt like Larry Holmes had used it as a punching bag. I shrugged my shoulders, which made the pain sing. Still, it was better than being raped or killed.

I picked up my boots and set off. It took me several minutes to get to the road and behind the wheel of my car. Unfortunately, they took the keys. Muttering at my stupidity for leaving them, I ripped the sparkplug cables from their bikes, tossed them into the woods, and shoved each one over. Feeling some satisfaction, I put on my boots and walked toward town.

Chapter 14
Summer of '59

The rolling thunder of heavy balls on wooden lanes and the brittle crash of pins greeted me as I opened the door. For all the noise, only four lanes were in use. I glanced at the clock over the shoe rental counter and saw it was a little past noon. The Temperance Bowl-A-Rama usually got busy with leagues around six o'clock and stayed that way until closing. I was there in search of Roscoe Gunn, our town's peculiar writer. He authored a series of books about Jack Hazzard, a private eye who was arrogant, obnoxious, and hard-drinking. From all I'd heard, Gunn shared those qualities. He wrote each day in the Gutter Ball Lounge, the dark room at the end of the lanes. It was a small bar, just big enough for a few tables, jukebox, and dartboard.

He sat at the table in the farthest, darkest corner, a cigarette burning in his left hand while he wrote with his right. A pile of papers was across the table next to an overflowing ashtray, a short, empty glass, and a porkpie hat. I watched him in his rumpled tweed suit. He'd write for a minute or two, stop, gaze at the ceiling, and then write more.

I approached his table and stood by his side, waiting for him to notice me. He kept writing as if I weren't there. Nor did I get a response when I cleared my throat.

I pulled a chair from the table and sat. "Excuse me, Mr. Gunn. I'd like to ask you a couple of questions."

The writer tensed. He lifted his gaze from his work, cigarette smoke intensifying an angry expression.

I filled the uncomfortable silence. "Uh, I want to ask a couple of questions. My name is—"

"I know who you are. You're Bloom's kid."

"Charly."

"Your dad's name is Robert."

"My name is Charly."

"Well, damn it, Charly, can't you see I'm working? Hit the bricks, kid."

"It'll only take a few minutes."

Gunn barked at the bartender across the room. "Damn it, Lou. Is this a bar or a kindergarten?"

Lou, a large bald man in a white apron and red vest, came over. He dropped a heavy hand on my shoulder. "All right, kid. Let's go."

"Wait," I blurted. "I can pay you."

Gunn considered me and waved Lou off. Plunging a hand into my pocket, I brought out a bunch of coins and dropped them on the table. He looked from them to me, disbelief on his face.

A moment later he burst into coarse laughter. "Damn, kid. You don't think much of my services, do you?" he asked, picking through the coins. "Tell you what, you can buy me a drink. We'll chat until I finish the drink, and then you take a powder. Capiche?"

"Huh?"

"Do we have a deal?"

Before I could agree, he was up and moved to the bar. I scooped up the rest of my coins and deposited them back in my pocket. Noticing his papers, I snatched a page and read.

Vincent was quite the cocksman.

I paused a moment, trying to figure out what that sentence meant. Seemed that I remembered Solomon talking about a type of sailor, a rank, that sounded like that. I continued.

He knew what to expect when his neighbor, Daisy, called and asked, "Vincent, can I get your help with something? Normally Paul handles it, but he's out of town for a few days." Paul was her husband, and him being out of town cemented Vincent's suspicions.

"I'll be right over," Vincent replied. Being tactful, he pretended not to know what she wanted. "Should I bring some tools?"

Daisy answered, "That won't be necessary. The back door is open."

Vincent took a navy shower, brushed his teeth, and splashed on cologne. He walked up the street and paused in front of Paul and Daisy's house. He looked around to make sure none of the neighbors were watching as he went up the driveway to the backdoor.

"Hello? Daisy?" Vincent called when he stepped into the kitchen.

She answered in a breathy voice. "I'm in the living room, Vincent."

He took the short hall, turned into the living room, and smiled at the sight of Daisy on the sofa, wearing only a string of pearls. She put a hand to her cheek in a mock expression of surprise that melted into a sultry smile as she reached to...

My face heated up. This had nothing to do with rank on a ship. Roscoe might write mysteries, but he wrote dirty stories too. Was he a sex fiend like Bobby had talked about? A desire to flee hit just as he dropped back in his chair, a glass of amber liquid clenched in one hand.

He saw what I'd been reading and gave me a hard stare. "What do you think of my prose?"

I wasn't sure what I felt, though a large portion of embarrassment was in the mix. My lips moved without forming words, so I looked down at the table, but there was Gunn's salty tale. I lifted my gaze, and though he didn't smile, I saw amusement in his face.

"Never read a dirty story, Charly?"

I shook my head.

"What? You've never looked at a men's magazine?"

My face flushed deeper as I thought of the girlie magazines I'd thumbed through at Bobby's.

"Well, after reading my work, do you have any questions?"

"I thought you wrote whodunits."

Roscoe said, "I mean about what Vincent and Daisy are up to."

"I know what they're up to," I said and thought, *Generally speaking*.

"Don't look so shocked," he said. "I write whatever pays."

"This pays better than whodunits?"

"Well, that all depends on how successful those whodunits are." He stopped, watched me, and scratched his head. "I can't believe I have to justify myself to a kid." He grabbed his glass and took a slug. "Look at it this way. I have two ways of making money through writing. The first is these dirty little stories. They're easy to write, and they're easy to sell, as long as I can come up with creative ways of describing assorted body parts." He shook his head. "Dignity goes right out the window when you start writing things like *his throbbing member* and *her silken womanhood*." He leaned toward me. "You're blushing redder than a stoplight." He picked up a few sheets of paper. "I may not be proud of these, but I'm damn well happy when I get a check for them." He lit another cigarette. "My second kind of writing is the mystery stuff, Jack Hazzard. Those I do brag about, even though they don't sell that well, which is why I have to write this." He tapped the pile of paper. "I sell most of these to publications like *Black Silk Stockings, Adam, Monsieur, 21.*" He took a drink. "Look, why are you here? I hear you're a hell of a pitcher. Why aren't you playing some ball on a sunny day like today?"

"Because I want to ask you a few questions."

"You've been doing that." Gunn held his glass up for me to see. "Just a couple of more sips."

"Yes, sir. When you write mysteries and all, you must think a lot about crime."

"I do."

"Solomon told me you used to work as a crime reporter."

"Also true." Gunn upended his glass.

"I want to ask what you think about those two missing girls, Sarah Mundy and Theresa Goodnight."

The writer choked on his drink and put it down. "You're annoying, aren't you?"

"So I've been told."

Standing, Gunn said, "Wait here." He pointed at his papers. "And don't read any more of that crap."

He returned with a new drink and sat, staring at me.

I said, "I'm trying to find out what happened to them."

He leaned over the table and pointed his finger at me. "You?"

"I figured with your experience, you might have some insight."

He leaned back. "Well, I haven't thought much about it, not theoretically."

I pulled the notebook and pen from my back pocket and dropped them to the table. "Can we talk about it?"

He sniffed. "Let me get this straight. You're trying to solve this... like a detective?"

"Yes, sir, I suppose so."

"Good lord, Temperance's own Nancy Drew." He stared at me, but I kept my face blank. He sighed, sat back, and said, "I figure Vincent and Daisy can get on without me for a few minutes."

I snickered, and for the first time, he offered a smile that was free of sarcasm. He looked to the ceiling again, and I figured he must keep his thoughts up high. "It's safe to assume that both cases are related, though the motive is unknown, right? I mean, there have been no ransom demands, have there?"

"Not that I've heard of."

"So it's not kidnapping for money. While there could be other possibilities, odds are it's a predatory kind of thing, maybe sexual," Gunn dropped his voice, "and a good bet neither will be found alive."

"Yeah," I sadly agreed.

"A person who commits a crime like that probably has a criminal record. While Sheriff Rysdale is a supercilious prick who couldn't find his ass with both hands and his pants off, checking records is easy, so I'm sure even he can handle it."

"Then what should I look for?"

"Well, it would answer many questions if you can figure out how he gets the children from the point of abduction to where he keeps them. The first one was at night, right?"

"Yes, sir. Took her right from her room."

"In Temperance, if it was late at night, there's little chance of anyone being out to witness the perpetrator getting the child from her house to a car. The other one, as I understand, was in broad daylight."

"She was at Town Center Park, right across the street from the sheriff's department. That was the last she was seen."

"Jack Hazzard might work it from that angle, try to learn how she was kidnapped from a busy park without anyone seeing a thing." His gaze wandered up again, and he rubbed at his chin. "Here's something else to consider—whoever took them needs a place to do whatever he does to them. If he takes them to his house, then odds are he lives alone."

"Like Mr. Altus," I said.

"Why him?"

I gave him a recap of what happened at Old Man Altus's house, ending with, "I made a fool out of myself."

"Adam blamed Eve. Eve blamed the snake. The snake didn't have a leg to stand on."

"What's that supposed to mean?"

Gunn said, "Look, you saw evidence that Elwood Altus was the snake, pretty damn good evidence, and if the sheriff wasn't so arrogant, he'd admit it too. And you did learn one thing."

"What?"

"You learned Elwood Altus is not the person responsible. Now you have to figure out who the real serpent is."

"Okay."

He thought for a while. "Yeah, if I were writing this, I'd have the detective focus on how he got the Goodnight girl out of the park while looking into where he could take them—abandoned buildings, or cabins, or barns, out in the woods somewhere, someone who lives alone, that kind of thing. But if you're playing Nancy Drew, I'd suggest you stick with the park question and leave the part about where he takes them to the professionals."

"Why?"

"Why? What happens if, in your junior G-man investigation, you luck on to where this man takes the girls? How much risk are you willing to take?" He looked at me. "You're a kid, Charly. If this guy knew you were on to him, you'd be dead, plain and simple. Stay safe and stick to the question of the park."

"I suppose." I thought a moment. "You think we'll ever know who's doing it?"

Roscoe thought and said, "Only if he makes a mistake next time or the time after that."

"You think he's going to keep doing it?"

"Without a doubt."

"Why do you think the Snatcher will take another girl?"

"The Snatcher, huh? Well, I think this person, this Snatcher, is insane, maybe not in a way that people notice, but he's driven to do these things."

"Why now?"

"Why not now?" Gunn tapped his pen on his open palm. "He's thought about it for a long time, fantasized about it. For whatever reason, he's stopped playing it out in his mind and is doing it for real. Now that he's up and running, I doubt he can stop, even if he wanted to."

"He started when that thing flew over town."

Gunn shrugged. "Who knows what sets madness into motion?" He put his glass down and collected the papers on the table and made a neat stack. "Goodbye, Charly." He stood, put on his hat, collected his papers, and walked from the Gutter Ball Lounge.

I followed at a distance and watched as he stepped from the Bowl-A-Rama and squinted into sunlight. I went to play Arabian Nights while thinking about what Gunn had said.

Chapter 15
Autumn of '82

While I held a bag of frozen peas to my eye, Grievous finished a cursory examination of my back. She was a true Renaissance woman. At various times in her life, she'd been a painter, a travel writer, a restaurateur, and—what I found most important at the moment—a nurse.

"We should take her to the hospital," Roscoe told his wife.

Grievous helped me get my shirt back on. "Honey, if you want to go, we'll go."

I said, "No."

"She's okay, Roscoe. No broken bones, just a bruise that's going to look nasty tomorrow. I'm not worried about her eye, but let's see if we can get the swelling down." She kissed me on the cheek. "Why don't you stay here tonight?"

"Thanks, Grievous."

Grievous came from Norway as a child, and her voice still held a Scandinavian trace. A solid woman, but not fat, her blond hair had faded to gray, and she was still beautiful. I hoped I'd be like her if I got to live that long, which, considering nights like this one, seemed doubtful.

Roscoe gave me a look.

"I'm fine, Roscoe."

"Fine? You've got a black eye."

"I should have gone with Kit out to the Thugs' house."

"Now that's where you're wrong," Grievous said and pushed my hand with the bag of peas back against my eye. "Kit can handle it. You need to take it easy."

"He looked mad. I hope he doesn't do anything stupid," Roscoe said.

Kit had just left Roscoe's with one of his deputies. I told them about Shorty's, meeting up with the Thugs, and them attempting to rape me, or kill me, or whatever they were planning. Kit used Roscoe's phone and called a few more deputies. They were going to meet up and pay a visit to the East Coast Thugs and arrest Preach and Weasel. He also called Rodney Darling, who promised to cut a new key, change my tire, and get the Firebird to Roscoe's by morning.

"I'm going out for a cigarette," Roscoe announced. Grievous didn't let him light up inside. "Want to join me?"

"Sure."

It was a little after three in the morning as we settled on his dark porch. A match flared, bringing a second of light, and then I found my gaze drawn to the lit cigarette tip.

"Sure you're okay?" he asked.

"I'll be sore for a while, but won't be the first time."

"You're lucky Billy Divit picked you up."

"Yeah." The overnight manager at the Econo Lodge, Billy Divit, was on his way to work when I flagged him down. He drove me to Roscoe's, who called Kit.

"Damn good thing you didn't wave down a carload of Thugs."

When I'd gotten a quarter of a mile from my car, a motorcycle rode up. Figuring it was Grizz, I hid in the tree line. He stopped at the car and toppled bikes for about twenty minutes, and then he roared past my hiding place. I assumed he found his boys all beat up and went to get a car or truck. I started walking again, and about fifteen minutes later, I flagged down Billy.

The orange tip glowed as Roscoe sucked on his Vantage. "Read about you in the paper this morning."

"What's the word on Ronnie Carson?"

"She's okay. I worked with her at the Charlotte Observer. She came up and took over the Temperance Mountain Times about a dozen years ago." He paused to inhale more smoke. "You didn't tell Kit everything, did you, Charly?"

I didn't answer immediately but finally said, "I gave him the general picture."

"Come on. What'd you keep from him?"

"Well, I told Kit that I'd fought back and escaped, but I didn't give him too much detail."

"What do you mean by that?"

"I messed up Preach's eye pretty good and put a steel-toed kick to his temple."

"Ouch," Roscoe said with admiration.

"Weasel got the worst of it. I just saw red after he clubbed me in the back and then announced he was going to rape me."

Roscoe paused a moment. "What'd you do?"

"Stabbed him in the foot."

"Damn, Charly."

"The knife might have gone clean through. Then I took the limb he hit me with and returned the favor."

Roscoe's cigarette flared as he took a particularly deep drag. "Yep, that's a scene I'll have to put in my next Hazzard's girl."

I slept in the Gunns' guest room and woke before Roscoe got up. Grievous was in the kitchen, getting a pot of coffee going. My clothes from the night before were torn and filthy, so I borrowed a few things from her, all too big, but with some tucking here and belting there, the skirt and blouse combination worked, sort of, and my boots provided a unique look to my ensemble. Grievous gave me some painkillers for my bruised back. They were stronger than aspirin, she promised, but would leave me clear headed. Though there was still some swelling around my left eye, someone would have to take a close look to see any bruising through the makeup.

I decided to stop by the sheriff's and see what happened with the Thugs. A deputy I didn't recognize was working and said that Kit left a little earlier. I headed over to his cabin after a quick stop at the inn to change into jeans and a T-shirt. I loved a warm autumn in the mountains.

Kit lived up on Doe Ridge Road, which, while technically still in Temperance, was on a small mountain. As I navigated the twisting gravel road, I got the feeling of being out in the wilderness. I passed a farmhouse and then an A-frame, climbed some more, and got to his place. It was a simple, two-story, saltbox log cabin with a deep, covered porch. I shut off the engine, and Kit stepped around the side of the house, shirtless and carrying an axe. He smiled and wiped at his brow.

"Hiya, Kit. You didn't have to strip down on my account," I said, getting out of the car.

He blushed, which was so damn cute on a manly man. "Cutting firewood. Doesn't seem like it now, but cold weather is coming."

"I was worried you'd be asleep. You had a long night."

He shook his head. "Still wound up. A little physical labor helps me relax. Come on in." He led me into his cabin. The first floor was one large open area. A handmade picnic-style table sat just to the right of the door, and he picked up a T-shirt there. There was a shine of sweat on his torso, and as he put the shirt on, I noticed that his muscles stood out after his chopping-block workout. His biceps filled the sleeves as he pulled the T-shirt to his waist. It was a size too small and fit him like a second skin. He turned and saw me watching. I forced my gaze away, and he clumsily puttered about a kitchen counter, preparing coffee.

"It'll take a minute," he mumbled and used his fingers to comb a fallen lock of hair back into place. "I need to wash up."

I grinned as he stomped up the stairs, amused at how easily he could be made self-conscious. My smile faded as feelings I thought were buried tried to rise to the surface. *Down, girl. That was then, this is now.* I took in the living area across the room, with its comfortable leather sofa and chairs, woodstove, and a built-in bookcase filled with paperbacks and hardbacks. Ahead, there was a door that opened either to a closet or the basement—I'd never opened it to see—and past that, the staircase. The room was immaculate, and I added neat freak to his endearing qualities. He'd be quite the catch for a single woman. He could have been mine.

I first visited Kit's cabin three years ago after I'd reconnected with him in Raleigh. There'd been sixteen years between then and high school graduation, plenty of time for a wild boy to turn into a gentle man and the towering ideal of a masculine male. He'd been in Raleigh attending a law-enforcement conference and had looked me up. Normally, I wasn't a big fan of reunions. There's more to my past that I'd like to forget than remember. But Kit called just as I'd closed a particularly difficult case, and I was in good spirits. We arranged to meet in the lounge at the Sheraton Raleigh, where he was staying. I got there early and bellied up to the bar for a drink. My jaw dropped when he walked up to me.

"Hi, Charly," he said, a crooked grin on his face. The weather had been cool, and he wore a green flannel shirt, new blue jeans, and cowboy boots.

The depths of his dark-brown eyes rendered me speechless. Finally, I found my voice and said, "Good lord, Kit. When did you turn into such a stud?" That was the first time I'd seen him blush, something that I'd since learned is easy to cause.

Other than the required queries concerning the health and well-being of each other's family members, we didn't talk about our mutual past, for which I was grateful. Our topics covered law enforcement, past cases, and places we'd been. Our conversation was helped along by copious amounts of alcohol. Though I'm sure I instigated it, I couldn't remember exactly how our friendly little get together turned into a mad dash for the elevator and room number 414, where we shared a passionate and sleepless night. Kit blew off the rest of the conference to spend time with me, much of it horizontally. I followed him when he returned up the mountain and shacked up at his cabin for a few days.

"Did you build it?" I asked the first time I crossed his threshold.

He nodded.

"No hometown winsome beauty up there keeping your bed warm?" I had asked, glancing to the ceiling.

He cracked a self-conscious grin. "Nope."

"Damn, Kit. A big hunk of beef like you, a good job, beautiful place. I'd think women would line up." That earned me another blush, and I attacked him right there. Somehow, we removed each other's clothes and made it to the sofa before we fell and injured ourselves.

As lust fueled our time together, a romance flowered.

My rumination ended as Kit clomped down the stairs. "Coffee's almost done. Want some?"

"Sure." I turned from him, worried that he'd look at me and know what I'd been thinking. Putting on a lighthearted air, I said, "I don't see any feminine touches around your domain."

He stepped into the kitchen. "I'm sure my love life didn't bring you out here. Probably something to do with motorcycle-riding fools."

"Yep." I sat at the table. "How'd it go?"

"Six of us hit their house at four a.m. Damn if they weren't still up, partying on their porch. There was Grizz—a.k.a. William Donovan—and a couple of other Thugs, Luke Beason and a skinny guy they call Bones."

"What about Preach and Weasel?"

"The only others were a couple of women who looked rode hard and put up wet."

"Do you think they were hiding inside?"

"Nope. Grizz was just as hospitable as could be and let us poke around indoors. A real pigsty, by the way."

I was angry that Preach and Weasel weren't there, but the smell of brewing coffee mellowed me. "They were wired last night, coke or speed."

"They were waiting for us, Charly. They hid anything they didn't want us to find."

"What'd Grizz say?"

"Said you left Shorty's, and Preach and Weasel left a little later. Grizz stayed. Said he had no idea they were going after you, and he hasn't seen them since."

"Yeah, right. They're most likely down the mountain, or on their way. They'll keep a low profile at one of their other chapters."

"That's what we figure. We've contacted the PDs in Charlotte, Greensboro, and Raleigh, and they'll look out for those two, but I wouldn't hold my breath."

At least they had some painful injuries to remember me by. "They didn't come for me because of the girls. Preach had a grudge and felt a rape would even the score."

The coffee finished brewing. Kit straddled the kitchen bench next to me and filled our cups. Our conversation dried up, and we self-consciously sipped our coffee. Kit yawned, and I turned to tell him to get some rest, but instead, my hand reached to his cheek, fingers lightly brushing skin and stubble. I knew I should've gotten up and said goodbye. It was still possible to leave, even sitting so close with my hand to his cheek. I could bail and save us both from turmoil. But then I looked in his dark eyes and leaned forward to push my lips against his.

I WOKE IN KIT'S BED. There was a soft breeze against my face, and I opened my eyes. Kit lay beside me, head resting on a hand, his face inches from mine. His breath warmed my cheek.

"When we make love, my favorite part is waking up next to you," he said, an easy smile on his lips.

His words were so sweet that I was scared to respond. And then I tried to be funny. "I'd tell you my favorite part, but you'd run me in on an obscenity charge."

He sniffed. "I love the smell of your skin." He pushed his face closer. "Your hair." Kit ran his finger around my face, finding the scar on my forehead and tracing it back and forth several times before kissing it. He tugged the sheet down past my breasts, and I awaited the feel of his lips on my nipple. Instead he kissed the scar on my collarbone. Was it his way of saying he loved me even for my imperfections?

Instead of asking, I made a joke out of it. "You're twisted."

"Me?" He slid a hand up my thigh. "You're the one who got things rolling on the kitchen table."

"I liked it, though that table was rough on my back," I said, still sore where Weasel hit me. I rolled to the side and gave him a look.

He tenderly ran a fingertip around the discoloration. "That's a hell of a bruise."

I rolled back for a quick kiss. "Yep. I need to pee." I tried to climb over him, but my left leg got tangled in the sheet, and it took a minute to work it free with my other foot.

His bathroom was the one room in his cabin I didn't like. It was too utilitarian. There was a narrow shower stall, tiny sink, toilet, a small place for towels, an even smaller place for toiletries, and that was it. The philistine didn't even have a tub. If he wanted a woman to move in, he'd definitely have to remodel. That triggered a memory of how things ended the last time, and I didn't want to go there. I finished in the bathroom and came out to find him sitting up in bed.

"You hungry?" he asked. "I can make omelets."

"Maybe," I said, wandering around his room. It was definitely a man's room, but unlike the bathroom, it was comfortable and inviting. The walls were dark wood, and the furniture even darker. I picked up items from his dresser top, looked at them, and put them back. I moved to a full-length mirror in a walnut stand and positioned myself so Kit could see the reflection of my naked body. I pretended not to notice him watching me and swayed my hips slowly back and forth. His gaze intensified as I lifted both hands and ran fingers through my hair. My left hand lowered to rest on my belly, and my right stopped at my breast so that my index finger could lightly brush my nipple. Keeping my fingers on skin, I lowered my right hand down past my breasts, my ribs, passing over my belly, and as I got to my mons pubis, I stopped and stepped from the mirror.

Kit groaned, but I kept my face turned away so he wouldn't see my smile—or maybe I should've let him see it. I was sure it was full of possibilities. There was a coat tree next to his mirror, holding a couple of jackets, a few hats, and his gun belt. I got the belt, stepped back to the mirror, and strapped it on so that it sat low across my hips, Kit's .357 heavy on my thigh. I grabbed his sheriff's hat and placed it on my head at a jaunty angle.

"Careful with my gun, Charly," Kit's voice broke.

I took a slow, sexy stroll over to him, my thumbs hooked into the belt. He was sitting up with the sheet across his lap, which I grabbed and pulled off like a bullfighter flipping a cape. I crawled onto the bed on hands and knees.

I said, "So you're the sheriff, huh?" Kneeling, I pushed Kit so that he fell back. "You probably think you're hot shit because you're the boss." I straddled his hips. "Let me show you what happens when a woman's in charge."

Chapter 16
Summer of '59

They upped the reward to five thousand dollars, which I thought showed just how desperate they were. I hadn't seen much of Micah Lee or Bobby. Micah Lee's mother was being a real keeper, and who knew what was up with Bobby. I visited Solomon, and he had copies of Sheriff Rysdale's reports. I read them and made notes in the notebook. The sheriff thought it important that Sarah Mundy's bedspread, blanket, and sheet were twisted on the floor in her room. He wrote that her mother said Sarah was *fastidious*.

"What's fastidious mean?" I mispronounced it.

"Fastidious," Solomon said properly. "She was fussy with her things, not sloppy. She wouldn't have left her blankets and all on the floor."

I noticed in the margin of the Theresa Goodnight report that the sheriff had written in a reference to the library books.

Solomon tapped the page. "He hadn't thought about the books until we told him. You're outthinking the pros, Charly."

"I don't know. I'm more confused than anything."

"Did you talk to Roscoe Gunn?"

I moved my tongue from one side of my mouth to the other. "He says if it was one of his books, Jack Hazzard would try to find out how the Snatcher got Theresa out of the park, while also looking for places he could take the girls."

"Makes sense."

"Yeah, well, if you think about it, there's about a million places that could be. I mean, think of all the old cabins and barns up in the mountains. And he said I shouldn't work on that angle because I'd be in big trouble if I stumble on to where he takes them."

Solomon nodded gravely. "He's right about that."

"I suppose."

"He's right." Solomon peered carefully at me. "I'm serious, Charly. You tend to only mind us grownups when it suits you." With a stern expression, he added, "On this one, you mind me, Charly."

SUNDAY MORNING, I GOT out of bed earlier than normal and asked my parents if I could go to Micah Lee's house and walk to church with him. Mom hemmed and hawed, but Daddy said I could if I went to Micah Lee's straightaway.

Mrs. Leigh opened the door after I knocked. "Good morning, Charly. You're here bright and early."

"I thought I'd walk to Sunday school with Micah Lee."

Concern creased her face. She looked past me at the sunny morning. "I suppose it's okay. Come on in."

She called upstairs for her son, and I asked to use the phone. Bobby answered, and I told him to meet Micah Lee and me on the way to church.

Micah Lee came downstairs tugging at his collar. He'd outgrown his gray Sunday suit so that several inches of socks and wrists were visible.

Mrs. Leigh whipped up some eggs and bacon for us and then proceeded to lecture us on the dangers of strangers. She worked herself up so much she was twisting her apron with both hands and her voice got squeaky high. We tried to leave, but she stopped us at the door and darn near repeated everything all over again before we finally made it out of the house.

On the sidewalk, Micah Lee ripped off his clip-on bowtie and unbuttoned the top button of his shirt. He gave me a sidelong glance, and I noticed his cheeks were red. "You look real pretty in your dress, Charlotte."

"Oh, good God," I blurted. As if I didn't already feel awkward wearing the damn thing. "Micah Lee, if you start making goo-goo eyes at me, I swear I'll give you a knuckle sandwich."

He didn't say anything and avoided my glare, so I knuckle-punched his arm.

"Ouch, Charly! That hurt!"

"Well?"

He kicked at a stone on the sidewalk. "Fine, I won't make goo-goo eyes at you."

Embarrassed, Micah Lee stalked ahead a few steps and was knocked ass over head by Bobby Whist. Their collision rolled them over the sidewalk and onto a lawn where they came to rest. I laughed at the sight of their arms and legs all tangled.

Micah Lee got away from Bobby and stood. "That's not funny, Bobby. Look, my coat's torn at the elbow, and I got grass stains on my shirt, Goddammit."

"If I was you, I wouldn't say Goddammit on my way to church." Bobby laughed. "Lightning will probably strike you as you set foot in the door."

Micah Lee's eyes widened as he considered the risk.

I noticed Bobby in his usual jeans and T-shirt and said, "I take it you're not going to church."

"Hell, no, Charly. I got better things to do. So what'd you want?"

I brushed some blades of grass from Micah Lee's back, and we began walking again. "I've been doing some thinking about the lost girls."

Bobby glanced at me. "That's all you been thinking."

"I was hoping you guys would help me."

"I can't. You know how my mom's being," Micah Lee said. "I'm surprised she let me walk to church without her."

"That's okay. Right now I just want you guys to think about it some, see if you come up with any good ideas," I explained.

"Like what?" Bobby asked.

"Our best chance of solving this is by figuring out how the Snatcher got Theresa Goodnight out of the park with no one seeing."

"That *is* weird," Micah Lee said.

"The other thing is to come up with a list of places the Snatcher could take the girls without anyone knowing. Is it someone who lives alone like Old Man Altus? Is it an old abandoned building some-place? Is it a cabin up in the hills, or does he just take them out to the woods somewhere?" Knowing that Solomon would be furious if he heard what I said next, I went on. "Once we have a list, we can prior-itize the places and start looking around." Thinking of the dream of the lost girls I had in the park, I said, "I got a feeling they were taken west."

Bobby looked at me. "Why west?"

I gazed at Cray's Hill. "It's just a feeling."

"That's dumb."

The church parking lot turned into a mini traffic jam after Sunday service, so many people chose to park on the surrounding streets. As we got closer to church there were more worshippers on the side-walks, so we dropped our voices.

"Okay, I'll think about it," Micah Lee said. "I'll make a list too. Hey, maybe he takes them to the school. It's summer, so no one's there. What if it's the janitor? He's creepy."

Bobby stopped to light a cigarette. He saw the disapproving stare from Mrs. Hightower across the street and blew a smoke ring for her benefit. "Just because school's out doesn't mean it's empty. The prin-cipal and some others are there even in summer."

"Oh."

"That's all right," I told Micah Lee. "That's the kind of thinking we need. Write your list, and then we can talk about it and see which places look good."

"I don't think I'll help," Bobby grumbled.

"They raised the reward to five thousand dollars," I said.

Micah Lee's eyes grew big. "Jiminy."

Bobby shrugged. "Sounds like a lot of work. Look, I got to go." Bobby turned up a street and walked against the flow of church bound. Way up the street, I saw Mrs. Whist's Plymouth at the curb and wondered how he got his mother up so early to drive him over.

"Think about it, Bobby," I called.

"He won't do it," Micah Lee said. "It's too much like homework."

I nodded, and we walked over the threshold of the Good News Baptist Church.

I could just tolerate Sunday school, though I didn't like how they treated us like little kids. On the other hand, they still gave us butter cookies and orange juice, and that was good no matter your age.

Mr. Cordis, the choir director, got the church services underway, leading the singers in a rousing version of "Old Time Religion." The pastor at Good News Baptist Church was Otis Winkel. He came to Temperance a couple years earlier when Reverend Lazarus Laws retired and moved to Florida. Reverend Laws had been a real hellfire-and-brimstone preacher, shouting and yelling, and most Sundays, he'd put other denominations in his crosshairs. I remembered the time he preached that, after the rapture, when we were safe and sound in the city of God, we'd look down on Earth and see fat Catholics in our homes, puffing cigars and drinking Irish whiskey. I asked my dad why the fat Catholics didn't stay in their own homes, and he laughed until Mom shot him a dirty look.

I'd heard it said that there were two kinds of Baptist preachers—the hummers and the honkers. Reverend Laws was the latter, honking declarations during sermons that dealt with the wrath of

God, the fear of God, and eternal damnation. Pastor Winkel was a hummer. He'd drag out words until they turned as smooth as cream. He hummed me to sleep most Sundays, at least until Mom or Daddy poked my ribs.

Pastor Winkel had been going on for about ten minutes. His holy humming provided a serene cloud for me to float on as my eyelids grew heavy. My perception changed as I drifted into that peaceful valley between wakefulness and sleep. The room turned misty, and colors brightened. Pastor Winkel's voice grew distant and soft. Across the aisle and a couple of pews up from mine, a girl stood and walked toward the back of the church, as if the air around her had thickened enough to slow movement. Her name was Lily Branch, and she was eleven. She wore a canary-yellow dress, her blond hair almost a match. As she moved, dust motes as big as blown dandelion seeds floated in the slanted sunshine coming through the eastern windows. She noticed my attention and smiled as she passed. The moment she went by, I snapped out of my daze. I turned as Lily went through the door that led downstairs to the community room, Sunday school classrooms, and the children's bathrooms.

Bored, I gazed out the windows until Pastor Winkel announced it was time to pass the offering plate. Mom handed me a dollar to put in, and the choir began "A Closer Walk with Thee," and the congregation joined in. After a few verses, movement caught my attention. It was Mrs. Branch, standing in a yellow dress that matched her daughter's. She looked at the back of the church and gazed about the congregation. She pushed past others in the pew, hurried down the aisle, and through the door Lily had used.

As I dropped the dollar in the offering plate, I wondered if Lily was having some kind of stomach problem. Maybe she decided it'd be more fun to play in one of the Sunday school rooms than to be up here listening to Pastor Winkel's lengthy sermon. Somewhere in my chest, I felt the first kernel of unease as I thought that maybe it was something much more disturbing. It didn't seem possible, not on a Sunday, not at church.

Leaning toward my mom, I whispered, "I have to use the restroom."

I stood just as the door they'd gone through opened. Mrs. Branch was pale, her eyes wide. She swallowed once and then said something that was somewhere between an announcement and a scream.

"I can't find my Lily."

Chapter 17
Autumn of '82

Kit slept. I could wear a man out. I got out of bed and looked for my clothes then remembered they were downstairs, scattered around the kitchen table. After I dressed, I drove back to the Temperance Inn and figured there was time for a bath before dinner. While I didn't carry a notebook to interview clients, witnesses, and suspects, I did use one for reviewing cases. In Dub's glorious bathtub, I went through a notebook that I bought at a farmers' market in Chapel Hill. The size of a paperback, the cover was purple paisley. The craftsman even made the coarse paper. Using the fountain pen my father gave me for college graduation, I wrote down all I'd learned, being careful not to get the pages wet. I notated what I saw, who I talked to, and what they said. When I finished, I read it through, making notes in the margins. I learned plenty of little things, but the total sum of progress felt like zero. Something about the East Coast Thugs kept gnawing at me.

Out of the bath, I wrapped myself in a towel and sat on the bed to continue my musings. Maybe I needed to step back and look at the town as a whole. But how? Temperance, to me, was like a photograph that had been double-exposed with another similar, yet different town. Twenty-three years ago, nobody in Temperance had a clue as to what was happening. I now knew that Sheriff Rysdale was in over his head. A competent investigator might have nailed the Snatcher right after Sarah Mundy disappeared. But that was looking at it in hindsight. There were plenty of crimes that appeared as if a mastermind were at work, but when the crime was solved, it turned out the criminal was simply lucky.

The phone rang, and I answered distractedly, "Yeah?"

"I thought you were going to stay for one of my award-winning omelets." Kit sounded like he was smiling.

Keeping my eyes on a page in my notebook, I said, "I wanted to go over some things." He didn't respond, and then I thought I had sounded cold. "Sorry, Kit, I was just reviewing some notes."

"Oh."

"I already ate. I'll take a rain check on that omelet, though."

"Yeah, sure." Kit paused. I wondered if he was waiting for me to fill the void, and then he said, "I was thinking, Charly. If you want, you can stay with me while you're in town."

With that, I was taken back three years, when things with Kit got too serious too fast. He had asked me to move in with him, and I gave him my standard speech about how I like being on my own, and how we should take our time. It had worked on other men, but back when I had said it to Kit, it sounded concocted and shallow.

I took too long to answer, and Kit muttered, "Never mind. Talk to you later."

"Wait, Kit—"

He hung up.

I rubbed my eyes, and all at once, I was lonely. It was my own damn fault. I shouldn't have jumped his bones. I closed my notebook, turned out the light, and rolled over. Sleep did not come easy.

THE MORNING BEGAN WITH a stop downtown. I wandered the park, which sure seemed bigger when I was a kid. I cast a wary eye at the sheriff's department across the street and wondered if Kit was in. If so, should I go talk to him? Not yet. Instead, I went over to

Le Bistro and looked at the park from that perspective. If Savannah Smallwood left the restaurant and walked straight across the street, she'd be at the playground. At twelve, she might have been too old for a swing set, teeter-totter, and merry-go-round. Perhaps she'd gone exploring around the park. That was what I would have done at that age.

"Hi, Miss Bloom."

I turned to see Kit's niece approaching. She wore the same outfit as when I first met her. "Hi, Violet. Coming in to work?"

"Another day, another dollar."

I had a couple of questions bouncing around my head and asked, "You have a couple of minutes to spare?"

Violet looked at her watch. "Sure."

"Were you working the night Savannah Smallwood vanished?"

"Uh-huh. We had to stay late and answer questions for Uncle Kit and his deputies."

"Tell me what you remember."

She worked her lips from side to side as she recalled. "I was working the dinner shift. I got in at four thirty. The Smallwoods came in about seven thirty. You've eaten here, so you know that it's not a rush kind of place. I'd say that the girl finished eating by eight thirty. I know it was dark out."

"You were their waitress?"

It was a sad thing to be connected to a crime against a child, and Violet said "Yes" like it was a burden. "She went to the park, and her parents finished their coffee about twenty minutes later. They paid, said they had a great dinner, and left. They came back ten minutes later asking if we'd seen their daughter. Her mother was close to panic. Artie called Uncle Kit right away."

"Artie?"

"He's the manager. He knew it was serious, but he didn't tell them about Copycat. He let Uncle Kit deliver that bad news. I felt so sad for them and kind of guilty. I didn't think to tell them about Copy-cat. If I had—"

"Don't go down that road," I told her. "Do you remember who worked that night?"

"Well, me and Artie." She touched a finger with each name. "Katie was the other server that night. Ben's our chef, so he was here. Luke was working line, and I think Gus was washing dishes and bussing tables."

"That's it? Doesn't seem like a big staff."

She pointed through the plate glass window. "It's not that big of a restaurant."

"Cozy," I said, looking in.

"Yeah, cozy."

"Can you do me a favor?" I asked.

"Sure."

"Ask them if they remember anything strange or out of the ordinary that night, anyone hanging around, that kind of thing."

"Okay."

I took one of my cards and wrote the number for the inn on the back and handed it to her. "If you come up with something, call this number. If I'm not there, leave a message with Mr. Mellerman."

I talked to people at the surrounding stores, shops, and business-es. Most were closed by the time Savannah Smallwood was abducted. The few that were around that night hadn't seen anything. I finally found myself outside the sheriff's office and decided it was time to face the inevitable. Taking a deep breath like I was about to plunge into cold waters, I pushed open the door and approached the deputy up front.

"Is Kit in?" I asked.

The deputy was reviewing some files and didn't even look up but pointed around the counter to Kit's office. His door was open, but I stood on the outside of the threshold and tentatively knocked.

Kit was filling some forms out at his desk. He looked up at me and back down to his work. "Hi, Charly."

"Hi, Kit." I took a couple of steps into his office.

For several seconds, the only sound was Kit's pencil scratching across the paper. "What can I do for you?" he asked, eyes on the paper.

"I was hoping that we could talk." He didn't respond, so I said, "Maybe later. I can see you're busy. I also wanted to know if I could go to the elementary school and see where the Regis girls were abducted."

Kit took a moment to finish writing. He picked up his phone in one hand and flipped through a Rolodex with the other.

He dialed a number, and when someone answered he asked, "Could I speak with Mrs. Avery?" A full minute passed. Kit kept the phone to his ear while looking everywhere but at me. He finally said, "Hi, Carol. It's Kit. One of my investigators would like to come by and see where we think the Regis girls were abducted." She talked a bit, and he said, "That'd be fine. See you then." Hanging up, he said, "She asks that we wait until all the children are gone. We'll meet there at five."

NEITHER KIT NOR I SUGGESTED we ride over together. Crazy. One day we were romping passionately in the nude, and the next we were as uncomfortable with each other as sixth graders on a first date. It was no wonder I wasn't a fan of relationships. I'd had few that lasted longer than a few months. Granted, I was the one who broke them off. I told myself it was because I liked being single, but there had been times, usually during those three a.m. introspections in bed, when I wondered if it was because I was afraid of what would happen to anyone I allowed to get too close to me.

Kit was waiting for me when I pulled up in front of my elementary alma mater. He gave me a curt nod and then introduced me to the principal. He then took me to where they thought the Regis girls were abducted.

"I'm assuming that there's beefed-up security," I said.

"Teachers watch the kids wherever they go. Additional teachers are on duty at the bus drop-off and pick-up, same with parent drop-off and pick-up. I have a deputy here when students arrive in the morning and leave in the afternoon."

Kit and I hopped the fence, and he showed me where they found Pedi Regis's shoe. We got back to Kit's LTD, and he drove to Weir Road, where they thought Copycat parked. How did he haul two struggling girls for a mile through the woods?

By the time we left Weir Road, Kit and I seemed more comfortable with each other, and I followed him out to a barbecue joint out on the west side of town.

At a table with a red-checked tablecloth, I said, "Remember when the only restaurants in town were the Pine Top and Beryl's?"

"I still hold Beryl's near and dear to my heart. That was the closest thing we had to an ice cream parlor."

A waitress brought us water glasses, with which we toasted the memory of Beryl's.

"I'm going to drop in on Handsome George tomorrow," I said.

"Good."

"Think he'll be happy to see me?"

"Maybe. Don't be hurt if he isn't."

"Yeah." I changed topics. "I have this gut feeling about the Thugs."

"That they're involved?" Kit asked.

"Yeah."

"There's nothing that points in that direction, other than Grizz talking to Piper Darling at Shorty's."

"I know. Like I said, it's just a feeling. I'm going to look into them a little more."

"I don't think they're connected, so don't waste too much time on them." Kit gazed at his food, glanced at me, and then down again. "When you stopped in today, you said we needed to talk. How about now?"

Yeah, I'd said that. But now, when we were getting along pretty good, it was the last thing I wanted. "How about we wait until—"

"Come on, Charly. Let's have it out. You and me, what happened yesterday, what happened three years ago."

I nodded. "Yesterday, I shouldn't have..."

"No, it was great. I just don't... I'm not sure what..." His hand was on the table and moved toward me.

I'd been in this situation plenty of times. If it went on, it would not turn out well. I put my hand over his. "You know what? Let's wait until this is all over, until we get Copycat."

He nodded, turning his attention back to his plate. What had started out as some damn good barbecue lost its appeal, and I was done eating. I drove back to the Temperance Inn, where I spent an hour trying to distract myself from thinking about Kit by reading Roscoe's story in Penthouse.

Chapter 18
Summer of '59

In the hubbub that ensued, I went and grabbed Micah Lee and dragged him downstairs. Men rushed around, calling for Lily both indoors and out. The women stayed up in the sanctuary, many of them trying to calm Mrs. Branch.

The Good News Baptist Church perched sideways on a hill, so that on the east side, the basement was truly a basement. On the west side, however, there was a door and several windows. I knew we had a few minutes before they got organized and kicked us out of the Sunday school area. The door to the girl's bathroom was propped open, and I noticed the window was open as well, so I shoved Micah Lee inside and followed.

"Look for clues," I whispered.

Micah Lee looked around the sinks while I checked out the two stalls. The first didn't offer up much, but in the second, I noticed that the roll of toilet paper had been unwound so that some had piled on the floor a couple inches thick. There was something by the back wall. I didn't want to disturb the pile of unrolled paper, so I went around the other side of the toilet, leaned over it, and put my hands against the stall wall to keep my balance.

"What are you doing?" Micah Lee whispered from the stall door.

"Look." I nodded to three wet red spots on the tile.

I stared until I realized I was holding my breath, and exhaled, feeling my heart hammer away. There was hushed conversation by the door, and I left the stall as Sheriff Rysdale and Deputy Atwater pushed through a small crowd. The sheriff looked awful, like he'd aged twenty years since I last saw him.

"Everybody, give the sheriff some room," Marty said, moving his arms like he was directing traffic.

I sheepishly held up my hand like I was in school. "Sheriff?"

He turned to me, and I noticed a tic in his right eyelid. "Get out, Charly." His harsh tone startled me.

I started out the door but first grabbed Marty's sleeve.

"What is it?" the deputy whispered.

I pointed to the second stall. "There's blood on the floor by the wall."

They made everyone go back up into the church, and a prayer service was held for Lily and her family. While the sheriff and Marty looked around, the auxiliary members interviewed churchgoers one by one before letting them leave. My notebook was at home, so I borrowed a pencil from my mother and an envelope she had in her purse. I listed the people who'd been in church, figuring if they were in church with me, then they couldn't have made off with Lily.

I heard a familiar gruff voice and turned to see Solomon roll through the door. The sheriff and Marty came from downstairs, spoke a few minutes with him, and went out. Solomon looked around the church, and with a grim expression, he signaled me to join him.

"Where are you going, Charly?" Mom asked as I stood.

I pointed to the door. "Solomon wants to talk to me."

"Why?"

"I don't know, Mom. But he's head of the sheriff's auxiliary, so I better go."

"Well..." She was shaken up. "Okay. But don't leave church without us."

I passed by Micah Lee and his mother in their pew. Mrs. Leigh's eyes were wide, and she held her Bible with shaking hands. Micah Lee gave me a little wave. I aimed a finger toward the front door, hoping he'd follow, but he shook his head and pointed at his mom.

"Hi, Solomon," I said when I reached him.

"This is some kind of mess, ain't it, Charly?"

I nodded.

"Every time a little angel disappears, I keep hoping I'll wake up to find it's all been a nightmare."

"Me too."

"The sheriff wants to talk to you."

"Me?"

Solomon took my hand. "This is wearing hard on him, so he's a bit edgy."

"Edgy?"

"He knows you've been looking into things, so be honest with him. Tell him whatever he wants to know."

"I will."

I pushed Solomon out the church and to the parking lot where the sheriff waited with Marty.

The sheriff turned, and in the sunlight, he looked even worse, his skin loose and pale, and there were dark circles under each bloodshot eye. His facial tic was still evident, and he hitched at his belt as he frowned down at me.

"Charly Bloom." I don't think I'd ever heard my name sound so unappealing.

"Um, Sheriff Rysdale."

He licked at chapped lips. "You think I can't solve this?"

That came out of left field and left me stammering until I managed, "I don't think that."

"Really? Because you sure as hell been sticking your nose where it doesn't belong." He waited for me to respond, but I was frozen like a rabbit facing a coyote. "Let's see. Figured out the library book angle, didn't you? Called Miss Grunwald to let her know you think I'm dropping the ball."

"I just wanted to see if Theresa Goodnight had checked out books."

"Then you tramped all over the park, ignoring me when I told you to stay on the sidewalks."

"No, sir, I didn't mean to disobey you."

"Let's not forget how you accused Mr. Altus." Sheriff Rysdale sneered. "And then you pushed your way into that crime scene"—the sheriff pointed at the church—"snooped around, even though you know you shouldn't have, right?"

I stood silent, eyes wide.

"Right?" the sheriff bellowed.

"Yes," I managed before the tears spilled over.

"You've been talking to others around town, haven't you?"

"Yes, sir." My face crumpled, snot loosened, and my eyes lost focus.

"Telling them that I'm incompetent, can't do my job?"

"No, sir, I wouldn't say anything like that."

Solomon gave Marty a look, and the deputy put a hand on the sheriff's shoulder and said, "Sir, we should talk to Lily Branch's family."

Breathing like a bull, Sheriff Rysdale pierced me with his eyes. "You stop meddling, Charly Bloom. Keep out of it." And he stomped back to church with Marty at his heels.

I spun to Solomon and blubbered, "Why's he mad at me?"

Solomon pulled me down into a hug. "I'm sorry, Charly. I didn't know he'd go off on you like that. I thought he was going to ask you about finding the blood."

I sobbed some and left Solomon's arms. "Sorry. I hate crying."

He handed me a handkerchief. "That's no problem. And don't take it personal. The sheriff is at his wit's end. He told me he hasn't had a good night's sleep in weeks."

"That's no reason to yell at me."

Solomon nodded. "All them things he was accusing you of, telling people he's incompetent and can't do his job? That's how he's starting to feel about himself. And on top of that, he's up for reelection next year. If he doesn't solve this, people will turn on him and vote him out even though he's been sheriff for almost twenty years. All I'm saying is he's under stress, so don't take what he says to heart."

"Okay." I nodded while wiping at my nose.

Solomon rolled back toward church, and a hand gripped my shoulder. I turned to find the SBI agent.

He leaned toward me and spoke low. "Charly Bloom, right?"

"Yes, sir."

"Special Agent Kennedy."

"Pleased to meet you," I said, feeling stupid because it was obvious I'd been crying.

"I know you want to keep looking into this." A protest formed on my lips, but he held up a hand. "I've been an investigator long enough to recognize your drive and instinct, but promise me that from now on you'll leave it to us."

I didn't know what to say.

"It's an ugly thing, what this Snatcher is doing, and we don't need any more victims. Each clue we find, each bit of evidence gets us a little nearer to this man. I've always seen it as some sort of intricate dance, because by its very nature, an investigation like this draws the investigators and the perp closer and closer to one another, circling round and round. And I can tell that this dance won't end until there's more blood. That's why you have to stay out of it. It would make me sad if you turned out to be the next missing girl. Promise, Charly? No more snooping around?"

What he said caused goose flesh to rise on my arms and on the back of my neck. "Yes, sir."

Still, could I stop? Would I? No, I'd only told him what he wanted to hear.

Chapter 19
Autumn of '82

There was a knock at the door, waking me. I sat up, turned on the bedside lamp, and listened. The knock repeated on the fire escape door. My little play date with Preach and Weasel taught me a lesson, and I took my gun, a .38 revolver, from my lock box in the bedside table drawer.

"Just a minute," I said, glancing at the clock, which showed it was just after eleven.

As I was in panties and a tank top, I slid on my white bathrobe and put the gun in the pocket while keeping a grip on it. I opened the door to find Kit, and he didn't look happy. He tromped past me into the room.

"By all means, come in."

He was in a white button-down shirt, some sort of rough weave that looked like it was made by local Cherokee artisans. "I can't do this, Charly."

"Do what?"

"I can't do my job, focus on this case, if you're going to play head games with me."

I wanted to be angry at his insinuation. Instead, I turned from him. "Head games?"

"What happened at my cabin."

I felt bad. "I'm sorry, Kit. It's my fault. I shouldn't have made a move on you. We both need our focus for the case."

"That's just it. Since we... you know... I've had that rattling around in my head along with the case. Maybe I'm just a dumb redneck—"

"Kit, you know that's not—"

"But I need you to spell it out for me, Charly. Either we're giving us, you and me, another shot, or we're not. I can't function if we keep blurring the lines."

I took his hand and led him to the one of the two small chairs at the table. They were so spindly I worried he'd break one when he sat.

"Kit, I found myself so attracted to you that I let myself lose control, and I'm sorry. It's not fair to you. We talked about this back when... well... you know? You told me you want a family. I don't. It's just who I am. Not to mention we have an entire state between us. Long-distance relationships are hard enough for people who really want it."

Kit had his elbows on his knees and stared down at the floor. "One of us could move."

I hated rehashing old arguments. "I told you three years ago, even if I wanted to leave Raleigh, which I don't, I couldn't make a living in a town this small."

He stood and started for the door. "I didn't mean you coming here."

"Hold up," I said, grabbing his arm. "You'd have moved to Raleigh?" He didn't answer but looked at me with a hurt expression. "But I thought with you being sheriff and all..."

"What's it matter? You never asked." Kit opened the door. "Look, Charly, I'm going to state it as plainly as possible. I can't afford to get distracted with figuring you out. From now on, we keep it professional." He glared at me, anger and pain all there in his eyes. "Got it?"

It took me a moment to respond. "Yeah, Kit. Got it."

I listened to his footsteps descend the fire escape, sat in one of the chairs, and felt miserable. As much as I wanted to be mad at him, I was angry at myself. I seduced him, and though there were no strings attached from my perspective, I didn't consider what he thought or felt. Kit was a great guy, the best. He was a list of paradoxes—incredibly strong yet gentle, handsome yet humble, angry at me while in love with me, even after three years. What would it be like if he did live in Raleigh? Would I sabotage any chance we had simply because that was my history? I was closing in on forty. Maybe it was time I tried to break that history.

I shook my head, deciding these were all things to work out once we'd put Copycat away.

I WOKE IN THE MORNING and moaned in ecstasy as I lay amidst the gazillion-thread-count sheets. Then I remembered Kit's late-night visit, and my mood darkened.

"Shit," I muttered and rolled out of bed. I grabbed a blouse from my bag and took off my tank top, turning to look at my bruised back in the mirror. That fuckin' Weasel really did a number on me.

I slipped on my blouse and strolled to a nearby diner to pick up a to-go breakfast.

I had a cup of coffee while I waited, grabbed my grub, and paid. There was a newspaper stand outside, and I fished a coin out of my pocket. I sat on a bench, put down the food, and read three stories dealing with the abductions. One headline screamed, *Snatcher's Burial Ground Discovered*. Kit was quoted on the discovery, the current crimes, and as to whether Copycat was imitating the Snatcher. Another was a background piece, with biographies on the lost girls, both from '59 and now. The third rehashed the investigation, highlighting how both the SBI and I were helping Kit.

When I got to my room, I cleared the small table for breakfast. While I was eating, I turned my thoughts to the case, particularly the two-wheeled grease monkeys known as the East Coast Thugs. I was doubtful I'd see Preach or Weasel again, but what about the other members? There was Grizz, the one they called Bones, and there was Luke Beason. Not much of a gang. Why would the Thugs want a chapter in this little town? A thought came to me, and I flipped through my notebook and read.

I went to the bedside table, picked up the phone, and called Kit at work. "Hey, Kit. How's it going?"

"What can I do for you, Charly?"

Okay, if he wanted to be strictly business, I could play it that way too. "What can you tell me about a Thugs member named Luke Beason?"

I heard him shift the phone from one ear to the other. "Beason isn't a member yet. He's a prospect. That means—"

"I know what it means." A prospect was low man on the totem pole of a club, a prospective member who had to go through a period of brutal hazing before he was either welcomed into the fold or cast off. He wouldn't have the full patch. Instead, he'd have the MC for motorcycle club, and a bottom rocker that said Prospect. "Does he have a job in town?"

"Well, yeah. He and the one called Bones work somewhere besides ECT Motorcycle Repairs. Bones is a stone mason for Booth Construction, Beason cooks at Le Bistro."

My heartbeat picked up a bit. "Do you have your niece's phone number?"

"Yeah, why?"

"I just want to check something."

He gave me her number, and I hung up.

I had that feeling in my gut that said I was on to something, and I dialed Violet's number. Her mother answered and yelled for her daughter.

Violet picked up the phone. "Hello?"

"Hello, Violet. It's Charly Bloom."

"I haven't had a chance to talk to everybody yet." She sounded defensive.

"That's okay."

"I did talk to Ben and Luke."

"What did they say?"

"Ben doesn't remember anything out of the ordinary. And I was wrong, Luke didn't work that night."

I sat up straight. "Oh?"

"He reminded me that he just popped in to get his paycheck. That's why I remember him being there."

This was interesting, but would it add up to anything? "What time did he come in?"

"I can't remember exactly, so it could have been anytime from when my shift began at four thirty until closing."

Keeping my tone neutral, I asked, "Do you remember him being there after the abduction?"

She was silent while thinking. "No."

"So somewhere between four thirty and eight thirty?"

"I guess."

So Luke Beason, a prospect for the Thugs, also worked at Le Bistro. Though he was off the night that Savannah Smallwood was abducted, he stopped in to get his paycheck. There was a connection there, but did it mean anything? If he went for his paycheck, did he see her leave the restaurant and take her because... why? Were the East Coast Thugs, as a group, abducting girls? Again, why? Human trafficking, selling them to the highest bidders, kiddie porn? On the other hand, it didn't have to be the club. It could just be Beason acting alone. I chewed a lip as I thought. How could I check his whereabouts during the other disappearances, and do it without him knowing? My best bet, I thought, was to see where he was during the Mani and Pedi Regis abductions. That window was fairly narrow.

Violet asked, "You still there, Charly?"

"I'm sorry, I was thinking. I hate to be a pest, Violet, but could I get you to do one more thing for me?"

"Sure." She sounded as if she was smiling. I think she enjoyed playing private eye.

"Can you find out who was working on the afternoon of..." I paused, looked at my notes, and gave her the date for the abduction of the Regis sisters.

"Sure. Past schedules are kept in a filing cabinet. Anyone in particular?"

"See if anyone working the night Savannah Smallwood disappeared also worked that date I just gave you between three thirty and four. Okay?"

"Okay."

Playing dumb, I asked, "Oh, and what was the name of the line cook who got his paycheck when the Smallwood girl vanished?"

"Luke Beason."

"Might as well check him too. Speaking of which, I have a good grasp of some of your co-workers," I lied, "but I don't know anything about Luke Beason. What can you tell me?"

"Well," she said, gathering her thoughts, "he's into motorcycles and rides with a gang called the Thugs."

"He's a member?" I knew he was only a prospect, but I wanted to see how much she knew.

"No. He wants to join, though. I tell him he's crazy."

"He's a local guy, right?"

"That's right. We went to the same schools, though he's older. I was a freshman when he was a senior, so he's twenty-four or twenty-five."

"How did he get in with the bikers?"

"I'm not sure, but he's been into motorcycles as long as I can remember, riding them since he was little, mainly dirt bikes," Violet said, adding, "Now he rides something he calls a sport—no, it's a sporter."

"A Sportster?" I ventured.

"Yeah, I think that's it."

"What's he look like?"

Again, she paused as she thought, filling the void with, "Well, he's good looking, I guess. I mean, some of the girls used to like him. He has that wild biker look now, long hair, and he doesn't shave much, so he's stubbly. He's kind of an average size and build."

"What's he like, personality and all?"

"He used to be okay, a nice guy," she said.

"Used to be?"

"Ever since he's been hanging with the bikers, he's kinda turned into a..." She stopped to come with the appropriate term. "A jerk."

"Like how?"

"Now he acts all macho, like he's looking to fight all the time. And he's always flirting with girls, but in a dirty way."

"Crude?"

"Very. And he's a smartass, even with Artie. Artie will fire him if he keeps it up."

"Thanks, Violet. Don't tell him I was asking, okay?"

"Sure."

"It'll be our secret."

"Yeah, okay. Mums the word." By her eagerness, I could tell she liked the idea of our sharing secrets.

THE FIREBIRD IDLED across the street from The Forum Theater. I spent countless hours there as a child, mesmerized by the action on the screen. Before the summer of '59, almost all those hours were shared with Micah Lee and Bobby. After the events of that summer,

I couldn't bring myself to return. Then, one chilly November day, Handsome George walked to my house and said he needed help. We walked back, talking about lots of stuff, but not anything that had to do with the Snatcher. *Ben-Hur* was showing, and I still remembered how exciting the chariot race was, and how Handsome George sat by me for the whole movie. In fact, he was by my side for every other movie I saw there.

The Forum Theater was now dying a slow death, losing business to a complex with four screens out on I-26. No longer able to afford first releases, they showed second-run movies. The marquee over the ticket booth said *Star Trek II: The Wrath of Khan*. Coming attraction posters behind framed glass announced that *Poltergeist* and *Grease 2* were upcoming features even though they'd been released months earlier. The ticket booth was empty, so I bypassed it and walked in. It hurt to see that the Forum had gone from majestic to gloomy.

"Charly Bloom, is that you?" Handsome George's sister was behind the snack bar.

"Hi, Mary. How are things?"

"Oh, same old. I saw in the paper that you were back."

We chatted over the counter for a bit until I asked, "Is George here?"

"In his usual spot."

I paused in the dark theater as Ricardo Montalban and William Shatner tried to outwit one other. I went down the center aisle about two-thirds of the way until I got to Handsome George. Still living up to his nickname, he stared at the screen.

I kissed his cheek. "Hi, George. It's me, Charly."

He didn't turn or acknowledge me. I crossed in front of him and sat in the next seat over. Mary took care of him and brought him to the theater every day so he could watch all the movies. She had a couple of theater seats taken out so they could move his wheelchair into place.

"I'm in town for a few days and wanted to see you."

He looked at me, and there was no recognition in his eyes. "I wanted to..." he mumbled. "I don't..." An explosion onscreen caught his attention.

I put an arm around him, rested my head on his shoulder, and cried a little. Senile Dementia was the name they gave it now.

I took his hand, and we watched the movie. Handsome George shifted, and I turned to see him looking at me with a cognizant smile.

"Where's Bobby and Micah Lee?" he asked.

I looked into clear, observant eyes, and it took me a moment to answer. "They couldn't come today."

"Want to help me clean after the show?"

"More than anything, George."

Clear eyes fogged, and he was gone. A vacant gaze lingered on me until the glow from the screen recaptured what little attention he had. Handsome George hit the nail on the head when he once told me that growing old ain't for sissies.

I returned to the inn, and Dub was at the desk. "Hi, Charly. Been reading about you in the paper." He wore a ball cap and overalls. I figured he was ready to tackle more weeds.

"You and everyone else." I took his one arm. "Come walk with me, Dub."

We went outside and wandered about the gardens and lawns.

"I can't remember the last time that it was this warm so late in the season," he said.

"I love it."

"Any day now, the weather is going to turn, and just like that"—he snapped his fingers—"you'll remember how cold it can get up here."

"Just send up another comforter, and I'll hibernate for the winter."

"How's the investigation?"

Wanting to use the right word, I filed through my mental thesaurus and settled on, "Vexing."

"Think there's any connection back to '59?"

"Sometimes yes, sometimes no. That's why I want to talk to you, so I can pick your brain."

"Pick away," he said.

"Back when we were kids, we knew just about everyone in town."

"That we did."

"It seems odd that nobody figured out who the Snatcher was."

"In retrospect it seems pretty obvious, huh?"

I stopped walking and turned to Dub. "What about now? Is there anyone that comes to mind who should be a suspect?"

"Town's grown. Don't know everyone these days." Dub stopped walking and gazed out over a steep, green lawn. "Ya know, Charly, I still have my service .45. If I knew who was taking those girls, I'd put the barrel to his forehead, pull the trigger, and rejoice at his earthly departure."

"And I'd help you mop up the mess. But there's a difference between knowing who it is and suspecting someone."

He shook his head. "I don't have a clue."

"Okay. What about those bikers, the East Coast Thugs?"

"Do I think they're responsible?"

"I just want to get your opinion," I said.

"Well, I wouldn't be surprised if they were dealing drugs, stealing stuff, something like that. But I can't see a whole group of guys preying on little girls. That seems like something one lone crazy person would do."

"How about just one of them?"

Dub didn't look convinced but answered, "It's feasible. But they've been in town four or five years. Why wait until now?"

"I don't know," I answered, wondering if I was spinning my wheels looking at the Thugs.

Chapter 20
Summer of '59

I walked home with my parents, others of the congregation doing the same, stone faced and silent. That another of Temperance's children could be snatched while we were all nearby was chilling. And the fact she was taken from God's house meant that nowhere was safe.

I spent much of the day writing. After I copied the names of the people who'd been in church into my notebook, I gave a detailed account of what had happened that morning. When I finished, I decided to look for Bobby and fill him in.

"Where do you think you're going?" Mom asked as I passed her and opened the door.

"I'm gonna hang with Bobby."

"No, you're not." She closed the door. "You're staying home. It's not safe out."

I remained at the door, looking out at the freedom that lay just over the threshold. Fearing the answer, I asked, "Stay home? For how long?"

"For the time being," she said and went into the kitchen.

I stood horror-struck. *For the time being?* If Mom said that, it meant it would be a long time, an eternity for a kid like me.

THAT NIGHT, I LAY BACK on my bed with notebook in hand. I'd gone over it about a gazillion times until the letters and words all seemed to blur together. I tossed it to the floor and got off the bed. I did a couple of laps around my room and finally settled by the window that looked into our backyard. Temperance was high up in the mountains, about thirty-five hundred feet above sea level. Sometimes, instead of clouds overhead, we were in the clouds, which was pretty much the same as wet fog. That was how it was that night, and our back-porch light did little to pierce it. I could make out the maple tree midway back in the yard, but nothing farther. With a combination yawn and groan, I rested my head against the window. My eyes lost focus, though I still watched the mist and how it changed. It seemed solid, then soft, then frozen, then in motion. When I noticed motion within the motion and shapes within shapelessness, I thought I might have slipped into sleep and what I saw was a dream. Sarah Mundy formed to the left of the maple tree and Theresa Goodnight to the right. The girls took several steps closer and looked up at me, appearing as they had in the park. A second later, another figure stood between them, a blond girl in a yellow dress. She gazed up with the same smile as when she passed me in church. They turned, and for a few seconds, they were no longer in my yard, but walking single file into the pathway through the park woods where the library books had been found.

I jerked awake, my head resting against cool glass. The backyard was empty. Still, I felt a deep sorrow because I thought that seeing her with Sarah and Theresa meant that Lily Branch was now dead.

THE WEEK PLODDED BY.

Mom knew Micah Lee was anchored to his mother, and that Bobby Whist was none too dependable as an escort. Home imprisonment was just another reason to hate the Snatcher. The monotony broke when Solomon came for a visit on Tuesday. Mom and I manhandled his wheelchair up the front steps so he and I could sit on the porch and drink lemonade.

"I'm going crazy, Solomon. Mom won't let me go anywhere."

"I understand how she feels. Young people of your gender are being targeted. It's normal that she worry. If the cabin fever gets too bad, call me. I'll come get you and treat you to a movie or something."

"Thanks." Though it was the total lack of freedom that truly bothered me, I'd take what I could get. "What's the sheriff learned about Lily?"

"That's what I came to tell you. No one heard or saw anything. Going by what you found in the stall, we do have a theory as to what happened." He drank from his glass.

I'd been thinking about it as well and had come up with my own theory. Lily, I thought, used the bathroom. The Snatcher came in through the window and hit her while she was in the stall, knocking her back. As she fell, she grabbed at anything, snagging the toilet paper, which was why it was all unwound on the floor. She struck the back wall and bled a few drops on the floor. Stunned or knocked out, the Snatcher carried her out the window to his car. And what Solomon told me pretty much confirmed that.

After he left, I stayed on the front porch until Mom ordered me inside, figuring if a child could vanish from church, a front porch would be easy pickings. I went into the backyard and rambled around the maple tree, thinking back to my dream of the three lost girls in the fog. Of course, there were no footprints. Neither dreams nor ghosts left that kind of evidence. I leaned against the tree, moving up and down like a bear scratching its back, and then sat against the trunk. The girls had been here, yet when they left, the scenery shifted to that one pathway into the park woods. Why? Was there significance in that? Was there any kind of significance in a dream?

By Thursday, I was climbing the walls. I talked to Micah Lee on the phone every day and was furious at Bobby for not coming over or even calling. On Friday, I phoned Solomon to take him up on his movie offer. We went by Micah Lee's, but his mother wouldn't let him join us. Though I was still angry, we stopped by Bobby's house. His mother answered the door in a bathrobe and had no idea where he was. Handsome George sat with us as we watched the matinee of a moonshine-running Robert Mitchum battling feds and gangsters in *Thunder Road*.

"Do you think we could swing by the library?" I asked Solomon as we got in his van. Seeing the girls in my backyard, and then the locale shifting to the path into the park woods gnawed at me.

"Picking up a book?"

"No, I'm curious about Town Center Park."

"The park?"

"You know, the history, how it got built, that kind of thing."

"This have to do with the Snatcher?"

"Yes," I said, watching him carefully.

Solomon sighed. "Charly, the sheriff told you to keep out of it."

"I'm keeping my investigation at a distance, like you said."

He was quiet a minute or two, and then Solomon unexpectedly turned right on Crown Drive. "I have a better idea. Do you know Augustus Ettinger?"

I thought a moment and said, "I don't think so. Who's he?"

Solomon reached out his open window to adjust his side mirror. "Augustus used to be the mayor back when the park was put in."

That was news to me. I'd figured the park had always been there. "And he's still alive?"

"That he is. He and I are about the same age, though Augustus lives at Golden Years Elderly Care Center. He's a sickly man, you see, but his mind is sharp," Solomon said as we turned into the visitor's parking lot.

I pushed Solomon toward the front door as he called out greetings to patients who sat in the sunshine out front. Inside, we paused at the reception desk.

"Good afternoon, Solomon," a nurse said.

"And to you, Norma. Do you know my friend Charly Bloom?"

"I think so," she said. "A local baseball legend." I blushed as I shook her hand.

Solomon said, "We're here to visit Augustus. Is he feeling up to guests today?"

"I'm sure he is. Check the activity room."

Solomon guided me down a carpeted corridor. We pushed through swinging double doors into a room that smelled of disinfectant and flowers. There were colorful bouquets all around. Large windows lined two walls, letting in abundant light. A radio played soothing orchestra music. Handsome George's mother sat in a wheelchair, looking into space, and we stopped to say hi. She smiled but didn't speak.

"There he is." Solomon pointed to a bald, bespectacled man in a shirt and tie who was nearly a skeleton. He sat in a wheelchair at a table with another man, playing checkers.

We arrived as Augustus reached a shaky hand to push a piece forward.

"Good afternoon, Augustus," Solomon said.

"Hello, Solomon," Augustus answered in a tremulous voice.

"This is Charly Bloom, and Charly, this is Augustus Ettinger."

"Mr. Ettinger, pleased to meet you."

"The pleasure is all mine, young lady," Mr. Ettinger said. He pointed at the man across the table and added, "My opponent, Sherwood Blankenship."

When the introductions were done, I asked Mr. Ettinger, "Solomon said you used to be mayor."

He nodded and pointed to the other man. "I was, and Sherwood was a city councilman back in the day."

Solomon asked, "Sherwood, would you mind if Charly had a little of Augustus's time?"

"Not at all," Mr. Blankenship said. "I'm tired of his cheating."

Mr. Ettinger wheezed, "Me? You're the crook."

"Never trust a politician," they said in unison, laughing slowly like old men do.

Sherwood collected the checker board and took it with him. I slipped into the vacant chair.

"If you two don't mind, I'm going to visit with Bernice Talbot over there." Solomon pointed to a woman gazing out a window. He winked and rolled across the room.

"To what do I owe the pleasure of your company?" Mr. Ettinger asked.

"Well, sir, I'm doing some research into town history, and Solomon thought you could help."

"I imagine so. I'm old enough to be history."

I smiled at his joke and asked, "Can you tell me about Town Center Park? You know, when it was first built."

"That bit of land used to be the most godawful mosquito-infested bog in the county."

"Really?"

"Oh yeah. If there was a heavy rain, it would flood, which meant the adjacent streets would be knee deep in water. That's why all the surrounding buildings were built up so high.

We put in the town's sewer system in the twenties. Anyone who wanted to say goodbye to their outhouses could hook up for a small fee. Somewhere around, oh, 1929, our town manager, Todd Wilson, God rest his soul, had the idea to connect the bog to the sewer so as to drain the marsh. Once we did that, the land dried out, and we put in the park."

My heart picked up its pace, though I worked at maintaining calm when I asked, "You put drains in the park?"

Augustus nodded. "Cleared out a couple of sections and put in two."

"Where?"

"Where they wouldn't be seen, and where the flooding was worst. It's where the woods are between the playground and north field."

Roscoe Gunn had told me that one way to solve this was to figure out how the Snatcher got Theresa Goodnight out of the park unseen. It was a wonder I didn't jump up and let out a whoop, because now I had a pretty good guess.

On the ride home, Solomon asked, "Did you learn anything useful?"

I almost told him my newfound theory. I felt confident I was right, but there was some doubt because I'd also been convinced that Old Man Altus was the Snatcher. And I was wary of what the sheriff's reaction would be. At church, he'd gone off on me like a bomb, and I wasn't eager to have that happen again. And truth be told, I wanted to look into it myself. I decided I'd think on it a bit before I told an adult.

"Not really," I lied. After a couple of minutes, I asked, "Solomon, how good a job did they do when they searched the park woods this last time?"

Solomon rubbed his chin, making a scratchy noise. "Pretty thorough. The sheriff had everyone line up, no more than ten feet between each person, and they took their time going through. Why?"

"No reason," I muttered, closing my eyes to mull it all over.

Chapter 21
Autumn of '82

In the morning, I made a reconnaissance run by the Thugs' house out in the country. I think a dream inspired me. In the dream, the Snatcher and Copycat were the same person and rode a motorcycle as big as a truck. The back of his jacket said Kid Killers MC, and the patch was a screaming skull in pigtails. He chased me through what seemed most of the night. I woke exhausted and cranky.

The old two-story structure that served as the Thugs' home sat back off the roadway. It hadn't seen a drop of paint in decades, and judging by the present owners, I knew it wouldn't get any until hell froze over, thawed, and froze again. The yard was pretty much dirt, weeds, trees, and debris. A timeworn and monolithic barn behind the house leaned noticeably to the right, looking like the next stiff breeze would bring it down. A quarter-mile farther on, I turned around and went back by, slower this time. I didn't see any signs of life. I headed back to town and the Thugs' motorcycle repair shop. As I pulled to the curb, Grizz came out, eyeing my Firebird.

"Sweet ride for a cop," he said, smiling as I got out.

"I'm not a cop, not anymore," I answered, pretending I didn't notice his *Free Moustache Rides* T-shirt.

He waved a hand dismissively. "A cop consultant, then. Hey, open it up for me."

"Sure," I said and popped the hood.

Grizz leaned his bulk over the engine, peering in. "Nice, Charly. How the hell you keep the engine so clean?"

"I have it detailed every couple of months," I told him.

"What's that run ya?"

"Plenty, but this is my pride and joy." I closed the hood, nearly catching a couple of his fingers. "So where are those two assholes?"

"Preach and Weasel?"

"Who else?"

"Don't know, Charly. They're on the run."

"Right," I said. "How about a tour of the shop?"

"Not much to it," he said and went back in.

I followed and saw that he was right. The front room was mostly empty, with a counter and a couple of old stools. There was a peg board behind the counter with a few items hanging there. I saw plug wires, gaskets, and such.

"Not much inventory," I said.

Grizz looked around. "Nah, not up here. We have more in the back. And if I need something that's not in stock, I special order it."

"How about a look around back there?" I nodded toward the doorway behind the counter.

"Nope," Grizz said. "You gotta be a brother to go back there. Seein' as you're just a citizen, this is all you get to see."

I waggled my fingers and said goodbye.

"Hey, Charly. Come back out to Shorty's and give me a rematch."

I stopped at the door and turned. "After what happened last time? I don't think so."

"Hey, neither of those bozos should've done what they did. And trust me, I won't let any other Thug do anything to you."

"We'll see, Grizz," I said and headed back to the inn.

I KICKED BACK ON THE bed in my room, made a quick call, and learned Violet was at work. I found a phone book in the drawer, called Le Bistro, and asked if she was busy. She got on the line a minute later.

"Violet, hi. It's Charly. Did you get a chance to look up that old schedule like I asked?"

"Mmm-hmm. Hang on." She put the phone down, and I waited until she came back. "Okay, let's see. Katie and Denise were waiting tables, Ben was cooking, Everett was on line, Artie was here, and Gus was pearl diving."

Having served at several restaurants, I knew pearl diving was slang for washing dishes. "What about Luke?"

"Nope, Everett was on line."

So Beason wasn't working when Mani and Pedi Regis were abducted. "Great. Thanks for checking. Hey, one more thing. Is Luke working today?" I wanted to see what he looked like.

"No, he's not on the schedule."

I hung up and closed my eyes, but the gears in my brain were whirring. The fact that Beason wasn't at Le Bistro when the Regis girls were abducted didn't even stack up as circumstantial evidence. What did I really have that made me suspicious of Beason and the Thugs? Nothing. I wanted to investigate the Thugs more, but if they had nothing to do with the missing girls, I'd just be wasting my time. No one else seemed to think they were worth looking into. I picked up the phone again, dialed, and was put through to Kit.

"Sheriff Haiselton."

"Hi, Kit. Still talking to me?"

"Sure, Charly. What's up?"

"I feel like I'm wasting your money. Anything new in the case?"

"Not really."

"I take it the SBI hasn't come up with much?"

"Caputo is still kicking around, but every avenue he's taken has led to a dead end. I told him about your interest in the Thugs, but he dismissed it."

I shook my head. "Figures."

"I'm meeting him a little later. Care to sit in?"

"I'd rather have a root canal. Let me know if he has anything."

WHEN IT BEGAN TO GET dark, I got in the Firebird and drove past the Thugs' house. There was activity. The porch light was on, I saw a few people moving around, and there were motorcycles parked in the dirt. I pulled over up the road and walked back to where I could peer past some trees. Grizz hiked a meaty leg over his motorcycle and sat. There was another hog, equally wide, with someone I didn't recognize on it. He was skinny. I recalled a member named Bones and figured that was him. Next to them, a young man of medium build was trying to kick start a thinner Harley. I knew motorcycles to a degree and recognized a Sportster. So that was Luke Beason. He was pretty much as Violet described, and I felt an instant distaste for him. He kicked again and failed to start the bike. Grizz and Bones laughed at him. I jogged back to my car, and just as I opened the door, I heard the Sportster fire to life, adding its rumble to the thunder of the other two bikes. I figured they'd be going to Shorty's, but they turned left out of the driveway and headed toward town. After a quick three-point turn, I was driving after them with my headlights off.

Once we got to Temperance, I switched on my headlights but stayed well back, letting other cars move between us. When it became obvious where they were going, I dropped back and waited twenty minutes and then parked a block from their repair shop. I pulled my hair into a ponytail and walked the rest of the way, keeping to the shadows across the street. When I got to where I had a pretty good view, I perched in a dark doorway and waited.

For a long time, nothing happened. Then a black step van drove up, parked in front of the shop, and honked. A minute later, a gate beside the shop opened. Beason stood there and signaled the driver in. I would have liked a tag number, but the driver turned off the lights, and I couldn't see it. Figuring I might get a chance if the brake lights came on, I took a couple of steps closer. Unfortunately, the van pulled in and out of sight before the driver hit the brakes. I turned my attention back to Beason, and it looked like he was staring directly at me. Or was he? Slowly, I backed fully into the darkness of the doorway, and he closed the gate.

I walked around the block. Behind the shop, on another street, was a small hardware store. I went behind it to a fence, pulled myself up, and looked into the Thugs' repair shop backyard. There was a back door, a couple of windows, and a bay door. Their motorcycles were parked there, but the van wasn't, so it had to have gone through the bay door. I went back to my dark doorway and waited, worrying that Beason truly saw me. He certainly hadn't raised the alarm if he did. Just to be safe, I left that spot and took a similar position farther up the block. I began nodding off after a couple of hours and had to occasionally stand to keep awake. Finally, I heard the gate opening. The step van rolled out and headed back the way it'd come.

When the street was quiet, I went to my car and headed for Kit's cabin but decided it would be better to talk by phone. I drove back to the inn and called him.

"Could be motorcycle parts," he said after I told him what I witnessed.

"Then why stay so long?"

"Maybe they were partying."

"Maybe, maybe not."

"Whatever it is, I'm about a hundred percent sure it doesn't have to do with why I hired you," Kit said.

Message received. "Goodnight, Kit."

My mind was too busy to sleep. I thought about what was happening now, and it always ended up meshing with events from 1959. I needed to sort everything out so that it all made simple sense and thought that maybe a night drive, or in this case an early-morning drive, would help me think. Remembering my adventure with Preach and Weasel, I took my lockbox, about the size of a small toolbox, out of a bedside table drawer. I put it on the coffee table, spun a three-digit number in the rolling combination on the front, and opened it. Inside were a canister of mace, brass knuckles, a knife, a baton, a flat sap, and my .38 revolver. I took the .38, gave it a once-over, checked that it was loaded, and put it in a holster that I attached to my belt. I put on a long cotton shirt to cover it.

Ten minutes later, I was down the fire escape and in my car. While the Firebird warmed up, I dug through my cassette tapes and chose Mountain's *Nantucket Sleighride* album. The cassette started at "The Great Train Robbery," and the raw rock 'n roll was the perfect accompaniment as I pulled out of the parking lot and headed out of town. After a few blocks, I saw there were at least two of us awake in Temperance. Headlights followed along behind me—someone delivering the morning paper, I thought. By the time I reached the city limits, they were gone. The twisting roads, rising and falling, were a balm to my unsettled mind. I found that instead of thinking about the case, I wasn't thinking about a thing, which, in and of itself, was good. It was like I was resetting my brain. Time passed, and the faster I went and the louder I cranked the music, the more relaxed I got.

Somehow, I'd meandered through various country roads and found myself on the gravel road that ran by Shorty's. Only I was coming at it from the other direction so that I was heading toward I-26. I swung wide around a curve and blasted by Shorty's. With their lights off and parking lot empty, it looked more like a deserted old cabin than a honky-tonk. I roared up to I-26 fast enough that my rear slid when I braked.

Yawning, I turned left and headed back toward town. Mountain's "Travelin' in the Dark" came to an end as I climbed to a little over fifty miles per hour. Before a new song began, I heard the roar of another powerful engine. Lights flared behind me, blinding me as they reflected in my rearview. The mystery vehicle accelerated, moved along my left, and slammed into my car. I flew off the road, headed straight for Morrison Gorge. I had no control as I wrestled the steering wheel and pumped the brakes. There was a quick glimpse of the approaching edge in my headlights, and then the Firebird spun a full three sixty. Again, I saw the gorge mere feet away before the car spun ninety more degrees and crashed to a stop. My limbs were locked, and I sat still, staring straight ahead. The headlights illuminated the hill leading up to I-26 just before the bridge. It took a few more moments for me to realize I wasn't breathing, and I sucked in air and then another breath and another until I was hyperventilating. My head dropped to the steering wheel, and I worked at slowing my heart and inhalations.

The nagging thought that whoever just ran me off the road might come down to finish the job inspired me to open the door and fall from the car. I landed on solid ground, and a quick inspection showed the lip of the gorge was three feet on the other side of the Firebird. I leaned in and turned off the ignition and killed the headlights. I knelt, pulled my gun, and stayed still for five minutes, then ten, but I didn't hear anyone approaching or a car up on the road. Turning on the lights again, I inspected the damage. The left side, from the door back, was badly dented by my assailant's vehicle. Around back to where the right rear rested against a solid pine tree, it was just as damaged or worse. I wanted to be angry that my Firebird was so fucked, but at the moment, I was too relieved to be counted among the living.

Well, I thought, *hoofing it to town from mountain roads is becoming a habit.* I kept hold of my pistol as I hiked up the incline to I-26.

Who had hit me and why? I thought about Luke Beason after he opened the gate for the step van earlier. He had stared directly at where I'd been hiding in the doorway. He and I were going to have to have a serious conversation soon.

Chapter 22
Summer of '59

"Can I go to the library?" The times I had asked that now numbered in the double digits. I added a drawn out, "Please?"

"Charly, I've told you no. I'm not letting you out on your own until they catch the Snatcher," Mom said.

I sighed loudly, picked up the kitchen phone, and called Micah Lee. I knew he couldn't go. I just wanted to pester my mom. "Hey, Micah Lee. Think your mother would let you go to the library with me? I can't go by myself." I nodded as he said what I knew he'd say. "Okay, bye." I hung up and repeated my sigh.

"Oh, give me the phone." My mother grabbed it and dialed. After a few beats, she said, "Ruby, hi. It's Grace Bloom. I'm fine, and you? I'm wondering if you could squeeze me in today? Mm-hmm, that'd be fine." Mom hung up and said, "I have a hair appointment in forty-five minutes. You can go to the library while I'm at Ruby's, but only if you stay inside."

"Thanks, Mom," I said and ran upstairs to get ready.

I was antsy on the drive over, and though Mom still acted perturbed, I could tell she was happy to get out of the house.

She pulled over in front of the library. "I'll be back in one hour."

I hopped out, a little annoyed that she stayed at the curb until I entered the building, though I went no farther than the foyer. Pulling out my notebook, I sat on a bench and went over my notes for five minutes. Then I got up and left the library, casting a wary eye for Mom, and focused on the playground across the street. After a couple of cars had passed, I crossed, went through the playground, and made for the third path. I slowed enough to look into the wild growth as I went but didn't stop until I got to where the books were found. Figuring there was a reason they were stashed where they were, I stepped into the woods. The going was slow because of vines, low limbs, and unsure footing, but I went less than twenty feet in when I came to a relatively open area that seemed to be the lowest bit of ground on that side of the path. I picked up a stick and scratched at the ground through the layers of leaves and debris. After a time, I lost patience and stabbed the ground. The end of the stick was firm and sank into the ground an inch or two with each jab, but at one spot I hit something hard. Thinking it was probably a rock, I stabbed the ground again, and this time, my stick sank a full six inches. Curious, I studied the ground, thinking it looked as if someone had scraped leaves and scrub together into one spot. I knelt and pushed away soil and pine needles, and after a minute, I uncovered a grated metal drain that was close to three feet across. I sat back and stared as a range of emotions from fear to the joy of discovery went through me.

I got down on my knees and peeked between the grates but could only make out darkness below. I squatted, grabbed the drain, and tried to lift it, but it was either too heavy or firmly sealed in place. My first instinct was to run over to Solomon's, but before I even started, I changed my mind. I wanted to make sure that both my friends were in on the discovery and got to share in the rewards.

Back at home, I tried calling Bobby.

"Hello," Bobby answered.

I'd been trying to get in touch with him for so long, I was surprised that he answered. "Hey, Bobby."

"Hey back at ya. What's buzzin', cuzzin'?"

I laughed. It was good to hear his voice. "Damn, I've been trying to call you for days. Where've you been?"

"Oh, you know, here, there, and everywhere. Sorry I haven't been by, but I've kinda been busy.

"That's okay. It's not like Mom lets me go anywhere. Can you come by today?" I asked. "I got something to tell you."

"Yeah, sure. Give me forty-five minutes."

I next called Micah Lee, and though I didn't tell him exactly what I'd found, I told him, "I've made a real discovery."

"What?" he asked.

"Look, Bobby's coming over in a little bit, and we'll swing by your house. I'll tell you both then."

Bobby showed up, and I thought that Mom was so sick of me that she wouldn't argue if I asked if we could go to Micah Lee's.

"As long as you go straight there and back." Mom held the door as we left. "And Bobby, you walk Charly home, you hear?"

"Will do, Mrs. Bloom."

Mom closed the door, and I swore I heard a big sigh of relief on the other side of the wood.

Micah Lee's mother served us peanut-butter-and-jelly sandwiches and these grody salads made from a scoop of mayonnaise on half a canned pear and sprinkled with shredded cheese. She had gotten the recipe from a magazine and was real proud of it. None of us ate it.

We bounded upstairs to Micah Lee's room, and I told them what I'd learned about the drainage in the park woods, and how I thought that was how the Snatcher made off with Theresa Goodnight.

Bobby listened, narrowing his eyes.

"That's crazy unreal." Micah Lee got all excited and jumped up on his bed. He pointed at me and said, "See, damnation, I knew you'd be a good detective."

"Cut the gas, Micah Lee," Bobby said. "We don't know that's how the Snatcher done it."

"It makes perfect sense," Micah Lee said.

"Drop dead."

Micah Lee jumped off the bed. "Drop dead twice."

"What? And look like you," Bobby answered.

"It was right past where the books were found," I argued. "I've thought it over, and I'm going to tell to Solomon."

"Why Solomon?" Bobby asked.

"Because I promised him that if I found anything, I'd tell him. I'll say we all figured it out. That way we can all be heroes."

"Or zeroes, if it turns out like Old Man Altus," Bobby countered.

Micah Lee's exuberance fell. "Yeah, maybe."

"I don't know," I said. "It's important. I shouldn't have waited this long, but I wanted to tell you guys first."

Bobby threw an arm over my shoulder. "C'mon, Charly, think about it. Solomon will tell the sheriff, and he's come down hard on you a couple of times already. If you're wrong on this, he'd go ape, might even lock you up for interfering with an investigation or something."

The possibility of another bad experience with the sheriff already sat heavy on my mind, but could I get arrested? "So what should we do?"

"I'm not sure. Let me think on it," Bobby said.

"Yeah, all right," I told him, "but tomorrow morning, I'm going to talk to Solomon."

"Okay," Bobby said and held out his hand. We shook on it.

We hung out in Micah Lee's room for a couple of hours until Mrs. Leigh kicked us out when she caught Bobby smoking.

He walked with me until we got within sight of my house, and said, "I reckon this is close enough," and took off as fast as the Road Runner. Meep-meep.

THE NEXT MORNING, I woke fighting the urge to sneeze. I opened my eyes, and there was Bobby leaning over me and tickling my nose with a small feather. I pushed his hand away and rubbed my nose.

"Damn, Bobby, you're such a lame-o," I whispered while laughing.

"Get up, Charly Bloom, private dick. I got to talk to you."

"Did you climb in?" I jerked a thumb at the window.

"Yep."

I sat up, wiped my eyes, and got a good look at him. He had a black eye and a freshly scabbed split lip. "Damn, Bobby, who gave you the shiner?"

"Who do you think?" He touched the tender skin around his eye. "Me and Winthrop got into it last night."

"About what?"

Bobby started to answer then stopped and looked down at the floor. He mumbled, "You know how Winthrop gets. Wasn't nothin'."

"Doesn't look like nothing. Did you get any licks in?"

"Not so's you'd notice."

I checked my clock. Mom would be in the kitchen, fixing Daddy's breakfast before sending him off to work. "Climb back down and go knock on the back door. Tell my mom you're meeting me, and I'll be down in a couple of minutes."

"What if I don't want to?"

"Mom will feed you breakfast."

His eyes lit up, and he scuttled out the window.

I went to the bathroom and cleaned up. I sniffed the pants and T-shirt I wore the previous day, and they didn't seem too bad, so I slipped them on. I ran downstairs in time to hear Bobby thank my mom through a mouth full of food.

"Hey, Mom. Hi, Bobby," I said.

Bobby mumbled something.

"Morning, Charly. What do you and Bobby have planned so early?" Mom asked.

"We're going over to Micah Lee's, if that's okay with you."

It had been a week and a half since Lily Branch got snatched. Though she still wouldn't let me go anywhere by myself, Mom's defenses had since declined, so I didn't have to beg as long as I was in someone's company. It was the Snatcher sex-fiend buddy system. In another week, I was sure I'd be able to do what I wanted, as long as another girl didn't vanish before then.

"Call me if you go somewhere else," she said and slid a plate of bacon onto the table.

"That won't happen," Bobby told her. "Mrs. Leigh has Micah Lee on a tight leash."

"I don't blame her," Mom said.

Bobby and I left for Micah Lee's. Mrs. Leigh made Bobby explain his black eye and split lip and then promise not to light up a smoke. Up in Micah Lee's room, Bobby stood by the open window and lit a Viceroy. He didn't think promises made to adults had to be honored.

Bobby told me, "I saved you some embarrassment with the sheriff."

"How?"

"After I left you yesterday, I went to the park woods and found the drain."

"So?"

"So I spent half an hour trying to get that hunk of metal up. I think it rusted shut over the years. No way anyone could open it."

"Didn't look rusty to me," I said.

"You're just too weak to lift it," Micah Lee said to Bobby.

"And you're weak in the head," Bobby answered.

I said, "Micah's not saying you're a weakling. It's just those things weigh a ton. Probably would take two grown men, or more, to lift it."

"Well, then there's no way anyone could hold a struggling kid in one arm and lift it with the other," Bobby said.

"I'm still going to tell Solomon," I said.

"Naw, Charly, don't." Bobby looked pained.

"Why?"

"Because it's stupid."

"No, it's not."

Bobby considered it and sighed. "Fine, Charly. If that's the way you want it. Let's go and see if all of us can lift it up."

"No way," Micah Lee said.

Bobby could see the wheels turning in my head. "Charly?"

"I'm up for it."

"Then you guys have to go without me," Micah Lee said, meaning there was no way his mother would let him go.

"You gotta come with us," Bobby said. "Wouldn't be any good if all three of us weren't there. Remember? We're going to be heroes."

"Rich too," I added. "Don't forget the reward."

Micah Lee looked beyond miserable. "I wish I could."

"Must be something we can do," I said.

Bobby took a last drag and tossed the cigarette butt out the window. "You can sneak out."

"At night?" Micah Lee asked.

"Sure. That'll give us plenty of time to look around."

"I don't know."

I poked my head out his window and said, "Come on. It wouldn't be the first time you've climbed down the trellis."

Micah Lee joined me and looked at the honeysuckle vines outside his window. "Yeah. I'm tired of being stuck inside all day. Once we're heroes, what can she do?"

Bobby threw an arm around Micah Lee's neck and pulled him close, giving him a knuckle rub. "That's the spirit. We go tonight."

"Tonight?" Micah Lee and I said at the same time.

"Hell, yeah. Why not? Let's meet at the swings at midnight, and don't tell no one."

"And bring flashlights," I said. "If we get the drain open, we'll go down and explore. You know it's got to be dark as hell down there."

Chapter 23
Autumn of '82

The next morning, Kit gave me a ride, while Rodney Darling followed in his tow truck. After we crossed the bridge, we turned around and pulled to the side of the two-lane blacktop.

"That's where you left the road," Kit said, pointing to the tire tracks through the high roadside grass.

We got out and joined Rodney at the top of the hill, looking down at my car.

"Damn," Rodney muttered.

"Yeah," I said.

If that pine tree hadn't been there, I would have flown over the edge and made a hard landing a hundred feet down in the French Broad River. All of a sudden, the sky seemed bluer, the clouds whiter, and the flora greener. I made a mental note to go to church soon and thank God for planting that particular tree.

Kit squatted and looked at the scene. "Run me through it again."

I shrugged and said, "I went for a ride—"

"In the middle of the night?"

"I was thinking about Copycat and couldn't sleep. A drive relaxes me, helps me think. I ended up on the other side of Shorty's, turned onto this road, and a few seconds later, I heard another car, lights came on, and wham."

"And you didn't see the other car?" Kit asked.

"Nope, just the lights."

"Did you see any other cars before this, while you were driving around?"

I thought for a moment. "No. Not out here. In town, I did."

Kit looked at me carefully. "Any idea who did it?"

As a matter of fact, I did have my suspicions, but I wanted to talk to Beason first, so I said, "Don't have a clue."

We went down, following alongside the torn path my car had left, and got to the life-saving tree. We kicked around my car for a few minutes, and then Kit and I headed back into town while Rodney began the job of pulling my car up the embankment and towing it to his garage.

"You're lucky Willie didn't shoot you," Kit said five minutes later as we drove past the old man's cabin. It was the first place I'd come to on my hike back to town. I'd had to bang on his door awhile, and he answered with a shotgun in his hands. But once I explained my predicament, the old black man made coffee while I called Kit. The sun was coming up once Kit arrived. We waited for Rodney Darling and went on out to the scene of the crime.

"Willie's a sweet old man. I'm going to bring him one of Le Bistro's apple pies."

"Why pie?"

"Apple pie. I had a slice. It's the perfect thank you."

After filling out a report at the sheriff's office, I declined an invitation to breakfast and had Kit take me to Darling's Garage. The sight of the once immaculate Firebird, heavily damaged on both sides, rekindled my anger.

"Something you ought to see," Rodney said. He led Kit and me to the wrecked left side and pointed. "Whoever ran you off the road drives a light-color vehicle, probably white." The impact left smudges of their paint on my car.

"Can you fix it?" I asked.

"I don't do body work, and to be honest, I wouldn't trust this car to the two garages up here that do. I'd suggest you either take it to

Asheville, or wait until you go down the mountain and have your guy do it."

I looked carefully at the car. "Are you saying it's still drivable?"

"Oh yeah," Rodney said. "The right rear fender was scraping the tire, but I pried it away. There's nothing else wrong. The frame's not bent, none of the lenses or lights were busted. Driver's-side door still opens okay. But if you don't want to drive it, we can get you a rental."

"No, no," I said and held out my hand for the keys. "I'll drive it." It'd keep my anger kindled and my focus sharp. As I walked Kit to his car, I asked, "Have you questioned Luke Beason about any of this?"

"Talked to him about the day Piper Darling was at Shorty's. Why?"

I was quiet for a moment. "What's he like?"

Kit shrugged. "Never knew him that well. Now that he's hanging with the Thugs, I'm getting to know him better. He's a punk who's getting in over his head and is going to wind up in real trouble someday. You think he has something to do with all this?"

"Who knows?" I answered, turning away so Kit wouldn't see the sadistic expression on my face. But I planned to find out.

I was exhausted as I pulled into the inn's parking lot and couldn't wait to fall into the big bed. But first, I had to make a call. I planned to be anonymous with a couple of general questions, but Violet answered at Le Bistro and recognized my voice.

"Hey, Charly."

"Hi, Violet. I want to ask you something, and I don't want you to tell anyone I asked."

It took her a moment to respond. "Okay?" She said it like a question.

"What time does Le Bistro close?"

"We stop seating at nine when the kitchen shuts down. Most people are gone by nine thirty, definitely ten."

"Is Luke working tonight?"

"Yeah."

"A secret, Violet."

"I know," she said.

HAVING GIVEN IT HARD thought, I decided to question Luke Beason out where I was run off the road. Maybe talking to him at the scene of the attempted murder would throw him off. That led to even more difficult brainstorming—how to get him out there. If I were a hundred percent sure it was him, I'd have no qualms about using one of my lockbox tools to incapacitate him, throwing him in my trunk, and driving him. But as much as I liked him for it, he was only a suspect.

I got to thinking about what Violet had told me about how he flirted in a crude, sexual way. A lot of guys his age, particularly ones who put up a tough-guy persona, tended to think more with their little heads than their big heads. Maybe sex would lure him out. In other circumstances, I could try the experienced-older-woman approach, but there was the chance he saw me when I was surveying the Thugs' shop. I was sure he and his club brothers talked about what I'd done to Preach and Weasel, so he'd be suspicious of anyone fitting my description. The best I could come up with was the secret-admirer ploy. I'd exploit his desire for sex and boost his ego at the same time.

I practiced speaking in what I hoped passed as a younger woman's voice. When I got to where it sounded natural, I called Le Bistro. A man answered, and I asked for Luke in my new, youthful pitch.

A minute passed, and then, "Yeah?"

"Luke?" I said in a hopeful tone.

It took him a second to respond. "Who's this?"

I produced a nervous laugh. "We went to school together."

"Oh, yeah?" His voice was friendlier. "Who are you?"

"Uh-uh, not yet. I saw you the other night."

"Where?" he asked.

"At the restaurant." Striving for flirty, I said, "You've gotten even more handsome."

He laughed. "Come on, who is this?"

"To find out, meet me tonight at Shorty's. We'll have a drink, you can give me a ride on your motorcycle, and we'll see what happens from there."

"Oh yeah?" His voice took on a hoarse quality. I was pretty sure I had him hooked.

"I'll be the girl with the red scarf. See you at eleven," I said and hung up.

I replayed the conversation in my mind and was fairly confident he bought it. But would he become suspicious as he thought about it through the evening? Oh well. If he showed up, great. If he didn't, I'd have a beer or two at Shorty's.

I threw on a dark windbreaker with deep pockets and put on my boots. After rummaging in my suitcase, I found the red scarf I'd brought and stuffed it in my jeans pocket. I got my weapon lockbox and opened it. The gun went into my belt holster, and I considered the other tools of the trade, settling on my flat sap. It was an updated version of the old sap, or blackjack. The head was loaded with lead shot, and there was a flat spring in the handle to give it that extra snap. It slipped it in my jacket pocket and relocked my box of toys.

At ten, I cruised through the parking lot at Le Bistro in my battered Pontiac. There were a few cars, and I spotted Beason's Sportster in the far corner. I pulled back onto the street and headed out toward Shorty's. As I approached to turn off from I-26 to the honky-tonk, I pulled to the side of the road across the street from where I'd been run off. My plan was to use the red scarf to flag down Beason before he got to the turn. I got out of the car and looked around. As dark as it was, and considering he only had a headlight on his bike, I'd have to stand right at the road and wave the red scarf. I turned back to my car and realized I'd made a miscalculation. If it was Beason who ran me off the road, he'd recognize my car as he pulled up.

"Crap," I muttered.

My eyes were getting used to the dark night, enough that I could tell that the woods began about twenty feet farther from the road. I got in the car and parked it as close to the trees as possible. The sound of an approaching vehicle got my attention, but I saw it was a car and disregarded it. I walked twenty or thirty yards in the direction Beason would be coming from and stood close to the road. When I thought he'd seen me across from the Thugs' shop, my hair had been in a ponytail. I bent over and rubbed my hair vigorously, plumping it out and hopefully presenting a totally different silhouette from what Beason had possibly seen.

I saw the lone headlight before I heard the motor. I shook my head one more time, took a step into the road, and waved my scarf. Though I felt pretty damn stupid waving that scarf at the roadside, I kept it up. He got closer, and the bike got louder. When he swept by me, I thought he'd missed me, but a split second later his taillight brightened as he hit the brakes. I walked toward him, and he got off, turning back to look at me.

"Hey," he called. "Is that—you?"

I imagined he could just see me approaching in the crimson glow of his taillight, so I waved the scarf over my head, and in my younger voice, I called back, "You see the red scarf, don't you?"

"All right, it is you," he said loudly and then shut off his bike, which killed his lights and placed us in darkness.

As I got close, I angled toward the woods and where I'd parked my car. I could hear his hot engine ticking and imagined that he'd been just as revved up.

"Thought I was meeting you at Shorty's," Beason said, watching my shape as he took off his helmet and put it on his seat.

I was parallel to him, about halfway to the woods, and without slowing, I said, "Change of plans. I have a blanket in my car up there. Let's spread it out, see what happens." I turned, walking backward, and added, "And then afterward, we'll go for a beer."

I was a feminine, mysterious figure, cloaked in the dark night, promising carnal delights, and Beason followed after me, laughing and asking who I was.

When I got to my car, I leaned back against the dented rear fender. Beason stopped in front of me, though it was too dark to make out his features. He stepped close to me, and I could smell a man who'd been working in a kitchen all night.

"I don't know who you are," Beason said. "But I still want a kiss."

He leaned down to plant a wet one on my lips, but I put a hand to his shoulder and held him back. "There's a blanket on the front seat. Why don't you get it?"

"Sure," he said. He opened the door, and the interior light switched on, seeming as bright as a lighthouse after so much time out in the countryside at night. "I don't see a blanket," Beason said and turned to me. I saw he wore a black leather jacket and chaps. His key-chain hung from his belt, and he wore heavy engineer boots on his feet. He pushed hair from his eyes and got his first glimpse of me in the light. His smile fell, and he squinted like he was trying to make sense of what he saw. "I thought you'd be—I mean—well—you're old." As he prattled on, I took the time to pull my hair back into a ponytail. "I don't mean you're old, but I thought you'd be—wait a minute." He stepped closer, his head turning one way and then another. His playful tone turned accusatory. "I know who you are."

I moved between him and his distant bike. "I'm Charly Bloom."

His eyes widened and then narrowed. "You're that bitch who spied on us last night, the one who sucker-punched Preach."

Crossing my arms, I said, "I did not sucker-punch Preach. I bounced his head on a table like a basketball. If he's telling people I sucker-punched him, it's because he doesn't want anyone to know he got beat up by a girl."

"Bullshit," Beason said, shoving me aside on the way to his bike.

He'd put his hands on me—let's call that assault—so I could respond in kind, and we'd call that self-defense. I stunned him with a kick to the shin, spun him so his back was to my car, and jabbed my index finger into the base of his throat just above the sternal notch. I pushed into the pressure point and backed him up. My other hand reached to his belt and took his keychain. I pressed him back against the car, behind the open front door. When I stepped back, he came at me with a wild punch. I easily dodged it and landed a quick snap-punch just below his nose. That was a painful spot, and he squealed. I sweep-kicked his feet out from under him, and he fell to the ground.

He clapped his hand over where I'd hit him and said, "You fuckin' bitch!"

I led with my knee and connected with his chin, holding back so I didn't do too much damage, just enough to knock his head back into the already dented fender. While he recovered, he shut up, but his eyes said he was somewhere between scared and pissed.

I took out my flat sap and waggled it in front of his eyes. "This is a flat sap. I can hit your body in certain places that will produce pain unlike anything you've ever felt. We're going to have a little talk, and you're going to answer honestly, or I'll show you how good I am with this."

He opened his mouth to speak.

"Uh-uh. Shhh. You've called me bitch twice already. If you say it, or any other gender-oriented slur, I will take Miss Flat Sap here and break one of your bones." I paused, letting the silence drive my point home. "Now you can talk."

"Can I stand?" he asked.

"No, I think you're fine where you are."

"Why are you doing this?"

"The Thugs have come up in my investigation."

He blinked in disbelief. "The lost girls?"

"Why would you say that?"

Nervous, he dug his hands into the turf at either side of him, pulling up clumps of grass. "I know who you are. That's why you're in town, isn't it?"

"Uh-uh. I ask, and you answer." I dangled his keychain in front of his face and then threw them behind me. "When we finish, you can go look for your keys."

"Fuck you." That earned him a quick flick of the sap against his jaw just under his ear. "Oh, ouch. Oh shit. Owww."

"Piss me off again, and tomorrow, you'll look like you've been worked over by several angry men, and I'll make sure word gets around that Charly Bloom did it. You think you'll get your Thugs patch if a girl stomps you?"

"Ah, fuck me," he said.

"Yeah, you're fucked. But it doesn't have to be so bad."

He'd pulled up most of the grass in reach, but like a child, his hands worked anxiously at the ground, digging and dropping handfuls of dirt. "What do you mean?"

"After we're done, no one has to know we talked, including your bros."

He wiped his forehead and nodded. "Yeah, okay."

"How long have you been prospecting for the Thugs?"

"About nine months."

"Why?"

He looked at me liked I asked the most stupid question in the world. "Why what?"

"Why do you want to be a Thug?"

He shook his head, funneling dirt from one hand to the other. "Always been into motorcycles. Always wanted to be in a club, be an outlaw biker. I used to drive to Asheville and go see the biker movies at the Park Drive-In."

"What do you drive besides your bike?"

"The Sportster's all I got."

"Would any of your bros lend you four wheels?"

"Maybe. Depends what I need it for."

"Who has a car?" I asked.

"Grizz has a '68 Goat."

"A GTO?"

"Yeah. Bones has a pickup on account of being a stonemason. Jelly's got a Nova."

"Who's Jelly?"

"One of the brothers."

"Any other cars or trucks?" I asked.

"There's an old Dodge pickup. It's the business truck."

I moved to the side to better see his face in the interior light. "Which one did you use to run me off the road?"

"What?"

I put a growl in my voice. "Why did you try to kill me last night?"

His face went blank, and he blinked three times before responding, "Kill you?"

"You should have stopped to finish the job."

"What are you—"

I held out a hand and said, "Shut up." A car turned out of the road that led to Shorty's. The last thing I needed was someone stopping to ask if we needed assistance, so I closed the door and squatted low. I stared at Beason and put a finger to my lips. The vehicle picked up speed, and as it went by, I stood and watched it travel down the road, making sure it didn't slow or come back. Keeping my eyes on the receding taillights, I opened the door for light.

I turned back to Beason, saying, "Let me ask you again, why—"

He had stood up while I was watching the car on the road, and he took a swing at me, which was funny because he was too far away for his fist to connect. Still, figuring he'd step closer for a follow-up punch, I went into a fighting stance, eyes wide open. I realized then I'd made a grave error. Beason wasn't taking a swing at me. He'd been sitting on the ground, pulling up grass and dirt. I'd thought it was nerves until he flung a whole fistful of dirt into my open eyes.

I felt the impact as the dirt struck, and my eyes stung. A second later, they burned. Knowing Beason was there, I forced them open but couldn't see a thing other than the glow from my interior light. A second later, I was hit in the stomach and flew backward. I lost my flat sap and landed on my back, unable to breathe. Beason was on top of me. He got off, and no matter how hard I sucked at air, it was like my throat was closed. Then I recognized the sound of my car door shutting. The engine turned over, and I heard Beason drive off.

I finally drew in enough air to mumble, "Son of a bitch," referring to both Beason and the situation in general. He must've charged and hit me in the solar plexus with a shoulder block. My eyes burned like hell, my stomach hurt, my breath was shallow, and I was pissed. Though I vowed to do major damage to Beason when I caught up to him, most of my anger was directed at myself. I couldn't believe I let him surprise me like that.

I finally got my breathing under control and wiped gently at my eyes, not wanting to scratch them and do permanent damage. Damn, it hurt. The dirt in my eyes and under my eyelids turned mucky as tears mixed with it. I could only open them for seconds at a time before the pain forced them closed. When I did open them, I wasn't sure if I was blind, or the night was simply too dark.

After long minutes of helplessness, I heard a distant engine. What if Beason was returning? What if he was taking my advice this time and coming back to finish the job? I pulled my gun. I might not be able to hit the broad side of a barn at the moment, but a couple of gunshots would probably scare him off. Still, I didn't want to push my luck, and cradling the pistol in both hands, I knelt low. The vehicle went by, and I could tell by the sound that it wasn't my car.

I needed to get somewhere to wash out my eyes, and the closest place was Shorty's.

Taking one slow step after another, I reached the asphalt. This was the third time I'd been stranded on these mountain roads, the second time in this general vicinity. I could've kicked my own ass, I was so angry at myself. Opening my eyes into a squint, the pain was tolerable, but I still couldn't see. I focused on walking so that my left foot was on asphalt and my right foot on dirt and grass, and slowly shuffled the couple of hundred yards to the turnoff to Shorty's. The gravel road was trickier to navigate, and I moved to the middle of it, hoping a drunk wouldn't run me down. The burning in my eyes lessened enough that I opened them a little wider. I got around a small curve and could make out distant lights. The colorful neon beer signs got brighter as I got closer. I shuffled through the parking lot, up the steps, and through the door, entering the ever-present fog of cigarette smoke.

I heard Tamara say, "Well, looky there. Temperance's own Wonder Woman."

I stumbled toward her voice, my arms outstretched.

"Honey, what's wrong."

"I can't see."

In a second, she was at my side and took an arm. "What happened, hon? You're a mess."

"I got into a tussle with someone. He threw dirt in my eyes and stole my car."

"Come with me." We passed through a door, and by the smell, I knew she'd led me into the ladies' room. She took my hand and put it on a faucet. "Here, wash your eyes out. The bathroom may not be clean, but our well water is."

I bent over and repeatedly splashed my face.

"Careful, hon. Don't rub your eyes."

I nodded even though I'd already thought of that. With each handful of water, the sting lessened.

I heard the door open, followed by a man's voice. "Hey, Tamara, I'll do the bartendin' until you're done in here."

"The hell you will, Grover. Nobody goes behind my bar. Won't kill you to wait." She kicked the door shut. "The fool would drink me dry if I let him back there."

"It's all right, Tamara. I can take it from here."

She passed me her bar towel, and I carefully dried my face. Eyes open into a squint, I could see Tamara, though she was blurry.

"Well, come out when you're done, and tell me what happened. Beer's on me."

She left, and I continued splashing water in my eyes. Even after I got most of the dirt out, I continued. Resigning myself to the pain, I looked in the mirror. My eyes showed more red than white. My anger at Beason flared briefly, but I put it away. I'd bring it back out once I found him.

Exiting the bathroom, I saw there were only a few people at the bar.

Tamara shook her head. "Honey, your eyes are redder than taillights."

"They don't feel so good either."

She scrutinized me and then smiled. Laying a towel on the bar, she said, "You ever done upside-down margaritas?"

"Yeah, but I don't think that's going to help."

"I don't mean for you to drink one. I mean, you know how you lean backward on the bar while the bartender mixes the drink in your mouth?"

"Yeah."

Tamara dug around under the bar and came up with a bottle of Visine eye drops. "Gets so smoky in here that I have to use this from time to time. Assume the upside-down margarita position, and I'll flush out your eyes."

I sat backward on a stool and leaned back until my head rested on the towel. Tamara used her index finger and thumb to gently hold my right eye open while she slowly squeezed half the bottle into it. The initial sting was agonizing but quickly lessened until it felt good. Then she did my left eye.

"How's that?"

I sat up, blinking. "It's better. Oh yeah, much better."

She handed me another bar towel and asked, "Miller, right?" She poured one and said, "So tell me what happened."

I wiped my face and took half the beer in one gulp. "I got into it with Luke Beason down the road."

"Luke?" She sounded surprised.

"Yep, and when I get my hands on his scrawny little neck—"

"But Luke was here a little while ago."

"Huh?"

"Ran in saying he needed a ride to town. Bert Deavers was heading that way and gave him a lift."

"The car that passed while I was on my ass. That must mean..." I ran out the door, ignoring Tamara's shouts. Those front steps nearly did me in, but I managed to keep my feet as I looked around the parking lot. A couple of trucks, a couple of sedans, that was all. "Shit." I went around the side of the bar and saw my car. I fought the urge to give it a hug, opened the door, and smiled at the sight of my keys in the ignition.

"Tamara, I need to use your phone," I said as I went back in, carefully tucking my keys into my pocket.

She put a black Bakelite phone on the bar, and I called the sheriff's department, but Kit wasn't in. I told them it was important that he get back to me at Shorty's. I hung up and tried his home, but he wasn't there either. Tamara slid another beer in front of me, and we talked a few minutes about what a lowlife Luke was until the phone rang. Tamara reached for it, but I grabbed it first.

"Kit?"

"Got your message, Charly. What's up?"

"I lied when I said I didn't know who ran me off the road. There's a good possibility it was Luke Beason."

"Why do you say that?"

As I started to relate what happened, everyone at the bar leaned toward me. "Hang on a second." I picked up the phone and moved as far down the bar as the cord would allow.

"I got this," Tamara said, grabbing some coins and moving toward the jukebox.

When the music began, I said, "Sorry, Kit. There are too many ears wanting to listen in."

"Where are you?"

"Shorty's," I told him.

"Can we talk now?"

"Yeah."

"Why do you think it was Beason?"

I didn't answer immediately. I wasn't sure how to say it but decided to jump right in. "He assaulted me a little while ago and took off."

"Assaulted you? Are you okay?" There was anger and concern in his voice.

"I'm fine."

"He assaulted you at Shorty's?"

"On I-26 where I crashed. That's why I'm at Shorty's."

"I'll put out an APB for his motorcycle."

"That's just it—he's not on his bike, at least not now. It's parked up on I-26," I said. Feeling like an idiot, I added, "Where I met him."

"Met him?

"I wanted to question him, you know, on the site of where I got run off the road."

Kit picked up on something in my voice. "He came willingly?" I didn't say anything. "Charly? What happened?"

I drained my beer. "Off the record?"

It took Kit a moment to say, "Fine, off the record. Just tell me what happened."

"I lured him out here, pretended I was a secret admirer who wanted to get to know him in a Biblical sense."

Kit groaned, and I had a mental image of him shaking his head.

"I had good reason to believe he was the one who ran me off the road. I was questioning him."

"How... intense was this questioning?"

"Pretty intense, I guess."

"Damn it, Charly. That makes anything he told you inadmissible, not to mention puts your ass in a sling."

"Well, he started it," I said, thinking how childish that sounded. "Look, he didn't say anything. I'd just started asking questions when he got the best of me and got away in my car."

"He stole your car?"

"Yeah."

"If you press charges, he can turn right around and claim you lured him out there so you could assault him."

"I got the car back. He drove it to Shorty's and caught a ride back to town with someone named Bert Deavers."

There was silence on the other end as Kit processed what I'd told him so far.

I said, "I'd love another shot at him."

"Yeah, when pigs fly."

"Come on, Kit."

He paused and then said, "In my interrogation room with me sitting by your side. If he's good for any of this, I don't want him getting off on technicalities because of your tactics. Dammit, Charly."

I deemed it best not to respond.

Kit asked, "Did you get any kind of read on him for the missing girls?"

Tamara slid another beer in front of me, and I nodded in thanks. "I didn't get a chance."

"I'll radio the boys to keep an eye out and bring him in. I'll tow his bike in, for that matter. But Charly, you tricked him to go out there and smacked him around. His assaulting you and taking your car could be nothing more than self-defense. And if you scared him enough, he'll go to ground."

"Shit."

"What's your gut say, Charly?"

"I'm still liking him for running me off the road and for abducting the girls," I said, though my confidence was waning.

"Okay, we'll bring him in and sweat him in a cell for the rest of the night. Come by in the morning, and we'll tag-team him."

"Sorry I screwed up."

He hung up without responding.

My vision was still blurry, but I refused to leave my car overnight at Shorty's, so I declined Tamara's offer for another beer and drove slowly back to Temperance, stopping to search for and finding my flat sap. Maybe I'd get to use it on Beason again.

Chapter 24
Summer of '59

Midnight rendezvous were for lovers, schemers, adventurers, and thieves. I was all of these. I loved my two best friends, sneaking out was our scheme, and the adventure was waiting for us underground. Hell, I was even a thief. I wanted to steal the Snatcher's freedom and see him locked up forever.

Figuring I could get a couple of hours' sleep, I went to bed at nine but was too fidgety. I tossed and turned until I heard my parents go to bed around ten. With a sigh, I turned on my bedside lamp and picked up *Auntie Mame* but couldn't get through two sentences without thinking about the night's coming quest. Instead of waiting, I put on my clothes and slipped new batteries into the Mastercraft flashlight I'd borrowed from my father's toolshed.

I spent the remainder of the time alternating my attention between the notebook and the clock and climbed out my window at eleven thirty. I crept around the house to where I'd stashed my bike for a quick getaway, pushed it out to the street, and pedaled to Micah Lee's. I pulled to the curb just as he climbed from his bedroom window.

I tiptoed underneath and whispered, "Pssst, Micah Lee."

He gasped and fell the remaining six feet, landing on his back. When he got his breath back, he asked, "What the hell you doing here?"

"Watching your swan dive," I answered.

We both snickered, humor fueled by sly night freedom. Micah Lee got his bike. My stomach hurt from restrained hilarity, and when we got far enough from his house, we both exploded with laughter.

We rode to the park as if we were setting out on a magical adventure and the whole world was frozen except for me and Micah Lee. Instead of black, everything had been brushed a dark blue. All we heard were subtle night noises and the hum of our wheels on pavement. We didn't see one car or another living being. In daylight, Temperance was a busy little town, but that night, at that particular moment, Temperance belonged to us.

We pedaled down the middle of the street, increasing speed as we went. Side by side, we bent over our handlebars and pumped our legs. We flew through intersections and past parked cars and dark houses. As if it had been planned, Bobby wheeled out of the dark as we sped through one intersection and pulled up alongside us. We were three kids free from grownups and with a calling to find a killer.

Bobby carried a long pole like a lance and shouted, "Got a pipe from behind Boone Plumbing to get the drain up."

We concealed our bikes behind the merry-go-round and continued in darkness until we made it to the park woods. Once on the path, I turned on my flashlight. Bobby had brought a kerosene lantern and paused to light it. Micah Lee pulled out some kind of toy gun and flipped a switch.

He saw us staring and said, "My Buck Rogers ray-gun flashlight." When we snickered, he said, "Hey, it's all I could get."

Bobby bumped Micah Lee's shoulder. "That's real good. You can zap the Snatcher."

"I wish. But it can change colors." He pushed a switch that moved colored lenses in front of the light.

"I like the red," Bobby said. "It's creepy."

Micah Lee swept nearby trees, the path, and Bobby, making them blood tinged. When he held it under his chin to make a scary face, I reached over and switched it back to normal.

"Come on." I led them up the path. The trees closed in, and the path narrowed, the night air no longer fresh but muggy and stifling. I pointed my flashlight into the woods. "It's this way."

"Are you sure?" Micah Lee asked.

I aimed my flashlight at a rock. "That's where they found two of the books."

"Which ones?"

"Which what?"

"What books did they find?" Micah Lee asked.

"*Curious George* and something called *Chouchou*. What's it matter?"

"It kinda makes it more real, you know?"

I thought a moment and nodded.

"Last chance to call it off," Bobby said.

Micah Lee looked like he was considering it, but I pushed into the wild growth, and they followed single file. I'd covered up the drain again after my discovery, just in case the Snatcher returned and saw someone had found it. Bobby had as well, so I put my flashlight down, making sure it aimed at the right patch of ground, and began sweeping aside leaves and dirt. Bobby set his lantern down, and Micah Lee put down his flashlight, and they helped me clear the drain. Bobby slid the pole in between the grates and pulled down on it, but it didn't budge.

"Gimme a hand," he grunted.

Micah Lee and I each grabbed a length and pulled. After a couple of seconds, there was a grating noise. The drain lifted an inch.

"Keep it up." Legs wide, I bent down and got my fingers underneath and pulled. I had a moment of panic when I thought of the terrible situation I'd be in if it dropped on my fingers.

"I got the pole," Bobby said through gritted teeth.

Micah Lee knelt next to me and got his fingers in as well. Groaning with exertion, we lifted the drain a few more inches. Bobby dropped the pole, moved next to me, and helped. We lifted it all the way back until it fell over.

"Messed up my fingers," I said. They seemed petrified in place, but I worked them until they started moving.

"That was damn heavy," Bobby said.

Micah Lee picked up his flashlight and aimed it into the hole, illuminating a concrete pipe almost large enough for us to stand in. "It's dry."

"That's 'cause it hasn't rained lately," Bobby said. "This pipe is runoff for the park. It runs into other pipes at each end. That's where the real sewer is."

"How do you know?" Micah Lee asked.

"Because I'm not a dumbass." Bobby handed me his lantern and sat with his legs in the hole. "There's a ladder here." He climbed down, and I followed, smelling nearby sewage.

"Any spiders?" Micah Lee called from above.

I swept the pipe with my flashlight.

"Ain't no spiders." Bobby's voice sounded hollow in the pipe.

Micah Lee descended, and I went west. "This way."

That pipe joined another. A few inches of brown water flowed south. This pipe was smaller, and we walked in a crouch with our legs spread and feet on each side of the runoff.

"Smells like shit," Micah Lee said.

"Gee, I wonder why," Bobby said.

"Grody," I mumbled.

We continued on, the kerosene in Bobby's lantern sloshing. Occasionally, we moved south but would head west again at the next cross tunnel. At least I thought we did. It was hard to tell. We hit a couple of pipes where the brown water was deeper, and had to roll up our pant legs. I had my old sneakers on, so I didn't mind much, but Micah Lee wore new ones.

"Something else my mother's gonna kill me for."

A couple of times, we came to what Bobby called *junctions*, concrete rooms with a number of pipes leading from them. He always acted like he knew which one to take.

Forty-five minutes into our underground adventure, Micah Lee asked, "Anybody else get the feeling we're on a wild goose chase?"

"And that we're going around in circles?" I added.

"We're not going in circles," Bobby said, his lantern sending up black smoke. "I'm guessin' we're close to Wallace Lake."

We stepped into another junction. A metal ladder cemented to the wall led up to a manhole lid. Three large pipes were set in three walls, including the one we'd just exited. Another wall had two small openings. I took my dad's flashlight and aimed it down the big tunnels then stood on tiptoe and shined the light in the tallest of the smaller pipes.

I saw something a short distance away. "Hey, there's something in here."

"What is it?" Bobby asked.

"It looks like..." I paused, not wanting to say what it resembled. "Give me a boost."

Micah Lee handed Bobby his ray-gun flashlight and held his hands low, fingers interlocked. I put a foot in, and Micah Lee boosted me up. I crawled into the hole, my flashlight before me.

"Yuck. Your shoes got sewage on them," Micah Lee said from behind me.

I scrabbled down the tunnel, the concrete hard on my hands and knees.

"What is it, Charly?" Bobby called.

"Just a minute," I said as I got closer. "It looks like... holy shit." All at once, it seemed I was alone, cut off from my friends, and the tunnel shrunk in on me. I grabbed what I found and shuffled backward as fast as I could in that confined space. "Oh shit, oh shit, oh shit," I chanted.

I pushed out of the hole so fast that I landed on my ass and dropped what I'd found. I pointed the flashlight at it—a children's picture book with a blue nighttime cover depicting an owl and a glowing insect. *Sam and the Firefly*.

Chapter 25
Autumn of '82

I was wound up after my encounter with Beason. The last thing I wanted to do was call it a night, especially when it'd been so counterproductive. My eyes were still sore, but I could see okay. I got an idea and drove past ECT Motorcycle and Small Engine Repair. Maybe Beason was hiding out there, and if not, I'd still like to check it out, especially after the late delivery I witnessed last night.

The place was dark and appeared locked tight. I made my way around the block and parked in front of the little hardware store. After shutting down the Firebird, I grabbed a flashlight from my glove compartment and got out. A strong breeze blew, and it was getting chilly. I paused, but the neighborhood remained quiet. Walking along the back fence, I found a pallet of pavers next to it. I hopped up, looked into the repair shop backyard, and didn't see any motorcycles, so I slipped over.

There was a lot of junk in the yard, mainly beer cans and bottles. There were also beat-up lawn chairs, a table, what looked like a fire pit, and other assorted crap. It was too dark to see in either of the windows, and both the back door and garage bay door were locked. Around the left side, there was nothing but a tangle of old bricks, lumber, discarded engine parts, and rusty pipes. I picked up a few pieces of wood, settling on a six-foot-long two-by-four. The garage bay door pulled up enough before the lock engaged, and the wood just fit but wouldn't slide in any farther. I went to the pile of debris, chose a brick, returned, and hammered the two-by-four in a good six inches. I straddled the lumber and gripped it, thinking how much

211

this would piss off Kit. I grinned and jerked up. The lock popped, and I fell on my ass. Standing, I returned the two-by-four and brick to the junk pile and brushed the dirt from my hands. Inside, I shut the bay door and turned on my flashlight. Rodney Darling's garage had two bays, both of them pretty grungy from lots of work. This garage bay, though not neat, just didn't appear to get much use. There was one Honda dirt bike balanced on a cinder block, the rear wheel off, and a couple of lawn mowers in the corner, but it didn't seem enough to earn the money needed to run a shop, much less make a living. I found a tall, multi-drawer Craftsman toolbox and went through it. The tools weren't well maintained or organized.

I made my way through three more rooms, and from what I saw, not much in the way of motorcycle or small-engine repair got done in this building. Though judging from the number of cans, bottles, and take-out boxes strewn around, I knew they spent plenty of time here. The shop was a cover for something. Thinking back to the night before, I went to the garage and pictured a step van parked in the bay. It would be a tight fit, and if they were loading or unloading something, they'd back it in. If they were unloading something, what would they do with it? I went into the next room, which looked like a living room of sorts, with a couple of lounge chairs, an overstuffed sofa, some TV trays, and a coffee table. The walls were festooned with posters and magazine pages of motorcycles and naked women. The floor was covered in linoleum, and in two places behind the sofa legs, the linoleum was torn.

"Interesting," I said to myself.

Leaning into the sofa, I pushed it back several inches, revealing a seam in the floor. I shoved the couch all the way back until a trapdoor was revealed.

"Bingo."

The door was heavy, but I heaved it up and over. A wooden stair-case descended into darkness. Flashlight in hand, I went into the subterranean gloom and flipped a light switch at the base of the stairway. The room was ten by twelve, had a concrete floor, and compared to the upper rooms, was meticulous. Half a dozen chairs, three to a side, surrounded a long table, and on top sat three sets of triple-beam scales—the basics needed to divide large shipments of drugs, in this case, cocaine. Boxes of plastic bags were stacked against the wall, as were boxes of lactose powder—what they probably cut it with. At one end of the table was what looked like a quarter of a kilo of coke that hadn't yet been cut and bagged. At the other end, they'd separated the three-quarters into several ounces, multiple eight balls, and a whole lot of grams. Remembering my SBI days, I did some quick math, and assuming they brought it in regularly, I thought the Thugs probably had a sweetheart deal of somewhere around fifteen to twenty thousand dollars per kilo. Depending how much they stepped on it, they could earn ninety to one hundred thousand dollars per kilo. If that step van visited often, the East Coast Thugs' drug-running operation through this little outpost in Temperance was earning them millions.

So the step van came, dropped off a few kilos or more, and picked up what they'd doctored and cut into smaller batches. Why the step van? My guess was the thing was loaded with tools and engine parts, with a clever hideaway for the drugs. When they dropped off a shipment, they picked up the cut cocaine and delivered it to Thugs chapters all up and down the east coast. If they got pulled and searched, they'd only find tools and engine parts. Why Temperance? It was an out-of-the-way location that was almost midpoint for all the chapters. Temperance was a distribution center.

I picked up a gram, stashed it in my pants pocket, and left the way I'd come, taking the time to close the trapdoor and push the sofa over it. The lock on the garage bay door was shot. Hopefully, they'd think it crapped out on its own. I got to my car and started driving, figuring I'd tell Kit about it when I saw him in the morning.

The night grew colder, and halfway to the Temperance Inn, I turned on the heater.

Chapter 26
Summer of '59

We stared at the book, none of us willing to pick it up. "How the hell did that get there?" Bobby asked. "How did..."

"It's time to tell Solomon," I said.

Bobby grunted, "Uh-uh."

"What do you mean uh-uh?"

Bobby turned his gaze from me to Micah Lee and back again. He licked his lips and pointed at the book. "That means the Snatcher brought that girl through here and got her through that pipe."

"So?" My voice was raspy.

"What if she's on the other side of that pipe, Charly?"

"She's not alive," Micah Lee whispered.

"I ain't stupid. I know that." His gaze fierce, tears pooled in Bobby's eyes and rolled down his cheeks.

Micah Lee stared at Bobby. "Why are you crying?"

"Because... because..." Bobby took a breath. "Just because."

I grabbed his shoulder. "We aren't abandoning her, Bobby. We're just going to get Solomon. He'll get the SBI agent and Sheriff Rysdale and come right back."

"Sheriff Rysdale don't know his dick from his nightstick. I don't care what you do. I'm going through the pipe to see if..." He paused and licked his lips. "See if that little girl is there."

I thought for a few seconds. "Okay. We'll follow."

"We will?" Micah Lee asked, eyes wide.

"No, you won't," Bobby said.

"What?" I asked.

"Let me go. I'll check it out. If it's safe, you come on over."

"I don't know…"

"I said you two wait."

I stared at him and the intensity in his eyes. "Okay. But dammit, Bobby, afterward we go get the sheriff."

Bobby stood there breathing hard. I gave him my flashlight and took his lantern, and without waiting for a boost, he pulled himself up and into the pipe. We used Micah Lee's ray-gun flashlight and watched his progress, though about all we could see were his ass and feet. He quickly got out of range for Micah Lee's toy, and we watched his silhouette backlit by the flashlight he held.

Bobby called, "I'm about there." Less than a minute later, he yelled back, "It's another junction, a big one."

"Is she in there?" I asked, hoping not.

"It's dark, and I can't see much from this angle. I'd climb out, but I don't know how to do it without falling on my head."

I grasped the bottom of the pipe and stood on tiptoe for a better view. I could just make out Bobby at the end of the pipe. "Be careful."

Then something happened. One moment, Bobby was there. Then his legs kicked, and he was gone.

"Bobby?"

He didn't answer, and my mouth dried.

"Bobby, did you fall?"

The silence was broken when Bobby shrieked, "No! Come on, please! Don't! Please don't!" I'd never heard his voice so high.

"Who? Who's there, Bobby?" I shouted.

There were sounds of a fight muted by the pipe and distance.

"Who is it, Bobby?" Micah Lee shouted in a shaky voice.

"No!" Bobby screamed.

A gun fired from the junction, and the struggling noises stopped.

"Bobby?" I called.

"Charly?" Micah Lee whispered. He sounded near panic.

I stared into the pipe, now totally dark. The Snatcher got Bobby. Then I realized I'd be dead if he pointed his gun down the pipe and fired. I ducked down. Claustrophobia struck then doubled and tripled in intensity. Underground was the last place in the world I wanted to die. They'd never find us. They'd just add our names to the list of lost children.

"What if he comes through?" Micah Lee asked in the darkness. I knew he meant the Snatcher and not Bobby. "Charly, I'm scared." He was crying.

"Me too."

"What are we gonna—"

"Shhh. Let me listen." I got up on tiptoe again, putting my ear to the open pipe.

There was noise from the other end. I heard mumbling, a couple of grunts, and what I swore was a voice muttering, "You dumbass." All that was followed by rhythmic steps on metal.

"Can you hear anything?"

"Shhh!"

There came a grating sound, low and metallic.

"Sounds like he opened the manhole cover. I think he's leaving."

"Thank God." Micah never sounded so sincere. "What now?"

I looked at Micah Lee and slowly shook my head. I didn't have a clue. I was too terrified to think. I looked down at my hand, and it trembled like I had palsy.

"Charly?"

I took a deep breath. Yeah, I was scared. So what? We had something we had to do.

I laced my fingers and held my hands down for Micah Lee to step on. "Let's go."

"What?" Micah Lee gasped.

"We gotta go help Bobby."

Micah Lee looked miserable. "Yeah, I guess so."

I handed him the ray-gun flashlight. He tucked it into his pants, and then I boosted him up, and he disappeared into the hole. My heart swelled at how faithful a friend he was.

Grasping the edge of the pipe, I hoisted myself up. "Right behind you, Micah Lee."

We headed into the tunnel. The possibility that the Snatcher was trying to trick us and would open fire at any minute made our passage feel as dangerous as crossing a thinly frozen lake.

Micah Lee stopped and whispered, "Charly, should I turn on the ray-gun flashlight?"

"No."

"Why not?"

"What if he's waiting? You want to give him a target?"

Micah Lee considered this. "I'll just hang on to it."

"Keep going."

We continued to shuffle in the darkness until Micah Lee got about five feet from the end of the pipe.

"What should I do?" he whispered.

I'd already thought about that as we made our crawling march and whispered back, "Get your flashlight ready. Crawl out of the pipe as fast as you can and drop to the floor. Turn on the flashlight right away. If he's there, shine it in his eyes. I'll follow you out, and maybe the two of us can take him."

I could hear Micah Lee swallow. "Okay."

"On three. One, two—"

"Wait. Do I go on three or wait for you to say go?"

"Dammit, Micah Lee. On three," I said through gritted teeth. "One, two, three."

Were it any other place and time, our shuffling rush would have been comical, but in the moment, it seemed frantic and desperate. Micah Lee fell from the end of the pipe and yelped when he hit the ground. I kept crawling. A second later, his flashlight flared. I pushed out the pipe, fell, and came up ready to fight. But the Snatcher wasn't there. Micah Lee stood motionless, holding the flashlight like a gun and illuminating blood smeared on the cement floor.

"That's Bobby's blood," he said in a daze.

"Gimme that." I grabbed the light from him and shone it around the junction.

"Where's Bobby?" Micah Lee said.

I aimed the ray-gun flashlight at the metal ladders leading up to a manhole cover. "The Snatcher must have taken him."

"Why?"

"I don't know." I put the flashlight on the ground. Balanced on the handgrip, it aimed straight up. "Come on." I pulled Micah Lee to the ladder and made him climb.

He got to the manhole cover and pushed on it. "It's too heavy."

I made him get to one side of the ladder while I got on the other. I lowered my head and put a shoulder to the steel disc. Micah Lee held one hand to it.

"We need to get it up."

Tears on his cheeks, he wrapped a leg through a couple of rungs and put both hands against the manhole cover. We pushed. Through desperation and adrenaline, we shifted it enough that I could squeeze out.

"Don't leave me, Charly."

I gave him a hand up and looked about the night, trying to figure where we were.

Micah Lee stared down into the hole and shivered. "Do you..." He stopped and wiped at his eyes. "Do you think Bobby's dead?"

He swayed back and forth, so I grabbed his shoulders. "I don't know. I hope not. All I know is that we have to get help."

He rubbed at his nose. "We're gonna leave without Bobby?"

"The Snatcher's got a gun. We'll get help and come back for him."

"Okay."

I worried that Micah Lee would start bawling, and I put an arm around his shoulder. "We need to be strong until we get help. Okay?"

He looked at me with puppy dog eyes and nodded.

"I think we're out on the county road."

Micah Lee looked around. "Yep."

"We can follow it in to town, or we can take a shortcut. If we cut through the woods there, north of the ridge, we'll come out at Wallace Lake. We can wake up Mr. Henderson at his store and call the sheriff."

"Okay."

There was a noise, a soft clump, behind us. I turned and looked up the road. A silhouetted figure stood close by. Not much more than a shadow, it shifted from one foot to the next.

"It's Bobby, isn't it?" Micah Lee asked.

The shadow moved toward us, and I pushed Micah Lee toward the woods, "Run."

Terror took root, and my brain shut down, as I ran as hard as I could. I lost track of time, but when I could no longer breathe and my tired legs felt as limp as rubber, I dropped to the forest floor and crawled behind a tree. My face and arms stung from scratches I got from limbs and sharp brush.

"Micah Lee," I whispered with a shaky breath. Somewhere in the back of my mind, I remembered him calling my name. I pushed myself up and looked the way I'd come. As far as I could make out, nothing moved, nor did I hear anyone walking or running about. I hoped that Micah Lee was okay. Gauging from the direction I'd come, and if I'd run straight, I estimated the route to take for Wallace Lake. I'd still make for Mr. Henderson's store and hoped Micah Lee did too.

It was a strange march through the woods, kind of like I was in a dream verging on a nightmare. I came to a point where the trees ended and saw I had angled too far south in my mad dash. I was atop the ridgeline, which meant I had to go north, I guessed about a half mile or so, before heading west again.

A limb snapped ahead of me, and I dropped to a crouch, peering around a tree into the night woods.

There was the unmistakable sound of two footsteps, and just when I tensed to run, a voice whispered, "Charly?"

I sighed and said, "Micah Lee, over this way."

Leaves crunched, and I watched a form take shape among the trees. It was too big to be my friend.

I turned and ran back south along the ridge line. The thought that the Snatcher knew my name spurred me on. Angling to the left, I hoped to go in a big circle until I was northbound. I'd run nonstop to Henderson's store. Though not closing the distance, the Snatcher stayed near enough for me to hear. At one point, I fell down a small hill. When I looked up, I saw him, a dark figure at the top of the incline. I got up as he started down after me.

Panicked, I fled blindly and ran right off the ridge.

Chapter 27
Autumn of '82

My room was so frigid that I woke during the night and got another blanket from the closet. In the morning, I stayed huddled in bed while calling down to the desk.

Dub answered, and I said, "It's freezing up here. Do something."

"Sorry, Charly. My furnace is giving me fits. Hopefully, it'll blow hot air by midmorning."

"What's the temperature?"

"Forty-two right now. It dropped almost thirty degrees from yesterday evening, and the weatherman says it's supposed to get colder tonight. Our Indian summer has ended."

My exertions from the previous night left me in need of a bath, and unlike the furnace, the hot water heater still did its job. By the time I got out of the tub, the bathroom looked like a sauna. I put on clothes, including a sweater and jacket, and got to the sheriff's department, hoping Kit found Beason. No one managed the front desk, and I headed for Kit's office. He wasn't there, and I noticed the meeting room door was closed. As I started for it, it was flung open, and what had to be every deputy under Kit rushed out.

SBI Agent Caputo exited, turned, and said, "I'll get on the horn and have a crew up here by this afternoon." His face was flushed as he rushed by, pretending not to see me.

Kit emerged, taking purposeful strides toward his office. "Come with me," he said, his face cast in stone. I trailed in his wake, and he shut the door. "You were right. Caputo is a fool."

I held up my hands in a *what can I say* gesture.

"A cocky bastard," Kit added.

"He's why I left the SBI."

Kit sat back. "Caputo is?"

"He got promoted to supervisor just as I was getting set to do some undercover jobs. He rescinded those orders and tried to put me on desk duty. I walked."

"How about that," Kit said. "No wonder you hate the man."

I kicked Caputo from my mind. "What's going on?"

"Another abduction," Kit said.

"Ah shit. When? Who was taken?"

"Pretty much like Piper Darling. Taken last night from her bedroom. Her parents discovered her missing at around six thirty this morning. Her name is Gili Acosta. I'm heading back to make sure every square inch of her home is looked at, inside and out." He paused. "Look, I unloaded on Caputo in there, saying he hasn't done shit for us, and if you'd been in there, I'd have said the same to you."

"I'm doing what I can."

He leaned over his desk, his eyes fierce. "And it's not enough." He sat back. "A few of us hit the Thugs' place late, but Beason had already been home and left again. Grizz and Bones were there. They claimed not to know where he went."

I chewed on my lip. "Makes me wonder."

"Wonder what?"

"What if my confrontation with Beason wound him up, and he needed some kind of release."

"So you think you stressed him out, the pressure built, and he abducted Gili Acosta because of it?"

"It's a theory." I stood and tossed the gram of cocaine on his desk. "Here."

"What's this?"

"What it looks like. I found it and a whole lot more at ECT Motorcycle and Small Engine Repair last night."

"B & E, huh? You were breaking all kinds of laws last night, weren't you?" Kit shook his head and shoved the coke in his desk drawer. "It'll have to wait."

"I know."

He sighed. "Copycat takes priority right now."

"I know."

Kit stood. "Why don't you follow me over to the Acosta house?"

"I'd rather find Beason."

He looked at me a moment. "No rough stuff."

"No rough stuff... unless necessary."

He grabbed his hat. "You want one of my boys to go with you?" Meaning he wanted to anchor me with a babysitter to make sure I played nice.

"That won't be necessary."

I made a quick stop at the Temperance Inn to pick up my .38 and drove out past Roscoe's to the Thugs' house. I parked by the porch, and when I got out, I saw a doorless shed next to the house, with three motorcycles sitting inside. An old Nova and beat-up GTO were in the yard. Neither of them had damaged right sides that would be consistent with running me off the road. I moved up the steps. A dented washing machine sat to the left of the door. The porch extended to the corner on the right side, where numerous kitchen chairs and a rocker sat. None of the windows were screened, and one had a dangling shutter on the side. The tin roof was discolored with age. I grabbed the old crystal knob on the ancient front door, turned it, and pushed the door open. As good as an invitation.

I went in. The main room was as much of a mess as expected. A narrow hallway led to a kitchen, where every flat surface was piled with dirty dishes, glasses, cans, bottles, and pizza boxes. I went back to the living room and took another hallway that ended at a filthy bathroom. I opened another door to see tangled blankets on a mattress on the floor and some porn scattered among biker magazines.

Back in the main room, I looked up the stairs. I guessed that was where I'd find Beason. I put a foot on the first step, and something hard pressed to the back of my head.

"I don't think anyone asked you to come in, Charly." His voice was gravel and smoke. "I could blow you away right now." Somehow, for all his girth, Grizz had snuck up on me.

"You could," I said, maintaining calm, "but I don't think Sheriff Haiselton would look too kindly on it."

"Who's to say he'd ever know?" Grizz pushed the gun barrel hard to my head and moved close. I saw his face from the corner of my eye. "I'd just keep it simple and bury you out back. Then I'd have one of my boys drive your car to a chop shop down the mountain. It'd take care of you and earn me a few bucks in the process."

I had no doubts that Grizz would shoot someone under the right circumstances, but for all his criminal potential, I didn't think he wanted the headache he'd get for shooting me here. I moved to face him, but he grabbed my arm. I yanked free and turned. As big as he was, the .44 Magnum he held made him seem gargantuan. He was tromping around bare-ass naked, save for a pair of gray socks. He started to say something, but I grabbed his wrist while pushing the gun away. I turned to the side and kicked, grinding my boot down his shin and stomping on his instep. Air rushed from his throat in a combination grunt and moan. The man was a giant, and I knew that if I lost the advantage, he'd crush me like a bug. I let fly a backhanded punch to his groin, and as he bent over, I delivered an elbow jab to his throat. In the next second, I held my Smith and Wesson snub-nose .38.

Grizz wobbled, dropped to his knees, and made guttural noises. I slid my hand down his wrist and yanked the .44 from his grip. He collapsed on his side in the fetal position, one hand at his throat, the other at his testicles.

I kicked back on the couch and studied his .44 Ruger. It was much more intimidating than my .38, which I returned to my holster. I rested the heavy piece on my knee and kept it pointed at the big man while waiting for him to recover.

Minutes passed, and I was surprised to hear him laugh. "Damn, girl, you are something else." He held out a hand and said, "Careful with that gun."

"Maybe you'd feel more comfortable if I took my finger out of the trigger guard."

"Sure would." He grinned and sat up. His eyes were bloodshot, and he was sweating and smacking his lips. Grizz was suffering a major hangover. I kept my finger on the trigger, and the gun aimed at his head. His smile vanished. "If that's how you want to play it."

"Hey, you made the first move," I said.

"Me? Who broke into whose house, huh?"

"Who was first to pull a gun?" I asked. Our banter reminded me of the arguments I used to have with Micah Lee or Bobby, arguments that generally began with, "Yeah, well, you started it."

Though the house was cold, he didn't seem to feel it, even naked. However, I found his overall obesity and genitalia surrounded by a coarse forest of pubic hair to be repulsive.

He said, "Look, I shouldn't have come up on you like that, but I'm a real grouch when I wake up, and your sheriff buddy kept me up 'til the wee small hours."

"So I heard."

"Come on, Charly. No hard feelings, huh?"

"Where's Beason?"

He cupped his testicles gingerly and winced.

"Where is he?" I repeated.

"Like I told the sheriff, I haven't seen that boy since last night. And why do you guys want him? Kit wouldn't tell me."

I ignored his question and said, "He hasn't come back since last night?"

"That's right. What'd he do?"

"You're lying."

"No, I'm not. He showed up here, took the truck, and left. I haven't seen him since. I told Kit all this. Why don't you talk to him?" Grizz dug a finger into his nose.

"Put on some pants, and come talk to me. Be good, Grizz, and I'll give your gun back."

He flicked a booger and shambled into the hallway, showing me his hairy ass. I thought about the possibility of Beason using the truck to abduct Gili Acosta. Grizz came back scratching at his massive beard. He wore what looked like the same clothes as when I'd first seen him at Shorty's. He bypassed me in stocking feet, boots held in one hand, went to the kitchen, and returned with a can of Schlitz. He tried to sit beside me, but I motioned with the gun to a chair. He went and sat there.

He opened the beer and took half in one gulp. "So what do you want with Luke?" There was a dusting of white powder on his moustache. A morning line to soothe that hangover?

I asked, "How well do you know him?"

"I've known the scrawny wannabe a couple years." Grizz picked up his spurred boot and put it on. He had a hard time getting his foot all the way in and stomped on the floor, making the spur sound like a dropped coin. "He had a Suzuki 185 that was giving him fits and came in the shop one day. Turned out to be a coil going bad." He got his other boot on. "That's when Luke started hanging out. A year ago, maybe not quite a year, I made him a prospect."

"What time did he leave in the pickup last night?"

He grabbed a crumpled pack of smokes and a book of matches from the coffee table. "One, maybe later." He ripped off the top of the pack and pulled out the last remaining cigarette.

"I think he's mixed up in something bad, and I want you to help me find him."

He looked at me and laughed. "Yeah, right. You know better than that. A Thug is true to his bros."

I put the .44 down on the coffee table. "Another girl was abducted last night."

His laughter died, and he stared at me. "You think Luke is doing it?"

"You tell me. Last night, Gili Acosta was taken from her bedroom sometime after Luke came home and got the truck. The third girl, Savannah Smallwood, disappeared near the restaurant where he works."

He lit his cigarette. "Well, if he's busy working, he can't go taking girls."

"He wasn't working. He stopped in for his paycheck while she was having dinner with her family. She went across the street to the park and hasn't been seen since. I doubt Luke has an alibi for any of the times girls were abducted."

Grizz furrowed his brow and nibbled at his lip. "Ah fuck."

"Help me on this."

"Luke's a bro. I can't rat him out. It's in our bylaws, for fuck's sake." He swallowed and looked at me. "Are you sure about this?"

It was nearly impossible to get one biker to incriminate another. Club brothers were so tight they squeaked. Unless... "He isn't exactly your bro."

"And why not?"

"He's a prospect. Not every prospect makes it into the Thugs, do they?"

"Hell, no."

"Are they your bros?"

"Fuck, those washouts?"

"He's a prospect, not a bro. And if he gets arrested for this, and you're protecting him, how much shit are you going to be in, huh? You're going to have cops all over this house." I added more emphasis when I said, "And all over your shop."

His face darkened.

"No telling what trouble it could cause the other chapters."

Grizz ran those possibilities through his mind then shouted, "Fuckin' prospects, more trouble than they're worth." He dumped a long ash on the floor, clamped the cigarette in his teeth, bent down, and grabbed a stack of magazines under the coffee table. He rooted through them, pulling a couple aside. He put the rest back and saw something else there, a paperback, and got it. "I like them big-titty magazines with hot, horny bitches, spreadin' their pussies for the camera. Grown women. But Luke, I don't know. This is some of the shit he's into."

He put the magazines and paperback on the table. One was called *Lollipops*, the other, *Tender*, and the book was titled *Daddy's Darling Daughter*.

"Kiddie porn?"

He didn't answer, just looked me in the eye.

Girls were missing, and this was Beason's porn. "Grizz, I think he's taking the girls."

Grizz sighed like a father who learned his son had gone astray. "I'll help you get him."

I stood up. "Where's your phone? I'll call Kit."

"Whoa, hold on a minute. I'll help you, but it has to be on my terms."

"Terms?"

Grizz emptied the beer, dropped his cigarette in the backwash, and got up. "If he's doing it, it's going to be bad news for the Thugs. And the guys at the other chapters are going to be pissed that they're suddenly under a damn microscope. Who are they going to take it out on? The guy who made Luke a prospect. It'll be different if I'm the one who helps you bring him in. If I do that, the cops will know the Thugs had nothing to do with what Luke was into and leave the club alone."

"Grizz, we need the sheriff to look for him."

"He's my prospect. I can find him. Guaranteed. Give me until six o'clock."

I knew that in his mind he was thinking about getting Beason before the cops went to search for him at the repair shop. "Don't fuck me over, Grizz."

"You can trust me on this, Charly."

No, I can't, I thought, but I wasn't going to debate the point. "What kind of pickup is he driving?"

"'64 Dodge, white with a faded blue roof. Name of the shop is on the sides."

"Wouldn't happen to be dented on the right side, would it?"

He looked at me a moment. "How'd you know about that, huh?"

"Because someone hit me, tried to run me into Morrison Gorge the night before last... someone in a white vehicle."

"No shit? Luke had it a couple of nights ago and said he hit a guard rail. That motherfucker." Grizz leaned forward, and I felt a stirring of respect when he said, "You don't think much of me, and I don't give a shit. But you can take it to the bank that I won't abide someone who goes after kids."

Chapter 28
Summer of '59

Black softened to gray and then lightened enough so I could see my surroundings. Everything was out of focus, and my head was all wobbly. I blinked several times and figured out I was sitting in the cave at Wallace Falls with Bobby and Micah Lee. They were yucking it up. How'd I get here? And then I remembered the Snatcher.

"Shut up," I hissed. "The Snatcher is looking for us."

"Snatch is another word for beaver." Bobby snickered.

Micah Lee clutched his gut and howled laughter.

"Shut up." They ignored me, and I closed my eyes to keep from losing my temper. When I opened them, I was racked with pain. I struggled into a sitting position, and the world around me pitched back and forth. I wasn't in the cave after all. I must have dreamed that. Opening my mouth to groan, I vomited instead. *Hello, dinner. Back so soon?*

I grabbed handfuls of pine needles, wondering why I was in the middle of the woods. Where were Bobby and Micah Lee? I opened my mouth to shout for them, but then I remembered the night, the sewer, the gunshot, the chase, and running off the ridge. I looked up and saw that I'd been lucky enough to go off where it sloped at a steep angle instead of a sheer drop. I must have rolled down, banging off rocks and sliding on scree. I ached all over, though the back of my head hurt most. Reaching up, I felt leaves and pine needles tangled in my hair then flinched when I touched the ball-sized lump at the back of my head.

Leaves crunched as someone walked to my side. I could see her out of the corner of my eye, but when I turned to her, she wasn't there. When I looked away, she reappeared. Okay, so I had a companion, but only seen in my side vision. I recognized her just as I had when I'd seen her in the park and then later in my backyard. She still wore plaid pajamas.

"Hello, Sarah," I croaked. "Are you really here, or is it 'cause I busted my head?" When she didn't answer, I looked directly at her, and like before, she was gone. I got to my feet, though it took time, and stood on shaky legs. Sarah was again at the edge of my sight. She motioned for me to go in a particular direction.

"What's it like being dead? Is it bad? Do you feel anything?" I couldn't help myself. Maybe it was my banged head, but my mouth moved nonstop, asking Sarah questions that went unanswered. "Is there a Heaven? Why ain't you there?" And as I blabbered, I followed her while keeping her in a lateral view. When she changed direction, I'd do so as well, keeping her to my side and continuing through the woods.

We'd been moving up for a time, and I figured out where we were. "We're on Cray's Hill."

We came upon a dark cabin by a barn, a pump handle between them. A big, dusty dog rushed from under the porch, his tail wagging. While Sarah stroked his fur, I stumbled to the pump and worked it until I was rewarded with cold mountain water. I drank, threw it up, and drank more.

Sarah motioned for me to continue walking.

"I'm sorry the Snatcher killed you." I moved unsteadily, wondering if this was what being drunk felt like. I pointed to the dog following us and said, "We got company." He caught scent of something and ran into the brush, barking furiously.

We reached the top of Cray's Hill and started down the other side, and I found that I was alone, abandoned by both Sarah and the dog. I wasn't scared because even though it was night, I could see pretty well. There was a nearly full moon glowing like the biggest night-light. When I got to the bottom, in the glade between Cray's Hill and Rock Ridge, a mist formed and moved in figure-like wisps. The woods on Cray's Hill stopped just behind me. A hundred yards ahead, Rock Ridge began to slope up and was bordered with a thick stand of pines.

Movement to my right caught my attention, and I spied another girl so far in the distance as to almost be a part of the dark. I moved toward Theresa Goodnight. She answered each step I took with one of her own. I supposed her shyness in life carried over into death, because even though I could look directly at her, she kept at a distance. She led me around the base of Rock Ridge before she stepped into a wall of trees.

I entered, pushing into the woods until I saw her disappear around a pine. I hurried, but she was gone by the time I got there. Looking around, I glimpsed her moving from tree to tree, and then she ducked behind a boulder. At the boulder, I saw her far away, pushing into some wild growth. Eventually, she led me around Rock Ridge and a good way up Hallow's Summit. I stepped from the trees into a clearing and saw what looked like the top of a castle on the other side of a hill. I started for it and came to the remnants of a brick road that led over a knoll. At the top, I saw that it curved toward a gate in a tall fence around the structure, which I recognized as the old textile mill. A pretty blonde in a canary-yellow dress appeared at my side.

"Hello, Lily. Where are you taking me?"

She pointed at the old mill, and we headed up the brick drive. A growing noise broke the forest silence, and Lily stepped into bushes. I followed as a car drove up, the headlights sweeping where I'd just been standing. The car parked at the bottom of the ruined brick road, the lights shut off, and the driver's-side door opened. I started to push out and get help, but Lily grabbed my arm with a cold touch. The car was too distant for the interior light to allow me to identify the driver as he shut the door and opened the trunk. He threw something over his shoulder and went up the drive. Though my night vision was good, I still couldn't make out who he was as he passed, but I was pretty sure the bundle over his shoulder was a body. He continued to the gate and then beyond, stopping at the fence and passing through.

After a minute, Lily and I walked toward the old mill. A short way past the gate, we came to a section of fence someone had taken wire cutters to, and I squeezed through. The sky was brightening, though it would be twenty to thirty minutes before the sun cleared Black Mountain to burn off the morning mist. I looked up at the old textile mill, an ugly brick building three stories high and stretching back a long way. Small windows were set at regular intervals down the length of the building, and as far as I could tell, each was broken. The architect had designed the roofline with battlements, giving it that castle feel. Three brick smokestacks rose like skeletal giants twice as high as the building.

Lily led me into a side door and through warrens of rooms. Some were empty, others contained ancient machinery, and some were littered with papers and raw materials. We stopped at a metal latticework gate that closed off an industrial elevator shaft, and I heard arbitrary sounds from the basement—something sliding across the floor, a metallic clank, and soft laughter. We went along a wall until we came to a staircase and descended. The dawn light dimmed to underground gloom. I couldn't see much and focused on Lily—the dead leading the blind. We turned into a long hall where a dull glow spilled from a distant door.

"Is that where the Snatcher is?" I whispered.

Lily was gone.

Chapter 29
Autumn of '82

The wind had picked up. It was bracing as I got out of my car at the Temperance Inn and ascended the fire escape to my private entrance. I opened the door to a warm, cozy room and silently congratulated Dub for fixing the furnace. I shed my jacket and sweater. My gun went back into the lockbox.

Yeah, I made a deal with Grizz, but I wasn't going to risk Beason getting away. I dialed the sheriff's department, and the dispatcher gave me the Acosta address. When I arrived, I discovered that Kit wasn't there, though one of his deputies took me in to meet the Acostas.

"This is Charly Bloom," the deputy said. "She used to be with the SBI, and she's helping us with the case."

I held out my hand, but because of the obvious horror and shock they were experiencing, neither seemed to notice. Mrs. Acosta's eyes were red rimmed from crying.

"Thank you for helping," Mr. Acosta said, his voice weak. He put his arm around his wife, and I wasn't sure whether it was to comfort her or to help each other stay upright.

I considered questioning them but decided it might be better to wait until the shock lessened. I turned to the deputy and asked, "Can you show me around, Deputy...?"

"Stines. Call me Van."

Van led me to Gili Acosta's bedroom at the back of the one-story house. One window facing nearby woods was open, letting in chill air.

"That's how he got in?" I asked.

"Yep."

The room was neat and girly, the bed unmade. "Is it like the other scenes?"

"In what way?"

"No leads."

Van looked surprised. "Haven't you gotten Kit's messages?"

"No."

"He called the inn and left word with Dub. There're a couple things."

I'd gone to my room and left it by the fire escape. I hadn't checked in with Dub. "What?"

Van got on a knee, lifted the bedspread out of the way, and pointed to a spot under the bed. "There was a rag here on the floor. We missed it initially. Neither Mr. or Mrs. Acosta recognized it. There was a strong chemical smell to it."

"Do we know what the smell is from?"

"Nope, but that's where the sheriff went. He's taking the rag up to Asheville himself. They're going to run it through the lab. Kit thinks Copycat dropped it during the abduction, and it got kicked under the bed."

"When will Kit be back?"

"He oughta be back in a couple of hours. He's hoping that if he takes it, he can get them to rush it through."

"You said a couple things. What else?"

Van pointed to the south. "A neighbor across the street and a couple houses down saw a truck parked out front. He heard it drive off a little later."

"What time was this?"

"Around three."

My heartbeat played tympani. "Did you get a description of the truck?"

"Not much. He didn't think it was important at the time. He said it was too dark to tell what color it was but thought it was an older model."

Van gave me the man's name, and I rushed across the street and knocked on his door.

When he opened it, I asked, "Peter Cordis?" His name was familiar.

"Yes."

"I'm Charly Bloom. I'm helping Sheriff Haiselton, and I'd like to ask you a few questions."

Mr. Cordis was shorter than me and in his seventies. What little hair he had was brown and combed over, covering a small percentage of his scalp. He looked up through his glasses and smiled. "My, my. Charly Bloom."

"Yes, sir."

"You don't remember me, do you?"

"To be honest, no. Though your name is familiar."

"I was choir director at Good News Baptist Church when you were a girl. Had supper at your house on a couple of occasions."

I remembered a younger Peter Cordis directing the choir. They wore navy-blue robes, but Mr. Cordis's was ruby-red and trimmed in gold. He was funny to watch and mesmerizing. He'd direct with hands flying and arms flapping, and the wide robe sleeves looked like cardinal wings. I half expected him to take flight every Sunday.

I gave him a wide smile. "Of course."

"Come in, come in." He ushered me in to his kitchen table. I declined anything to drink, and we sat.

I touched his hand. "I want to thank you for helping us."

He looked out the kitchen window that faced in the direction of the Acosta house. "If I'd had any idea what was going on, I'd have done more."

"Don't sell yourself short. This is the most we've gotten at any of the crime scenes. I know you've already told the sheriff what you saw, but would you mind repeating it for me?"

"Of course not. About three this morning"—he pointed to the kitchen window—"I looked out there—"

"What were you doing up at that time?"

"Seems the older I get, the less sleep I need. Most nights I go to bed by ten, but dang if I'm not wide awake at two or two thirty. I get up and putter around the house, read, do some housework. If I'm lucky, I can fall back to sleep around five and catch another hour or two."

"Okay, so you woke up, got out of bed, and...?"

"Well, I came in the kitchen to make some tea, looked out the window, and saw the truck in front of Tom's—Mr. Acosta's house."

I stood and wandered around, got a feel for the kitchen, and looked out the window. "Things are different at night, Mr. Cordis. At night, with the light on in here, you wouldn't be able to see out the window."

Mr. Cordis grinned and pointed a finger at me. "You're good. When you were a kid and solved the kidnappings, I knew big things were ahead of you." He got up and went to the stove. "I have night lights around the house, including this one I leave on every night." He switched on a dim light under the hood over his range. "It's low wattage, and when going around the house at night, I don't turn on much else. That's why I could see out the window."

"Show me where the truck was parked."

He joined me and pointed. "See at the edge of their lawn where those big bushes are?"

"It wasn't parked right in front?"

"Nope. Looking back, hindsight being twenty-twenty and all, I'd say they parked there so as not to be seen if the Acostas looked out."

"Which way was the truck facing?"

"This way."

"And you couldn't tell what color it was?"

"You know how colors turn to gray when it's dark out."

"Could you tell if the roof was a different color than the rest of the truck?"

"Well." He scratched his cheek. "No one asked me that." He thought a second. "Now that you mention it, I think it was darker."

Another step closer to proving it was Beason. I was actually feeling optimistic about the case. "Then what happened?"

"I made my tea, sat here at the table, and planned out my day. Ten minutes later or thereabouts, I heard an engine start."

"What did you do then?"

"Nothing, I was just sitting and..." His gaze shifted from me to across the kitchen.

"What is it?"

"Now that you ask, I got up to wash my cup just after the engine started."

"Which way did the truck go when it left?"

"The way it was parked, it drove by the house."

"Did you see it again as it went past?"

He tapped his lips as he thought. "I just remember seeing it at the curb."

"I understand, but if you're already up and the window is right there, it'd be reflex to look if a truck goes by."

"I don't remember, but..." Mr. Cordis stopped talking. He stood and pointed a finger as he remembered how he walked from the table to the sink. He paused, turned his head to the left, and looked out the window. "Well, I'll be. I did look, for just a second. How did you know?"

"It makes sense."

"And you know what? There was writing on the door, like it was a work truck."

I felt like I was in the final laps of winning a race.

"Did you happen to notice any dents or damage to the truck?"

"No, couldn't see it that well."

Back at the Acosta house, I pulled Van to the side and asked him if he could get in touch with Kit.

"I can call the lab in Asheville and see if he's still there. If he's on his way back, it would depend on if he was in radio range or not."

"Luke Beason. Do you know him?"

"Yeah, Ellen's boy. Sheriff has orders to bring him in for questioning."

"If you talk to the sheriff, tell him that I'm convinced it's Luke."

Van opened his eyes wide and gazed down at the floor, processing what I told him. "Luke? Luke Beason?" He looked back up at me. "Yeah, I'll tell Kit."

Chapter 30
Summer of '59

At some point, I'd have to move, but my feet were like magnets on metal. Facing the lit room down the hallway, I could make out pipes under the ceiling and rubble on the floor. There were a couple of reflective puddles in the long hallway from water that leeched in from somewhere overhead. I heard a drip and saw ripples in the nearest. With a deep breath, I forced myself to take a step, and then another. As I tiptoed, an image came to me of Elmer Fudd hunting "wabbits," and a nervous giggle escaped my lips. I paused and listened. Nothing. I started again, making my way down the hall, fingertips brushing the left wall, going slowly, so very slowly.

Someone spoke. "What? What do you want?" I recognized Micah Lee's voice.

My head swam, and I had to lean against the wall to keep from falling. That was Micah Lee that the Snatcher had pulled from the trunk and carried up to the old mill. I had run off and left him alone in the woods. It was my fault he'd been snatched.

From down the hall, Micah Lee pleaded, "Please let me go. I won't say nothing."

There was a smack, and I imagined an open palm against Micah Lee's cheek. He whimpered, sniffed, and said in a pathetic voice, "What'd you do that for?"

"Listen to me, you little faggot." There was something about that voice. "Look at me. Damn it, look me in the eyes so you'll know I'm telling the truth. I'm going to kill you."

"But—but why?" I could picture Micah Lee's face all scrunched up.

"You ain't a girl, and I ain't queer, but we'll have us some fun anyway."

A second later, Micah Lee screamed.

"That's it, you shit. Scream like a girl. I like that." He had a lisp. *Thath it, you thit. Thscream like a girl.* The Snatcher was Winthrop Whist. I'd always known he was nuts, but this crazy? Crazy enough to have killed those girls? Kill his own brother?

Micah Lee screamed again.

I ran down the hall, splashing in one of the puddles and hoping Winthrop didn't hear.

"Show me what you got. Come on, you little fruit."

He hit Micah Lee again, but this time it wasn't the open-handed slap. This was the meaty thud of a fist in a stomach. Micah Lee grunted, was quiet for several seconds, and then sucked air.

"Shit, you ain't even got any hair down there, little queer."

I got to the door, squatted, and peeked inside. Winthrop stood in front of Micah Lee, who was naked and tied to an old straight-back office chair. Winthrop was in full greaser regalia—leather jacket, jeans, and engineer boots. He bent over, cupping his crotch through his jeans, and reaching with his other hand to squeeze Micah Lee's penis.

Micah Lee screamed, and I turned away.

The room was dimly lit by a handful of candles. It looked like a storeroom filled with all manner of old chairs, desks, cabinetry, bookshelves, and shadows. There were stacked filing cabinets far enough from the wall for me to fit behind. As quietly as possible, I crossed through the door, stepped into the room, and hid behind the cabinets. A pain like a hot needle drove into my head. Dizziness washed over me, so I knelt. The feeling ebbed, and I caught my breath. The room was damp, like the cave at Wallace Falls, and smelled of mildew.

The cabinetry had been carelessly stacked with spaces between, and I peeked through just as Winthrop punched Micah Lee in the face. There was a crunch, and a second later, his nose streamed blood.

"Look at me," Winthrop demanded.

Micah Lee squealed, his head wonky on his neck.

Winthrop clutched his chin. "Yeah, there it is. You're heading in the right direction." He let go and swung a roundhouse against Micah Lee's left ear.

Micah Lee screeched, "Help me! Somebody help me!"

Winthrop laughed. "There ain't nobody to hear you."

I walked the length of the cabinets and came out in a dark pocket twenty feet from the candles. I went farther into the darkness, past chairs and desks, stopping when I got to a tipped-over chair with two legs missing. Dropping to my hands and knees, I felt around until I located one of the chair legs. It was solid and heavy.

Grasping it, I started for Winthrop. He teased Micah Lee and hit him more. He groped my naked friend and called him names. Each step brought me more into candlelight. Five feet from my goal, I froze. It seemed impossible that I could do anything to hurt the Snatcher. I looked into the darkness, wondering if I could retreat without notice. When I turned back, Winthrop was staring at me, his eyes boring into me like the twin barrels of a shotgun. He charged, and I swung. It was as simple as that. I hit him square on the side of the head, and he fell to the floor.

I looked down at Winthrop. He was the Snatcher, and I'd laid him out with one swing of a chair leg. But it wasn't over yet. Micah Lee and I needed to get out.

I turned from Winthrop and went to Micah Lee, who gazed out from his bloody face with big eyes. "Look out."

Winthrop was trying to get up. I stepped to him and kicked his shoulder, knocking him back.

He glared with pure hatred. "I'm gonna kill you, Bloom."

"No, you're not," I said and slammed the chair leg on top of his head.

I stared at Winthrop's crumpled form. I hadn't known that people knocked unconscious sometimes snored, but he was sawing some big logs. The chair leg dropped from my grasp, and I knelt before Micah Lee.

"You're not dead?" Micah Lee spoke through bloody teeth. The left side of his face was swollen though not yet bruising. His lip was split, and his nose crooked to the side. The blood from his broken nose covered his lower face and chest.

"Nope."

"He said you fell off the ridge by Wallace Lake."

"I did, but I'm still alive. Can you believe it?"

He smiled, a bubble of blood grew from one nostril, and I gave him a hug before starting to work at the rope tying him to the chair.

"I can't believe he shot Bobby, shot his own brother," Micah Lee said.

"He's crazy, Micah Lee. Crazy as a loon."

"Crazy as a peach orchard boar," he agreed.

"Crazy as a June bug in May."

He grinned through his broken face. "Crazy as a soup sandwich."

I giggled. "Crazy as a shithouse rat."

Micah Lee snickered then barked a laugh, spraying his blood on my face, which made me laugh louder. We looked at each other through our terror-induced elation. Him, naked, all beat up, and tied to the chair. He looked at my face, freckled with his blood, and at my injuries from the tumble down the ridge, and our laughter waned to gentle smiles.

"I love you, Charly."

"I know. I love you too." The ropes were big and coarse. "Let me see if I can find something to cut these with."

A quick search revealed nothing sharp, so I rummaged through Winthrop's pocket and was rewarded with his switchblade knife. The handle was mother-of-pearl, and I pressed the brass button, which released the blade with a snick.

As I sawed through the rope, Micah Lee stiffened.

"Did I cut you?" At that moment, I realized that Winthrop was no longer snoring.

There was a flash of white, and my vision faded to black.

Chapter 31
Autumn of '82

Waiting for Kit to return, I went out to examine the ground where the truck had been parked and the area outside Gili Acosta's window. Though my watch said it was three, it was getting dark. The wind was blowing through the trees hard enough to make limbs wave.

"Looks like a storm's coming," Van said, joining me.

I zipped up my jacket. "It's cold."

"Might see flurries."

"Excuse me." Mrs. Acosta popped her head out the door. "There's a call for you, Miss Bloom."

Expecting it was Kit, I followed her to the kitchen and picked up the phone. "Are you back?"

"Back? Back and forth, up and down, give and take. It's all about balance, isn't it?" It was Grizz.

"How'd you know where to find me?"

"I been looking all over. Finally called the sheriff's, told them I was a big shot with the SBI and had to get in touch with you right away. They told me where you are."

"What do you want?"

"I think I know where Luke took the girl." He sounded proud of himself.

This could mean we might get this girl in time. With a sense of urgency, I asked, "Where?"

"Uh-uh. Remember our deal. I help bring him in, and that keeps the cops off my ass."

"If you know anything, you better—"

"That's just it, dumbass. I do know, and I'm heading there now. You can come or not."

I pondered my options and said, "Where?"

"Do you know where everyone parks out at Wallace Lake?"

"That stretch of county road closest to the lake?"

"Meet me there at four o'clock. Alone." He hung up.

I found Van, reiterated what he was to tell Kit, and added that I'd be swinging by the inn, and Kit should try calling me there as soon as he got back. The reason I wanted to go by the inn was because I trusted Grizz about as far as I could throw his corpulent ass. I wanted to pick up a weapon or three. Even more than that, I wanted to dress warmer. The temperature was near freezing, and there was a stiff wind. It'd be bitterly cold at the lake.

Dub sat at the desk and told me Kit had called a couple of times and left messages, which he handed to me. One was about the rag, the other about Peter Cordis. In my room, I undressed, and then redressed in warmer clothes, including long johns and thick wool socks. A pair of jeans and a flannel shirt went over the long johns, a heavy sweater over the shirt, and then my neck-to-knee ski-jacket over it all. I found my knit cap tucked into the corner of my suitcase and retrieved my .38, slipping it into the deep righthand jacket pocket. I thought that if Grizz had something nefarious in mind, he'd come at me hard, so I brought my KA-BAR combat knife. The sheath clipped to my belt, and the jacket hid the seven-inch blade.

Still no call from Kit by three-forty.

I went downstairs and found Dub. "If you hear from Kit, tell him that I'm going to meet Grizz out at the lake."

"Are you sure that's smart?" Dub asked.

"I know it's not. That's one of the reasons I'm telling you, in case something happens to me. But Dub, if what Grizz told me is on the up and up, I just might close the case this afternoon."

"Hang on a second." Dub left the desk and went in the back room. He came back gripping something. With a couple of deft moves, he flicked open a butterfly knife. He flicked it again and handed it to me closed.

"I already have a knife."

"Take two. I had this one in 'Nam, and it brought me luck."

I raised an eyebrow and looked at his armless shoulder.

He said, "Better than dead."

I leaned over the counter and kissed his cheek. "Thanks, Dub."

This visit to Temperance reminded me of the affection I held for my one-armed innkeeper. When I returned to school in the fall of '59, I found myself the center of hushed attention. Everyone knew what had happened, and it seemed I was constantly stared at. Dub and Kit came to me one day and asked what it was like to be tortured. I knew it seemed offensive, but after a week of silent stares, I welcomed their frank curiosity.

Cautious, I asked, "Why do you want to know? Are you writing a book?"

Kit, a pain in the ass back then, gave a hint of his future self when he answered in total sincerity, "No. We just want to know what happened to you, Charly. What it was like."

I wanted to answer in a way that would make them understand, but all I could come up with was "It was bad. Really bad."

They nodded as if that explained it all.

Dub then put a hand on my shoulder and said, "Wanna get up a game after school?" A simple question unless you were a kid and could decipher all the meanings it implied—*we're sorry it happened, we're still here for you,* and *remember we're your friends.*

Slipping the butterfly knife into my back pocket, I left the inn and walked out to a light flurry. The afternoon sky was dark enough that I turned on my headlights. I hoped it stayed a light flurry, but by the time I pulled behind Grizz's GTO out near Wallace Lake, the snow fell heavier.

The GTO exhaust belched black smoke, and I saw Grizz's silhouette inside. I got out, walked to his car, and tapped on the window. He looked at me and held up a finger. He brought up his other hand, which gripped a small square of mirror with two lines of cocaine laid out. He took a rolled-up dollar bill and snorted. Poof, gone in a second. He rolled down the window a couple of inches, and pinching at his nostrils said, "A little snow for the snow. Get in, and I'll turn you on to a couple of rails."

I bent down to the gap in the window. "Don't do drugs in front me, Grizz."

He grinned, eyes alight. "Whatcha gonna do? Bust me?" He shut off the GTO, though it took a few chugs for it to die. The chassis wobbled and squeaked as Grizz got out.

He held out his arms. "Welcome to winter wonderland."

"Yeah, well, I prefer coconuts and palm trees."

He walked to me, and the sound of his spur on the road cut through the wind. He threw an arm over my shoulder like we were old buddies and said, "I bet you were the type of kid who liked snow—sledding, snowballs, snow forts."

I shrugged off his arm. "Where's Beason?"

"A little birdy told me he saw something over there." Grizz moved his head, signaling the direction of some woods on the other side of a grassy field that was getting a dusting of white.

"What?"

Grizz didn't answer but said, "Come on." He headed across the field.

I reached into my jacket pocket and thumbed off the safety on the .38. I hurried to catch up to Grizz. "No more secrets. Where are we going?"

He looked at me from the corners of his eyes. "I'll be open with you, okay? But you can't use anything I say to cause me trouble. Luke, however—I don't care what happens to that shit."

"Yeah, okay."

As we crossed the field, Grizz's fat thighs and long strides produced a rhythm as the fabric of his pants rubbed together. "Luke and Preach are tight. Preach is kind of like his mentor, showing him how things are done in the club. After that unfortunate evening when Preach and Weasel got a little rough with you, someone"—by the way he looked at me, I knew he meant himself—"decided those two should hang out at one of the other chapters until things cool off."

"That's what I figured."

"You fucked Weasel up good, and he didn't have no problems with leaving, but Preach wanted to stay, and when he gets his mind made up, he can be damn stubborn."

"Why'd he want to stay?"

"Mainly to have another go at you."

"Holds a grudge, huh?"

"He's not like us. This morning, I held a gun to your head, and you cracked me in the balls, and yet here we are, taking a stroll through a meadow like a couple of sweethearts. Weasel was in no shape to ride, so we loaded their bikes into the pickup, and Jelly drove them down the mountain. Before they left, I saw Preach take Luke to the side, and they were whispering, *pssst, pssst, pssst,* conspiring something. So I went over and reiterated that Preach would not return until I gave the okay."

"And what does that have to do with us hiking through a field in a snowstorm?"

"I went by Shorty's and asked around about Luke. One of the bar rats said he saw Preach's bike parked right over there by the trees."

"You think he came back, and Luke is with him?"

"Yep."

"And that they're both involved in the lost girls?"

Grizz didn't answer directly but said, "Preach is pretty nuts."

"So I noticed. But I don't see his bike," I said as we got close to the trees.

"Me neither."

I looked a little farther up the tree line. "Hold on."

"What?"

I hurried, Grizz breathing heavily behind me. Twenty yards later, we stopped at Preach's bike lying on its side.

"I'll be damned," Grizz said and reached for it.

"Leave it," I ordered.

Grizz stepped away. "Hate to see a bike on its side."

I looked around the trees and back to the fields and saw tire tracks in the grass. A car or truck had been out here. A little more snow, and I'd have missed the tracks and the motorcycle.

"Why here?" I asked.

"Follow me," Grizz said.

We headed into the woods, and I unzipped my jacket so I'd have quicker access to my KA-BAR.

"You grew up here, Charly. I bet you spent many a summer day at Wallace Lake."

"Uh-huh."

"There's the falls and the swimming area."

"Right."

"There's also little hidden areas, like private coves where you can party, and you don't have to worry about anyone seeing you."

I looked around the woods. Though I had thought we were just pressing blindly through the trees, I saw we were actually on a small trail, and I knew that at the end of the trail was the secret beach I shared with Micah Lee and Bobby. The recognition was so instant that it shocked me into immobility. The last time I'd been here was with my two best friends.

"What's the matter?" Grizz stopped and looked at me.

"I just realized where we're going."

"Oh yeah? The hidden beach?"

"We..." I forced myself to move. "A couple friends and me—this was our hangout."

"No shit? We found it and started coming out to party. Sometimes bring town girls out for a fuck, pardon my French. Preach, Bones, and Luke built a little party shack out here, and I bet that's where we'll find Luke and the girl."

I pushed past Grizz and jogged down the trail, ignoring him when he asked me to wait. As the trees thinned, I slowed and crept up to what was once our secret beach. Their shack was in some trees, so it wasn't visible to anyone in a boat. It was an eight-by-ten piece of crap, slapped together with scrap lumber. There was one door, no window, and a black pipe sticking through the roof. My focus returned to the secret beach, and rage twisted my gut. They'd trashed the place. There were so many empty beer bottles and cans that I thought the Thugs must shed them like a mutt sheds fur. There was other assorted junk, lawn chairs, and a fire pit.

"You think he's in there?" Grizz caught up to me.

Approaching the shack would be a perfect time for a double cross. Grizz didn't notice as I took the .38 from my pocket. I turned and pressed it to his stomach. "Hand me your gun."

He looked down at my gun and back up at me. "Hey, I brought you out here. Don't you trust me?"

"Give me your piece."

"Fuck." He reached into his jacket and removed his cannon.

I took it and returned the .38 to my pocket. With my other hand, I pointed at the pipe extending up from the roof. "A chimney?"

"Yeah. We got a wood stove in there. But there's no smoke. He might not be here after all."

"You wait here."

"Yeah, yeah, whatever."

I moved close to him. "Let me ask you something."

"What?"

"If you're setting me up, do you want me to take you out with a head shot or a heart shot?"

Without waiting for an answer, I turned and approached the shack. My eyes constantly moved, looking for telltale signs of occupation or movement. My ears picked up my hushed footsteps, Grizz's panting, and the gentle lap of water against the shore. I could smell the lake and traces of burnt wood from the fire pit and perhaps from the woodstove in the shack. Though grateful that there were no windows for my approach to be seen through, there was a little open space between the door jamb and upper part of the door, and I corrected my course so that it kept me out of view.

I pressed my back against the wall and looked to make sure Grizz stayed put. He gave me a feminine little wave, and I rolled my eyes. I started toward the door, all the while listening for movement. I paused, studying the latch so I wouldn't have to fiddle with it. It was the kind they sold at hardware stores for gates. Grabbing the handle, I pressed the latch, pausing when there was a click. After ten seconds, I pushed the door open and took a step from the wall, the .44 trained on the doorway, or what one of my firearm instructors referred to as the "fatal funnel." As I stood to the left of the doorway, I took little steps to the right, the gun at the ready, clearing the room a bit at a time. The room was full of murky shadows, so I watched for movement more than anything. Once I cleared the door, I stepped in and swept the area, gun ready.

There was a smell of stale piss, body odor, and trash. Wood was stacked near a wood stove, and a twin-size mattress sat on the floor, upon which a motionless body lay face up.

I aimed at the figure and shouted out the door. "You have a flashlight, Grizz?"

A few moments later, he was peeking in. "A small one on my key-chain."

"See who's on the mattress."

His keys jingled, and there was a small cone of light. He stepped in and illuminated Preach, naked, eyes wide, and with a round hole centered just above his brow.

Chapter 32
Summer of '59

I woke to something soft pressing into my face and a flaring pain at the back of my head that was ten times worse than before. Blinking failed to bring my sight into focus, so I closed my eyes and took a deep breath. When I reopened them, a fleshy button danced before me and pushed against my cheek.

"Go on. Suck it, you little whore."

"What?" I leaned my head back, and the simple movement produced nausea. I thought I'd vomit.

"Lick it, Bloom."

My eyes focused, and I blurted, "What the hell?"

Winthrop, half-naked, made little hops from one booted foot to another. Blood from where I'd clubbed him etched his forehead and ran past his nose and down his chin. Clothed in a T-shirt and a jacket but no pants, he appeared so bizarre that I thought I must be dreaming. I tried to push his tiny dick away as he rubbed it across my lips, but I couldn't lift my hands. They were tied to the chair arms.

Seeing his thing jiggle at me brought back what I'd read in Roscoe's story. "Vincent might be quite the cocksman, but you sure aren't."

He quit his movements and stepped back. "Huh?" Other than my daddy, and a couple of boys I spied on swimming naked at Wallace Lake, I hadn't seen any cocks, but I could tell his was too small, smaller than my little toe. His ball sack was as tight and tiny as two cherry pits. A boy as old as him should be hairy down there, but he was bare.

I nodded at his crotch. "Isn't that little thing supposed to be hard?"

A tangle of expressions crossed his face. Confusion danced with embarrassment, paranoia fused with shame, and it was all mixed with cold fury. Winthrop let loose and swung an open hand against my head. It wasn't a fist, but it did a number on me.

"Leave her alone." The words were mumbled.

I glanced past Winthrop and saw that Micah Lee and I were each tied to chairs a couple feet apart, facing one another like bound mirror images. Micah Lee looked so damaged I feared that he'd die if he didn't get to a doctor. He slumped in his chair. Blood from a dozen wounds wet his body. I noticed his ankles were no longer tied to the chair legs, and looked at my own wrists. Winthrop had used those ropes to bind me to the arms of my chair.

Winthrop bent to take my right nipple in his mouth. He bit. The pain was electric, like he'd used scissors on my flesh, and I shrieked.

"Stop it!" Micah Lee shouted.

Winthrop did, long enough to turn to him with a grin and then bite my left nipple.

As my scream died, Micah Lee coughed and said, "You know the reason his pecker isn't hard, Charly?"

Winthrop released me and spun.

"Why?" I managed.

"Well, he spent a whole lot of time messing with me when it was just us."

"Shut up," Winthrop growled.

"You think Winthrop's queer for you?"

"Shut up."

"I think ol' Winthrop oughta go hang out at that pervert park down in Charlotte. That'd give him a woody," Micah Lee finished with a pained laugh.

Winthrop roared unintelligible words. His switchblade appeared in his hand. He flicked it open and drove it into Micah Lee's thigh. Micah Lee screamed so pure and high that it pushed me to lose consciousness for a moment. I awoke to vise grips at each side of my head that turned into Winthrop's strong hands. His face was an inch from mine.

"You think I'm playing with you? I'm gonna kill you, but not 'til I hurt you, and then hurt you more, and when I see in your eyes that you know there ain't no hope, then I'll kill you."

Micah Lee tried to speak, coughed, and swallowed. "Winthrop, you're just a dumb punk."

Winthrop gripped the knife handle and twisted. Micah Lee wailed in agony, and his head fell to his chest. Winthrop grinned like he'd done something clever.

Micah Lee coughed, lifted his face, and smiled, which was the bravest thing I'd ever seen. "Bobby told me what your daddy liked to do to you. Want me to tell Charly?"

Winthrop grabbed Micah Lee's little finger and jerked it back, snapping it like a breadstick. Micah Lee's scream was silent, and when it ended, he looked at me through tears.

He moved his lips several times until he said, "Ya see, Winthrop and his daddy would—"

Winthrop pulled a pistol from his jacket pocket, the pistol that Bobby had told us about, the one Micah Lee and I wanted Bobby to borrow so we could shoot it. He put it to the side of Micah Lee's head and pulled the trigger. There was no thunderous bang, just a sad little pop, and my last good childhood friend was gone.

Chapter 33
Autumn of '82

We hiked back to the cars, and Grizz rode with me to a nearby convenience store.

He contemplated Preach's murder and every now and then muttered, "Motherfucker."

Outside the store, I pressed the cold payphone receiver to my ear and called Kit. He was back and relieved to hear from me. I gave him a quick synopsis of what happened. I hung up, and Grizz came out of the store with a couple of Pabst tall boys, draining the first in one long pull. He held out the other to me, which I opened and took a swig from. I handed it back, and he finished it. We got back in my car and drove to the lake to wait for Kit.

After I pulled behind Grizz's car, I handed him his .44. "Probably a good idea to hide this and your stash in your trunk."

"Yeah," he said and went to put his gun and cocaine under the spare tire.

The wail of Kit's siren was heard a full minute before he arrived. Snow fell, and chill gusts blew the flakes about the road. Getting out of the Firebird, I looked out at the field with its growing pockets of white.

Rubbing at his nose as he returned, Grizz muttered, "I hate snow."

Kit pulled up behind me, his flashing lights diffused by the storm. He got out and walked to us, never taking his eyes from Grizz. Since I had already told him the CliffsNotes version of what happened over the phone, he took charge without asking a thing.

Kit pointed at Grizz and said, "You wait here. When my deputies arrive, show them the way." He turned to me without waiting for a reply. "Take me to the shack."

We crossed the field at twilight, though with the storm, it had seemed like a perpetual twilight for the past few hours.

"Why the hell are you going off in the woods with Grizz? Alone? Christ, Charly. Have you forgotten what happened with Preach and Weasel?"

"Of course not. I came armed. What'd you find out about the rag?"

"Couldn't get results right away, but the lab boys say they'll rush it."

We stopped at Preach's motorcycle, and after a minute, we continued. Though it was darker in the trees, they cut the wind, and there wasn't as much snow. Since I led, Kit handed me his flashlight and followed until we got to the secret beach.

"I'm not familiar with this part of the lake," he said, taking his flashlight back.

"I used to come all the time with Micah Lee and Bobby. It was secret and beautiful. Those assholes trashed it."

Kit directed the flashlight beam to the shack. "That's it?"

"Yeah."

Kit entered, and I stood by the door as he turned the flashlight around the small room and then fixed on Preach's corpse. He scanned down the body.

"Odd," Kit mumbled.

"What?"

"All his tattoos. A lot are the traditional things—roses, daggers, skulls. Mixed in are things that would be better scrawled on a bus station bathroom wall, and then there are Bible passages."

I moved beside him, and he pointed at the open Bible on Preach's chest.

"Leviticus 19:28," he read.

"That scripture means you're not supposed to get tattoos."

"Why would he have a tattoo that says don't get tattooed?"

"Preach was crazy. He claimed that God set him on Earth to intentionally commit sins so as to demonstrate to the rest of us what we should not do."

"Really?"

"Seemed earnest about it too."

"Great job if you can get it," Kit muttered and focused on the bullet hole. There were two tracks of dried blood. One went up his forehead into his hair. The second trailed down past the inside of his left eye, his nose, and off his cheek.

"Small caliber," I said.

Kit lifted Preach's head enough to see there was no exit.

"Let me see your flashlight." I aimed it at his leg. "Look."

Another Bible had been tattooed on his upper thigh. At the top of the page was a childish rendering of an erect penis. Below that were three passages—Matthew 18:6, Luke 17:2, Mark 9:42.

I handed the flashlight back to Kit and said, "Give me a pen and some paper."

He took a small notebook and a pen from a shirt pocket and handed me the pen. He ripped a sheet from the notebook, and I copied the scriptures.

"What do you think those mean?"

I shook my head. "Considering the picture at the top of the page, something to do with adultery or lust. I'll check it out." I pushed the paper into a pocket and gave Kit his pen.

"So walk me through this again," Kit said. "Grizz called you because..."

"I went to their house looking for Beason. He wasn't there, so I talked to Grizz, told him that there'd been another abduction, and I suspected Beason. If Beason was a full patched Thug, Grizz wouldn't have said anything, but since he's only a prospect, Grizz showed me some kiddie porn that Beason's into."

"Ah shit."

"He told me that Beason damaged their shop truck, claimed he'd hit a guard rail. He had it last night, and when I talked to Peter Cordis, he gave a similar description of the truck, down to the lettering on the side. Grizz talked to someone who saw Preach's motorcycle out by the tree line. He said Preach and Beason were tight, a mentor-and-protégé type of thing, and since this is a party spot for the Thugs, he deduced that Beason was with Preach and the Acosta girl out here in the shack."

Kit moved the light around the room and then walked to the corner nearest the woodstove, where there was a pile of clothing. He examined each piece and set it down next to the original pile. He went through what I presumed were Preach's jeans, leather jacket, and sleeveless denim jacket with his patch on it.

Kit stopped and mumbled, "Dear God, help us." He held up a child's pajama bottoms. Next, he brought up the top. He picked up a black shirt, which he moved to the other pile.

"Wait," I said.

"What?"

I grabbed at one of the shoulders of the shirt and pulled it away from the other. On the breast, in gold lettering, it said Le Bistro.

We went out and waited for Grizz, who arrived with four deputies and Special Agent Caputo in tow. Kit stepped to the door of the shack, pointed at Grizz, and said, "Come in for a minute."

Grizz's eyes widened in surprise.

Kit aimed the flashlight at Preach's head. "A small caliber. Mean anything to you?"

Grizz nodded, his lips twisting into a scowl. "Luke has an old Colt .22."

Kit shoved Grizz toward the door, and we stepped out.

"Van," Kit called, "Mr. Grizz here is going to be agreeable and help us out, aren't you?"

Grizz looked at him suspiciously. "Yeah, sure."

"Good. Grizz is going to ride in the back of your car. Take Special Agent Caputo with you." He looked to Caputo, who nodded. "Have Willits and Franklin meet you at the Thugs' house. Search the place and property, and see if Beason is there."

"Come on, Sheriff. He ain't there."

Kit removed his hat. "We're going to get a look at your house, either willingly or with a search warrant."

"Fine," Grizz said.

"Van, Caputo, come with me a minute," Kit said and, with an imperceptible move of the eyes, indicated I should join them. We got into the shack, and Caputo looked down at the corpse with an unpleasant expression. "I want you to give Grizz a little surprise," Kit whispered.

Van grinned. "I love surprises."

"After you search the house, put him in the backseat of the cruiser, and announce that you want to look at their repair shop." Kit looked at me, and we smiled at one another. "Make it sound like you guys are going to breeze through to make sure Beason isn't there. But leave him locked in the backseat. Where will they find the goods, Charly?"

"They have a living room area just off the garage bay," I whispered. "Move the sofa, and you'll find a trapdoor down to the basement and at least a kilo of cocaine."

That got Caputo's attention.

"Then bring him in and lock him up, along with any other Thugs you come across," Kit said.

As we stepped from the shack, I figured Caputo was already scheming on how to take credit for the drug bust.

Van walked up to Grizz. "Ready, big man?"

Caputo grabbed Grizz by his meaty upper arm. "Let's go."

Grizz called back in raspy good cheer, "See ya, Charly."

"Later, Grizz." I wondered how cheerful he'd be if he knew the shit storm he was in for.

As they walked away, I heard Grizz tell Caputo, "Let go of my arm, or I'll snap you in two like a Popsicle stick."

I grinned when Caputo dropped his hand.

Kit called one of the deputies over and introduced us. "Everett here is a deacon at Good News Baptist."

"That's my old church," I said.

"So I hear. Come join us Sunday."

"Maybe I will."

Kit put a hand on his shoulder. "Everett, you still carry a Bible in your squad car?"

"Always."

"Would you run and get it for us?"

"Right away."

"Timson, get in there with your flashlight. The body is on the mattress. There's a pile of clothes in a corner. Don't touch anything, but see if there's anything else of interest." Kit turned to me. "Come on."

We walked to the lake's edge and stood in silence. The wind made small waves, and the snow had picked up. The swirling flakes were hypnotizing as they blew about until they hit the lake and melted.

"Things are coming to a head," Kit said.

"Feels like it," I agreed.

"How do you think it went down?"

I pulled my knit cap lower on my head. "Beason got away from me and went home for the truck. He knew about Gili Acosta—maybe he's been stalking her, already picked her out. He goes there late, takes her, and brings her out here. Preach is supposed to be lying low at a Thugs chapter far away. Instead, he wants revenge for me kicking his ass, so he comes back to Temperance and hides out here in the shack. Maybe he helped Beason get Gili Acosta or was already here when Beason showed up with the girl. They may have been in on it together since the beginning. Either way, they had some kind of disagreement, and Beason shot Preach.

"I sure hope I'm wrong, but with Gili Acosta's pajamas mixed in with Preach's clothes and Beason's shirt..." As much as I didn't want to finish my thought, I went ahead and said, "I think she was raped."

Kit made a face like he tasted something bad. "I hope you're wrong too."

We headed back to the shack.

"Now what?" I asked.

"Now we wait for the coroner and start an intense search for Beason." Kit looked at me. "You did good, Charly. You can head on back to the inn. We'll take it from here." A particularly strong gust blew in our faces, and Kit shoved his hands in his jacket pockets. "At least one of us will be warm."

"Yeah, okay. After Everett gets back with his Bible."

I perched on the bricks that ringed the fire pit and hunched low, trying to stay warm. Finally, Everett jogged through the trees and held up a well-thumbed Bible. "Here ya go, Sheriff."

Kit took it, and I stood next to him. "Thanks, Everett. What are those passages again?" he asked me.

I fished the paper out of my pocket. "The first is Matthew 18:6." I took the flashlight while Kit turned through the pages.

"...but whoever causes one of these little ones who believe in me to sin, it would be better for him to have a great millstone fastened around his neck and to be drowned in the depth of the sea."

A sick feeling settled in the pit of my stomach, and I looked at my scrap of paper. "Luke 17:2."

Kit turned pages and read, "It would be better for him if a millstone were hung around his neck and he were cast into the sea than that he should cause one of these little ones to sin."

My mouth was dry as I said, "Mark 9:42."

Kit flipped the Bible pages. "Whoever causes one of these little ones who believe in me to sin,it would be better for him if a great millstone were hung around his neck and he were thrown into the sea." Kit closed the Bible with a thump, and we stood without speaking.

I cleared my throat. "Considering his screwed-up belief that he's supposed to sin to show others what not to do, I'd say he considered that Biblical confirmation to molest children."

Chapter 34
Summer of '59

Did I scream, or was the high-pitched note blaring inside my head? My mental newsreel replayed Micah Lee's death in slow motion, and I saw the pistol inches from his ear. Winthrop's finger tightened on the trigger, and the hammer fell. My imagination took liberties and showed the bullet leave the barrel to penetrate Micah Lee's head. It didn't look violent, more like a magic trick, until the bullet exited the other side, taking cranial matter with it. Time froze, and everything stopped. Bits of skull, brain, and sprays of blood hung in midair. And then Micah Lee was there, my Micah Lee, whole and healthy in a goofy plaid shirt, rolled-up jeans, and sewer-stained shoes. He sat in the same chair as dead Micah Lee, both occupying the same space until my Micah Lee stood, looked at his beaten body, and shook his head.

"Can you believe this, Charly? Damn, I don't want to be dead."

"I don't want you dead either." Tears and snot flowed down my face. "Are you really here, Micah Lee? Or is it because my head is so busted up?"

"I imagine I'm all in your head." He strolled around the chair, studying his corpse. "There aren't any do-overs this time. Damn." He paused and looked at me. "You can win, you know."

"How?"

"Jeezum, Charly. This is Winthrop we're talking about, dumb as can be."

"Dumb as a stump post," I agreed.

Micah Lee grinned. "Dumb as a box of rocks."

266

I smiled back. "Dumb as a sack of hammers."

"Dumb as a clump of hair in a clogged drain."

"Dumb as a mule and twice as ugly."

We laughed hard, and I closed my eyes.

"What the hell are you laughing at?" Winthrop stared at me like I'd just blasted the trouser-trumpet during a funeral.

"Micah Lee?" I muttered and saw the sad, slumped form of a dead boy with a knife in his thigh.

"You are crazy, aren't ya, Bloom?"

Winthrop looked at the corpse, and I tugged against my restraints. The knots binding my wrists had been rushed and were large and clumsy. The right one wasn't tight at all. In fact, it was loose. I pulled again, and my hand half slid out.

Placing his hand over the exit wound in Micah Lee's head, Winthrop rubbed it in a circular motion and then rubbed over Micah Lee's chest and stomach, smearing blood like a child finger-painting.

Winthrop was oblivious as I tugged my right hand free. Standing on shaky legs, I grabbed the knife in Micah Lee's thigh and yanked it out, producing a sucking sound as the blade pulled from meat and muscle. Winthrop made a strangled noise and came at me. I brought the knife up to my left shoulder and swung it into his thigh in almost the same place he'd planted it in Micah Lee's leg. Winthrop's scream rivaled an opera singer, and he collapsed.

I thought it was my anger that kept me focused as I gripped the knife and sawed through the rope binding my other wrist. "Shut up, Winthrop. You sound like a little girl." I started to run from the room, but my body didn't cooperate, and I ended up on the floor, the knife clattering away and disappearing into shadows. This was it. I doubted I could get up before unconsciousness closed in, so I closed my eyes and surrendered.

Then I heard a familiar sound and put my ear flat on the cold concrete. Just like I had at Town Center Park, I could hear the inner workings of the world. Whether it was because I was below ground or due to my physical condition, the noise was louder—gears meshing, chains rattling, clockworks clicking, pendulums whooshing. I wasn't sure what it meant, just that it was important. Another sound, my heartbeat, joined with the inner workings, beating randomly and out of sync. Winthrop cried and moaned, and I knew that he'd come for me soon. Still, I lay, listened, and discovered that the inner workings ran at their own beautiful rhythm. And then my heartbeat found that same rhythm and merged with it. In tempo, I found the strength to stand and run from the room.

I did a good job retracing my way to the stairwell and went up them as fast as my unsteady legs would allow, escaping darkness for daylight. Up on the first floor, I turned in a direction I hoped would lead to an exit, but stopped. If I ran out into the woods, I'd be in the same fix I was in earlier, and I didn't like my odds of getting away from him in the daytime. An idea bubbled in my brain, and I figured that since I'd been leaving my fate in the hands of ghosts, real or imagined, I might as well fly by the seat of my pants once more.

I returned to the stairway and heard Winthrop cussing and bustling around below me. "How ya feeling, Winthrop?" I yelled down the steps. "Bet your leg hurts plenty."

"You're dead. Do you know that?" From his tone, I could tell he said it through clenched teeth. "But when I get you, dyin' is going to be a long time coming. I'm going to—" There was a crash, and I pictured him falling in the darkness below.

I laughed, trying to make it as bright and cheerful and loud as I could. Then I went up the stairs. Winthrop started to climb, so I bypassed the second floor and continued up to the third. At the top of the stairs, my stumbling presence scared birds nesting in the ruins. The stairway opened to a large room that was a couple thousand square feet, maybe more. The roof had collapsed long ago. Decades of rain and snow had poured in, rotting the floor and the floors below it. It might even be where the water in the basement leaked from. Besides collapsed roofing, the debris in the room included bricks from crumbling walls and glass shards from broken windows. Across the room was another door, but there was a massive hole in the floor about two-thirds of the way to it. That must be where the teenagers had fallen through in the forties, and if the floor had been bad then, a decade's passage would make it much more treacherous.

My half-baked scheme seemed pretty stupid then, but Winthrop, huffing and cursing, was closer, so I started across, plotting my way where the floor looked most solid. I made for piles of bricks, figuring if the floor could hold them, they could take an additional ninety pounds.

I was halfway across when Winthrop said, "Hey, Bloom."

I turned and saw him aiming the pistol at me. There was an explosion, and then I was on my back, staring up at the sky. The realization that I'd been shot arrived with pain. It felt like my chest had blown up. I couldn't breathe, couldn't move, and I lay there in agony. For whatever reason, Winthrop stayed by the stairs. My breath returned in shallow gasps, and I lifted my head.

Winthrop grinned. "I'm a pretty damn good shot, ain't I?"

I tried looking at my wound, but it was too high on my chest. From where the pain was centered, I thought he'd gotten me on the left side, near my shoulder. My left arm was useless, so I rolled to the right and used my right hand to push myself into a sitting position. Winthrop aimed, fired, and missed, hitting a pile of bricks behind me. I scooted back on my butt, screaming when he fired and missed again. I got to the bricks and climbed the waist-high pile then rolled painfully down the other side, putting the bricks between us.

Panting, I looked around for an escape route. The door was still a ways off. I'd be a target for Winthrop if I tried for it, and from the way I felt, I'd be a slow-moving target. Plus, I'd have to circumvent the hole in the floor, which would give him that much more opportunity to shoot me. The nearby wall had windows, but a jump from the third floor would kill me.

"Bet your chest feels worse than my leg, huh, Bloom?"

I crawled a little up the pile of bricks, peeking over them. Winthrop, with a bloody face and leg and a nub of genitalia, fired, sending up shards of brick.

"I got one more shot, Bloom. I'll save that for when I'm done with you. *Bang!* Right in the eye."

I figured that if he was saving that bullet for later, then maybe I could make it to the door, so I struggled to stand. For a couple of seconds, everything around me swayed. I regained some balance and knew I'd been wrong. I wouldn't be able to run for the door after all, or anywhere else. The long night, the injuries—I was spent. Staggering on trembling legs, left arm hanging useless, I'd soon be too weak from blood loss to do anything but die. If I was going to do something, now was the time. Acting as if dizziness had gotten the best of me, I half collapsed on the bricks and then pushed up again, relishing how the rough surface of a brick felt in my right hand. Winthrop couldn't see it because that hand was hidden by the brick pile.

"You ain't lookin' too good, Bloom."

"Not feeling great, neither," I answered weakly. "I'm done, Winthrop. I don't have anything left in me. You win."

He stood there, suspicion working through that peanut he called a brain.

"Hell, if you were close enough, you'd see it in my eyes, Winthrop. Isn't that what you said? You wanted to see surrender in my eyes? It's plain to see, if you get close enough."

He still didn't move.

"Goddamn you, Winthrop, if you're too much of a coward to come get me, at least use that one bullet and put me out of my misery."

"I ain't a coward."

"Prove it, you chicken shit!" I screamed at him, and then I swayed to the right and almost fell.

Winthrop smiled that evil grin of his and started toward me. "You're gonna wish you'd kept your mouth shut, Bloom. I got things I'm gonna do to you that'll take hours and hours, if you don't die on me first."

He got closer, and I prayed that the floor would open underneath him and gravity would suck him to a crashing death. No such luck. He limped on, gun hanging at his side, describing in detail what he had planned. I stood still, head down, gripping the brick like a baseball. When he was twenty feet from me, I stepped back with my right foot, moving into a throwing stance.

"Whoa, Bloom. You gonna fall on your ass?" He chuckled.

At fifteen feet, I lifted my head, gauging distance and trajectory. At ten feet, I wound up like a one-armed pitcher, and that was when Winthrop saw the brick. I hurled it before he got the gun up, and it struck him square on his face. He spun to my left, and I got another brick and pitched hard and low, taking him on the knee of his injured leg. He didn't fall, I'd give him that, but he stumbled farther to my left.

I looked carefully at Winthrop, staggering, eyes squinched shut, gun up and pointing at nothing. And in this mental snapshot, I saw how the hole in the floor was just a few feet behind him.

"Now, Charly. Do it now." I don't know if it was Micah Lee's voice or my imagination, but it got me to move.

I charged around bricks and sped headlong toward Winthrop. At impact, I turned my head to the left and ducked, leading with my right shoulder. It felt like I'd struck a tree, and fresh agony surged from my wounds. I kept pumping my legs, charging forward while Winthrop hit at me with his free hand. The gun discharged its final bullet, and a line of fire opened on my forehead, but I kept on, even as blood ran into my eyes, until I slipped and fell to my knees short of my goal.

With the remainder of my strength, I wiped my eyes and looked up as Winthrop regained his balance inches from the hole. He didn't appear much better than I felt. The first brick had smashed his nose, and blood flowed. He blinked his vision clear, laughed in triumph, and disappeared as the floor collapsed.

I managed to crawl on my right elbow and knees and peered over the edge. Blood from my forehead fell into empty space, through the holes in the second and first floors, to the basement, baptizing Winthrop's body. His limbs twisted in broken angles, and the shaft of a textile machine impaled his chest. My breath became shallow, and my vision went out of focus, so I pushed from the edge and curled up on the floor, waiting to die. I heard someone say my name.

My eyes focused, and looking up, I beheld one more ghost, blood on his face and clothes. "Bobby? I'm so sorry," I managed before falling headlong into unconsciousness.

Chapter 35
Autumn of '82

I hiked up the path, through the woods, and across the snow-covered field. Grizz's GTO sat by the road, parked in front of my car. I had to give Grizz credit. He led me to the certainty that Copycat was Beason. Grizz helped the investigation big time, and if I got the opportunity, I'd say so at his arraignment.

I shut myself inside the snow cocoon of my Firebird and turned the ignition. It didn't care much for cold weather and struggled at first, warming up to a low-timbre idle. I switched on the wipers, and after several passes, the snow brushed off. I put the car in gear, made a U-turn, and headed back to town. The rear-wheel drive was awful in this kind of weather, so I took it slowly.

The steep incline of the Temperance Inn driveway got the best of me. I attempted it twice, but both times, the Firebird's wheels couldn't get traction on the snow, and the tail end slid back and forth. So I parked at the diner and hiked back. I wouldn't have been surprised if the weather reached blizzard conditions later in the night.

I figured I'd fall right to sleep once I got in the warmth of the bed under the down comforter. It didn't happen. My mind kept replaying the events of the day, and when I finally considered surrendering and getting up, I fell asleep.

I dreamed of Micah Lee with the Snatcher in the underground room at the old mill. I woke crying. Outside, the wind screamed, and I guessed it was up to gale force. I hoped that Kit and his men were finished out at the crime scene, but that was about all the sympathy

I spared for them before I turned over, clutched the pillow, and read-ied myself for another plunge into slumber land.

As I waited for sleep, I focused on the sound of the wind, its many layers, how it rose in pitch and then dropped, how there was a melody to it. Mixed in with all that, I noticed there was a rhythm as well, pronounced and regular. I wondered if something metallic was blowing against the side of the inn or tapping against the fire es-cape outside my room. It turned into one of those annoying sounds I could almost name, something I couldn't quite remember. Then I thought it was something I'd heard recently. Though I was under a warm layer of bedding, my body went cold, and I gasped as I recog-nized the sound of Grizz's spur tapping against the floor.

"I take it you're awake?" he said.

I played it cool, like there was a drug-running biker king lounging in my bedroom every night. "Anyone ever tell you to knock?"

"You're one to talk. Besides, it's colder than a witch's titty out there. I didn't want to freeze waiting for you to wake up."

It sounded as if he was sitting in the loveseat that was toward the right-side foot of the bed. I wondered how long he'd been there. Slow as to be silent, I began to move out from under my blankets toward the left side of the bed.

"Didn't know you had a key," I said.

I heard the smile in his voice. "Don't need one. I'm a man of many talents." He paused and then conversationally threw out, "Hey, I'm pissed at you."

"Why's that?"

"Because we had a deal. You double-crossed me." He didn't sound all that mad.

"I didn't double-cross you."

"You didn't know that, after they searched my house, they'd move on to the repair shop?"

"I knew, but our deal was that I wouldn't pass on anything you told me. You didn't tell me a thing about cutting drugs at your shop."

"The sheriff told you what they found?"

"I already knew." I got all the blankets and sheet off. The cold was sharp on my flesh. I didn't think there was any way I could get off the bed without the mattress groaning, so I'd wait until the right moment and jump, hoping I pounced instead of tumbled. "See, I had a little chat with your prospect..." I leaped from bed and locked into a fighting stance. *Bring on the fat bastard.*

A light snapped to life. Grizz sat on the loveseat, his hand at the lamp on the table next to it. He wore a shit-eating grin and ground his teeth, his wide eyes glowing like black jewels. I stood my ground, wondering whether to charge or try to get to my weapons.

"I come in peace." He held his leather jacket open, showing me the .44 in the shoulder holster. "If I was coming for you, you'd be got." He took his gun out and flipped it so he was holding the handle out to me. "Shit, you've had this thing so much, I feel like it's mostly yours."

I took it from him.

"Go on, finish your story," Grizz said and ogled me as I put on my robe.

"After talking with Beason—"

"Wait, how much did he tell you?"

I smiled, letting him think that Beason told me everything.

"That little son of a bitch."

"Well, here's what you'll find important. I broke into your shop, looked around, and found the trapdoor leading down to your cutting room. I'm the one who told the sheriff."

"Fuck!"

"So how come you aren't locked up right now?"

He smiled. "I knew something was up. That SBI clown couldn't keep his mouth shut. On the way to the house, he kept saying how we'd look through it and then go to the shop and do a quick sweep to make sure Luke wasn't there. He kept going on about a *quick sweep*. What a dipshit. I knew I was toast. I wasn't sure what to do, but I found a note from Luke that helped me make up my mind."

"A note? Saying what?"

"Saying he's into some shit and needs my help."

"Where is he?"

"We'll get to that. See, back at our house, we have a special mail-box."

"A drop box to hide messages?"

Grizz tapped his nose. "The way shit's been falling, I don't suppose it matters. It's one of the bricks in the fireplace. You can wiggle it out and in, and if we have a message we want to keep between bros, we put it there.

"Anyway, we get to the house. Bones was there and freaked when I told him more cops were on their way. The SBI guy wanted to look around, and he made Bones go upstairs with him. I stayed down with Van. Van went into my bedroom, and I took that time to see if there was anything in the mailbox and found that note from Luke. I knew I was shit out of luck and that they'd find the basement at the shop. I decided to do what I could to shave off some hard time. While Van was back in my room, I snuck out and took Bones's truck. So once again, I'm going to help you get Luke, and we're going to bring him in together."

"We tried that."

"It's different this time."

"How so?"

Grizz leaned forward. "I've already seen him—and the girl. She's still alive."

"What?" He'd seen her and left her with him. I shouted angrily, "Why didn't you save her?"

"I would have if I could have. He had his gun and kept that little girl in front of him. He wouldn't come out all the way. I never had a chance at him."

"All the way out of where?"

"To learn that, you have to come with me now."

I pushed his gun into his mitt-sized hand and got dressed, ignoring him when he waved a dollar bill and said he'd slip it into my panties if I came closer. He watched with approval as I opened my lock box and got my gun, flat sap, and KA-BAR knife. Once everything was in place, I patted it all to make sure they were secure, and I felt something in my back pocket. It was the butterfly knife that Dub gave me.

I was ready to rock.

Chapter 36
Summer of '59

I woke later when someone shouted, "She's alive!"

Handsome George Crow cradled me in his arms as he rushed out of the old mill. I tried to explain what happened, but it came out as garbled nonsense.

"Shhh. It's okay, Charly. We've got you. You're going to be fine."

My eyes focused, and I saw that he was crying, and that set me to crying too. Someone ran up to us. It took a moment to recognize Roscoe Gunn. I was touched that he'd come.

"Shot me in the head," I mumbled.

"What?" Roscoe asked. "Hold on a moment, George."

Handsome George stopped, and I thought about how content I felt in his arms.

Roscoe examined my head. "It's just a scratch, Charly. The bullet grazed you." Thinking I couldn't hear, he whispered to Handsome George, "A half inch more, and it'd be over."

I accepted the news with the same lack of scrutiny as I'd given the ghosts.

The gate was open. Handsome George and Roscoe had either gotten the key or used a bolt cutter. We hurried down the brick drive. I couldn't hold up my head anymore, and it fell so that I saw Solomon's van next to Mrs. Whist's car. Solomon was half out the driver's-side window, yelling at Handsome George to hurry. I passed out but woke again in the back of Solomon's van with my head in Handsome George's lap. Roscoe was at my side, holding my hand.

I tried to speak, failed, and tried again with some success. "Solomon?"

From up front, he answered, "We got you, Charly. You're going to be fine."

"Solomon?" I repeated.

"What is it, Charly?"

"I'm not sure I want to be a detective anymore."

MY INJURIES WERE BAD, and the damage to my head was the worst. Three days later, I woke up, but I remained in a hospital bed for eight more days. I was poked and prodded, swabbed and stuck. They'd shaved all my hair, and my head was wrapped in a turban of bandages. For all they did to nurse me to health, there wasn't anything they could do for my broken heart. The deaths of Micah Lee and Bobby had shattered it beyond repair.

The sheriff came to the hospital. Someone, probably Solomon, had told my parents how the sheriff had treated me, and my father refused to leave me alone with him. Sheriff Rysdale didn't bully me with Daddy at my side. I told him everything, except about the ghosts.

When Solomon first visited, all I could do was cry, and he did the best thing possible, which was to hold my hand without empty words of comfort. Handsome George was a regular visitor, as was Roscoe Gunn. I asked questions, but Solomon said that there'd be no discussing unpleasant topics while I was in the hospital. When I got to where I could move about, they allowed me to shuffle solo into the bathroom. My first glimpse in the mirror made me gasp. My head was swollen like a melon. The left side of my face was one big bruise, all purples, browns, and yellows. I had some nasty scratches on my right cheek, but what frightened me were my glazed eyes. They were dull, almost colorless—not my eyes at all.

I was released and taken home. The first thing I did was lie down on my own bed. My father came in and sat beside me. He reached for my face. I think he wanted to stroke it, but it was so beat up that he took my hand instead.

"When you're ready to talk, let me know," he said.

"Do you mind if I talk to Solomon about it?" My question hurt him, I could see, and I wanted to take it back.

"Sure, Charly. I'll give him a call. You just rest now."

It seemed as if I closed my eyes, slept for a moment, and opened them, but I'd really slept almost a full day.

My father was again by my side. "Solomon is out on the porch. Think you can make it?"

I nodded, and he helped me dress and get down the stairs. As we got to the first floor, Mom rushed from the kitchen, hugged me, and gave me a light kiss on my cheek. She went back to the kitchen, and by the time I hobbled out to the porch, she followed with a tray of cookies, a pitcher of iced tea, and two glasses. I sat in the rocker next to Solomon's wheelchair. A couple neighbors strolled by, staring at us like we were circus freaks.

After a few minutes of silence, Solomon spoke. "It's a helluva thing."

I said, "Yeah."

Solomon poured the tea, handed me my glass, and sipped from his. "Can I ask you a question?"

"Sure." I expected him to ask if I was all right, or if Winthrop had raped me, or if I remembered any of it.

Instead he said, "Are you a better person because of Micah Lee and Bobby?"

There was no doubt as to the answer, yet I chewed on the question a full minute. "Yes."

"Then to have them both in your life was a blessing. When you get sad because of what happened, remember that they were a gift to you, Charly Bloom, from God himself."

I wanted to cry but was too tired.

"Are you ready to talk?"

I rocked in my chair and gazed out to the sunny day. "Yes."

"At the hospital, you told Sheriff Rysdale about what happened, about how you'd come up with the sewer theory, snuck out, and everything that happened."

I nodded.

Solomon rolled to the railing and looked out onto the street. "It was Mrs. Leigh who sounded the alarm. She woke with a bad feeling, went to check on Micah Lee, and found his bed empty. She called Sheriff Rysdale, and he called me. I was the one who thought to check on you and Bobby too. With all of you gone, I knew you three were investigating some crazy lead." He wheeled his chair to face me. "Why didn't you tell me?"

Solomon glared at me, his lips twisted into a scowl. I'd never seen him so angry, and it shocked me. But I managed to say, "I was going to, but I wanted to be a hundred percent sure. I was scared the sheriff would yell at me again or maybe worse." I thought to hold back the rest, but I didn't want to lie to Solomon. "And well, we wanted to be the ones who found out who the Snatcher was."

Solomon's expression softened, and he shook his head. He looked out to the street. "Duke Bernard from up Cray's Hill called the sheriff. Said his dog was barking to beat the band. Thinking a bear might have been sniffing around his hens, he got up and saw someone in the distance making off with his dog."

"He's a good dog."

Solomon looked at me and scratched at his beard stubble. "We figured it was you guys and moved our search up there and to the surrounding roads. Devon Littlefield was the one who discovered Ellen

Whist's car down from the old mill at dawn. There was blood in the backseat. He couldn't raise anyone on his walkie-talkie and had to drive back a ways before he could. Handsome George, Roscoe, and I were nearby in the van. We rushed over and found you barely alive, Winthrop dead, and Micah Lee—poor kid." Solomon paused. "The sheriff, some investigators from down in Charlotte, and a couple of SBI agents have been going over the old mill with a fine-tooth comb. That's where Winthrop took the girls, where he killed them. What we don't know yet is what he's done with their bodies."

"Bobby?"

Solomon spun in his chair and rolled up close enough to put his hands on my knees. "Are you sure you want to know right now?"

I nodded.

Solomon took my hand. "Someone found where a manhole cover had been removed, and they found Theresa Goodnight's library book, a lantern, a toy gun—"

"It's a flashlight," I interrupted.

"Well, we found all that and blood. We didn't find Bobby."

Tears came without shame, without sound.

"From what you've told the sheriff and what we've pieced together, we think that Winthrop killed his brother and then went after you and Micah Lee. You got away, but he got Micah Lee. We think that somewhere between there and Hallow's Summit, he hid Bobby's body, probably in the same place he put the girls. The sheriff is confident we'll find them soon."

Sheriff Rysdale's confidence wasn't worth shit.

Chapter 37
Autumn of '82

We went out on the fire escape. The wind ripped the door from my grasp, slamming it against the building. Grizz shut it. There were already several inches of snow on the steps, and I saw the tracks Grizz left coming up. The stairs were slick, so I held on to the banister with both hands as I descended. Grizz clomped down, and his one spur sang *ta-ching* with every other step. Bones's truck was rumbling in the middle of the inn parking lot.

"I left it running so it'll be toasty inside," he said.

The truck was a year or two old, and Grizz said he set it to four-wheel drive. Still, we slid down the driveway into the middle of the street. The snow was thick and wet, and Grizz turned the windshield wipers to their fastest. He pushed a cassette into the player, and Steppenwolf blared from the speakers.

As we drove from the inn, I lowered the volume and said, "Did you do that on purpose?"

"What?"

"Cue the cassette to play 'Snow Blind Friend.'"

He smiled. "Trying to be poignant."

Grizz headed west, and I said, "Tell me where we're going."

He kept his eyes straight ahead, though how he could see anything but churning snow, I didn't know. "Someplace near and dear to you, darling. The old mill."

"They demolished that years ago."

"True. But when I got out there, Luke popped up from the ground like a whack-a-mole. Not all the basement caved in. I think he has her in a room down there."

"You think?"

"I didn't go in, remember? He stayed at the entrance with the girl, holding his .22."

"Is there a plan bouncing around in your head?"

"I told him I was going to get some supplies, come get him, and we'd drive down the mountain and set up shop with another chapter. I pointed out that now is the perfect time to go, that with the storm, the cops won't be out looking for us."

"What about the girl?"

He shook his head in distaste. "He's planning to kill her before we leave."

"Damn it, Grizz. You left her with him?"

"I told you, Luke didn't give me a shot at him. But I did tell him not to do anything to her until I got back." He dropped his voice. "Told him I wanted a piece of her myself. He'll wait."

It was time I took charge. "Park where he can't see us, which, with the storm, won't be too far. You go first. I'll follow close enough to see where you go. If he leads you down to the room, I'll wait a few minutes and follow you in, and we'll take him down."

"Sounds good."

"First and foremost, keep the girl safe."

"If I can. Now shut up. I want to hear 'Hippo Stomp.'" Grizz cranked up the music.

Twenty-three years had passed, and instead of a hot summer, we were in the midst of a blizzard. Still, I felt like I was on my way to revisit the dread and heartache I'd experienced with the Snatcher. The drive turned into a white-knuckle thrill ride over Cray's Hill and Rock Ridge, and the trip up Hallow's Summit felt like the slow climb of a roller coaster right before it plummeted. Grizz parked at the base of the drive leading up to where the old mill used to stand.

"It's blowing even harder up here," I said.

Grizz dropped a meaty hand to my shoulder. "Let's get this peckerwood, save the girl, and be the heroes we deserve to be." Nostalgia kept working at me. What Grizz said reminded me of how Micah Lee, Bobby, and I wanted the same thing with the Snatcher—to save the girls and be heroes.

We opened our doors and stepped into the maelstrom. The wind raced down Hallow's Summit, shrieking and howling and driving the snow sideways. I pulled down my cap and zipped the jacket to my chin. Not wanting anything to encumber my use of weapons, I didn't bring gloves, so I pushed my hands deep in my pockets.

Grizz went up the hill and turned into an indistinguishable shadow. I rushed to follow. Two-thirds of the way up, I slipped and fell to my knees. Wincing, I got up, and Grizz had vanished into the storm. I ran. A couple times, I glimpsed a shape and went that way, not knowing if it was Grizz or the storm creating phantoms out of wind and snow. When I started to worry about getting lost, I found myself at the top of the drive. Going left, I ran into a vertical metal pole, what was left of the chain-link fence that once surrounded the old mill.

With some confidence, I carried on to where the old mill once stood, but a new sound came through the screaming wind. I stopped and listened for several seconds. It was either a crying child or the wind playing a cruel joke. The sound came from my right, on the other side of where the fence once stood. The wind and snow blew in my face. I walked hunched over, hands guarding my eyes as I tried to see. The crying grew louder. She was nearby. I ran into the wind, ignoring the sting to my eyes. The wall of frenzied white broke here and there as I passed shapes that were barely recognizable as trees. I made her out. She was huddled on the ground next to a tree, just a lump until I got close enough to see a frightened girl wrapped in a thin blanket. Terrified eyes watched me approach. I dropped to her side and hugged her, feeling her tremble. At first, I scared her, but then she threw her arms around me and cried. Underneath the blanket, she was naked. The poor thing must've been freezing. I hoped frostbite hadn't set in.

"Come on, sweetie. Let's go."

"I can't," she whimpered. Then I saw the chain. One end encircled the tree trunk and was secured with a padlock. The other end looped around Gili's neck, another lock holding it in place.

"Shit," I muttered, wondering if there were any tools in the back of the truck.

Gili looked at me like she wasn't sure I was real and reached a hand to touch my face. Her gaze traveled over my shoulder, and her expression contorted into raw terror. I glanced back and saw Grizz approach through the blowing snow.

"It's okay, sweetie. He's with me. We're both here to help."

She shook her head vehemently.

I grabbed her shoulders as Grizz moved behind me. "Really, Gili. He's big and scary, but he's okay."

Grizz began to sing, of all the things, and with his hissing voice, it sounded like part of the wind. A new chill grew within me, as cold as the night, as I thought the song was one I knew. Feeling like someone in a jungle who heard the low growl of a tiger behind them, I slowly stood.

Still singing, Grizz grabbed me from behind, lifted me from the ground, and clamped a wet cloth over my face. A strong chemical odor made me gag. I kicked my heels against his shins and knees, but he didn't lessen his grip. His arm encircled me, though I jerked my left arm free. The chemical in the rag made my head spin as I threw elbow punches into his fat. He grunted but held firm. Stars exploded in my vision. He pulled me higher, squeezed me tight, and sang directly in my right ear. Although injury changed his voice, I now knew who was singing. I tumbled into unconsciousness to the accompaniment of The Everly Brothers song, "All I Have to Do Is Dream."

Chapter 38
Autumn of '82

Consciousness came in waves. I woke but couldn't open my eyes, and then I passed out again. Awhile later, I could see but couldn't lift my head, and oblivion returned. I woke and lost consciousness, back and forth, awake and out cold. Each time, I was aware of more—of sitting in a chair, of darkness, of the cold, damp, a concrete floor, of a crying child. And then I was aware of a three-hundred-fifty-pound nightmare crouching at a nearby wall. There were some flickering light sources scattered about, but they were inadequate to illuminate him as he squatted in a patch of shadow. I remembered what happened that moment I slid into unconsciousness, how I grasped his true identity as he sang that song. It was the one we sang to tease Micah Lee whenever he went on about his latest crush. All at once, it felt as if someone punched my stomach from the inside, and I threw up. I tried puking to the left, but some ended up on my naked thigh.

"A side effect of my knockout recipe. It'll pass."

"Bobby?" I managed.

He lifted his obese form and stood but stayed in the gloom. "Took you long enough."

"How did you—how?"

"It's easy to fool the willing."

I felt awful, sicker than sick. "What was on that rag?"

He took a step closer, his spur sounding like a blade, and though his body stayed in shadow, his face was illuminated in wavering light.

"My own mixture. Mostly chloroform and formalin, a dash of gasoline, and a couple of other chemicals added to the mix."

I vomited again.

"Chloroform works but takes too damn long. This'll put a kid right out. You fought it longer than I thought. Winthrop liked to punch them, but that wasn't reliable."

My head dipped and nodded like a ceramic bobble-head doll. Bobby had dragged me down to one of the remaining basement rooms. It was smaller than the one Winthrop used so long ago. A few candles were placed around me, but farther in the dark were indistinct forms and shapes, and I heard Gili crying softly. I sat, hands tied behind the chair-back and ankles bound to the chair legs. The bastard had taken off my clothes, and I was freezing.

As his chemical bomb left my system, the significance of Bobby, alive, intensified. "Bobby," I moaned then cried like a heartbroken school girl. Behind the beard, behind the fat, and in his eyes, I saw Bobby Whist. He was my childhood collaborator in mischief, my confidant in all secrets. I felt more comfortable with him than anyone, including Micah Lee. Bobby accepted me for being me because I accepted him for being him.

"Bet this is a real déjà vu for you, Charly."

"I thought you were dead." I stated the obvious. "I thought Winthrop—"

"Killed me? My own brother? Nah. We just fooled you. Fooled everyone." He stepped from the shadow. My gun was tucked in his belt next to a small-caliber pistol and my flat sap. My clothes were piled on the floor. Bobby picked them up in one hand and tossed them behind me. Reaching into a back pocket, he took out my KA-BAR knife and dropped to his knees. He pushed my legs apart and dumped a pile of cocaine on the chair seat between them. Like a chef dicing onions, he used the KA-BAR to chop and shape the coke into a thick line. Closing one nostril with a finger, he pushed his head into my thighs and snorted up half. He repeated it with his other nostril. After a second, he jumped up, electrified, and dragged a chair closer.

In a psychotic Ricky Ricardo impersonation, he said, "Lucy, I got some 'splainin' to do." He set the chair a couple of feet from me and straddled it backward. "Let me tell you what really happened back in 1959.

"You know Daddy was a piece of shit, and Mama climbed into a bottle to get away from him. She was a comatose drunk, and Daddy was a mean drunk. Me, I'm a happy drunk. Life is grand and everyone is my friend—well, unless someone pisses me off. Okay, I admit I do enjoy kicking ass when I've had a few. So maybe I am my daddy's boy. Hell, I bear his mark, scars on my back from his belt. But no matter what I got, Winthrop got worse. Daddy marked him with his belt, too, but also with electrical cords, clothes hangers, his open hand, and closed fists. I don't know why Winthrop made Daddy so angry. A psychiatrist might say he was transferring his guilt about raping his boy into anger at the boy he raped. There, I said it. The cat's out of the bag and turned into the elephant in the room. When Daddy came home drunk and pissed off, and Winthrop had done some misdeed, real or imagined, Daddy would take Winthrop out to his shed in the backyard. That's where he stowed all his tools, fertilizers, and as we discovered, where he kept his dirty magazines and pistol. I'd sometimes sneak out and go listen at the shed door. First off, Daddy would cuss Winthrop, shouting at him to take off his shirt. Then the whipping began, each crack answered by a cry. It was different for me. He only punished me in the house, not the shed. I suppose I should be thankful for that.

"Another difference was Daddy would tell Winthrop, 'Take them pants off, boy.' Other times, I'd hear him say things like, 'Don't you tell nobody, 'cause we're blood, and blood sticks together.'

"There'd be grunts and mumbling and Winthrop crying. I was mystified as to how he could wail on Winthrop's butt with no smack.

I picked the lock one time and got an eyeful of what Daddy was doing to him. He raped Winthrop, and did so until the night he was called out to work on a power line and was so drunk he electrocuted his sorry ass.

"I ain't going to lay all the blame on Daddy. It was obvious that Winthrop was different. Lots of folks said he was stupid, but that's because they didn't know how devious he could be. He had a bad temper. He didn't sleep much, two hours a night, maybe three. I'd wake and hear him through the walls, pacing his room and muttering. There was one more peculiarity to Winthrop. He had a kid's dick. No shit. Even at seventeen, you'd swear he had the dick of a five-year-old. I've looked into it over the years, done some research, and there are several medical conditions that can explain it. Considering his other peculiarities, I think Winthrop suffered from something called Prader-Willi Syndrome, which covers his tiny dick, his rage, what some might call his borderline retardation, and why he couldn't sleep.

"When Daddy took the dirt nap, I was hoping Mama would get off the bottle, but she was already a boozing zombie. That was when Winthrop began to flex his freedom, and instead of pacing his room at night, he'd go out and have adventures. He'd tell me about things he'd seen peeping into people's windows, about vandalizing cars and property, killing cats and dogs, all kinds of stuff. Winthrop found Daddy's stash of dirty magazines and looked at those things day and night. Sometimes, I'd find him with his pants down to his ankles, studying those pictures, and pulling on that nubby excuse for a cock. He'd yank and twist and jerk and pinch, and that thing would stay just as small and loose as a grub worm.

"I told you that Daddy liked to put it to Winthrop. Combine that with Prader-Willi, and I think by the time he was seventeen, he was trying to show himself, and in a convoluted way, everyone else, that he was a straight, manly, heterosexual male. But our father taught him sex was rape. And Winthrop had the intellect of a child, the emotions of a child, and the genitals of a child, so because of all that, he chose children to be his lovers.

"When summer break started in '59, and we were all out at Wallace Lake, celebrating, Winthrop was hiding behind a tree, watching Sarah Mundy play in her yard. He later told me that when that thing flew over, he knew. What everyone took as a UFO or meteor, Winthrop took as a sign that it was time he got to work.

"Two weeks later, he put a ladder up against the Mundy house, crept through her window, and took her out to the old mill, where he tried to rape her. He couldn't get it up and got so frustrated that he beat her to death with a brick."

Chapter 39
Autumn of '82

"Huh?" Bobby grunted and was silent a minute before saying, "I'll ask." Bobby looked at me. "So what do you think?"

The sting of chemicals made my voice hoarse. "What your father did was evil, but what Winthrop did to those girls, what you're doing to girls now, perpetuates it."

"Ah, the curse of the continuing cycle." He chuckled.

"None of this is funny, Bobby."

"I find it downright hilarious."

"Why didn't you tell someone?"

Stalking over, he put a hand on each of my thighs and brought his face inches from mine. His fingers dug into my flesh as he shouted, "Because he's my brother!"

Though the chemical taste lingered, I'd shaken the mental effects. I knew Gili's fate and mine, and I knew there was more he wanted to share. The math was simple—the more he talked, the more time before he killed us.

"I want to know," I said, and he returned to his chair.

"The day after you, me, and Micah Lee looked for Sarah Mundy, Winthrop came and got me. Said he wanted to show me something. He loaded a pick, a shovel, and a bag of lime from Daddy's shed into the trunk and drove me out to the old mill. Imagine my surprise when he proudly pointed to the bloody body lying on the concrete floor. Sure, I'd known Winthrop had a few loose screws, but it was then that I knew just what he was capable of. He was full of pride as he knelt and poked at her, pinched her dead flesh as he gave me a blow-by-blow account. In his version, it was her fault he couldn't get it up, and she deserved what she got. Winthrop made me touch her. She was so cold. She stared at nothing, fear frozen on her face, her skull cracked open. He kissed her, and then he made me do the same, forcing my head down, pushing my mouth against her dead lips, laughing at me when I puked my guts up.

"He wanted me to help get rid of her body, and we argued about it. At one point, I threatened to tell on him, but he said that I couldn't, that because we were blood, I had to help him. Finally, he swore that he wouldn't kill any more girls if I helped bury her. We rolled her into an old tarp, carried her out to the car, and put her in the trunk.

"Funny that it took twenty-three years for anybody to find that grave. Winthrop had seen an old gangster movie where they got rid of bodies by dumping lime on them, so we poured some over her and filled in the hole. Afterward, he said he felt like an outlaw, like John Dillinger or Billy the Kid. I just felt sick. I kept rubbing at my lips, trying to get rid of her taste.

"After Daddy died, Winthrop and I spent a lot of time in his shed. Like I said, that's where we found his porn stash, but we also found maps of Temperance that Daddy used working for the city. One set was of the sewer system. I guess that was when Winthrop started planning on the next girl. Remember Sheriff Rysdale having the town meeting with all the kids? Winthrop told me later that day that he had a joke he was going to play on the sheriff to make him look like an idiot. He wouldn't tell me what it was, said it'd be funnier to just show me.

"The next day, we parked out on the county road and hiked through the sewers to the park. We came up and waited. We saw her coming with her books. Winthrop acted like we were just cutting through the woods, going in the opposite direction, and me, I wanted to shout at her to turn around and run. I think she saw that in my

expression when we got close enough, but before she could do anything, Winthrop popped her good, and she dropped. Winthrop told
me to get rid of the books, and I shoved them under a big rock. Then
he changed his mind and told me to give him one for a souvenir. He
dropped the girl into the drain and put a bunch of leaves and stuff
on the grate, and we climbed in after her and slid the grate into place.
He carried her through the sewers until we got to the car. That was
about the time Winthrop found Daddy's gun in a box in the shed under a bunch of his tools. He tied her to a tree and used her for target
practice. He stood too far away and missed her every time. He handed me the gun and told me to reload it. While I did that, he took half
a dozen steps closer to her. For a minute, while I stood behind him, I
thought about putting the gun to his head and pulling the trigger. I
could have ended it all right then. I'd have saved Theresa Goodnight.
But I didn't. That night, we put her in the hole with Sarah Mundy
and a fresh dusting of lime. He said he'd only done it to make the
sheriff look like an idiot, and he promised me, again, that he wouldn't
kill any more girls.

"But of course, there was Lily Branch. Don't know if you remember or not, but that morning I walked with you and Micah Lee to
church, I met Winthrop up the street. He told me what he had in
mind and how I had to help because if he got caught, I'd be in trouble
too. He was right. I knew about the other two and never told anyone,
never tried to help them. I remember being numb as he parked in the
back of the parking lot, where it swung around behind the church.
Everyone was praying and singing, and we hung around outside the
girls' bathroom window. We watched Lily come in and go into a stall,
and I realized I was kind of looking forward to it. We slipped in,
and Winthrop moved me in front of the stall door and pantomimed
throwing a punch. I shook my head no, but he gave me a look that
said he'd kick my ass if I didn't. As soon as she opened the door, I let
fly with a fist. Trouble was, I didn't knock her out. She screamed. It

was loud, and I was sure we'd get caught, but everyone upstairs was singing and didn't hear. Lily kept screaming, so I hit her again, and she slammed into the wall and sat, but she was still awake. Winthrop pulled me out of the stall, moved in, and kicked her. He got her out the window, to the car, and up here."

"Why..." I stopped for a few heartbeats to keep from sobbing. "Why kill Micah Lee? Why pretend to help us search the sewers?"

"Because it wasn't supposed to happen like it did. Winthrop wasn't supposed to be there." He sighed and looked unhappy. "Do you remember when you figured out how the Snatcher used the sewers? You told me and Micah Lee and said you were going to tell Solomon about it."

"I remember. You made me wait a day."

"I went home and told Winthrop, and he freaked out. He knew you'd been playing detective. Hell, you had that intuition or feeling or whatever, that the lost girls were somewhere west of town. That scared Winthrop, and the fact that you learned about the sewer really worried him. He thought if you could figure those things out, you'd find out about the old mill, and from there, you'd learn he was the Snatcher. That was when he said he should kill you next."

"And you went along with it?"

"No! I tried to change his mind. Thought I did. We argued for hours, we fought, we compromised, and fought again. Winthrop finally agreed that I would go with you and Micah Lee into the sewers. We'd wander around down there for hours, and we wouldn't find a thing. After that, it'd be easy to convince you that you were wrong, and you wouldn't tell any grown-ups about the sewer."

"But Winthrop lied to you, didn't he? He went down too." Bobby didn't answer, and I tried to speak calmly. "I know things aren't going to turn out well for me. But Bobby, I want you to do me a favor, as an old friend, my best friend. I want you to let Gili go."

Bobby laughed. "Yeah, right." His eyes sparkled in the candle glow. "You want to know what happened that night, or don't you?"

"I think I've figured it out."

"You do, huh? Well, you always liked solving mysteries, so go ahead."

"You thought you were leading us on a wild goose chase. Winthrop had other plans and used the library book as bait. You didn't crawl through that pipe to look for Theresa Goodnight. You went to try and stop your brother. But there was a gunshot... and blood. What happened?"

Bobby stared over my head and said, "Before I had a chance to try and stop him, he swung Daddy's pistol into my head. I went out, and either he fired the gun to make you think he killed me, or it went off when he hit me." Bobby held up his hand and showed me the big scar. "My first knife wound. Winthrop sliced it open."

"Why?"

"He knew you'd come through that pipe for me. He wanted you to think he'd killed me. It was part of his game."

I got angry at how we'd been played. "Winthrop was sick white trash."

Bobby's voice turned into a growl. "Don't call my brother names. He couldn't help it." He breathed and calmed some. "He put me over his shoulder, carried me up the ladder, and took me to where he'd parked the car. Then he went after you two. He got Micah Lee, brought him back, and shut him in the trunk. Then he went for you. But later, when I woke up, he said that you'd run right off the ridge like Wile E. Coyote off a cliff."

"Your brother screwed up. He should have checked on me."

Bobby ignored my criticism. "We drove toward Hallow's Summit, and I argued for him to let Micah Lee live. He finally lost patience, stopped the car, dragged me out, and left me by the side of the road while he drove up to the old mill with Micah Lee in the trunk."

Bobby was cool and calculating, but I figured that Gili and I had a better chance at survival if he was angry. Yeah, he was scary when he was pissed, but maybe he'd make a mistake if his emotions got control of him. So I said, "One of the best things I ever did was what I did to your brother."

He lifted an eyebrow. "Killing Winthrop?"

"Yes."

"You enjoyed killing my brother?"

"I liked killing him very much."

Instead of raging, Bobby stood and smiled. "See. We're not so different, you and me."

"We're very different."

Chuckling, he took a candle, walked into the shadows, and lit a few more. Gili was on her back on top of an old blanket that covered a raised concrete area about as big as a small bed. Her wrists were bound together and tied to a metal ring in the wall. A ragged bedroll covered her until Bobby yanked it off. She was naked, and her ankles were tied to different corners of the concrete table.

"I don't know." Bobby ran a finger over Gili's torso, making her whimper. "You liked killing Winthrop very much. I'll like killing this one very much."

I shouted, "Leave her alone!" He looked at me with quizzical amusement. "You haven't finished telling me what happened. Where did you go? How did you fool everyone into thinking you were dead?"

He flipped the bedroll back onto Gili. Back in the chair, he said. "I walked all the way to the old mill. When I got there, I heard gunshots from the third floor and ran up in time to see my brother fall through the floor. You collapsed, and I stood over you. Do you remember that? You opened your eyes and said my name."

"I thought you were a ghost."

Bobby smiled. "I heard Handsome George and Roscoe calling for you, so I ran and hid. And you know what? When they got you in the van and raced down the mountain to save you, I was right there with you, Charly. Remember Solomon's van and the handles he put on it so he could climb in and out easier? I jumped up on the back bumper and held on to those handles.

"I got off when he slowed for a turn near town and ran to my house. Around noon, there was a knock at the door, and I hid in the hall closet. Mama woke up and opened the door to Sheriff Rysdale and a couple other men. He told her Winthrop was dead, that her oldest boy was the Snatcher. Then he told her that they thought Winthrop had killed me as well. They told her that you killed Winthrop. They left, and she shut herself in her room.

"I was scared because you saw me. I worried that you'd think I helped Winthrop lure you into the sewers, helped him kill those girls. And even if you didn't, the sheriff might think I helped and send me to prison. I had to leave Temperance."

Between the cold and the ropes cutting off my circulation, my toes and fingers were numb. While he'd been running on, I'd tried loosening the knots binding me. "How can a kid just up and leave town?"

"You remember my momma's cousin who visited once? Tommy Donovan? He rode from Charlotte to Temperance on his motorcycle? He was the first biker I'd ever seen."

"That's when you started to slick your hair back."

"Yeah, because that's how Tommy did it." Bobby's eyes glazed over. "That's when I knew I'd grow up to be a tough guy, a biker."

"Congratulations on living up to your potential."

Bobby smiled. "You were always good at slinging sarcasm. Anyway, Mama passed out later that day. I went through her stuff and found a stash of about fifty bucks. That night, I stole a car." He grinned. "Shit, I just remembered something. I stole Ol' Man Altus's car, just to fuck with him one last time. I drove to Asheville that night, slept at the bus station, and took a bus to Charlotte the next day. Tommy Donovan seemed happy to see me. I told him about Winthrop killing little girls, and he didn't like that one bit. Then I told him how Winthrop had been killed and how Mama was such a drunk she couldn't take care of me. I said I was afraid people would come after me because of what Winthrop did."

"He took you in?"

"Because of blood, Charly. He said we were blood, and blood is more important than anything. I changed my name to Billy Donovan, and it wasn't long until most people thought of me as the son of Tommy Donovan, president of the Charlotte chapter of the East Coast Thugs."

"You became someone new? Just like that?"

"Pretty much. Tommy had connections for forged paperwork. I went to school in Charlotte. Not that I wanted to, but Tommy said a kid who didn't go to school would draw unwanted attention. I was the club mascot for the first few years, got my patch when I was eighteen, and reached the rank of sergeant-at-arms at twenty."

"How'd you end up back in Temperance?"

Bobby stood and walked around the room. "We got a new national president who decided it was time we started making real money. We moved pot for a while, but we really raked in the cash when cocaine became the popular drug of choice. We have a business agreement with some Columbians who ship it to various points along the east coast. Initially, our base of operations was outside Wrightsville Beach. Made sense, right? Offload to a cutting house. Problem was, that's what law enforcement expected. They found out where we were set up and made a bust. We had a big meeting with all the club officers. It was my idea that once the uncut coke made the coast, we move it all the way to the mountains. The cops wouldn't expect that. I said

I knew just the place to cut and distribute from. I know the area and was put in charge of this little operation."

"You're the one who ran me off the road?"

"Of course. Preach and I."

"Preach?"

"Yeah, I know. You think he went down the mountain to hide. Truth is, he stayed up here, floating between the party shack and the old mill. You see, he and I had a special partnership of sorts. Anyway, you spied on us when a shipment arrived. Luke saw you watching from across the street. I didn't know exactly why, whether it was for the drugs or the missing girls. I just knew I had to shut you up. I got Preach, and we parked half a block from the inn, trying to figure out how to take you out. Of course, he's all for a brutal rape and murder. But lo and behold, you go for a late-night drive. We trailed you out of town, killed our headlights, and followed along. The old shop truck looks like a beater, but it's got a 427 big block engine under the hood. Runs like a bat out of hell. When you turned onto I-26 toward Morrison Gorge, we knew that was our opportunity. You were damn lucky that tree stopped you."

"Okay," I said, controlling my rage. "I can understand the drugs, the motive for running me off the road. But why did you start copying your brother? Why kill Preach? I'm assuming that was you too. Shit, Bobby, if the Thugs find out what you're up to, how you're endangering their drug operation, you'll be a dead man."

"I know that." He grabbed my face with his giant hand and squeezed. He spoke slowly as if talking to an idiot child. "But blood is more important than anything, and Winthrop is my blood."

My wrists burned where the rope cut into them, but still I worked my hands back and forth, getting the smallest amount of free play. "What are you talking about?"

Bobby looked up, his eyes going from side to side. "Can I tell her?" He waited a beat. "Ah, come on. She'll be dead anyway. What can it hurt?" He paused and smiled like a kid as he returned his attention to me. "You don't hear him, do you?"

"Hear who?"

"Shhh." He put his finger to my lips, and his eyes went wide. "Listen."

I didn't know what I was listening for, but I only heard my heartbeat, Bobby's panting, and the sound of the storm raging.

Bobby nodded, thinking I heard whatever he wanted me to hear. "Winthrop talks to me. We're taking girls again."

Chapter 40
Autumn of '82

"You're crazy," I said.

Bobby laughed in wheezing bursts. The more he laughed, the funnier he found it, until he doubled over and tears rained down his cheeks. He sucked in a few gulps of air while shaking his head and stood.

All I could think to do was stall while working at the ropes. "How did Winthrop come back?"

Bobby knelt in front of me and described it in awed sincerity. "I was graced by fate, Charly. It was a miracle. We were at Shorty's, me and some bros, and I got sick of everyone's bullshit. Then I got to thinking about when you and me were kids. I kind of got depressed and wanted to be by myself. When I get like that, I like to take a ride out here to the old mill, or what's left of it. Halfway to Hallow's Summit, the night came to life with streaks of light, and at first, I thought I was hallucinating. Then I remembered something in the news about a meteor shower.

"I found a spot outside the old mill with wide-open sky and stared up. It was amazing. Beautiful. Objects blazed from horizon to horizon, east to west, in all colors, scorching through the heavens. I could feel a charge in the air, like a static-electric hum.

"The weirdest thing happened then. Someone breathed in my ear. And then I heard a whisper. The voice was too soft to understand, but it scared the shit out of me. I jumped up, ran around the old mill, fell into a damn hole, rolled down a staircase, and landed on wet concrete. It was too dark to see, but looking up through the hole, I could still see the meteors in the sky. I got my lighter out and flicked it. I was in a hallway, though most of the roof and walls had collapsed. I got to a doorway and saw that the ceiling beyond the door had collapsed as well. There was nowhere to go except to climb out the way I fell in. I turned to the staircase and saw something bone white next to the bottom step. It was a four-inch long piece of mother-of-pearl. I dug into dirt, broken bits of concrete, and bricks and uncovered a rusty knife missing one white grip."

In solemn awe, Bobby said, "It was Winthrop's switchblade."

Bobby pulled the old knife from a pocket, held it up, and gazed at it. "The discovery filled me with... with jubilation. I felt so much joy that I cried. I admit it."

He pushed the button, and the blade flicked out. "This knife hums with energy. You can feel it." He held the flat of the blade against my cheek. "Right? You can feel it?"

I didn't answer, but he didn't seem to care. He shut it and returned it to his pocket.

"Later that night, as I held the knife, I heard a voice, a whisper. It had to be Winthrop. Who else? I knew it was time to kill again. I saw Piper Darling at Shorty's the next day, and it was like old times. I could have worked alone, but Winthrop, back then, liked to bring me along, and I knew someone who'd be game.

"Preach has been in and out of jail since he was eighteen, and in juvie before that. You know his *I sin so others won't* spiel? He was sincere. He was raised by some crazy-ass preacher, and that crazy continued on down the line. His favorite sins were those of a carnal nature, the more perverse the better. And how he loved kids. Before he joined up with the Thugs, he worked with an outfit that made kiddie porn and shipped photos, magazines, and peep shows all up and down the east coast. Believe it or not, of all the things he's been arrested for, Preach never got nabbed on a sex crime. I'm sure Kit checked our records, so while there was plenty to read, there was nothing that would link us to child abductions. When I brought it up with Preach, I appealed to his ego, how he had experience procuring kids for those photo shoots and films. He was raring to go, though he wanted us to move the kids down the mountain and sell them to people he knew in the business.

"After I killed Piper, he realized I had other things in mind, and since *thou shalt not kill* is on God's top ten, he had no problem with it. Something else came with my killing of her. I could hear Winthrop a little better. He was loud enough that I could make out a few words, enough to know I had to do it again. The sisters at school were a piece of cake and just as sweet, and after we put the second one down, I could hear Winthrop like he was standing next to me.

"As for that kid from out of town, Luke, Preach, and I were driving from the shop, and Luke asked to stop in at the restaurant to get a paycheck. That's when we saw her. Winthrop whispered to me, told me to take Luke home, go back, and get her. I looked at Preach, and he grinned. It was like he read my mind.

"As for her"—he gestured toward Gili—"we cruised neighborhoods in the shop truck until we saw a kid we both agreed on and followed her home. Last night, we peeped in windows until we found her room. After everyone had gone to bed, we went in and got her. Preach wanted to start on her right away, but I told him we'd wait until the next night. Then we'd take her up to the old mill and go at her all night long.

"I dropped him and the girl at the secret beach and told him to hogtie her. I got home, and Luke runs in, all panicked, says they're coming for him for stealing your car. I told him to go out back and hide in the barn. A little later, Kit shows up with some deputies. If he'd gone around back, he'd have found both Luke and the shop truck in the barn. That's where I parked it after fucking up the side, running you off the road. Kit leaves, and then you show up. I'm worrying again, thought you'd figured out I was Copycat, which is why I greeted you with my .44. But like Kit, you were looking for Luke.

"That gave me an idea. You left, and I went into Luke's room and got his gun. Then I went out to the barn and told him the cops were looking for him in the shop truck, and he should take my GTO, drive up to the old mill, and lie low in one of the basement rooms. While he did that, I drove the shop truck out to the party shack. You suspected Luke, and you already knew that he and Preach were tight, so there was one more thing to do to make everyone certain that Copycat was Luke. At the party shack, I told Preach that I was too horny to wait, and we'd take that little bitch there and then. We stripped her, and I told Preach to go first. He got buck naked, and I shot him with Luke's gun." Bobby laughed and looked at Gili. "She peed herself."

"Beason isn't involved, is he?"

"Not willingly." He stepped into the shadows and dragged out something heavy wrapped in a tarp. "Didn't you think it was a little too easy convincing me it was Luke? Didn't it seem odd to you that I'd turn on a bro so quick?" When he got the tarp into the light, he unwrapped Beason, who was shirtless and beaten. A bandana gagged him, and his hands and feet were bound. He saw me and made muffled sounds from behind the gag. Bobby reached in a pocket for a cigarette. He lit it, kicked Beason in the stomach, and threw the tarp over him.

"So that wasn't his kiddie porn?"

"Oh man, we got so much perverted shit floating around the house that I just grabbed what would convince you it was him. I brought the girl up here, kicked Luke's ass, took his Le Bistro shirt, and tied him up. The girl too. I stashed the shop truck up here in the woods and drove the GTO back out to the secret beach to put Luke's work shirt in with Preach's clothes and the girl's PJs. Then I went and called you and met you at the lake." He dragged Beason back into the shadows.

"You gave me and Winthrop the idea to pin it all on Luke. Find-ing Preach dead by Luke's gun just solidified everybody's suspicions. Everyone will believe it. Planting his shirt out at the shack was a stroke of genius, don't you think? Here's how it'll look when we're done here. Poor ol' Sheriff Kit will think Luke abducted you and the girl. They'll think he raped and killed her, and then killed you with his gun, courtesy of the .22 slug they'll dig out of your brain." He pat-ted the small-caliber pistol on his belt. "Then the story's hero, me, will explain how I figured out where Luke was, I came to save you and the girl, but got here too late. I'll say Luke pulled his gun on me and I blew his head off with my .44. That's what they'll believe. I know I'm going to do time for the coke, but since I'm the one to end Luke's reign of terror"—he winked—"that ought to put me in good light with the court for a reduced sentence. When I get out, Winthrop and I will wait for another sign in the sky that tells us to start again."

"Bobby, Winthrop is gone."

Bobby pointed to the girl. "Winthrop wants you to watch me do her."

"Winthrop is in your mind. Let us go, and I swear I'll do all I can to get you help."

Bobby walked to Gili, pulled the bedroll from her body, and shouted, "I don't want your help!" He crushed out his cigarette on Gili's ribcage. She shrieked and bounced on the concrete bed like she was being electrocuted. Bobby's eyes were on fire. He rushed forward and backhanded me hard.

Chapter 41
Autumn of '82

My chair fell to the side when Bobby hit me, and my head bounced on the concrete. Blinking several times, I saw Bobby set more candles around the concrete bed upon which Gili was attached. He added more and more until he must have had thirty or more candles blazing on the floor, set on boxes, and several in a niche in the wall overhead. Bobby turned my way and sat on the concrete bed between Gili's feet. He worked to remove his boots, his spur singing when he dropped that one to the ground. He got the other boot off and stood, socks on his feet, and took off his clothes. Gili's head was up, and she watched him in total terror.

"Don't do it, Bobby," I pleaded. "Don't hurt her."

He stopped and stared at empty air a moment. "Winthrop says I'll do more than hurt her. He says I'm going to take her through a tour of all kinds of pain."

He got down to his crusty jeans. As he removed his belt and kicked off his pants, he gazed down on his victim. Compared to him, she looked like a baby doll before a fat, fleshy bear. I yanked at the ropes and tried to kick out. Bobby approached and towered over me. He stroked his erection while studying my face. I would have given anything for one chance to take him down. And then I remembered something. I extended my hands back as far as possible and felt about with my fingers, but I only touched cold concrete.

Bobby finished his scrutiny and asked, "How ya doin', Charly?" He kicked my chest, and it felt like my heart exploded. When he returned to Gili, he said, "Hey, sweetie pie. Your momma must give you a pretty pill every day 'cause you're so bee-yoo-tee-ful." He stroked the girl's cheek.

I sucked a shallow breath. Bobby's kick knocked me back a foot. My fingers twitched, and I felt cloth instead of concrete. My hands moved about, shifting the clothing, feeling it. The first garment was my jacket—not what I needed. My fingers next touched my sweater.

"Shit," I said to myself.

I kept moving material and searching until I grabbed a handful of denim. Dub's butterfly knife was in my pants pocket. After another ten seconds, I had the knife in my fingers. Checking on Bobby, I saw him stroking Gili's hair, his face just over hers. He moved to her side, facing away from me.

Normally, I'd have the blade open in a second, but my fingers were numb. I worked one handle from a side of the blade and ignored the pain when I sliced my index finger. It took me a little longer to free the other side of the blade and move the handles into place. I'd worked enough free play into the rope that I could saw at it. I freed my hands and, without taking my eyes from Bobby, cut through the ropes binding my ankles to the chair.

I rose into a predatory stance, blood rushing in my ears. My grip tightened on the knife, and I studied Bobby as he looked down on Gili, his back to me. Adrenaline pushed through me like hot steam. My body hummed with strength and sensation. Grinning fiercely, my face a tight mask, I ran. Gili saw me, and her eyes fueled my determination. A feral scream, my war cry, filled the room. Bobby started to turn, but by then, I was on his back. My left hand gripped his tangled hair, and my legs clasped around his flabby hips. Before he could react, I plunged the butterfly knife deep into his neck and pushed it out the front of his throat with a spray of gore.

Bobby grasped my wrist and threw me from his back like I weighed no more than a kitten. I hit the hard floor and lost the knife. Bobby lifted me and rushed me backward until my body slammed into a wall. He pinned me there, my feet kicking well above the floor. His right hand gripped my throat, thumb and fingers almost encircling my neck. Fixing me with a furious glare, he squeezed.

Then he made a leaky, bubbling noise. His countenance turned puzzled, and he moved his mouth but only achieved more bubbling. His left hand moved to his throat then away, and then he gazed into his blood-slick palm. He dropped me, and I fell hard. I looked up from the floor at Grizz's obesity painted with a red wash from his neck. Swaying, he attempted to speak, fell to his knees, and collapsed into a heap next to me. His feet twitched, and his legs randomly kicked.

I forced myself up and rushed to Gili. "It's okay. It's okay," I repeated for myself as well as her. I searched the floor until I found my KA-BAR and freed her. After lifting her from the concrete bed, I took her to my piled clothes, picked through them until I got my jacket, and wrapped it around her. I righted the chair and sat her on it then put my socks on her feet, though they were much too big.

Whimpering, she peered past me to Grizz. I turned and saw that he no longer moved.

"Gili, it's okay. He's dead. The bad man is dead. Stay in the chair," I said and tried to wipe Bobby's blood from my body with my long johns. I slipped on my pants, sweater, and boots, and stamped my feet to get my circulation going. I went through the pile of Bobby's clothes and came up with my .38, Beason's .22, and Bobby's .44. I could hardly lift his big gun with my tired arms and frozen fingers, so I dropped it in the shadows and tossed the .22 next to it. Across the room, I freed Beason from the tarp. His eyes were wide as I bent over him with my KA-BAR and cut his bindings. He stared at Bobby's corpse not five feet away.

There was a click as I pulled back the hammer on my .38 and pushed the barrel to his forehead. "I'm too tired for bullshit. If I think you're going to try something, I'll drop you right now."

He started to shake his head but stopped because of the cold steel pressed above his brow. "No, no, no. I'm not gonna do anything. Holy shit. I didn't know all this was going on. I swear to God."

I lowered the gun and nodded at Gili. "See her? You're going to go with her out to the truck, drive slowly, and safely down the mountain, and take her to the sheriff's office. You'll tell them what happened and where I am. Understand?"

He swallowed and nodded.

"If you don't, I will hunt you down and kill you."

"I'll do it, I swear."

I went through Bobby's pants pockets, found the truck keys, and tossed them to Beason.

"Why don't you come with us?" he asked.

That was a damn good question. No one would understand that I couldn't leave Bobby. Though he'd turned into a monster, as a child, he'd been a friend I loved like a brother. It was *that* Bobby I was staying with.

"Just go," I told him and then knelt in front of the girl. "You're going with Luke. He's going to get you back to your mommy and daddy. All right?"

Her eyes lit up at the mention of her parents. Luke picked her up. I led them from the room and followed a hallway to some stairs. We went up and out into the snow. I had no idea how much time had passed since Bobby had brought me here, but it was still dark out.

"The truck is parked at the base of the drive." I pointed then watched a few moments as Beason carried the lost girl to safety.

I made my way back down to the basement room, stood over Bobby, then sat next to his still body on the cold floor. As I waited for Kit to arrive with his deputies, I spoke through chattering teeth. It was a one-sided conversation between old friends who knew each other in childhood, who shared secrets and dreams, friends who once thought that nothing would ever come between them. I spoke of the great events in our childhood, of Micah Lee, of how I wish we'd been like Peter Pan and the lost boys and never had to grow up.

Chapter 42
Autumn of '82

The few days since I killed Bobby had been disjointed, and I fought to keep anxiety from overwhelming me. It felt like I had important things to do, things that I'd neglected, but there wasn't anything. I was simply coming down from a crazy adrenaline high fueled by bad things.

Right after they brought me back to town, they checked me out at the hospital. I was fine, at least physically. The next day, I gave an official report to Kit and then went to the Gutter Ball Lounge at the Temperance Bowl-A-Rama. At least Roscoe's interview might pay off with royalties. Today, I did something I'd put off since arriving in Temperance. I drove my battered Formula 400 out to Passage Point Cemetery to visit my parents, Solomon, and Micah Lee. Even though it was cold, I sat at Micah Lee's grave and told him everything that happened and how I couldn't comprehend the juxtaposition of our childhood friend Bobby with Grizz the monster. I cried for some time.

I didn't plan on a particular destination when I left the cemetery, but I ended up in front of Kit's cabin. After some deliberation, I got out and tried his front door. It was unlocked, so I went in and called him at his office. I told him I was at his cabin and wanted to say more but cried instead. Twenty minutes later, he rushed through his door, hugged me, and then led me upstairs. We lay together a long time in the warm comfort of his bed, naked and holding one another. When I put my head on his chest, his heart beat in that same rhythm I remembered from when I was a child and listened to the inner workings of the world. That rhythm began my healing.

Later, once we dressed, Kit walked me to my car. "You going to be all right, Charly?"

I turned to him and took his hands in mine. "Want to know something funny?"

"What?"

"I think what happened set my priorities straight. I think a future with you—you know, you and me together—would be a good thing."

Kit looked me square in the eyes and asked, "Are you sure?"

I took a moment to think about it and didn't feel that fear of a relationship anymore. I couldn't help but smile. "I think so."

Kit returned my smile. "We'd be a hell of a team."

I laughed at the thought of us as a couple. Hoping that Kit wouldn't think I was already backing out, I asked, "Can you give me a little time to get used to the idea?"

Kit took me in his arms, and we kissed. Then, still holding me, he said softly, "Take as much time as you need, Charly. You're worth it."

I went back to the inn and packed. Dub walked me to my car, gave me a parting one-armed hug, and watched me drive out of his parking lot. I drove from town and began my descent to the flatlands, thinking how I always left Temperance with a sense of loss. In an attempt to shake the melancholy, I turned on the radio but could only get one station out of Hendersonville. After a couple bad pop songs ending in a commercial break, I pushed a cassette into the tape player. As the Allman Brothers started "Whipping Post," I cranked up the volume and pushed the accelerator to the floor.

About the Author

Andrew Nance is a writer, actor, and amateur historian. He spent over twenty years working in the radio industry up and down the east coast and still keeps his hand in as a volunteer at a local college radio station. He's had two young adult books published including *Daemon Hall* (Henry Holt Books for Young Readers), which was named an American Library Association Quick Pick for the Reluctant Reader, a New York Library Book for the Teen Age, and was nominated for an Edgar Award in YA, and for the ALA Teens Top 10 for 2008.

Andrew lives in St. Augustine, Florida with his family and can be heard playing jazz on Mondays from 5-7pm EST on WFCF, which is available on iHeartRadio online.

Made in the USA
Columbia, SC
07 November 2018